Praise for *The Carrier*

'Do not think you have worked out where the plot is going and how it is going to end. Hannah is masterly at leading the reader down the wrong path and here she excels once again.'
Sunday Express

'Another massively intriguing premise from Hannah, with plot threads that spin out in all kinds of unusual and surprising directions . . . A hugely confident, beautifully written and bold mystery . . . Another gripping triumph.' *Heat*

'This poet and crime writer again confirms in this, her eighth novel her fluent writing skills, taste for complicated layers and deft hand with character, not to mention a knack for producing compelling openings. It is a mature work – full of confidence and intrigue.' *Daily Mail*

'A tale of the power that weakness and passivity can have over strength and action, and how theories of love and duty can lead us astray . . . Intriguing.' *Guardian*

'A leading writer of psychological suspense . . . her books are so distinctive that they deserve to be placed in a separate sub-genre of their own . . . as ever, Hannah excels.' *Spectator*

'It is brilliantly constructed, and it had me, screaming, on the edge of my chair' *Reader's Digest*

'Such is the author's command of the narrative, we . . . find ourselves glued to the page . . . Compelling.'
Daily Express

'. . . ly original . . . Hannah has once again ripped up the . . . ustry-standard "A to Z of writing a Whodunnit" and audaciously charted her own course . . . to produce a novel that is a classy, compulsive and chilling literary triumph.'
Irish Independent

'Another gripping puzzle of a novel from one of Britain's best crime writers' *Image Magazine*

Praise for Sophie Hannah

'For those who demand emotional intelligence and literary verve from their thrillers, Sophie Hannah is the writer of choice.' *Guardian*

'One of the great unmissables of this genre – intelligent, classy and with a wonderfully Gothic imagination.' *The Times*

'Sophie Hannah has a poet's eye, and she creates characters and settings of closely observed complexity in her psychological mysteries.' *Daily Telegraph*

'[A] challenging storyteller and anything but predictable . . . I felt quite bereft on reaching the final page.' *Irish Independent*

'Sophie Hannah has quickly established herself as a doyenne of the 'home horror' school of psychological tension, taking domestic situations and wringing from them dark, gothic thrills' *Financial Times*

'Hannah takes domestic scenarios, adds disquieting touches and turns up the suspense until you're checking under the bed for murders' *Independent*

'Stunningly clever and compelling' *Heat*

'Hannah excels at dissecting human behaviour, and the way she describes little acts of cruelty can send real chills down the spine.' *Psychologies*

'The queen of the ingenious plot twist' *Good Housekeeping*

'It's a given that nothing will be as it seems in the latest psychological thriller from Sophie Hannah, who marries complex plots with crisp, conversational prose' *Marie Claire*

Also by Sophie Hannah

Little Face
Hurting Distance
The Point of Rescue
The Other Half Lives
A Room Swept White
Lasting Damage
Kind of Cruel

About the author

As well as writing psychological thrillers, Sophie Hannah is a bestselling poet and an award-winning short story writer. Her fifth collection of poetry, *Pessimism for Beginners*, was shortlisted for the 2007 TS Eliot Award. She won first prize in the Daphne du Maurier Festival Short Story Competition for her psychological suspense story *The Octopus Nest*. Her psychological thrillers *Little Face* and *Hurting Distance* were long-listed for the Theakston's Old Peculier Crime Novel of the Year Award and *The Other Half Lives* was shortlisted for the Independent Booksellers' Book of the Year Award and a Barry Award. *The Point of Rescue* and *The Other Half Lives* were adapted for television as *Case Sensitive*, starring Olivia Williams and Darren Boyd.

Sophie lives with her husband and children in Cambridge, where she is a Fellow Commoner at Lucy Cavendish College.

More information about Sophie can be found at www.sophiehannah.com or you can follow her on Twitter: twitter.com/sophiehannahCB1.

SOPHIE HANNAH

The Carrier

HODDER

First published in Great Britain in 2013 by Hodder & Stoughton
An Hachette UK company

First published in paperback in 2013

2

For Peter Straus, my lovely agent
who has magic powers

Why are you still here, Francine?

I've always believed that people can will their own deaths. If our
minds can make us wake up exactly a minute before our alarm
clocks are due to go off, they must be capable of stopping our
breath. Think about it: brain and breath are more powerfully linked
than brain and bedside table. A heart begged to stop by a mind
that won't take no for an answer – what chance does it stand?
That's what I've always thought, anyway.

And I can't believe you want to stick around. Even if you do, it
won't be up to you for much longer. Someone will kill you. Soon.
Every day I change my mind about who it will be. I don't feel the
need to try and stop them, only to tell you. By giving you the
chance to take yourself away, out of reach, I am being fair to
everybody.

Let me admit it: I am trying to talk you into dying because I'm
scared you'll recover. How can the impossible feel possible? It
must mean I'm still afraid of you.

Tim isn't. Do you know what he asked me once, years ago? He and I
were in your kitchen at Heron Close. Those white napkin rings that
always reminded me of neck braces were on the table. You'd got
them out of the drawer, and the brown napkins with ducks around
the border, and slammed them down without saying anything; Tim

I

was supposed to do the rest, whether or not he deemed it important for napkins to be inserted into rings only to be taken out again fifteen minutes later. Dan had gone out to collect the Chinese takeaway and you'd marched off to the bottom of the garden to sulk. Tim had ordered something healthy and beansprouty that we all knew he'd hate, and you'd accused him of choosing it for the wrong reason: to please you. I remember blinking back tears as I laid the table, after I'd clumsily grabbed the bundle of cutlery from his hands. There was nothing I could do to rescue him from you, but I could spare him the effort of putting the forks and knives out, and I was determined to. Little things were all Tim would let us do for him in those days, so Dan and I did them, as many of them as possible, putting all the effort and care into them that we could. Even so, I couldn't touch those wretched napkin rings.

When I was sure I wasn't going to cry, I turned and saw a familiar look on Tim's face, the one that means 'There's something I'd like you to know, but I'm not prepared to say it, so I'm going to mess with your head instead.' You won't be able to imagine this expression unless you've seen it, and I'm certain you never have. Tim gave up trying to communicate with you within a week of marrying you. 'What?' I asked him.

'I wonder about you, Kerry,' he said. He meant for me to hear the pantomime suspicion in his voice. I knew he suspected me of nothing, and guessed that he was trying to find a camouflaged way to talk about himself, as he often did. I asked him what he wondered, and he said loudly, as if to an audience stretching back several rows in a large hall, 'Imagine Francine dead.' Three words that planted an instant ache of longing in my chest. I so much wanted you not to be there any more, Francine, but we were stuck with you. Before your stroke, I thought you'd probably live till you were a hundred and twenty.

'Would you still be scared of her?' Tim asked. Anyone listening who didn't know him well would have thought he was teasing me and enjoying it. 'I think you would. Even if you knew she was dead and never coming back.'

'You say it as if there's an alternative,' I pointed out. 'Dead and coming back.'

'Would you still hear her voice in your head, saying all the things she'd say if she were alive? Would you be any freer of her than you are now? If you couldn't see her, would you imagine she must be somewhere else, watching you?'

'Tim, don't be daft,' I said. 'You're the least superstitious person I know.'

'But we're talking about you,' he said in a tone of polished innocence, again drawing attention to his act.

'No. I wouldn't be scared of anyone who was dead.'

'If you'd be equally afraid of her dead, then killing her would achieve nothing,' Tim went on as if I hadn't spoken. 'Apart from probably a prison sentence.' He took four wine glasses with chunky opaque green glass stems out of a cupboard. I'd always hated them, too, for their slime-at-the-bottom-of-your-drink effect.

'I've never understood why anyone thinks it's interesting to speculate about the difference between murderers and the rest of us.' Tim pulled a bottle of white wine out of the fridge. 'Who cares what makes one person willing and able to kill and another not? The answer's obvious: degrees of suffering, and where you are on the bravery–cowardice spectrum. There's nothing more to it. The only distinction worth investigating is the one between those of us whose presence in the world, however lacklustre and chaotic, doesn't crush the spirit in others to extinction, and those about whom that can't be said, however kind we might want to be. Every murder victim is someone who has inspired at least one person to wish them out of existence. And we're supposed to sympathise when they meet a bad end.' He made a dismissive noise.

I laughed at his outrageousness, then felt guilty for falling for it. Tim is never better at cheering me up than when he sees no hope of consolation for himself; I'm supposed to feel happier, and imagine that he's following the same emotional trajectory. 'You're saying all murder victims are asking for it?' I willingly rose to the bait. If he wants to discuss something, however ridiculous, even now, I debate with him until he decides he's had enough. Dan does too. It's one of the many million odd forms love can take. I doubt you'd understand.

'You're assuming, wrongly, that the victim of a murder is always the person who's been killed and not the killer.' Tim poured himself a glass of wine. He didn't offer me one. 'To cause someone so much inconvenience that they're willing to risk their liberty and sacrifice what's left of their humanity to remove you from the face of the earth ought to be regarded as a more serious crime than taking a gun or a blunt instrument and ending a life, all other things being equal.'

By inconvenience, he meant pain. 'You're biased,' I said. I knew Dan might be back any second with the food, and I wanted to say something more direct than I'd normally have risked. I decided that, in starting this extraordinary conversation, Tim had given me his tacit permission. 'If you think of Francine as a spirit-crusher, if the only reason you haven't killed her is that you'd be more scared of her dead than alive . . .' I said.

'I don't know where you've got all that from.' Tim grinned. 'Hearing things again?' We both understood why he was smiling: I had received his message and would not forget it. He knew it was safe with me. It took me years of knowing Tim to work out that change is never what he's after; all he wants is to stow the important information with someone he can trust.

'You can leave her more easily than you think,' I told him, craving change – the enormous, irreversible kind – more than enough for both of us. 'There doesn't have to be a confrontation. You don't need to tell her you're going, or have any contact with her after you've left. Dan and I can help you. Let Francine keep this house. Come and live with us.'

'You can't help,' Tim said firmly. He paused, long enough for me to understand – or misunderstand, as I knew he'd insist if I made an issue of it – before adding, 'Because I don't need help. I'm fine.'

I overheard him talking to you yesterday, Francine. He wasn't weighing his every word, planning several conversational moves ahead. He was just talking, telling you another Gaby story. It involved an airport, of course. Gaby seems to live in airports, when she's not in mid-air. I don't know how she can stand it – it would drive me insane. This particular story was about the time the scanning machine at Madrid-Barajas ate one of her shoes, and Tim was enjoying telling it. It sounded as if he was saying whatever came to mind without censoring himself at all. Nothing contrived, no element of performance. Very un-Tim. As I eavesdropped, I realised that any fear he once had is long gone. What I can't work out is: does that mean he's likely to kill you, or that he needs you to live forever?

I

Thursday 10 March 2011

The young woman next to me is more upset than I am. Not only me; she is more upset than everyone else in the airport put together, and she wants us all to know it. Behind me, people are grumbling and saying, 'Oh, *no*,' but no one else is weeping apart from this girl, or shaking with fury. She is able to harangue the Fly4You official and cry copiously at the same time. I'm impressed that she seems not to need to interrupt her diatribe, ever, to gulp incoherently in the way that sobbing people normally do. Also, unlike regular folk, she appears not to know the difference between a travel delay and bereavement.

I don't feel sorry for her. I might if her reaction were less extreme. I feel sorriest for people who insist they are absolutely fine, even while their organs are being consumed at great speed by a flesh-eating bug. This probably says something bad about me.

I am not upset at all. If I don't get home tonight, I'll get there tomorrow. That will be soon enough.

'Answer my question!' the girl yells at the poor mild-mannered German man who has the misfortune to be posted at boarding gate B56. 'Where's the plane *now*? Is it still here? Is it down there?' She points to the concertina-walled temporary air-bridge that opens behind him, the one that, five minutes ago, we were all hoping to walk along and find our plane at the end of. 'It's down there, isn't it?' she demands. Her face is unlined, blemish-free and weirdly flat; a vicious rag doll. She looks about eighteen, if that. 'Listen, *mate*, there's hundreds of us and only one of you. We could push past you and all get on the plane, a load of angry Brits, and refuse to get off till someone flies us home! I wouldn't mess with a load of angry Brits if I were you!' She pulls off her black leather jacket as if preparing for a physical fight. The word 'FATHER' is tattooed on her right upper arm in large capital letters, blue ink. She's wearing tight black jeans, a bullet belt, and lots of straps on her shoulders from a white bra, a pink camisole and a red sleeveless top.

'The plane is being rerouted to Cologne,' the German Fly4You man tells her patiently, for the third time. A name badge is pinned to his maroon uniform: Bodo Neudorf. I would find it hard to speak harshly to anyone named Bodo, though I wouldn't expect others to share this particular scruple. 'The weather is too dangerous,' he says. 'There is nothing that I can do. I am sorry.' A reason-based appeal. In his shoes, I'd probably try the same tactic – not because it will work, but because if you possess rationality and are in the habit of using it regularly, you're probably something of a fan and likely to over-value its potential usefulness, even when dealing with somebody who finds it more helpful to accuse innocent people of hiding aeroplanes from her.

'You keep saying it's *being* rerouted! That means you haven't sent it anywhere yet, right?' She wipes her wet cheeks – an action violent enough to be mistaken for hitting herself in the face – and whirls round to address the crowd behind us. 'He hasn't sent it away at all,' she says, the vibration of her outraged voice winning the sound war at boarding gate B56, drowning out the constant electronic pinging noises that announce the imminent announcements of the openings of gates for other flights, ones more fortunate than ours. 'How can he have sent it away? Five minutes ago we were all sitting here ready to board. You can't send a plane off to anywhere that quickly! I say we don't let him send it away. We're here, the plane *must* be here, and we all want to go home. We don't care about the sodding weather! Who's up for it?'

I'd like to turn round and see if everybody's finding her one-woman show as embarrassingly compulsive as I am, but I don't want our fellow non-passengers to imagine that she and I are together simply because we're standing side by side. Better to make it obvious that she's nothing to do with me. I smile encouragingly at Bodo Neudorf. He replies with a curtailed smile of his own, as if to say, 'I appreciate the gesture of support, but you would be foolish to imagine that anything you might do could compensate for the presence of the monstrosity beside you.'

Fortunately, Bodo doesn't seem unduly alarmed by her threats. He has probably noticed that many of the people booked onto Flight 1221 are extremely well-behaved choirgirls between the approximate ages of eight and twelve, still wearing their chorister cassocks after their concert in Dortmund earlier today. I know this because their choirmaster and the five or six parent chaperones were reminiscing proudly, while we waited to board, about how well the girls sang something called 'Angeli Archangeli'. They didn't sound like the sort of people who would be quick to knock a German airport employee to the ground in a mass stampede, or insist on exposing their talented offspring to dangerous storm conditions for the sake of getting home when they expected to.

Bodo picks up a small black device that is attached to the departure gate desk by a length of coiled black wire, and speaks into it, having first pressed the button that makes the pinging noise that must precede all airport speech. 'This is an announcement for all passengers for Flight 1221 to Combingham, England. That is Fly4You Flight 1221 to Combingham, England. Your plane is being rerouted to Cologne airport and will depart from there. Please proceed to the baggage reclaim area to collect your bags, and then go to wait outside the airport, immediately outside the Departures Hall. We are trying to make the arrangement that coaches will collect you and take you to Cologne airport. Please make your way to the collection point outside the Departures Hall as soon as possible.'

To my right, a smartly dressed woman with postbox-red hair and an American accent says, 'We don't need to hurry, people. These are hypothetical coaches: the slowest kind.'

'How long on the coach from here to Cologne?' a man calls out.

'I have no details yet about the timetable of the coaches,' Bodo Neudorf announces. His voice is lost in the spreading ripple of groans.

I'm glad I can miss out on the visit to Baggage Reclaim. The thought of everyone else traipsing down there to pick up the luggage they waited in a shuffling, zig-zagging, rope-corralled queue to check in not much more than an hour ago makes me feel exhausted. It's 8 p.m. I was supposed to be landing in Combingham at 8.30 English time, and going home for a long soak in a hot bubble bath with a chilled glass of Muscat. I woke up at five this morning to catch the 0700 from Combingham to Dusseldorf. I'm not a morning person, and resent any day that requires me to wake up earlier than 7 a.m.; this one has already gone on too long.

'Oh, this is a fucking joke!' Psycho Rag Doll pipes up. 'You have got to be shitting me!' If Bodo imagined that by amplifying his voice and projecting it electronically he could intimidate his nemesis into silent obedience, he was mistaken. 'I'm not going to collect any suitcases!'

A thin bald man in a grey suit steps forward and says, 'In that case, you're likely to arrive home without your bag. And everything in it.' Inwardly, I cheer; Flight 1221 has its first quiet hero. He has a newspaper tucked under his arm. He grips its corner with his other hand, expecting retaliation.

'Keep out of it, you!' Rag Doll yells in his face. 'Look at you: thinking you're better than me! I haven't even got a suitcase – that's how much you know!' She turns her attention back to Bodo. 'What, so you're going to unload everyone's cases off the plane? How does that make sense? You tell me how that makes sense. That's just . . . I'm sorry for swearing, but that's just fucking plain stupid!'

'Or,' I find myself saying to her, because I can't let the bald hero stand alone and no one else seems to be rushing to his aid, 'you're the one who's stupid. If you haven't checked in a bag, then of course you're not going to collect any suitcases. Why would you?'

She stares at me. Tears are still pouring down her face.

'Also, if the plane was here now and could safely fly to Cologne airport, we could fly there *on* it, couldn't we?' I say. 'Or even fly home, which is what we'd all ideally like to do.' *Shit.* Why did I open my mouth? It's not my job, or even Bodo Neudorf's, to correct her flawed thinking. The bald man has wandered away with his newspaper and left me to it. *Ungrateful git.* 'Because of the weather, our plane can't fly *into* Dusseldorf,' I continue with my mission to spread peace and understanding. 'It's never been here, it isn't here now, and your suitcase, if you had one, wouldn't be on it, and wouldn't need to be taken off it. The plane is some-where in the sky.' I point upwards. 'It was heading for Dusseldorf, and now it's changed course and is heading for Cologne.'

'No-o,' she says unsteadily, looking me up and down with a kind of shocked disgust, as if she's horrified to find herself having to address me. 'That's not right. We were all sitting there.' She waves an arm towards the curved orange plastic seats on their rows of black metal stalks. 'It said to go to the gate. It only says that when the plane's there ready for boarding.'

'Normally that's true, but not tonight,' I tell her briskly. I can almost see the cogs going round behind her eyes as her mental machinery struggles to connect one thought to another. 'When they told us to go to the gate, they still hoped the plane would be able to make it to Dusseldorf. Shortly after we all pitched up here, they realised that wouldn't be possible.' I glance at Bodo Neudorf, who half nods, half shrugs. Is he deferring to me? That's insane. He's supposed to know more about Fly4You's behind-the-scenes operations than I do.

Angry Weeping Girl averts her eyes and shakes her head. I can hear her silent scorn: *Believe that if you want to.* Bodo is speaking into a walkie-talkie in German. Choirgirls nearby start to ask if they'll get home tonight. Their parents tell them they don't know. Three men in football shirts are discussing how much beer they might be able to drink between now and whenever we fly, specu-lating about whether Fly4You will settle the bar tab.

A worried grey-haired woman in her late fifties or early sixties tells her husband that she only has ten euros left. 'What? Why?' he says impatiently. 'That's not enough.'

'Well, I didn't think we'd need any more.' She flaps around him, accepting responsibility, hoping for mercy.

'You didn't *think*?' he demands angrily. 'What about emergencies?'

I've used up all my interventional capacity, otherwise I might ask him if he's ever heard of a cashpoint, and what he was planning to do if his wife spontaneously combusted and all the currency in her handbag went up in smoke. *What about that emergency, Bully-breath? Is your wife actually thirty-five, and does she only look sixty because she's wasted the best years of her life on you?*

There's nothing like an airport for making you lose faith in humanity. I walk away from the crowd, past a row of unmanned boarding gates, in no particular direction. I am sick of the sight of every single one of my fellow travellers, even the ones whose faces I haven't noticed. Yes, even the nice choirgirls. I'm not looking forward to seeing any of them again – in the helpless, hopeful gaggle we will form outside the Departures Hall, where we will stand for hours in the rain and wind; across the aisle of the coach; slumped half asleep at various bars around Cologne airport.

On the other hand. It's a delayed plane, not a bereavement. I fly a lot. This sort of thing happens all the time. I've heard the words 'We are sorry to announce . . .' as often as I've seen the flecked grey heavy-duty linoleum flooring at Combingham airport, with its flecked blue border at every edge, for contrast. I've stood beneath information screens and watched minor delays metastasise into cancellations as often as I've seen the small parallel lines that form the borderless squares that in turn make-up the pattern on a million sets of silver aeroplane steps; once I dreamed that the walls and ceiling of my bedroom were covered with textured aluminium tread.

The worst thing about a delay, always, is ringing Sean and

telling him that, yet again, I'm not going to be back when I said I would be. It's a call I can't face making. Although . . . in this instance, it might not be so bad. I might be able to make it not so bad.

I smile to myself as the idea blooms in my mind. Then I reach into my handbag – not looking, still walking – and close my hand around a rectangular plastic-wrapped box: the pregnancy test I've been carrying with me for the past ten days and never quite finding the right moment to do.

I often worry about my tendency to procrastinate, though I'm obviously putting off tackling the problem. I've never been like this about anything work-related, and I'm still not, but if it's something personal and important, I'll do my best to postpone it indefinitely. This could be why I don't weep in airports when my flights don't depart on time; delay is my natural rhythm.

Part of me is still not ready to face the test, though with every day that passes, the whole rigmarole of weeing on a plastic wand and awaiting its verdict starts to seem more and more pointless. I am so obviously pregnant. There's a weirdly sensitive patch of skin on the top of my head that never used to be there, and I'm more tired than I've ever been.

I glance at my watch, wondering if I've got time to do this, then tut at my own gullibility. The American woman was right. There are no physical real-life coaches on their way to rescue us. God knows when there will be. Bodo didn't have a clue what was going on; he fooled us all into assuming he was on top of the arrangements by being German. Which means I've got at least fifteen minutes to do the test and phone Sean while the rest of them are retrieving their luggage. Luckily, Sean is easily distracted, like a kid. When I tell him I won't be back tonight, he'll gear up to start complaining. When I tell him the pregnancy test was positive, he'll be so delighted that he won't care when I get back.

I stop at the nearest ladies' toilet and force myself to go in, repeating silent reassurances in my head: *This isn't scary. You already know the result. Seeing a small blue cross will change nothing.*

I unwrap the box, take out the test, drop the instruction leaflet back in my bag. I've done this before – once, last year, when I knew I wasn't pregnant and took the test only because Sean wouldn't accept my gut instinct as good enough.

It's not a cross, it's a plus sign. Let's not call it a cross: bad for morale.

It doesn't take long before there's something to see. Already, a flash of blue. Oh, God. I can't do this. I only slightly want to have a baby. I think. I actually don't know at all. More blue: two lines, spreading out horizontally. No plus sign yet, but it's only a matter of time.

Sean will be pleased. That's what I should focus on. I'm the sort of person who doubts everything and can never be uncomplicatedly happy. Sean's reaction is more reliable than mine, and I know he'll be thrilled. Having a baby will be fine. If I didn't want to be pregnant, I'd have been secretly guzzling Mercilon for the past year, and I haven't.

What?

There is no blue cross in the wand's larger window. And nothing is getting any bluer. It's been more than five minutes since I did the test. I'm not an expert, but I have a strong sense that all the blueness that's going to happen has happened already.

I am not pregnant. I can't be.

An image flits through my mind: a tiny human figure, gold and featureless, punching the air in triumph. It's gone before I can examine it in detail.

Now I really don't want to speak to Sean. I have two disappointing pieces of news to deliver instead of one. The prospect of making the call is panicking me. If I have to do it at all, I need to get it over with. It seems hugely unfair that I can't deal with this problem by pretending I don't know anyone by the name of Sean Hamer and disappearing into a new life. That would be so much easier.

I leave the ladies' toilet and start to retrace my steps to the Departures Hall, pulling my BlackBerry out of my jacket pocket. Sean answers after one ring. 'Hi, babes,' he says. 'What time are you back?' When I'm away, he sits and watches TV in the evening with his phone next to him, so that he doesn't miss any of my calls or texts. I don't know if this is normal loving partner behaviour. I'd feel disloyal if I asked any of my friends, as if I was inviting them to slag Sean off.

'Sean, I'm not pregnant.'

Silence. Then, 'But you said you were. You said you didn't need to do a test – you knew.'

'You know what that means, don't you?'

'What?' He sounds hopeful.

'I'm an arrogant fool who can't be trusted. I really, really thought I was up the duff, but . . . obviously I was wrong. I must be feeling hormonal for some other reason.'

'Don't take the word of one test,' Sean says. 'Check. Buy another one. Can you buy one at the airport?'

'I don't need to.' *Of course you can buy a pregnancy test at an airport.* I tell myself Sean doesn't know this because he's a man, not because he has no desire to venture beyond our living room, and spends every evening on the sofa watching sport on TV.

'If you're not pregnant, why are you so late?' he asks.

I'd like to blame the weather conditions at Dusseldorf airport, but I know that's not what he means. 'No idea.' I sigh. 'Speaking of late, my flight is too. The plane's been rerouted to Cologne – we're about to set off there on a coach. Allegedly. Hopefully I'll be back at some point tomorrow. Maybe very late tonight if we're lucky.'

'Right,' Sean says tightly. 'So, once again, my evening goes up in smoke.'

Be soothing. Don't argue with him. 'Shouldn't that be, once again *my* evening goes up in smoke? I'm the one who's probably going to spend tonight sleeping upright in the passport control booth at Cologne airport.' I hate myself when I use sentences that begin, 'I'm the one who . . .', but I have a strong urge to point out that it is not Sean who is trapped in a large building full of electronic bleeping noises and strangers' echoing voices, about to be shunted off to another similar bleeping grey and white neon-lit building. Sean is not the one struggling with the sense that he is being slowly disassembled on a molecular level, that his whole being has become pixellated and won't attain proper personhood again until he next walks through his front door. If he were ever to find himself in that situation, and if I happened simultaneously to be sitting on the couch drinking beer and watching my favourite kind of TV, I like to think I'd show some sympathy.

And, pregnancy test notwithstanding, I'm still an arrogant fool who thinks she's right about everything. I've tried to be humbler, but, frankly, remembering you might be wrong is not easy when the person you're arguing with is Sean.

'*Hopefully* you'll be back tomorrow?' he says. In the few seconds since he last spoke, he has been shovelling Carlsberg-flavoured fuel into the furnace of his indignation. 'What, you mean it might be the day after?'

'This may come as news to you, Sean, but I'm not exactly a big cheese at Cologne airport. They don't have to run all their flight schedules past me. I'm a powerless passenger, just as I am at Dusseldorf airport. I've no idea when I'll be back.'

'Great,' he snaps. 'Will you bother to ring me when you do know?'

I resist the urge to crush my BlackBerry against the wall and reduce it to fine black powder. 'I suspect what'll happen is they'll tell us one thing, then another, then something different altogether,' I say patiently. 'Anything to keep us at bay while they desperately cobble together a plan for getting us home, and we stand outside the closed Duty Free shop, shaking its metal grille and begging to be allowed in before we die of boredom.' I haven't given up hope that Sean might notice I'm not enjoying myself this evening.

'You don't really want me to ring you every hour with an update, do you? Why don't you look on Flight Tracker?'

'So you don't care enough to keep me updated, but I'm supposed to sit by the laptop, looking—'

'No, you're not *supposed* to do that. You can accept that I'll be back soon, but that neither of us knows exactly when, and just deal with it like a grown-up.'

Sean mutters something under his breath.

'What was that?' I say, reluctant to let an infuriating statement go unheard and uncontested.

'I said, who's the carrier?'

I stop walking.

It's a shock to hear the words spoken so casually. It makes me think of other words, ones that will always live in my head even if no one ever again speaks them aloud to me.

i carry your heart with me, i carry it in my heart . . .

I clear my throat. 'Sorry, what did you say?'

'For fuck's sake, Gaby! Who. Is. The. Carrier?'

An image of Tim storms my mind: at the top of a ladder at The Proscenium, looking down at me, holding a book in his right hand, clutching the ladder with his left. He has just read me a poem. Not *i carry your heart*; a different poem. By a poet who died young and tragically, whose name I don't remember, about . . .

My skin starts to tingle with the weirdness of coincidence. The poem was about a delayed train. I don't remember any of it but the last two lines: 'Our time, in the hands of others, and too brief for words'. Tim approved of it. 'See?' he said. 'If a poet has something important to say, he says it as simply as he can.' 'Or she,' I said petulantly. 'Or she,' Tim agreed. 'But, rather like a poet, if an accountant has something important to say, he says it as simply as he can.' Who but Tim would have thought of that response so quickly?

Tim Breary is The Carrier. But Sean can't possibly mean that.

'Are you asking which airline I'm flying with? Fly4You.' *Who's the carrier?* Why would he choose to put it like that? There's no way he can know. If he did, he'd come straight out with it. Wouldn't he?

You're being paranoid.

'Flight number?' Sean asks.

'1221.'

'Got it. So . . . I guess I'll see you when I see you.'

'Uh-huh,' I say lightly, and press the 'end call' button. *Thank God that's over.*

I've sometimes wondered if the moving walkways in airports are there to fool us into believing the rest of the floor isn't moving backwards. I am still not where I need to be, and feel as if I've been walking for years, following the many signs directing me to Departures. Very soon, seeing the word won't be enough to keep my spirits up. I might start to cackle like a deranged witch-monster and crab-walk sideways in the opposite direction, for the sheer hell of it.

I turn a corner and walk into an arm with 'FATHER' tattooed on it. Its red-eyed owner has stopped crying. She's tearing into a box of cigarettes the size of a small suitcase.

'Sorry,' I mumble.

She backs away from me as if afraid I might hit her, stuffs the half-unwrapped Lambert & Butlers back into her shoulder bag and starts to move in the direction of the signs that point the way to further signs. The reassuring sensation of a cigarette between her fingers is less of a priority, it seems, than getting away from me.

Is it possible that my self-righteous dressing-down scared her? I decide to put it to the test by picking up my pace. It's not long before I'm level with her. She glances at me, speeds up. She's panting. This is ridiculous. 'You're running away from me?' I say, hoping it will help me to believe the unbelievable. 'What do you think I'm going to do to you?'

She stops, hunches her shoulders: braced for attack. She doesn't look at me, doesn't say anything.

I help her out. 'You can relax. I'm relatively harmless. I only had a go at you to stop you laying into Bodo.'

Her lips are moving. Whatever's emerging from them could be meant for me. This is how a member of an alien species would look if it were trying to communicate with a human being. I lean in closer to hear her.

'I have to get home tonight. I *have* to. I've never been out of the country on my own before. I just want to be home.' She looks up at me, her face white with fear and confusion. 'I think I'm having a panic attack,' she says.

You bloody fool, Gaby. You chased this girl. You initiated conversation. All she wanted was to avoid you – an arrangement that could have benefited you both – and you blew it.

'You wouldn't be able to speak if you were having a panic attack,' I tell her. 'You'd be hyperventilating.'

'I am! Listen to my breathing!' She grips my wrist, locking her fingers and thumb around it like a handcuff, pulling me towards her. I try to shake her off but she doesn't let go.

'You're out of breath from running,' I say, trying to keep my cool. How dare she grab hold of me as if I'm an object? I object. Strongly. 'You're also a heavy smoker. If you want to improve your lung capacity, you should jack it in.'

Anger flares in her eyes. 'Don't tell me what to do! You don't know how much I smoke. You don't know anything about me.'

She's still clutching my wrist. I laugh at her. What else can I do? Prise her fingers off one by one? If it comes to it, I might have to.

'Could you let go of me, please? The profits from the sale of the cigarettes in your bag alone will see Lambert & Butler comfortably through the next twelve global recessions.'

She screws up her forehead in an effort to work out what I mean.

'Too complicated for you? How about: your fingertips are yellow? Of course you're a heavy smoker.'

Finally, she releases me. 'You think you're so much better than me, don't you?' she sneers: the same thing she said to the bald man with the newspaper. I wonder if it's an accusation she levels at everyone she meets. It's hard to imagine the person who might encounter her and be beset by agonies of inferiority.

'Um . . . yes, probably,' I say, in answer to her question. 'Look, I was trying to help – bitchily, I suppose – but, actually, you're right: I really couldn't give a toss whether you continue to breathe or not. I'm sorry if I offended you by making a joke you're too thick to understand . . .'

'That's right, you're *so* much better than I am! Little Miss Stuck-Up Bitch, you are! I saw you this morning – too up yourself to smile back when I smiled at you.'

Little Miss? I'm thirty-eight, for Christ's sake. She can't be more than eighteen. Also, what's she talking about? 'This morning?' I manage to say. Was she on my crack-of-dawn flight from Combingham?

'So much better than me,' she repeats bitterly. 'Course you are! I bet you'd never let an innocent man go to jail for murder!' Before I've had a chance to absorb her words, she bursts into tears and flings her body against mine. 'I can't handle much more of this,' she sobs, wetting the front of my shirt. 'I'm falling apart here.'

Before my brain produces all the reasons why I shouldn't, I've put my arms round her.

What the hell happens now?

2

10/3/2011

'So,' Simon said slowly. He was watching Charlie, who wasn't watching him back. She was staring at, but not really seeing, a programme on TV, and trying to act naturally. Like someone who wasn't keeping anything secret. The programme was one in which celebrities experienced life in an African slum before hurrying home to Hampstead the minute the cameras were switched off.

'So, what?' she asked. She hated keeping things from Simon; he'd successfully indoctrinated her over the years, instilled in her the conviction that it was his God-given right to know everything, always. To distract him, she pointed to the screen. 'Look – are those living conditions any worse than ours? I mean, I know they *are*, but . . . we should go and buy some wallpaper next time we've both got a day off – or one of those roller thingies, at least, and a tub of white paint.' She was sick of the lounge walls being a hotchpotch of faded colours no one had wanted for years: a jagged crest of 1970s wallpaper here, a peak of old plaster there. The clashing, unevenly stripped collage effect looked like a psychedelic mountain range, and sometimes felt like a form of visual torture. 'You're staring at me,' she told Simon.

He looked pointedly at his watch. 'I'm wondering what time we're expecting your sister.'

'Liv?' Could Charlie be bothered to deny it? 'How did you know?'

'You're on edge, and you keep picking up your phone.' He stood up. *Great*, thought Charlie. *Another nice, relaxing conversation.*

'You're obviously expecting something to happen. I know Liv's in Spilling today, I know you met her for lunch . . .'

'She's late,' Charlie said, frowning. 'She was supposed to be here between eight thirty and nine.'

Simon pulled open the curtains and leaned his back against the window. Drummed his fingers against the sill.

If he wanted to look out for Liv, he was facing the wrong way. Charlie waited, certain that her sister was the last thing on his mind, grateful to be spared a rant about unexpected visitors. Simon saw no moral difference between a family member turning up unannounced to say a quick hello and grab a cup of tea, and an invading horde holding aloft burning torches as they battered down your front door, intent on razing your home to the ground.

'Why'd you forgive her?' he asked.

'Who, Liv?'

He nodded.

'I didn't exactly forgive her. Well, I never told her I did. I just . . . slid back into seeing her.' Charlie hid her face in the neck of her favourite slobbing-around jumper. She'd stretched it so much over the years, it was probably now capable of being slipped over the heads of three or four people at once, if they stood close enough together. The roll neck in particular was badly prolapsed. Through its wool, Charlie said, 'No formal absolution was ever granted.'

'One minute you hate her because she's started seeing Gibbs, the next minute you're back to talking to her most days like nothing ever happened. And she's still seeing Gibbs. Even planning her imminent wedding to another man hasn't stopped her.'

Charlie could feel her chest and shoulders stiffening. 'Do we have to talk about this?' she said.

'Gibbs is still married, we still work with him. Liv's still invading your territory – that's how you saw it when they first got together, anyway. They still got it on at our wedding, she still hijacked a day that should have been about us and made it about her.'

'Thanks for the reminder. When she turns up, I'll spit in her face. Satisfied?'

'I'm asking what changed.'

'Well, let's see. Gibbs is now the father of premature twin girls, as cute as they are fragile.'

Simon looked impatient. 'You know what I mean. Gibbs is a dad since last month. You forgave Liv last year.'

'No. I didn't.' Charlie walked over to the window, pushed him out of the way and pulled the curtains closed. 'If she turns up now, tough. She's missed her chance. What you call forgiving, I call burying my head in the sand and trying to pretend the past never happened. And let's throw in the present for good measure. Pathetic, isn't it – the lengths a person will go to in order to hang on to a sister?'

Simon picked up the remote control. He flicked through the channels for a few seconds before pressing the 'off' button. 'You're dodging the question,' he said. 'Suddenly you're prepared to bury your head and make the best of Liv in spite of her transgressions when you weren't before. How come?'

'I don't know.'

'You don't, but maybe I do.' He sounded pleased, as if he'd been seeking her uncertainty all along. 'Was it because . . .' He broke off and started to turn in a small circle beside her, like a mechanical toy that was running out of battery power. His states of emergency always began in the same way: twitchy, erratic movements that dwindled to stillness as more and more energy was diverted to the racing brain.

'Simon?'

'Hm?'

'Are you trying to *guess* why I started talking to Liv again?'

'No. The opposite.'

'What does that—?'

'Shh.'

Charlie had had enough. 'Your pawn is going to the kitchen to consume alcohol while loading the dishwasher,' she said. 'If you want to carry on playing, you'll have to bring the game in there.'

Simon beat her to the lounge door and slammed it shut, trapping her in the room. 'The dishwasher can wait,' he said. 'Did you forgive her because you realised your parents aren't getting any younger, and when they die, Liv'll be the only family you'll have left?'

'No. But, again, thanks for the cheery reminder. Maybe Gibbs' and Liv's relationships will both break up, they'll marry each other, and I'll get to be beloved auntie to the premature twins. Or at least tolerated sister of homewrecking slapper stepmum.'

'Stop dicking about. No? You're saying that's not the reason you forgave her? So what was?'

'Oh, God, Simon, I don't *know.*'

'Was it because she had cancer when she was younger? You were worried it'd come back if you were too hard on her?'

'No! Absolutely not.'

'Two nos. Okay, so: why did you forgive her?'

One, two, three, four . . . The trouble was, you could count to ten and still find yourself married to Simon Waterhouse at the end of it. 'Is there a history of dementia in your family?' Charlie asked.

'I know I keep asking, but please, can you try to think? Don't let yourself off the hook so easily.'

'If I don't, who will? Not you. I could waste my whole life dangling from your hook. That wasn't an innuendo, by the way.'

'Think really hard. There must be a reason, and deep down, you must know what it is, or else . . .' He stopped. Bit his lip. He'd said more than he'd intended to.

'Or else . . .' Charlie concentrated on trying to guess the end of his sentence instead of tackling his question, since she was almost certain he wasn't really interested in her feelings towards Olivia. To ransack her brain for the right answer only to have him ignore its emotional content entirely would be too frustrating. 'Ah, I get it,' she said. 'This isn't about me and Liv. It's about one of your cases. Let me guess: someone's been murdered. And . . . somebody's confessed. But they're saying they don't know why they did it. You thought you'd worked out motive, but when you suggested it to them, they denied it – said no, that wasn't why. You think if this killer knows why he *didn't* do it, that must mean he knows why he *did* do it. You're wrong.'

'Is that what your sister told you?' Simon asked angrily. 'What Gibbs told her?'

'No. All my own work,' said Charlie. 'I've banned Liv from talking about your and Gibbs' cases since she stuck her oar in last year. She's been pretty good about it.'

'Then how—'

'Because I'm tied to you by invisible chains. Because I've ditched all parts of my own brain that aren't immediately necessary, in order to make space to carry around in my head a gold, glowing replica of *your* brain, so vastly superior.'

Simon frowned. 'What crap are you talking now?'

Charlie shoved him out of the way, opened the door and headed for the kitchen, which, this evening, felt less like a room in its own right and more like unnecessarily elaborate packaging for a bottle of vodka. 'I know how your mind works, Simon. I don't know why that surprises you. Once the guinea pig knows it's a guinea pig – much harder to surprise aforementioned pig. What? What are you thinking?'

'You really want to know?' He followed her into the kitchen: a new space to confine her in if she said the wrong thing. 'I'm thinking, no one who isn't a woman should ever have to talk to a woman.'

Charlie grinned. She took a glug of Smirnoff straight from the bottle. 'That's funny,' she said. 'You have no idea how most women talk, so you assume I'm representative. I don't talk anything like a woman. More like a . . .' – she cast about for an appropriate metaphor – '. . . really badly treated disciple of an unhinged messiah.' She giggled at the horror on Simon's face. 'And whenever I can I talk like you, in the hope that you'll hear me. Like now. You're wrong: it's perfectly possible not to know why you did something, but to know for sure that it wasn't for reason X.'

'I don't believe it is,' said Simon. 'Not unless you've got an inkling, deep down.' He knocked his closed fist against his chest. 'Somewhere in here, you know why you forgave Liv. If you didn't, you wouldn't be able to say that it wasn't for either of the reasons I suggested, not for sure.'

'Yes, I would.' Charlie put down the vodka bottle, pulled open the dishwasher. 'Think of something you've done and not known why.' After a long silence she added, 'And then tell me.'

'I've tried it on me and proved myself right. If I don't know why, then I don't know why not.'

'Really? What example did you use?'

Simon hesitated. Obviously nothing that might exempt him from answering sprang to mind. 'Proust,' he said eventually. 'Why do I let him get away with it? Why do I never go to HR, tell them what goes on behind closed CID doors? I should. No idea why I don't.'

'Perfect.' Charlie rubbed the palms of her hands together. 'Is it because there's a Persian cat in the Human Resources office, and you're allergic to cats?'

Even in conversation with his wife, in the safety of his own kitchen, Simon hated the unexpected. His mouth set in a grim line. 'You're being deliberately unhelpful.'

'Like you were, with the cancer idea? I'm supposed to believe my disapproval could provoke new cancer in my sister?'

She watched Simon's controlled exhalation with satisfaction. His turn to practise counting to ten. And when he got there, he would find himself still married to Charlie. 'There's no cat in the HR office,' he said. 'And I know I'm not allergic to cats. You can't claim that a known falsehood—'

'I've just proved that it's possible, in some circumstances, to know what your motivation *isn't* without knowing what it is. I rest my case. Put these away.' She handed Simon two clean pasta bowls, steaming from the dishwasher. 'There are some reasons we have that we know about, some we have that we don't know about, and some we *don't* have, which, when we hear them, we recognise as reasons we would *never* have because they're not the sort of thing that would ever cross our minds.'

'Let's say you've killed someone, all right?'

'Can you put those bowls away before you get distracted and drop them?'

'You admit it.'

'I admit it,' said Charlie. 'It was me.'

'I ask you why. You say you can't tell me – there is no reason. You don't know why. You just did it.'

'Did I plan to do it?'

'You say not. It was spur of the moment. Imagine I suggest to you a reason why you might have done it, and it's a reason that, if you confirm it, might get you a lighter sentence or even keep you out of prison if you're lucky.'

Charlie raised her eyebrows. 'What, you mean that perfectly acceptable motive for committing murder that judges and juries are so lenient about?'

'A motive that'd make it not murder, but a less serious crime. Maybe.'

'But . . . it wasn't my real motive?'

Simon considered her question. 'Either it was, and you're pretending it wasn't, or it wasn't and you're not willing to pretend it was to avoid jail time. In either case, why?'

Charlie smiled. 'Or . . .' she said. Simon stared at her expectantly. 'You're not going to like it,' she warned him. 'It's as devious as it is unlikely.'

'Tell me. You know how I feel about Occam's Razor. The simplest answer *isn't* usually the right one. Devious and unlikely is everywhere.'

'You ought to launch your own theory: Occam's Beard, you could call it. Okay, let's say your killer could halve the time he spends behind bars by confessing his true motive, the one you suggested to him. If he's desperate or a pessimist he might go for that. But if he's confident and a good liar, he might deny his real motive and insist as unconvincingly as he can that the crime he committed was full-on murder. Part of that implausibility might include pretending he has no idea why he did it.'

Simon was nodding. 'If he keeps saying he doesn't know why, and I suspect him of lying, I start to think he's not the killer, he's covering for someone. Exactly what I've been thinking. If I find someone else to pin it on, then he doesn't go to jail at all: he gets to be innocent of the greater crime rather than guilty of the lesser one.'

'Simon, it's so unlikely – that it'd occur to him, that he'd have the nerve to carry it through. He'd have to know there was someone else who could have done it, someone with motive and opportunity. Even then, he'd assume you wouldn't be able to prove it, wouldn't he? Any proof there is will point to him, the real killer.'

The doorbell rang, then rang again straight away, more insistently. 'Granted, it's a top idea,' Charlie called over her shoulder as she went to answer it. 'Sadly, it's my idea, not your suspect's.'

'Don't let her in!' Simon bellowed.

'Shout a bit louder and you might drive her away before I get there.'

More ringing of the bell. Charlie swore under her breath as she opened the door. 'Sorry, you've missed your slot. You'll have to make another . . .' *Appointment.* The last word didn't make it.

The woman standing on the doorstep in the driving horizontal rain wasn't Liv. Charlie didn't know who she was, though there was something familiar about her. Yet this was a face she had never seen before, Charlie would have sworn to it.

'Are you Sergeant Charlie Zailer?'

'Yes. Who are you?'

'My name's Regan Murray.'

Don't know the name, don't know the face. And yet . . .

'I'm looking for DC Simon Waterhouse. I know he lives here.'

As if Charlie was about to deny it. 'Simon,' she called, without taking her eyes off their visitor. 'Regan Murray's here to see you.'

At least she didn't need to worry about what she normally worried about. Regan Murray wasn't attractive; no one could think she was. She had a severe face, especially for a woman. Her eyes were too small, her forehead too dome-like.

She was bound to be something to do with the Don't Know Why Killer. Charlie realised she'd been assuming this hypothetical person was a man. Could Regan Murray *be* the Don't Know Why Killer? If she hadn't yet been arrested or charged . . .

'Who?' said Simon.

Not wreckage washed up on the doorstep by the latest case, then. Come to think of it, how did Ms Murray know Charlie's name too, and that she and Simon lived together? There was also the coincidence of the timing: Liv, who'd said she was coming, hadn't turned up, and this stranger had. 'Has my sister sent you?' Charlie asked. Was that why she looked familiar? One of Liv's old school friends?

Simon appeared by her side. 'I don't know any Regan Murrays,' he said to the one in front of him.

'This is a little bit awkward. Can I come in?'

'Not unless you give us a good reason,' Charlie told her.

'Not unless anything,' said Simon. 'I don't know you.'

Listen to us, Charlie thought. *Host and hostess of the year.* This was what happened when you dealt with dangerous, untrustworthy people every day of your working life.

'You do know me,' Regan Murray protested, pushing the door open as Simon tried to close it. 'Or, rather, you'd know my name – what my name used to be. Murray's my husband's name, which I took when we got married, and Regan . . . it wasn't the name I was born with. If you'll let me in, I'll explain.'

'It might have to work the other way round,' said Charlie. 'You've got about ten seconds.'

The woman shielded her eyes from the rain with her hand, so that she could get a better look at Simon as she spoke to him. 'Fair enough,' she said. 'I'm Amanda Proust. Your boss's daughter.'

3

Thursday 10 March 2011

'Lisa? It's me. You're not going to fucking believe this. Guess where I am now? On another fucking coach. Yeah. Yeah, that's right. All of us, on coaches taking us *away* from Cologne airport, when we've just spent two fucking hours getting there. They've said the crew that's supposed to be flying us home have gone past their limit, or something. What? Dunno. Everyone's saying we're off to a hotel, but no one really knows anything. No, I dunno. I'll ask Gaby. Lisa says, is there anyone on here from the airline who might know what's going on?'

'No one,' I say. 'Just us and the driver. Who speaks no English.' No point in shielding Lisa from the awful truth. When we boarded this coach for the first time, outside Dusseldorf airport, I assumed Bodo Neudorf would be coming with us. He seemed to be very much one of the gang at that point: helping elderly passengers and children up the steps, leaning in and counting us all every so often, as if the trip to Cologne airport was his own personal project. I assumed he would wish to oversee it from start to finish, but apparently not. When the door finally slid shut he was on the wrong side of it, having delegated the job of being our reassuring Fly4You liaison guy to nobody.

I turned and watched his lean, straight-backed figure shrink into the distance as we drove away, and was struck by the deceptiveness of appearances. It looked as if we had abandoned him, but he would be fine; we, on the other hand, were alone, all two hundred of us – alone in a hollow, uncontoured way that felt endless, a way that someone like Sean wouldn't be able to imagine and has certainly never experienced. No one has, unless they're a regular air traveller. Or perhaps severely depressed, or terminally ill and on the brink of death. There is nothing more isolating than hurtling through a stormy German night with a random collection of anxious strangers, all chasing the rumour of a plane.

'Lisa says, how can the crew have gone past their flying limit when they've been sitting on their arses necking cups of tea and waiting for us all night? She says it's not like they've been flying anyone else around to kill time, is it? Someone's been lying to us!'

Lisa: thirty-three-year-old nail technician with two toddlers from a previous relationship, now married to Wayne Cuffley and stepmother to twenty-three-year-old Lauren Cookson, who looks much younger than she is, and whom I am currently sitting next to. I'm on her Jason side, not her Father side. The Jason tattoo is even bigger, with red hearts on green stalks inside the holes of the 'a' and the 'o'. Jason is Lauren's caretaker-cum-gardener-cum-handyman husband. He has done the Iron Man Challenge three times.

It would be hard to overstate how much I have learned about Lauren and her family in the past two hours – more than I would have thought possible. All she knows about me is the one detail I have volunteered: that my name is Gaby.

'The time they spend hanging around Cologne airport waiting for us counts as time on duty,' I tell her. 'Do you really want someone who's been awake too long to fly you home?'

'I don't care who flies me home, long as someone does,' Lauren says shakily into her phone. 'Lisa, I swear, I'm going crazy here. I'm panicking. I need to get home. What? Yeah, course I will.' She clutches my arm. 'Lisa says I have to stick with you.'

Thanks, Lisa.

'What? No, I can't. Oh, Lisa, don't ask me that – if I told you, it'd do your head in. It's doing my fucking head in. Jason thinks I'm at Mum's. No, he doesn't know I'm in Germany. Don't tell Dad, will you? He'd only worry – he's as bad as Jason. What? No, I told Jason I'd be back by half eleven, quarter to twelve.

He's going to go mad when I'm not back by then. What am I going to do? I'm on a coach being carted off somewhere, I don't even know where . . .' She starts to cry again. 'What? Yeah, all right. Yeah, I will. Just . . . don't say anything to Dad, will you? Cheers, Lisa.'

No! No! Don't go, Lisa!

'I have to try to keep calm,' Lauren tells me, wiping her eyes. 'Easy for her to say. I'm not good at being calm. Especially when I don't know where I'm going, or how I'll ever get home, if I ever will. It's lucky you're looking after me. If I was on my own, I'd go apeshit.'

Tell her. Tell her, now, that you're not looking after her, that you never agreed to do anything of the sort.

'I'm stressed, that's what it is,' she says. 'This is what I get like. Jason's not frightened of anything, he never panics, but me? I lose it when I get stressed, big time.'

I push away a barrage of self-pitying thoughts along the lines of 'When do I get to cry and physically assault strangers?' and 'Why can't I be looked after?' Ten more minutes of Jason-this-but-I-that might actually make my head explode. I've already heard that Jason doesn't mind rain and snow, but Lauren hates both; Jason can sleep brilliantly on coaches, but Lauren can't; Jason's good at planning whereas Lauren can't think more than two minutes ahead; Jason knows what to do in a crisis and Lauren doesn't.

And I've missed another opportunity: failed for the third time to ask her to leave me alone, to make it clear that I'm not responsible for her. I should have done it when she fell into my arms sobbing, but I didn't. I should have done it when she rang Lisa the first time, as the coach set off from Dusseldorf airport, and told her she'd made a new friend: a nice middle-aged lady called Gaby who was looking after her. I didn't.

Is Jason intelligent enough to realise that if you describe a thirty-eight-year-old woman as middle-aged, she's more likely to want to kill you than help you? Because Lauren isn't.

'What am I going to do?' she asks me.

There's a book in my bag that has magic powers: at least three hundred pages I haven't yet read, and the ability to make this all-night coach ordeal bearable. What's stopping me from getting it out and opening it? Is it my reluctance to discover what 'apeshit' means to somebody whose idea of normal involves wailing in public? If I make the decision to disappoint Lauren, I'll have to suffer the consequences for God knows how long. There can be no getting away from her until we land in Combingham.

Or do I want her to carry on burdening me with her problems so that she'll owe me – so that I won't feel rude when I ask again about the innocent man who's going to prison for murder? I've already asked about him once, at Dusseldorf airport. I asked as soon as I humanely could, after I'd disentangled myself from our awkward embrace and she'd pulled herself together a bit. She clammed up. 'Nothing. Forget it,' she said. So far, I haven't been able to. Perhaps she'll let her guard down and bring it up again if I encourage her to talk.

'Jason doesn't know you're in Germany?'

'No. I've never lied to him before. Four years we've been together. This is the first lie I've told him. I couldn't tell him the truth.'

'Why not?'

'Because. I couldn't. Keep your nose out, all right?'

I can't force her to tell me. Although her mouth is at least as much to blame as my nose is. She shouldn't have mentioned her about-to-be-wrongly-convicted acquaintance if she wasn't prepared to share the full story.

I look at my watch. 'You're not going to be back by quarter to twelve UK time. It's impossible.'

'I know! That's what I'm saying: Jason's going to go mental.'

'What will he do?'

'He thinks I'm at my mum's. He's going to ring her, isn't he? Obviously. And she's going to tell him I'm not there. They'll both go off their heads. Believe me, you do *not* want to see Jason angry. Or my mum, for that matter.'

'Which one are you more scared of?' I ask.

She looks at me, puzzled, as if I've introduced a topic that's unrelated to what we were talking about. 'Jason. I'm not normally scared of Mum, not unless I've been taking the piss and she's going to find out.'

Impatience buzzes in my veins. I'm going to have to skip a stage. 'Ring your mum,' I say. 'You haven't lied to her yet, so you're still in credibility credit. You've told her nothing, right? As far as she knows, you're at home with Jason this evening. Ring her now, tell her the truth. Get her to ring Jason and say you're at her house, you've got food poisoning, you can't come to the phone . . . Et cetera.'

'What do you mean, I haven't lied to Mum?' No one else on the coach is speaking at all. Everybody is listening to Lauren's shrill voice; it's better at travelling than she is. 'Course I've lied! I've said I'm at her house – how can I tell her that without letting on that I've lied?'

'You haven't lied to *her*. You haven't told *her* you're at her house, have you?'

Lauren inspects me disdainfully. 'Well, I couldn't do that, could I?' she says. 'Mum's at her house. She knows I'm not there. She can see with her own eyes.'

Deep breath. 'I know that, Lauren. My point is: if you tell her the truth now, confide in her about how you've had to lie to Jason . . .'

'No.' She shakes her head vigorously. 'She'd ask me why.'

Aha. Progress. 'And you don't want to tell her?'

'Maybe I could tell her, but not with you right in my face, not with all these people earwigging. Thinking they're better than me.'

'Oh, give it a rest,' I snap before I can stop myself.

'What?'

'Your favourite refrain: "Everyone thinks they're better than me". Does the innocent man you're sending to prison think he's better than you?'

'I told you: I don't want to talk about that.'

'Oh, sorry,' I say casually. 'I must have forgotten.'

'No,' Lauren mutters after a few minutes. 'He's one of the few people that doesn't think it.'

And you're rewarding him by letting him go down for murder. Interesting. In the silence that follows, I wonder if I will try to do anything for this unidentified innocent man once I get back to England. Probably not. What could I do? Go to the police and tell them what I know?

Yes. I could do that. Whether I will or not is another matter. In situations of severe abnormality, I find it hard to imagine what I might do once restored to my normal setting. Sean doesn't understand this. Many times he's berated me over the phone, when I've been in an airport or a train station or a car hire office, for not knowing if I will or won't want dinner when I get home.

'It's not me sending him to prison,' Lauren says sulkily, doing a convincing impression of someone who does, in fact, want to talk about it. 'Do I look like the police?'

'Letting him go to prison, sending him there – is there a difference?'

'Yes, there is. There's a fucking big difference.' She passes her phone from one hand to the other and back again.

'Can you stop swearing? Give me that fag packet from your bag – I'll write down twenty new describing words for you to learn.'

'I'll do what I fucking well want, Little Miss Stuck Up Bossy Bitch.' She shakes her head. 'Sending him to prison'd be . . . it would be . . . not the same as . . .'

'Here's what you're trying to say,' I chip in helpfully. 'Actively doing harm to someone is more morally culpable than failing to step in and prevent harm done by others. Right? The difference between positive and negative responsibility; sins of commission versus sins of omission. Yes?'

'Are you always like this?' she sneers at me. 'I feel sorry for whichever poor sod's married to you.'

The coach slows down. Its engine makes a noise that's halfway between a rumble and a belch. If the driver were sitting closer to us and spoke English, I might wonder if he was waiting to hear my response to Lauren's insult.

'I'm not married,' I tell her. 'And what you feel is embarrassed because you didn't understand what I said, even though it's so simple, an egg sandwich could understand it. And before you ask me again: yes, I do think I'm better than you. I wouldn't take it too personally, though. Secretly, I think I'm better than a lot of people. You might too if you were me. Eight years ago I founded a company that invented a part for a surgical robot: a tactile feedback glove, it's called.'

The coach picks up speed. Thank Christ. Now I can admit to myself that I was worried by the belching noise; it sounded ominously breakdown-esque. Mercifully, the engine now sounds as if it's in tip-top nick and we are racing into the night once again. Soon we'll arrive at a hotel and I'll be able to crawl into a minibar and a nice clean bed.

I carry on telling Lauren about myself and my achievements, lowering my voice so that no one else hears. 'My company was bought by a bigger one for a staggering amount of money. Close to fifty million dollars. I didn't get that money personally – well, I got a decent chunk, but my investors got most of it – but it did leave me wondering why so many people don't ever really try and achieve anything big, creatively. Anything world-changing. I'm not talking about you – I wouldn't expect you to be scientifically innovative, because you're obviously not clever enough, but other people I know, people I was at university with. Potentially brilliant people. Why don't they try to do more?'

Lauren is gawping at me, her mouth open. 'Fifty *million* dollars?' she says.

I ignore her. I was enjoying my uninhibited monologue, and I hadn't finished. 'I think I'm better than those people because they seem to want to go through life expending minimum effort, and

I think I'm better than you not because you're thick, which isn't your fault, but because you were mean to Bodo Neudorf. And to the bald man.'

'Bodo what? Who?' Lauren looks around as if expecting to see somebody she hasn't previously noticed. 'What bald man? What are you on about?'

'Cast your mind back and work it out, or remain ignorant,' I say, happy to demonstrate that what goes around comes around. *Tell me about Mr Innocent-of-Murder and I'll remind you of the man you savaged earlier this evening, the one who had his name clearly printed on his lapel badge.*

'I don't think tonight's a one-off for you, is it?' I say. 'I know our current situation is far from ideal, but I bet you're mean and sweary even during the good times.'

No reaction at all.

'The reason I don't mind saying all this to you is that you're so stupid,' I go on. 'It's like talking to a piece of cardboard. No ramifications whatsoever. You're not going to ramificate; you don't know what it means. You don't know which of the words I use are real words and which I'm making up. I bet you've got the memory of a bottom-set-for-remembering-how-to-swim goldfish. Soon you'll be telling me I'm looking after you again, having forgotten everything I've just said.' I smile at her, feeling quite forgiving now that I've unburdened myself.

'You're a fucking cheeky cow, that's what you are,' Lauren announces after a short silence.

'That's what I am,' I agree. 'Well done. See, you have no trouble defining me without reference to Jason. Perhaps you could try doing the same with yourself.'

She stares down at her phone, holding it with both hands. 'Don't speak to me, all right?'

Jason. Now there's a strange thing. 'I don't get it,' I say. 'You've never been abroad on your own before, you're talking about panic attacks, you've lied to your husband, taking a significant risk that he'll find out, since planes are delayed all the time . . . Why? What did you have to do in Germany that took less than a day and justified the risk?'

'Why don't you mind your own business? How do you know it took less than a day?'

I close my eyes. *You mentioned seeing me this morning. But you might not remember having said it, so let's not over-complicate things.* 'No suitcase,' I say.

'So? You've not got one either!'

I open my eyes, and the nightmare is still real. My whole world is still a coach. The moronic Lauren Cookson is still my significant other. 'That's because I, too, have been in Germany just for the day,' I say patiently. 'And I'll happily tell you why.'

'Don't bother,' Lauren snaps.

'All right. I won't.'

Behind me, a young girl's voice pipes up. 'Daddy? Are you awake now?' One of the choirgirls, probably; I didn't see any other children waiting to board apart from a tiny baby.

Her father clears his throat. 'Yes, darling. What is it?'

I steel myself, expecting her to say, 'The two women in front of us are being hateful to each other and it's scaring me.'

'You know how Silas wants to be a famous footballer when he grows up?'

I relax. Lauren is jabbing at her phone with her thumbnail. A few seconds later she says, 'Mum? It's me, Lauren.'

'He wants to play for Manchester United,' says the choirgirl.

'Well, I'm sure whatever team he plays for will be lucky to have him.' The father sounds worried. I imagine he has woken up, looked out of the coach window and seen the same blank blackness and absence of informative landmarks that we're all seeing.

Or perhaps he's wondering how significant a hindrance the name Silas might be for a boy whose ambition is to be a sports legend. Parents are such arrogant idiots. I'm delighted I'm not about to become one.

'Mum, I've got myself in a right mess here. I'm in Germany.' Lauren is crying again. 'Yeah, Germany. No, I'm not in England.'

This is likely to be frustrating. She's going to take half an hour to tell her mother what I could summarise in twenty seconds, but, as a self-confessed hostile stranger, I can hardly hold out my hand for her phone and say, 'Here, let me.'

Should I ring Sean? Other women in my situation would want to phone their partners – for company, for comfort. Those would be the ones with partners who wouldn't immediately launch into yet another accuse-athon.

'I can't tell you now. I haven't told Jason. No. Jason doesn't know I'm in Germany, I've not told him. What? I can't say. No. Not till I see you. I'm on a coach with loads of people earwigging everything I say. Our plane's delayed, and now they're taking us to a hotel. It's horrible, Mum. I've been having a right panic attack. I've got a friend, though, that's one good thing – an older lady. What? She's called Gaby. Yeah. She's looking after me. She's being brilliant. You'd get on with her. She's saying everything you'd say.'

What? Oh, for goodness' sake.

'If Silas did play for Manchester United . . . Dad?'

'Hm? Sorry, darling, I was just trying to get a sense of where we are.'

'If Silas played for Manchester United, would you support them, or would you still support Stoke City?'

'Mum, listen, I need you to ring Jason for me. You're going to have to make-up some bullshit. I've told him I'm at yours. Yeah. You'll have to tell him I've got sick and can't talk. Tell him I'll be back in the morning.'

I tap her on the arm, shake my head.

'Hang on, Mum, Gaby's saying no.'

'If you were sick you wouldn't know when you'd be better,' I say. 'Tell her to tell him you'll ring him as soon as you're well enough – hopefully tomorrow morning, but you can't be sure. Keep it vague.'

Lauren nods. She passes on a less coherent version of my instructions to her mother. If she's lucky, they'll work.

I have just helped the willing facilitator of a serious miscarriage of justice to avoid getting bollocked for lying to her husband. If asked why I did it, I don't think I'd be able to explain. Oh well. Since I'm doomed to live out the rest of my days on a German coach, I don't suppose it matters much.

'Ah, this must be the hotel!' the man behind me says to his daughter. Other people have spotted it too. Exclamations of relief erupt all over the coach. I wipe the condensation off the window, take one look at the building we've pulled up outside and wonder what's wrong with them all. All this inconvenience, and Fly4You couldn't even put us up somewhere decent? We're to spend the night in this squat, grey, featureless building with tiny windows, by the side of a dual carriageway?

'Lauren.' I jab her in the ribs with my elbow.

'I've got to go, Mum, we're at the hotel. I'll ring you in a bit. But you'll tell Jason, yeah? Yeah, I'll stay with Gaby.' She drops her phone into her bag. 'Thank fuck for that,' she says. 'Here at last. My mum says I have to make sure I stay with you.' She stretches her arms above her head, releasing a gust of sweat mixed with floral deodorant.

'We're not staying here,' I decide aloud.

'What do you mean we're not staying here? Why have they brought us here, then?'

'Everyone else is staying here, but you and I are going to find ourselves a different hotel. A better one. This one looks like condemned council flats.'

'What fucking planet are you on? It's the middle of the night!'

'Trust me: this place will be bad in every way.' I pull my BlackBerry out of my bag. 'We'll find the nearest five-star hotel to Cologne airport.'

'Five-star hotel?' Lauren does a whole-body twitch, as if I've given her an electric shock. 'Are you shitting me, or what? I can't afford to stay in a five-star hotel! I'm a care assistant. I don't earn that kind of money!'

'I'll pay for everything. I'll pay for your room.' *Which I'll try to ensure is several floors away from mine.* I'm starting to crave space – specifically, space that doesn't contain Lauren. 'My treat.'

'*No!*' She bursts into tears.

I'm so taken aback, all I can do is stare at her. 'No?' Her reaction makes even less sense to me than my offer. Why aren't I taking this opportunity to go my separate way? There's nothing stopping me from finding a five-star hotel on my own.

Except that I've heard her tell two people that I'm looking after her. And her mother and stepmother both seem to think she needs to stay with me.

In my real life, I wouldn't put up with it; in this alternative universe, my role seems to be to supervise Lauren with a view to improving her. I can think of lots of ways: first break down her resistance to good hotels, then boost her vocabulary, then tackle her willingness to see blameless men framed for murders they haven't committed . . .

'No!' She shakes her head vigorously, sobbing. One of her tears lands in the corner of my eye. 'No. I'm not the sort of person who stays in a five-star hotel.'

'All right, forget it.'

'I can't do it. I wouldn't know what to do.'

'You'd do exactly the same—'

'No! I can't!'

'Fine. It doesn't matter. We'll stay here. Lauren? I'm sorry, just . . . pretend I never said anything. This hotel will be fine.'

She wipes her eyes, mollified. 'It looks all right to me,' she says, assessing it through the coach window. 'I hope it's got something I can eat. I'm starving. Haven't eaten a thing since six o'clock last night. I've not been able to face the thought of food.'

'You were nervous,' I tell her. 'About whatever you had to do today, about lying to Jason. Now you're on your way home, you're starting to feel better. And hungrier.'

She gives me an odd look, then nods. Barely.

What illicit reason could a twenty-three-year-old care assistant have for needing to come to Germany for the day? A lover? Wouldn't she have wanted to stay at least one night, if so? Perhaps she and Jason are one of those couples that never spend the night apart. Sean would approve. He ought to move in with them and form a threesome; they'd probably annoy him less than I do.

Eventually, there's a gap in the line of moving people filing off the coach. 'Come on,' I say. My legs buckle when I try to stand up.

'I can't feel my arse, I've been sat on it for so long,' Lauren announces. She stands, pulls off her silver bullet belt and stuffs it in her bag. Her jeans slide down to reveal sharp hip bones, a red thong and a tattoo of some parallel wavy lines. I don't know if this is purely decorative or if it means something to Lauren; to me it says, 'This accommodation has a swimming pool'.

Sean would claim this is my fault, not the tattoo's: I spend a disproportionate amount of time surfing where-to-stay websites because my work involves so much gadding, swanning and galli-vanting – three words Sean prefers to the more simple 'travelling'. For Christmas last year, I bought myself an antique gold St Christopher medal that I wear on a thin white-gold chain around my neck whenever I swan or gad, even though I am not at all religious. I needed something to make me feel better about all the time I spend surrounded by the flecked and speckled wall and ceiling tiles of airports, so I developed a relationship with St Christopher that involved him accepting my atheism and me redefining his role a little: the patron saint of gallivanters with whiny selfish partners.

Lauren and I are among the last to get off the coach. Two other coaches are parked alongside it: limping, yawning people spill out of all three vehicles. On our way into the hotel, we pass a crying woman who is holding up a very old man. 'Come on, Dad,' she says. 'We're here now. You'll be in bed soon.'

'Look at them, poor sods,' Lauren says to me. 'It's terrible,

Sophie Hannah

what those bastards have done to us tonight. They fucking owe us, big time. I haven't got a toothbrush with me or anything.'

'The hotel should have some,' I say. *Though probably not enough for all of us.* I try not to think about the top drawer of my bedside cabinet that contains at least seven unused miniature toothbrush-and-toothpaste sets, collected from various airlines' business-class goody bags over the years. Next time I travel – in six days' time, another dawn-cracking day trip, to Barcelona – I'll bring them all with me, just in case my flight is delayed overnight and six unstable dimwits decide to appoint me as their primary carer.

'Why would a hotel have toothbrushes?' Lauren asks, looking puzzled. 'Don't people normally bring their own?'

St Christopher? Do you want to field this one?

The hotel reception area is packed. Lauren and I can only just get in. We're standing at the edge of the built-in brown welcome mat. The automatic doors keep half closing on us, then springing open again as they sense the presence of bodies. I catch a glimpse, in the distance, of a plump blonde woman behind a desk. She is speaking, but I can't hear what she's saying.

'Why "FATHER"?' I ask Lauren, looking at her arm.

'It's my dad,' she says.

'Whose name is Wayne. Do you call him "Father"?'

'No, course not.' She giggles. 'I call him "Dickhead" most of the time. I love him to bits, though. He wanted it to say "Father". Wayne could be anyone, couldn't it? It was my birthday present to him, for his fortieth. He's always wanted me to have his name tattooed somewhere on me. Somewhere decent – he's not like that, or anything. Lisa had one saying "Husband" at the same time.'

A low rumble is making its way towards us from the reception desk through the crowd of bodies: the sound of mass discontent, growing louder as it approaches. *Bad news.* The first distinguishable words I hear come from the American woman with the dyed red hair, who is standing about a metre in front of me: 'They can't do that. They can't make us.' She turns; of course she does. In this kind of situation, people know it's their duty to pass on the misery as soon as they've received it. 'Unbelievable! They haven't got enough rooms,' she tells all of us who are behind her. 'Anyone who's on their own has to share. With someone they've never met before!' She lets out a cackle of outrage and throws up her hands. 'I can't see Hugh Grant anywhere in this crush, so . . . I'm out of here, gonna find a hotel with room service, satellite TV and a spa. I'm done with Fly4You.'

She's saying all the things I want to be saying. Except the bit about Hugh Grant – I'd prefer the young David Bowie, but he's not here either. I want to be walking away, like the redhead, out of this crappy hotel. So why aren't I? I *can't* – cannot, will not – share a bedroom with Lauren.

I feel something around my wrist. Her. She's handcuffed me with her fingers again. 'Don't you even think about it,' she says tearfully. It ought to sound like an order she has no right to give me, but all I hear is desperation. Something bad has happened to her, I think suddenly. It isn't only the delayed plane. She's trau-matised; that's why her reaction to hearing that the flight had been rerouted to Cologne was so over the top. *Something to do with her reason for coming to Germany. Maybe something to do with a murder.*

Does her mother know what's wrong with her? Is that why she told Lauren to make sure she stayed with me? Is the former Mrs Wayne Cuffley, first wife of "Husband", so worried about her daughter that she's pinning all her hopes on a woman she's never met?

'Promise you won't go off and leave me,' Lauren hisses reproach-fully, as if her imagining my betrayal and it happening are one and the same.

'I promise,' I say blankly. Part of my brain has gone numb. There's no way out. A sleepover with Lauren Cookson in the worst hotel in Europe. No point thinking about it. Not when you have to do it.

4

10/3/2011

Simon was making coffee for Regan Murray, spilling water and granules everywhere. Subconsciously-deliberately, Charlie guessed, so that he'd have to waste ten minutes cleaning up after himself, and perhaps make the drink again because his first attempt was a mess. Waste wasn't the word Simon would have used: in his book, if it succeeded in postponing a difficult conversation, it was time well spent.

Was there any reason to assume the conversation with Proust's daughter would be difficult? Stupid question.

'Better ring your sister and tell her not to come,' Simon said in a monotone. 'What did she want, anyway?'

'You're asking me *now*?' Charlie nodded towards the closed door. To consolidate their image as ungracious hosts, she and Simon had left Regan Murray alone in the lounge and shut themselves in the kitchen.

'She's an intruder. Let her wait. What does Liv want, and why the secrecy?'

'Not secrecy – reluctance to get involved,' said Charlie. 'On my part. Liv wanted me to ask you. I said no, because I knew there was no point, you'd never agree. If she wants to try and persuade you, that's up to her.'

'So she said she'd come round tonight. And you didn't tell me.' Simon was picking up individual granules of instant Kenco and transferring them from the worktop to the mug. Some were too wet from the pools of water they'd been lying in; they'd lost their solidity, and smeared across his fingertips.

'Like I said, I wanted nothing to do with it. But—'

'Tell me, for fuck's sake.'

'Give me a chance! I was about to say, let's skip the bit where we demonstrate that what I want couldn't matter less, since we're short of time. Liv wants to beg you – wanted me to beg you on her behalf – to go to her and Dom's wedding.'

Simon looked up. 'Why wouldn't I? I'm married to you: her sister. You're going, aren't you?'

Charlie was surprised. 'Yes, but I assumed, and Liv assumed, that you'd be giving it a morally judgemental wide berth. Have you decided you approve of infidelity?'

'Not my infidelity, not my business.' Simon picked up the mug. Water dripped from it onto the floor. He tilted it to wipe its bottom on his shirt, spilled coffee on his trousers, put the mug back on the worktop. 'What do you think I'm going to do? Co-opt Liv and Dom's wedding into my courageous moral odyssey by boycotting it? That'd make me a pompous arsehole. Which I'm not.'

'Since when?' said Charlie. 'No one notified me.'

'Very funny.'

'It wasn't meant to be. All right, since you're full of surprises tonight: Liv also wanted me to ask you if you'd read something. At the wedding. I told her there was no way you'd stand up in front of a crowd of media luvvies and lawyers . . .'

'I'll read,' said Simon.

'You *will*?'

'Why me, though? She's got plenty of people to choose from who love the sound of their own voices – all her friends.'

'She came over all coy when I asked her why you. I think she wants to show you off: her brother-in-law, the brilliant detective.'

'As long as I don't have to introduce myself, say my name, any of that shit. If all I have to do's walk up to the front, read, go and sit down, I'll do it. I'll read a passage from *Moby-Dick*.'

He sounded enthusiastic, for Simon. Charlie felt guilty. 'Not quite,' she said.

'What do you mean?'

'She wants you to read something else. And I'm not telling you what it is.'

'Why not?'

Because I'm incapable of relaying the information in a neutral tone of voice. Because I think it's utterly ridiculous, and I don't want to influence you.

'Well?' said Simon. 'I'm waiting.'

He wasn't the only one. Charlie glanced at the closed kitchen door. She was starting to feel jumpy. 'Can we discuss this later?' she said. 'Don't you want to know what our intruder wants?'

Simon turned away. 'Why's she got two names?' he said.

'You're asking the wrong person, Simon. She's sitting just through there. I'm sure she'd be happy to tell you.'

'How does she know our address? What's she doing turning up here at ten o'clock on a Thursday night?' He often referred to particular hours of particular days in a way that implied they were only acceptable if nothing at all happened in them. He could be alive, awake, bored out of his skull, but still nothing was allowed to fill those prohibited zones. Other more fortunate diary slots – nine on a Monday morning, say – were allowed to contain events. Charlie had never got to the bottom of this peculiar time apartheid, and now wasn't the moment.

'If I'm reading, I'm reading what I want to read,' Simon said quietly.

'What? Oh.' He was back to Liv's wedding. At which there was zero chance of his being allowed to read any part of *Moby-Dick*.

'She looks like him. It's like having a piece of him in the house.'

Back to Proust's daughter again. Switching between subjects so quickly wasn't like Simon. Nor was it like him to be diverted from obsessive thoughts about an ongoing case. He was more anxious than he was willing to acknowledge, and there was no need for it. 'Tell her you're not prepared to talk to her and ask her to leave,' Charlie suggested.

The kitchen door swung open. Regan Murray stood on the threshold. 'Please don't,' she said. 'However much you might want to.'

'Our mistake was to let you in,' said Charlie, putting herself between Simon and this diluted female version of the Snowman: a protective barrier. 'There's no reason for you to be here. Any communication that needs to take place between Proust and Simon can happen at work. They have no personal relationship outside work, and I'm pretty sure whatever you want to say is something personal, which makes it something we don't want to hear.'

Regan stepped sideways so that she could see Simon. 'You asked why I've got two names, and how I knew your address.'

'Did you have your ear pressed against the door?' Charlie asked.

'I got your address from my mum's address book. I have two names because—' She broke off with a sigh. 'Well, the surname part's obvious. Murray is my married name.'

'That makes a good tongue-twister,' Charlie told her. 'You could even add a bit: "Murray is my married name, I married Mr Murray". Did you know opera singers repeat tongue-twisters before concerts, to make their lips more flexible? I heard it on the radio.'

'I changed my first name to Regan two months ago. Dad doesn't know. Neither does Mum. I didn't want to be Amanda any more because my father chose that name for me, so I changed it. It's easy enough to do. Not so easy to tell my parents.' She smiled at Simon, who was resolutely not looking at her. He'd been staring at Charlie since Amanda-Regan had walked in, as if he wanted her to take care of the situation. Not, obviously, by prattling on about tongue-twisters, though Simon would have been the first to admit that it was impossible to get to the good ideas unless you went via the bad ones.

'Is that my coffee?' Regan asked, pointing to the mug.

Charlie handed it to her.

'Thank you. Are you familiar with the name Regan?' she asked. 'From *King Lear*?'

'And from every council estate in the Culver Valley,' said Charlie.

'Regan is Lear's spineless traitor daughter who doesn't love him but pretends she does.'

'You chose Regan over Goneril?' *Yes, this is really happening. You are standing in your kitchen, beside a statue of your husband, debating King Lear's baby name choices with Proust's daughter.*

'I'm too spineless to tell my father I've changed my name,' Regan said to Simon, ignoring Charlie completely. 'He'd ask me why, and I'd be too frightened to tell him the truth. I'd end up hating myself more for creating another opportunity for him to win.'

The thing about people who hate themselves, Charlie thought, is that you totally identify and sympathise at the same time as massively not wanting them as house guests. 'Don't you think it's weird that the expression "son of a bitch" is so well known, but no one ever calls anyone a "daughter of a bastard"?' she asked, looking around. *All responses welcome. The more the merrier.* 'Is it some kind of odd sexism, do you think?'

'I'm terrified of him,' Regan went on. 'Have been for forty-two years. And if I don't want him to know I've changed my name, I can't tell Mum either. She's his faithful lackey. They both want me to carry on being scared of Dad. It suits them fine. If I wasn't scared, I might start telling the truth about my childhood.'

Charlie tried, subtly, to fill her lungs with plenty of oxygen for the ordeal ahead. This was potentially worse than anything she could have imagined, in that it threatened not to finish soon. Childhoods, typically, were eighteen years long.

'I grew up in a totalitarian regime,' said Regan. 'There's no other way to describe it. I don't think I need to describe it, not to you two.'

Thank you, Lord.

'I'm sure you can imagine what I went through. You know what my dad's like.' Regan took a sip of her coffee, winced, then tried to hide it. 'The reason I'm here – and I'm sorry it's so late on a weeknight, I'm sorry I didn't write or ring first to ask if it was okay. For weeks I didn't think I'd be brave enough to contact you at all, and then tonight, when I realised I was, I knew I just had to do it, before I woke up and found I'd turned into a coward again.'

'The reason you're here?' Charlie prompted.

Regan rewarded her with a small smile, for saying something sensible, finally. 'I'm trying to come out from under the shadow. You know? With the help of a good therapist, I'm trying to build myself a proper life, build myself into a proper person.'

'That's been on my to-do list for years,' said Charlie. 'It's making the time, though, isn't it?'

'Can you give the mockery a rest?' Simon muttered.

'It's okay,' Regan told him. 'I know I'm putting you both in an awkward position by sharing this with you. You have to say something, and what can you say?'

Charlie could think of lots of things. They all had the word 'fuck' in them.

'Go on,' said Simon.

Regan looked stunned by this encouragement to speak. It took her a few seconds to recover from it. 'Thanks,' she said. 'Well . . . it's still early days. I'm nowhere near ready to confront my dad, but I'm taking steps in that direction. Important steps, my therapist says. Choosing a name for myself that isn't the name he gave me was the first one.'

'Regan's a baddy in *King Lear*,' Charlie pointed out.

'When you're brought up by someone like my father, you feel like a baddy every time you have a thought or feeling about him that isn't hero-worship. Like a traitor. Regan is who I am at the moment. When it no longer feels like me, I'll change my name again.'

Charlie laughed. 'And your shrink's given this her stamp of approval? I'd get a new shrink.'

'Will you shut up?' said Simon. 'You know nothing about it.'

Not quite true. Last year, thanks to one of Simon's cases, Charlie had met a psychotherapist who'd talked a lot of sense: a woman named Ginny Saxon. Ginny had offered an interpretation of Simon: why he was as he was. Charlie had never told him. She didn't know if she ever would. She couldn't decide if it would be helpful or harmful to pass on Ginny's theory about the psychological syndrome he might be suffering from. She'd have liked to ask someone's advice, but if she couldn't tell Simon, she certainly couldn't tell a third party. For several months, she'd been wishing she didn't know anything about it herself, as if wishing could make the knowledge go away.

'Step two is this,' Regan was saying. 'Coming here, meeting you, Simon. I know it sounds mad, but . . . you matter to me. You're my symbol of courage, in my head – the only person who's ever stood up to my dad. Openly, I mean. Lots of people loathe him and do nothing about it – everyone he knows, apart from my mum – but no one's ever told him what they think of him to his face apart from you.'

Simon cleared his throat. 'How do you know I've done it?'

'Dad talks about you a lot,' said Regan. 'Mainly to Mum, but also to me, sometimes. He always says the same thing: that he's only ever been loyal and supportive and encouraging to you. That you throw it back in his face every day, betraying and insulting him whenever you can.'

'That's not how it is. Or how it's ever been,' Simon said woodenly. Charlie wanted to help him, but she could hardly advise on how best to conduct the conversation while it was still in progress, and once it was over it would be too late. He needed to decide: either not to engage at all, or to immerse himself wholeheartedly and in the manner of a human being.

'He doesn't understand why you're so ungrateful,' Regan said. 'He thinks he couldn't possibly have been a more nurturing, fairer boss.'

'He's lying.'

'No,' Regan said vehemently. 'It's what he believes. He also believes he couldn't have been a better father to me. Want to hear what his idea of good fathering involved?'

'No.' Simon's voice was uneven. 'I want you to leave and not come back.'

Charlie watched the colour drain from Regan's face. 'Simon, don't be a twat,' she said.

'Don't worry, Charlie. I'm not going to fall to pieces. One good thing about being Giles Proust's daughter is that, when someone *else* savages me, it has next to no effect. It seems so . . . watered down.'

'He doesn't mean to be so . . .' Nasty wasn't the right word, not when Simon was frozen solid with shock and embarrassment. There was no right word.

'I meant what I said before,' Charlie told Regan. 'I'd be suspicious of any shrink who thinks that changing your name every time you reach a psychological milestone is a good idea. If you call yourself something stupid for no other reason than to spite your dad, he's winning.'

Looking at Simon but speaking mainly to her own ego, she added, 'I *do* know a bit about this kind of thing. I'm part of a regional suicide prevention forum. I talk to a lot of counsellors and therapists.' Charlie remembered too late that many of these people had, at one time or another, stressed the importance of never uttering the word 'suicide', not unless an at-risk nominal said it first. The word 'nominal' was overused in the suicide prevention literature that Charlie frequently had to plough through. It meant 'person'.

To Regan she said, 'I understand that you admire Simon because he stands up to Proust, but what do you want from him, other than to tell him that?'

'Only to talk. About what we've both been through, if that doesn't sound too dramatic.' She made it sound like the humblest request in the world. Poor woman. She wasn't to know that Simon would rather hand over all of his vital organs and his much-loved and much-Sellotaped copy of *Moby-Dick* than admit to a stranger that he had 'been through' anything.

'I'm still at the stage where I need to prove to myself every day that I'm not an evil defector,' Regan said. 'It would really help me to hear you describe what working with my dad is like – both of you. Maybe it would help you too. We've all been bullied by the same bully, right? For years.'

'I don't mind swapping Proust horror stories,' said Charlie, wondering if her willingness would make any difference to Simon. It might be fun, she thought, though she knew Regan was seeking a far less frivolous commodity: confirmation of the most important truth in her universe.

'It's not happening,' Simon said. 'You've got twenty seconds to get out.'

To Charlie's surprise, Regan nodded. 'That's the reaction I was expecting,' she said. 'If you change your mind, you can contact me at work: Focus Reprographics in Rawndesley.'

'He won't change his mind,' Charlie told her.

'He might once he understands I'm on his side,' Regan said, talking to Simon about himself in the third person. 'You've got a case at the moment: Tim Breary. Wife Francine, had a stroke that left her bedridden? And he's confessed to murdering her, and claims he doesn't know why he did it?'

Fuck, did this woman have a death wish? Simon's face had turned dark and stiff with fury. And Charlie knew the name of the Don't Know Why Killer: Tim Breary.

'There's something you should know that you don't,' said Regan. 'When Breary was first interviewed, you weren't there, were you? Sam Kombothekra and Colin Sellers interviewed him. Dad said it wasn't complicated enough for you: no mystery, an immediate confession.'

Interesting, Charlie thought, that Proust, like Simon and Gibbs when it suited them, shared confidential details of cases with non-colleagues: his wife and daughter, and God only knew who else. Funny that he'd neglected to mention this, on the many occasions that he'd threatened Simon with disciplinary action for telling Charlie too much.

'You only started to take an interest when you found out the motive had gone missing,' Regan went on. 'Dad's not happy about your newfound enthusiasm for the case. He's got his confession and he wants it off his desk, so he told Kombothekra and Sellers to leave you and Gibbs out of the loop. He had them alter the evidence. And here I am: telling you something that could land him in prison.' Regan exhaled slowly.

'Your shrink would be proud of you,' said Charlie. There was something wrong with the story, in spite of the convincing detail about Gibbs also being excluded. Yes, Proust would know that Gibbs would go straight to Simon with the truth. But Sam would too, Charlie was sure. Sam Kombothekra tampering with the evidence in a murder case? No way. And Proust was far too canny to give Sam and Sellers that kind of power over him – the power to end his career. Was Simon thinking all this as well?

'That first interview with Tim Breary – the transcript in the file isn't the one that was there originally,' Regan said. 'Less than two hours ago, I heard Dad boasting to Mum about knowing when to have the guts to bend the rules. It was pretty sickening, though no more so than all the other conversations my parents have. They're all about her reflecting him back to himself in the most flattering way possible.' Regan put her mug down on the worktop. 'I'm no detective, but if Dad cares that much about you not finding out, it must be important, right?' She turned and left the room: the woman who was so terrified of her father that she would give two people who hated him the chance to destroy him and explain that it was all his daughter's idea. Charlie wasn't sure she believed it.

The front door slammed shut.

'She's lying, Simon. She wants you to go after her so that she can lie a bit more.'

Simon picked up the cup Regan had been drinking from and hurled it at the wall. He was out of the house in seconds, leaving the front door swinging open and cold air and rain blowing in. Leaving Charlie covered in cold coffee, surrounded by pieces of broken mug. Not that she cared about that. She tried not to care also, as she heard him yelling hoarsely into the night, that he had never once chased after her while calling out her name as if his life depended on finding her again.

5

Friday 11 March 2011

There is only one bed in this airless attic room. It's a small double, the size of a sofabed, and partly covered with a single duvet. Only one pillow. No cupboards or drawers, just open shelves, on which I see no spare blankets, no cushions, nothing useful. I conduct an anti-inventory: no minibar, no kettle, no sachets of tea or coffee, no telephone, no bedside tables, no reading lamps, no television, no room service menu. In the far wall, there's a door that has had one of its corners shaved off and been squashed in under the eaves. I assume and hope this means we at least have an en-suite shower room. I know without looking that if we do, it will be roughly the same size as Lauren's brain.

'What the fuck is this?' she says, looking around. 'Oh, someone's taking the piss now! There's only one bed. What are we going to do?'

'We're going to make the best of it, because we have no choice,' I tell her. At home, Sean and I sleep in a bed that's seven feet wide, a super-king. When we were buying it, Sean said he thought a king-size would do. I overruled him.

I consider telling Lauren she can have the bed and I'll have the floor, then change my mind. I wouldn't be able to get to sleep, and I need to; even three or four hours would be something. I have no idea what tomorrow has in store. I need to look after myself so that, whatever happens, I'll be able to deal with it.

I am having the thoughts of a disaster survivor, trying to think no further ahead than the next small chunk of time and what actions and decisions it requires.

'I'm not sleeping in a bed with a woman.' Lauren folds her arms in protest. 'Or with a man, unless it's my Jason. He'd go apeshit.'

'Sleep on the floor, then,' I say, praying she'll agree.

'Fuck off! Look at the state of that carpet. There's chewing gum been stamped into it over there. It's filthy. What about finding another hotel, like you said?'

'That was a good idea two hours ago.' In the time it took the receptionist to arrange for all the rooms to be made up and to allocate keys, we could have driven back to Dusseldorf airport. Not that there'd have been any point. Somehow, it feels as if there's no point being here either, in the vicinity of Cologne airport. Getting home, at any time, by any means, feels very unlikely, though logically I know it will happen. 'I'm too tired now,' I tell Lauren. 'I'm not willing to lose any more sleep time. The coach is collecting us at seven.' *Allegedly.*

Lauren's lower jaw starts to twitch. 'You can have the duvet and the pillow,' I tell her. 'I'll use my coat as a blanket.'

'No! I'm not having this! They're bastards, doing this to us.' She tries to push past me. 'I'm going down to the lobby to tell that woman . . .'

'She's not there any more. Once we were all sorted with rooms, she left.'

'How do you know?'

'How do you *not* know?' I snap. 'She told us that was what was going to happen . . .'

'I didn't hear her.'

'. . . and then we saw her leave. Until 6 a.m., this is an unstaffed hotel.' One of my favourite details of our situation that I intend to include in all future tellings of this horror story is that breakfast is scheduled to start at seven on the dot: exactly the time that our coach will be departing for Cologne airport. The receptionist smiled as she presented us with this news, knowing that it didn't affect her; she would be able to have breakfast.

'All right, prove it!' Lauren's eyes light up suddenly. 'If there's no staff here now, let's smash the place up,' she says in a rush of excitement. 'Smash down doors until we find another bed!'

I cover my face with my hand and rub my forehead hard with my index finger. 'Lauren, I want you to listen carefully. You have a choice now. I'm going to get into that bed . . .' – I point to it – '. . . and go to sleep. You can either do the same, or you can fuck off and do whatever you want, on your own. What you can't do is anything that prevents me from sleeping, because if you do that, I promise you, I will make you sorry you ever met me.' That would have sounded more threatening if I hadn't yawned while saying it. Oh well.

I brace myself for the inevitable flood of tears. Instead Lauren says, 'If we're going to share a bed, you have to swear you won't lay a finger on me. And I'm not taking my clothes off.'

I hold up my hands. 'I promise to make no romantic advances. Really, you couldn't be safer. Even if lesbianism overpowers me in my sleep, my good taste will hold firm and protect us both.'

Lauren's eyes widen. She backs away from me.

'What? You're shocked to hear the word "lesbianism" spoken aloud in polite society? Sorry, I forgot to brush up on my bigotry before I set off this morning. If I'd known I'd be meeting you, I'd have given it my all.'

'Can't you talk in a way I'll understand?' Lauren says quietly.

'Yes. Night night – do you understand that?' I kick off my shoes. Fully clothed, I lie down on the far side of the bed, cover myself with my coat and close my eyes. I'd have liked to brush my teeth, but the receptionist ran out of toothbrush-and-paste packs before Lauren and I reached the front of the queue.

'Gaby?'

'What?'

'I'm starving. I feel sick and dizzy. I need something to eat.'

I wonder if I can get away with pretending to have fallen asleep after I said, 'What?' It's worth a try.

'Gaby? Gaby! Wake up!'

Fooling a fool is no fun. It's too easy. I open my eyes. 'There's a petrol station across the road from the hotel,' I say. 'Why don't you go and buy something there? Take the room key.'

'I'm not going on my own!'

'Why not?'

My callous suggestion that she should plunge herself into solitude for the next five to ten minutes has activated Lauren's inner sprinkler system: she's crying again. 'They might not speak English. I've never been to a foreign shop on my own.'

If I had the energy, I would kick myself. I knew she was hungry – she mentioned it earlier. I should have sent her to buy food while I waited in the queue.

'Please, Gaby. Come with me. Then I swear I'll let you sleep.'

I sit up. Dizziness makes my head spin. I clutch at what might be the corner of a silver lining: I can eat something too. I haven't noticed my hunger until now. I've been trying to lull myself into an insensate trance state in order not to notice how I feel about what's happening to me.

'Okay. Let's go,' I say, pulling my shoes back on. 'What are you going to get? I hope they've got hot fattening things and a microwave. I fancy a burger, and a Yorkie bar for pudding.'

Lauren screws up her face in distaste. 'They'll have something English, do you reckon? Foreign food turns my stomach.'

'That's ridiculous. Cheeseburgers don't have passports.'

'What, so liking the food in your own country's ridiculous, is it?' She turns on me. 'It's the Germans that are ridiculous! The only music I've heard all day since I got here is English music – every car stereo that drives past. They've got their own language, but they listen to our music. How daft is that?'

Well, you know the Germans – no nationalistic pride, that's their problem. That's what I say in my head. To Lauren, I say, 'I think I'm going to get a can of Coke as well.' I am learning the rules of moronic dialogue: when answering feels impossible, present an unconnected random statement as if it's relevant to the topic at hand.

Inside the petrol station, soaking wet from the rain, Lauren and I are reunited with the three football shirts from boarding gate B56 at Dusseldorf, the ones who were hoping to get drunk at Fly4You's expense. This is what I like to see: ambition steadily maintained until the goal is reached. These men have not allowed exhaustion, depression or a better idea to divert them from their course. They are at the till, euros out, sixteen cans of beer stacked up on the counter in front of them, still joking about how legless they will soon be. I wonder if this is the way it works for most heavy drinkers: that it's not so much the alcohol itself that's the attraction, but rather the comedy goldmine it represents, the opportunity to say a dozen times, 'How shit-faced are we going to be after all these?'

'There's sod all here I can eat,' Lauren says, looking around miserably.

I pull open the fridge door and take out the only two remaining sandwiches. There is nothing potentially hot on offer, and no microwave. 'Ham or tuna mayo?' I say. 'I'm happy with either.'

'I don't eat sandwiches,' says Lauren.

'On principle?'

'What?'

'Why don't you eat sandwiches? A ham sandwich, on white bread: about as English a snack as you could hope to find. What's the problem?'

She wrinkles her nose. 'Don't know who's had their dirty fingers all over it. I'm all right. I'll just get some Pringles.'

'You need more than Pringles,' I say, spotting my mistake as soon as the words are out of my mouth. *Remember: you don't care about this woman. You don't care if she eats weeds from the petrol station forecourt, or drinks five litres of diesel.*

I will not slip up again.

'I'll get the big size,' she says. 'It's massive. No way I'll be able to eat all them Pringles.'

'I'm going to get the tuna sandwich, because it's the most nutritious and filling thing here,' I say in my capacity as positive role model. 'And some Häagen-Dazs as a treat.' I open the freezer and pull out a tub of Cookies & Cream flavour.

'What's Haggendass?' Lauren asks, unable to make the connection between the word and the thing in my hand that isn't a sandwich.

'Posh ice-cream,' I tell her.

'Ooh-ooh!' she says sneerily, loud enough to turn the heads of the beer collectors. 'How la-di-fucking-da are you?'

'Better la-di-fucking-da than mardy-fucking-brat, that's what I always say. Actually, I don't say it, ever. Normally, I say things like, "So, what are the optimal kinematics for the end-effectors?" Except tonight there's no point saying any of the things I might normally say, because the only person listening to me is a thick parochial bigot.'

'You mean me, don't you?' Lauren says with a triumphant glint in her eye, as if she's caught me out.

One of the football shirts elbows another and says, 'Sounds like it's about to kick off over there. With those two lasses, over there.'

No, actually, it sounds as if the brief kick-off has already fizzled out. And your friends shouldn't need directions, being neither blind nor deaf. If they can't work out which argument you're referring to, what makes you think pointing will make a difference?

Am I the odd one out – not only in this petrol station but in the world? Are most people more like Lauren than like me? It's a scary thought.

'Go and get your Pringles. I assume I'm paying for them?' She hasn't brought her bag or a wallet with her.

'Got no euros left,' she says. 'I need a drink too. Can I have a Diet Coke?'

'No. You can have a normal Coke. If I'm paying, I'm choosing.'

'You what?' She laughs at my outrageousness. 'You're a cheeky cow, you are.'

'You're pin-thin, and you haven't eaten for more than twenty-four hours. You could do with the calories. Plus, Diet Coke's full of aspartame, which is bad for you. Side effects include acting like a dick at Dusseldorf airport.'

Worry shrivels the smile on her face. 'I drink Diet Coke all the time. It's all I drink.'

'Forget it. I was kidding.'

'You what?'

'I was making a joke. Don't you know anyone who does that? You don't have a sense of humour, but Jason does – that sort of thing?'

'You don't know Jason,' she says suspiciously, as if she fears that I might.

'I know. Forget it. Really. I'll stop . . . verbally sparring with you and just accept that there's no way to make tonight fun.'

'So can I have a Diet Coke?'

'No. I was serious about that. In fact, forget Coke as well. Get a bottle of freshly squeezed orange juice. And grab two tooth-brushes and some toothpaste from over there.' I point.

She picks up a can of Diet Coke and holds it defiantly.

'It's orange juice or nothing,' I say firmly. 'In twenty years' time, when you're on your deathbed, you'll be able to tell your great-grandchildren that you once tried vitamin C, one rainy night in Cologne.'

I choose a Coke for myself and pay for our food and drinks. It's raining even harder as we run across the empty dual carriageway back to the hotel. In our room, I sit down on the rancid carpet and tell Lauren to do the same, so that we can dry off a bit before getting into bed. It would make sense for us to dry our clothes on the radiators overnight – one of the best features of this room is that it has radiators – and sleep in our underwear. What are the chances of my being able to suggest this and not be mistaken for a sexual predator whose sole aim is to supplant Jason in Lauren's affections? If I have to sleep in a tiny bed with a cretin, I'd like not to have to do it in wet clothes.

Lauren spits a mouthful of orange juice back into the bottle. 'I'm not drinking *that*,' she says. 'It's disgusting. Got stuff floating in it.'

I'm glad she made us go out; I feel better now that I'm eating. The tuna sandwich is chilly and soggy, but it's tackling my hunger, and I'm able to get through it knowing that there's Häagen-Dazs at the end of it.

I ought to switch on my phone, see if Sean's left the string of messages I switched it off to avoid. I don't have to speak to him. I can send a quick text giving him the basic facts. He'll have gone to sleep by now, anyway.

I look up and catch Lauren staring at me. 'What?'

'In twenty years' time, I'll be forty-three,' she says. 'Why would I die when I'm forty-three?'

I'm so shocked, I nearly inhale the tuna that's in my mouth. I manage to swallow it instead. She must have remembered what I said from the petrol station and worked it out. I want to say well done, but that would be patronising, and I don't want to be – not at the moment. Though I'm sure I will again soon.

'No forty-three-year-olds have great-grandkids,' Lauren announces.

'No. You're right. See what happens when you switch on your brain? You can win arguments.'

'So what were you on about?' she asks, stuffing a handful of broken Pringles into her mouth.

'I was joking.'

'How's that funny, saying something that's not true?'

I balance what's left of my sandwich on my wet trouser leg, unwilling to let it touch any part of the hotel room. 'I was mocking you for being a working-class cliché, and being generally sarcastic and horrible. Me, I mean, not you. It's a way of keeping my mind active. I could read my book instead, but you'd keep interrupting me.'

'What d'you need to read a book for?' Lauren asks.

'Hanging around with you makes me feel as if my IQ's dropping,' I explain. 'I'd like to give it a boost.'

'Your IQ – listen to you!' She grins suddenly. 'I can't wait to tell my Jason about what you're like. Two things I'm going to say: she's a snooty cow, I'll say, but she's all right really. Underneath.'

'He'll feel as if he's known me all his life.' I smile back. 'Look, Lauren, you're not going to die when you're forty-three, but if you carry on smoking at the rate you do, and if you don't eat healthy stuff, ever, you might well die younger than you otherwise would. And . . . you also might have children too young, and get trapped with *your* Jason. He doesn't have to be yours, you know. He could be somebody else's.'

'What are you saying?'

Exactly what I was wondering myself. 'You have choices. You don't have to do what all your friends do.'

'What do you mean, I'll get trapped with Jason? He's my husband. I want to be with him.'

I abandon the remains of my tuna sandwich and move on to the tub of Häagen-Dazs. For once, I think Lauren might have made an excellent point. 'Sorry, I mistook you for me,' I say. 'I'm the one who should ditch her partner and definitely not have a baby with him.' I can't believe I said that out loud.

Only to Lauren. It doesn't count.

Still. I've never even said it to myself before.

'What's your husband called?'

'We're not married. We just live together. Sean.'

'Don't you love him?'

'I don't know if I do any more. Even if I do, it's not enough.'

Lauren laughs. 'You say some freaky things, you. How can love be not enough? It's, like, the most you can care about someone, isn't it?'

'I don't find him impressive or admirable. I can't convince myself that I don't deserve better.' *A proper, self-sufficient grown-up. Someone capable of spending up to four evenings a week alone without complaining.* A sudden surge of anger makes me say, 'If I weren't so busy with work, I'd have got my act together and left him by now.'

Have I turned myself into a procrastinator for Sean's sake? To spare his feelings, because I know I don't want to be with him any more?

Thank God I'm not pregnant. Thank God my flight home was delayed. This is a chance.

'Maybe you deserve better than Jason,' I tell Lauren. 'Is he kind to you? Does he treat you well?' *Or is he a bully, or violent? Is that why you mistake verbal abuse from a stranger for the comforting care of a new friend?*

'He's just a bloke, isn't he?' Lauren looks away. 'They're all pretty much alike.'

I decide not to press her for more details. I don't think I'd like them if I heard them.

'I once knew a man who was nothing like anybody else I've ever known, male or female,' I tell her, slipping free of my usual controls. 'I'd have married him like a shot.' *And had his name tattooed on my upper arm, both my arms.* Sometimes I think that there is nothing I wouldn't do, absolutely nothing, if I could have Tim.

'What happened?' Lauren asks.

'I fucked it up, then blamed Sean.'

'Blamed Sean? Why, what did he do?'

'Nothing. But I've found a way round that: it's called being unfair.'

'So what about the other one?' Why does she look and sound so avid? Having shown no interest in me up to this point, she's suddenly staring at me wide-eyed, as if my theories about my love life actually matter to her. 'Is that why you've not married Sean, because you're still hoping to pull him?'

I laugh. The word 'pull' in connection with Tim is absurd.

Lauren shoves more crisps into her mouth: enough to reveal that she expects to be listening and not talking for the foreseeable future.

'Tell me about your man first,' I say. 'Not Jason – the innocent one who's going to prison for murder.' Lauren isn't a bad person. She seems to have a strong sense of fairness, even if she does wave it around irresponsibly in public places. And something else that's just occurred to me: willing and enthusiastic participants in miscarriages of justice wouldn't typically use that form of words: 'let an innocent man go to jail for murder'. That's the sort of thing you'd say if you were against, not in favour. And Lauren wouldn't be in favour. Incredible as it sounds, I feel I know her well enough to be able to say that. I don't believe she would stand by and let someone be framed for murder unless she felt she had no choice.

Unless she can't go to the police with the truth, because she's too scared of what the real killer might do to her. Could that real killer be Jason, her husband?

Or am I leaping to crazy conclusions?

Lauren stands up. 'You won't let it go, will you?' she says bitterly. She brushes Pringle crumbs off her fingers onto the carpet, picks up her bag and heads for the door with the missing corner. Before I have time to apologise – insincerely, since I don't believe anyone would let it go, and nor should they – she's locked herself in the bathroom.

Hasn't it occurred to her that I could easily go to the police? I more than could, I decide: I will. I'm not scared of Jason Cookson; he has no hold over me. No one should do time for a crime they haven't committed.

The lines from the poem I half remembered at Dusseldorf airport come back to me again: *Our time in the hands of others / And too brief for words.* How can I have forgotten the rest? I don't like to think I've lost anything that came from Tim. They were someone else's words originally, but when Tim read me the poem at the Proscenium, they became his.

I pull my BlackBerry out of my bag and switch it on. Ignoring the symbol telling me that I have voicemails, I hit the internet browser button and type the two lines I remember into the search box. The first result that comes up is the one I want. I click on it, and the poem appears on my screen like an old friend. 'Unscheduled Stop', it's called, by Adam Johnson.

> I sit in the Charles Hallé
> At windy Manningtree,
> While gulls enact their ballet
> Above the estuary.
>
> 'We seem to have a problem . . .'
> A faltering voice explains.
> I spy, along the platform,
> A sign: 'Beware of trains'
>
> And picture you, impatient,
> In the car park at the back
> Of a gaudy toy-town station,
> Or craning down the track
>
> As the afternoon rehearses
> An evensong of birds –
> Our time in the hands of others,
> And too brief for words.

To my horror, I find that I am crying. I can see Tim at the top of the Proscenium's ladder, can hear him telling me that the poet was dying when he wrote the poem. It's his voice in my head, reading the words of each verse aloud.

I wipe my eyes briskly, hoping Lauren won't emerge from the bathroom any time soon. The older I get, the longer it takes me to lose the crying look.

Who is The Carrier?

I have to stop this. Now.

I'm about to turn off my phone when I have an idea: would an internet search track down Lauren's wrongly convicted man? Unlikely, since I don't know his name.

Unless Lauren's name would do the trick. Even more unlikely: 'Lauren Cookson, wife and protector of the real murderer, Jason Cookson, stood by and did sod all to prevent police from arresting someone who had nothing to do with it.'

Still, I type Lauren's name into the search box because it gives me something to think about that isn't Tim. Quicker than the blue line of a pregnancy test, the result I'm looking for comes up: 'Lauren Cookson, her 23-year-old care assistant . . .'

I press my hand over my mouth to make sure no noise escapes, nothing that might alert her. Has this been in the local papers, the ones I never read? On the local news that I never watch because I'm too busy? I click to read the whole article.

God oh God oh God. This can't be right. Cannot be happening. I've had this exact feeling before, so I know that when what's unfolding in front of your eyes is simply not possible, you still have to deal with it. You have to think and act and breathe, and sometimes speak, even though you no longer believe in the world that contains all these things.

It would be ideal in so many ways if this were to turn out to be a dream. It would mean I'm asleep now, for one thing; I've wanted to be asleep for a long time. Only, can I swap this nightmare for a dream that doesn't make me want to scream until I wake up?

My eyes skid over the story, disorientated, trying to take in what they can. 'The body of Francine Breary, 40, was found by Lauren Cookson, her 23-year-old care assistant . . . husband Tim Breary has been charged . . . DS Sam Kombothekra of Culver Valley CID . . .'

The words won't lie still and let me read them. I'm going to black out. I have to close my eyes.

It's Tim. Lauren's innocent man is Tim Breary.

POLICE EXHIBIT 1432B/SK – TRANSCRIPT OF HANDWRITTEN
LETTER FROM DANIEL JOSE TO FRANCINE BREARY DATED
22 DECEMBER 2010

Francine,

I don't want to write this letter, and you're never going to read it.
Not exactly the most promising start.

Who am I writing it for? Kerry's the one who asked me to do it.
For Tim's sake, she said, so a better answer might be Tim,
except he'll never read it either. Kerry says that doesn't matter.
He'll know it's there, she says, like he knows her letters are
there. He might read them and he might not. Kerry thinks
there's a good chance. I disagree. And, since I said I'd only do
it if she promised not to read what I wrote, and I have to say I
trust her on that, I'm fairly sure I'm now writing a letter no one
will read. That idea is supposed to make me feel free to say
whatever I want, but, as I told Kerry, I don't think that works
unless you have something you want to say, and I don't.
Generally, I only bother saying things to people I like who might
listen to me. You never fell into either of those categories,
Francine.

So, I have two options, I suppose. The cop-out would be to put a
blank sheet of paper in an envelope, seal it, write 'Francine' on it
and shove it under your mattress. Sorry – it's not yours, and never
will be, even if you lie on it for the rest of your life. It's Kerry's
and mine, on loan to Tim (that's right, Francine: to Tim, not to

you) for as long as he needs it, and that's the only reason you have the use of it. This seems as good a moment as any to make it clear that if it weren't for Tim's decision to move back in with you and look after you when you had the stroke, Kerry and I wouldn't have got involved. You'd have had no money and no support from us. Just so you know: Tim's the one we'd do anything for. He's the reason you're in the lap of luxury with your own round-the-clock care assistant. You're the one we'd do nothing for.

Looks like I did have something I wanted to say after all.

Well, this piece of paper's no longer blank, so if I'm going for option one I'll have to start again with a new piece, and not start writing next time round. I don't think Kerry would check. She trusts me. As she should, since I never lie to her. Even if she looked, I don't think a sealed envelope would make her suspicious, though I know she doesn't put her letters to you in envelopes. She leaves them open and accessible, so that Tim can read them.

She believes she's found a loophole in his policy. Direct communication about anything personal has always been forbidden (well, not forbidden so much as evaded, but it amounts to the same thing), but if Tim can read her letters secretly and replace them without ever having to admit he's read them, that's a different scenario. He might find it acceptable. If Kerry's theory's right and Tim avoids conversations about feelings because he's not prepared to risk becoming emotional in front of anybody, this is the perfect solution. Personally, I'm sceptical. I think Tim's as afraid of feeling the difficult stuff in private as he is of looking weak in public. That's why he tried to kill himself. He'd succeeded in escaping from you, Francine, and from me and Kerry and everyone else who knew him, but he couldn't escape the contents of his own head and heart. (He would say, 'Are you being superstitious again about the muscular organ that pumps blood around my body?')

It's a pity I'm not allowed to read this letter to you, but Kerry

says I mustn't, and she's the fairest and wisest person I know.
That's not to say I always agree with her: I don't think there
would be anything wrong with making an exception and reading
you extracts at least. You should know about Tim's suicide
attempt. You deserve to know that being married to you has that
effect. You're a tyrant. Were, I mean, before the stroke. Kerry
and I agreed on that definition of you about six months after
you and Tim married. 'A tyrant is anyone whose death would
free somebody,' Kerry said. 'Even only one person.'

I blame you for what Tim did to himself, though he laughed at
me once when I told him this, and said, 'No aspect of my behaviour has anything to do with Francine, now or ever. I ignore her
as scrupulously as you ignore my free will.' Seeing that I wanted
to pursue it further, he forcefully changed the subject. Later, I
puzzled over what he might have meant, and came to this
conclusion: he didn't have to marry you. He could have left you
at any time. Or he could have stayed with you but stood up to
you when you tried to micro-manage every facet of his life. When
he finally walked out on you, he could have gone straight to Gaby
Struthers and told her she was the woman he loved and wanted
to be with. He needn't have turned his back on his friends and
his career, rented a hovel of a bedsit in Bath, logged on to the
internet five months later in search of advice about how to slit
his wrists in a way that would guarantee his death. At every stage
he had choices – that was what he was trying to tell me. To an
external observer, it looked as if he obeyed your orders slavishly
until the day he left you, but Tim chose to define it differently.
He liked to think he disregarded you entirely, and picked the
course of action that was best for him every time. If that
happened to be whatever would keep you happy and therefore off
his back, then the benefit to you was a side effect. Kerry's sure
this is how he saw it, and I agree with her.

Has he told you about trying to end his life, Francine? Maybe
he has. He talks to you now in a way that he didn't before,

when you could answer. He didn't tell me and Kerry when he rang us out of the blue, after no contact for five months, and said in his normal tone of voice, 'I suppose you're too busy to come round, aren't you?', as if we were still regularly in touch and nothing had changed. Kerry said we weren't too busy. There was and is no such thing in our world as being too busy for Tim. You wouldn't understand, Francine, but he's our only family. All three of our actual families are worse than useless – quite a lot worse. We have no one but each other. I've come to the conclusion that people who suffer our particular type of deprivation tend to gravitate towards one another: those of us looking for water that can be thicker than blood is for most people, if you get my drift.

Do you know the story of Tim and his family? Has he told you yet? Post-stroke, I can't see why he wouldn't.

I knew it was Tim on the phone from the way Kerry sat upright and waved frantically at me, signalling emergency. We hadn't heard from him since the letter he'd written us when he left you and Heron Close, informing us that we'd never see him again, consoling us with the assurance that we were better off without his third-rate presence in our lives.

'Where are you?' Kerry asked him. 'Give us an address. We're on our way.' The address was in Bath, three and a half hours' drive from Spilling. It was eleven thirty at night. We knew we would miss work the next day. Neither of us cared. Kerry suggested this might be the perfect opportunity to both hand in our notice. We were about to become very rich thanks to Tim, and Kerry was convinced that his unexpected phone call meant that we would need to abandon our regular lives for the foreseeable future and devote ourselves entirely to helping him. 'He wouldn't have rung if his situation wasn't desperate,' she said on the way to Bath. Having delegated the driving to me, she was taking care of the worrying.

I tried to disagree. 'He might just have missed us and fancied getting in touch,' I suggested. 'No,' Kerry said. 'Whether he fancied it or not, he wouldn't have allowed himself to do it unless he'd reached a crisis point. And this is Tim we're talking about. He'd need to recognise it as a crisis – think how bad it'd have to be for that to happen. If it wasn't life or death . . .' I heard her exhale, trying to breathe her anxiety out. 'Tim isn't an undoer. He makes the most uncomfortable beds, then lies in them until his whole body's riddled with bedsores.' 'Nice image,' I joked, trying to lighten the mood. I suspected she was making a fuss about nothing, but she wasn't having it. 'Think about it,' she said. 'Marrying Francine, letting Gaby disappear out of his life. It's one of his rules: he doesn't value or like himself, so he's rigid about what he will and won't allow himself to do.'

You used to have a fair few rules yourself, Francine: no shoes in the house after you bought 6 Heron Close with its immaculate oak engineered flooring; no putting anything damp to dry on a radiator (why the hell not?); no food or drinks in the lounge; no having the central heating and the gas fire on at the same time, even when the cold's getting into minus degrees; no opening a suitcase to pack for a holiday, and certainly no entering a supermarket, without first making a list. Once in a supermarket, no buying anything that isn't on the list. And then the subtler never-directly-stated rules that governed the psychological lives of all those around you: no preferring anybody to you, no finding anybody more interesting than you, no being closer to anybody than to you. No suggesting, ever, that Tim might want to come round on his own if you were busy on a particular evening, or that if you needed to go into the office one Sunday, Tim might like to come out for lunch with Kerry and me rather than sit at home alone doing nothing, for no reason other than to ensure you didn't feel excluded. We had to remove a hell of a lot more than our shoes for you, Francine. We had to shed our authentic selves (yes, I know that sounds intense, but a) no one will ever read this, and

b) I don't give a toss). The constantly looming threat that was that you would ban Tim from seeing us: one of us would slip up and do something that made it clear that the three of us were closer to one another than any of us was to you, and that would be it – Tim wouldn't be allowed to see us again. None of us was prepared to risk that. Without Kerry and me, Tim wouldn't have had anybody in his life apart from you. So we swallowed most of the conversations we'd have liked to have, and sat there like robots, saying the kinds of things we thought would meet with your approval. In our fucking socks, most of the time.

Apart from making us remove our shoes when we were in your house, you couldn't dictate what Kerry and I wore, but Tim wasn't so lucky, was he? Before he met you, he wore young duffer clothes, always: old-fashioned tweedy suits with waistcoats that made his clients look twice at his face and wonder if this might be an exceptionally young-looking seventy-year-old. The clothes might have looked strange on anyone else, but they suited Tim. Instead of looking like a relic from a bygone era, he looked exactly as everyone knew he was meant to look, and, even weirder than that, he somehow made everyone around him look wrong. I freely admit that shortly after Tim's company merged with mine, I started to dress more traditionally, influenced by him. The irony is that I still dress that way, even though Tim hasn't for years. When he got engaged to you, Francine, you told him he looked like Colonel Mustard and bought him a whole new wardrobe of clothes that would make him look exactly like everybody else. Tim didn't seem to mind. When I asked him about it, he smiled and said, 'Francine cares more than I do about what I wear. She thinks it matters; I know it doesn't.' I was unwilling to let it drop. I said, 'She also cares more about getting married. You don't really want to do it, do you? So why are you?' 'Because I said I would, and she wants me to,' Tim explained, as if it made sense. 'You're right, she cares more. It seems fair that the one who takes the greater interest should have their way, don't you think?'

But there was more to it than that, Kerry says. In contrast to Gaby Struthers, who adored Tim and believed he was special (and therefore she couldn't be trusted), you behaved as if you thought he was a useless piece of rubbish, which tallied with how he saw himself. You were forceful, too – determined to impose your will. Kerry thinks that's why Tim married you and stayed with you. You always seemed so intent on improving him. Maybe he hoped you'd succeed.

'But she's so relentlessly horrible to him,' I pointed out. 'He has zero freedom. I'd give up all hope of improvement and reclaim my life at this point, I think.' Kerry told me I didn't understand. 'Tim has no interest in self-ownership,' she said. 'Who'd want to own a product that they perceive as among the most flawed on the market? Francine convinced him early on that his life was more her project than his. He doesn't think sufficiently highly of himself to treat himself to a second chance.'

She said a similar thing on the way to Bath, about Tim having phoned us out of the blue, five months after writing to us to say he was exiting our lives forever. 'I'm sure he knew within days that banishing himself was a bad move, but this is Tim. He believes that if he forces himself to live with the consequences of his cock-ups, he's at least keeping himself in line. Only utter desperation would provoke a U-turn on this scale – a late-night phone call, a summons halfway across the country, with no notice.'

I sort of knew she was right. Or maybe that's hindsight. I think I can remember being on the verge of saying, 'But he's U-turned before, when he left Francine,' and then stopping myself when it occurred to me that in his farewell letter to us, Tim had written, 'Francine might contact you with a hysterical and asinine account of my having left her. If she does, do your best to impress upon her that I've done no such thing. What I am doing is no reflection on anybody else, nor is it something I am doing "to" anyone, as all but the most ego-ridden will appreciate. I decided it would be beneficial for me and for those close to me if I were to isolate myself, and so that's what I've done. And, more importantly, it's all I've done. I have not left my wife.'

'Only Tim,' I said to Kerry. Or perhaps she said it to me. We said it to one another all the time, and still do. 'Only Tim would leave his wife, then claim emphatically that he hasn't left her, and mean every word of it.'

We arrived at Tim's flat at 2.30 a.m. on the night of the surprise phone call, having done most of the journey at an illegal ninety miles an hour. Kerry put her hand on my arm as we pulled up outside number 8 Renfrew Road. 'Prepare yourself,' she said. 'I don't know what we're going to find, but it's going to be bad.' The house was a shabby Georgian carve-up on a street that was basically a hill, nearly too steep to park on. The front door was standing open, but the effect was the opposite of welcoming. It was more suggestive of none of the residents caring enough to shut it properly. The communal areas were disgusting. The thread-bare carpet was every shade of stamped-in mud, the walls were cracked and damp-stained. The place smelled of a mixture of stale urine and wet dogs. Kerry and I tried not to touch the banister as we walked up the stairs. Tim had one of the two rooms on the top floor, he'd told us on the phone. We assumed it was the one with the open door, from which music was drifting out onto the windowless uncarpeted landing: classical. Songs, in German, a male voice. I looked at Kerry. I probably raised my eyebrows somewhat optimistically. Tim used to listen only to classical music before he met you, Francine – before you called it depressing, and banned it. Kerry shook her head: no cause for optimism. That was when I realised that the guy singing sounded pretty desolate. 'Tim,' Kerry called out.

'Come in,' he called back cheerfully. The music was turned right down, as if to make way for friendly conversation. Once again, I started to doubt Kerry's take on the situation. It would be exactly like Tim, I thought, to make us drive for three hours in the middle of the night and then greet us with ordinary banter, taking up where we'd left off as if we all still lived round the corner from one another.

I saw how wrong I was when Kerry and I walked into the bedsit. Tim was sitting on the bed wearing only boxer shorts and a T-shirt. Next to his feet were pools of blood and a small knife, the sort you'd use to chop garlic. The puddles weren't huge but they weren't small. It was a slow-drip-from-the-ceiling volume of liquid, I remember thinking at the time, as if the roof of Tim's building had a few broken tiles and had leaked red rain in several places.

I freely admit that I was useless, Francine. I froze. Did nothing, said nothing. Well, not quite nothing: I did a lot of looking, staring. So much that I can see the scene clearly now, years later. There were cuts to Tim's wrists, bloodstains and streaks all the way up to his elbows. His skin had a green tinge to it. He'd also cut at his ankles and heels, hence the blood on the floor. The room that contained him was in as sorry a state as its occupant. There was mould growing up the walls, and several of the windowpanes were cracked. Two corners of the ceiling were sporting cobwebs the size of hammocks: thick, grey rope-like constructions that must have been there for years. It horrified me to think that Tim had rented the room in this condition, that he hadn't even cleaned away those enormous webs. 'Because he planned to do nothing in that bedsit but decline and die,' Kerry explained later.

'Don't come near me,' Tim ordered us, picking up the knife. 'You'll get wet and sticky.' It looked and sounded to me as if he was threatening to harm himself further if we approached him physically, but I could have been wrong about that.

Kerry was brilliant, Francine. Acted as if nothing remarkable or upsetting had happened, as if this was just a practical issue that we could easily deal with. 'I can tell you now that none of those

injuries is fatal,' she said matter-of-factly to Tim, striding away
from him and over to the table where his laptop sat open. There
was a pen and a notepad next to it, with something that looked
like a list on the pad, dotted with flecks of red where Tim had
bled as he wrote. Kerry fiddled with the keyboard and the screen
came to life. 'Were these your instructions?' she asked.

'They're rubbish,' Tim said. 'If they were any good, I wouldn't still
be here.' The sickly greenness of his skin became more
pronounced every second. How did Kerry know he was in no
danger of dying? I wasn't so sure. The blood was flowing, there
was no doubt about that. Kerry had her phone out. 'Don't phone
an ambulance,' Tim snapped at her. 'I'm sure it's going to happen
soon.' I remember feeling as if someone had poured a bucket of
icy water into my stomach. Was that why Tim had summoned us:
to watch him die? Did he want us there for moral support? Didn't
it occur to him to wonder about the effect it might have on us?

Kerry snapped back at him, 'I will phone an ambulance, and you'll
shut up.' And she did. And Tim let her. She asked him when he'd
done it. 'Half past ten?' he said speculatively. Every few seconds
he gripped his knees as if they were the part of his body that hurt
most. '"Happy slashing"?' Kerry read aloud from the website. I
shuddered when I heard those words – literally, a whole body
shudder. I wished the internet had never been invented, and hoped
that everyone who put suicide instructions on it would practise
what they preached and die, in pain and soon. I knew the second
I heard the words 'happy slashing' that I'd never be able to get
them out of my head, and I was right: I never have been able to.

Kerry told the ambulance people it was urgent: a man had cut his
wrists and ankles and was losing blood. 'I'm glad you didn't tell
them I tried to kill myself,' Tim said. 'Didn't you?' I asked him. He
dodged the question, saying, 'Spilled blood is visible, cuts are
visible. Intentions are not visible. Better to stick to the facts.'
Kerry told him again to shut up, and that there was no way he'd

done this to himself at half past ten. 'You did it half an hour ago, after I rang you to say we were twenty miles away. Didn't you?'

Do you think that's what happened, Francine? Has Tim told you? Not that you'd be able to tell me if he had. I'd love to know, though. Did he do it as late as possible, so that we'd be in time to save him? Was that his plan all along? If he wanted to live, why not skip the wrist- and ankle-slashing altogether? Wouldn't someone like Tim have chosen a more dignified way to cry for help? Or did he mean to kill himself and fail? In which case, why not admit it, say, 'I can't even kill myself properly, I'm so useless'? Rubbishing himself has been one of Tim's favourite hobbies for as long as I've known him. I said that to Kerry, and she said, 'But he's also proud. You've heard him insist that he doesn't miss Gaby. He rubbishes himself in the abstract – "I'm third-rate, I'm unorig-inal" – while defending his craziest behaviour like a zealot and insisting he's never made a wrong decision.'

While we waited for the ambulance, Kerry interrogated Tim, trying to get a coherent account out of him, her tone strongly implying that she didn't believe a word he said. She sounded almost like you, Francine, and told me later that she'd hoped to increase Tim's chances of survival by forcing him to use his brain to defend his story. 'Why did you write out your wrist-slitting instructions by hand, on paper?' she asked him. 'Why not just read them off the screen? You wanted to kill time, didn't you? Kid yourself you were working towards your goal. You'd made a few tentative cuts and you were putting off making any more.' Tim's responses were inconsistent. He strenuously denied putting anything off, but also wouldn't admit to having tried to take his own life. When the ambulance pulled up outside, siren wailing, he said, 'Why am I being saved, exactly? "I do not approve, and I am not resigned", as a poet once said. That poet was Edna St Vincent Millay.'

You never approved of Tim's love of poetry, did you, Francine? You thought it was effeminate. When he joined the Proscenium Library, he didn't tell you. He knew you'd say it was a waste of money and sulk until he 'decided' to give up his membership.

Tim was furious with Kerry and me, once he heard the footsteps of the ambulance team running up the stairs and realised he was unlikely to die. 'Why all this effort and fuss for me?' he demanded. 'Does someone in Spilling have some VAT they need to claim back? Are all the other accountants busy? I'm not going back there, you know. It's not safe for me to go anywhere near Francine. You're deluding yourselves if you think you can move me in with you, unless you have a house I know nothing about that's nowhere near the Culver Valley.' After saying this, his eyes started to close and he seemed to be drifting off. Kerry burst into tears. I wondered what Tim had meant about it not being safe for him to go near you, Francine: safe for him or safe for you? The ambulance people rushed into the room and started to do their stuff, and it was a huge relief not to be responsible any more. I put my arms round Kerry, but she was too busy to be comforted – she was already planning. 'We have to leave Spilling,' she said. 'We'll sell up, buy a house miles away from Francine.'

Well, we did. And we took Tim with us. We didn't think we'd ever come back, but then you had your stroke and here we are. Tim claims we're here because of you – another of his convenient distortions. You could be anywhere, couldn't you? We could all tell you that you were in the bedroom of a house in Spilling and you wouldn't know any different. The move back was nothing to do with you, Francine. It was all about Gaby Struthers.

Signing off for now,

Dan

6

11/3/2011

The rain from the night before had stopped. Charlie opened the door to a few unconvincing patches of sun and a twitchy Sam Kombothekra, whose nervousness and guilt couldn't have been more obvious. 'I wanted to catch Simon,' he said.

So Regan hadn't lied. And Sam was here to do the right thing. 'You're too late,' Charlie told him.

'He's not due in till midday. He's set off already?'

If she said yes to this, she'd be giving a false impression: that Simon was on his way into work. He'd left clear instructions: she wasn't to reveal his whereabouts or plans, but she also wasn't to lie. 'He's not here,' she said. 'That's all I can tell you. Just don't expect him to turn up for business as usual. Don't expect his cooperation or respect from now on, either.'

Sam sighed heavily, rubbing a hand across his face.

'What the hell were you thinking, Sam? Scheming with Proust and Sellers against Simon? And Gibbs.' About whom Charlie didn't care because her sister cared too much, but still. 'Doctoring interview transcripts, leaving out—'

'Hold on a minute, Charlie. That's not—' Sam broke off and shook his head. Laughed. 'Proust told Simon, didn't he?'

'No. Sellers? No. You won't guess who told us if you try for a million years. And now I'm going back to bed. I've got the day off, I didn't get to sleep till five, so . . . bye.' Charlie tried to close the door.

Sam grabbed it and held it open.

'Is that your I-expected-better-of-you disappointed parent face?' Charlie asked him. 'If so, it's only a matter of time before your boys develop a crack habit, let me tell you.' She tried again to close the door; Sam stopped her a second time. He looked confused: she couldn't possibly really want to shut him out, could she?

He's a good person. You've always thought so.

Is that how it works? Charlie wondered: first build up a reputation for goodness, then behave however you like, confident that no one will recognise any behaviour that belies your label and assigned category? She wasn't sure she had the energy to redefine Sam, not after she'd gone to the trouble of defining him once already. Who had time to re-evaluate these things? Forming judgements about people wasn't supposed to be like dusting or stocking the fridge: something you had to do over and over again.

Sam turned and looked at his car, parked on the road, then back at Charlie. 'Come with me,' he said. 'You'd be a huge help. I could do with talking things over with someone who's coming at it afresh.'

Go with him where? He'd hardly invite her into CID, her former workplace. So where? Curiosity was an unfortunate character trait for a police sergeant who was no longer a detective and had the day off.

'Thanks for remembering to mention what's in it for me,' Charlie said. Though she could see one advantage of going with Sam: she'd be able to make sure he wasn't headed for the same destination as Simon: HMP Combingham, to talk to Tim Breary. Unlikely. Prisons didn't admit visitors without notice, unless those visitors were called Simon Waterhouse. Charlie knew, and Sam would know, that he wouldn't be able to get her in. Which meant that today wasn't her day for meeting Tim Breary, the Don't Know Why Killer.

Charlie heard herself say, 'I regret walking out of my job in CID and leaving it wide open for you to walk into.'

Sam smiled. 'You've never told me that before. But I've always known.'

'I could live with it when I thought you were saintly and more deserving than me, and a good balance for Simon, but now?' She shook her head, knowing she'd regret giving voice to the secret she'd kept carefully locked inside for years. Already, she could feel her resentment swelling, taking shape in the world outside herself.

'Nothing's changed,' said Sam. 'Get dressed. I'll explain on the way.'

'On the way to where? I haven't agreed to come with you,' Charlie pointed out. 'I'm more fucked off with you than I've ever been, and you're inviting me for a day out?'

'The Dower House, home of Kerry and Dan Jose. Wear something . . .' Sam changed his mind about whatever he'd been planning to say. 'Doesn't matter. Wear anything. Not too smart, though. Nothing intimidating or policey.'

Charlie knocked on his forehead as if it were a door. 'I'm angry with you, Sam. I don't want to go for a drive, and I don't want to spend my day off doing your work. Fuck, you're as bad as Simon.' Didn't Sam used to listen to what people said to him? Had working with Simon changed him? Charlie felt treacherous considering the possibility. Simon broke rules, but only . . .

Only when the rules were wrong?

'If you're still angry fifteen minutes after we set off, I'll stop the car, ring a cab to bring you back, and pay for it myself,' said Sam. 'Deal?' It was a deal Simon wouldn't have offered and wouldn't have honoured, and was therefore irresistible.

Charlie groaned as she headed upstairs. 'Pushover,' she muttered. 'Doormat.'

'Reasonable and flexible,' Sam amended.

'Hah! We both know that's not true. Clothes: lefty-liberal caring?'

'Do you have anything like that?' Sam sounded doubtful.

'No. Only chainmail with torture instrument accessories,' Charlie called down from upstairs. She brushed her teeth, washed her face, and put on her favourite bright red lipstick too quickly, so that it looked as if her mouth had brushed against an open wound. She swore under her breath – a calming mantra – as she removed the red smudges with water and a tissue. She wondered if Sam was hoping somebody would confide in her today, someone who wouldn't in him, or hadn't so far.

The Dower House. Kerry and Dan Jose. Charlie had attended a conference at a hotel called The Dower House once, during her former life as an academic. In Yorkshire; she couldn't remember where exactly, but she thought it might have begun with a 'K'. She'd asked a member of staff about the hotel's name, and ended up on the receiving end of a social history lecture that was long, tedious and mildly offensive in that it took for granted that everybody came from a wealthy country-estate-owning family, though both the woman delivering the lecture and Charlie, the only two participants in the conversation, quite clearly did not. Still, it was thanks to that woman's memorable pretentiousness that Charlie now knew that a dower house was where an estate owner's wife moved when she was widowed, once the estate owner had died and the larger manor house had to be passed on to the son and heir.

Charlie didn't think it likely that any of that applied to Kerry Jose, especially not if she was married to the still-alive Dan Jose. She pulled grey wool trousers and a sage-green V-necked lambs-wool jumper out of a drawer – no abrasive fabrics, softness to signify empathy – and felt excited about doing what she still thought of as proper police work, though in the small compart-ment of her mind that she maintained as strictly rational, in which her permanently ailing sensible streak occasionally barricaded itself in order to survive, she knew there was more to policing than catching murderers. There were other kinds of killers to apprehend that CID wouldn't look twice at. That was why Charlie had made a beeline for the regional suicide prevention forum when the chance arose.

She was as opposed to self-murder as she was to all the murders that were officially labelled as such. *Yes, in any and all circum-stances; yes, even in cases of pain and terminal illness – what's wrong with shitloads of morphine? Enough to remove pain and even consciousness if necessary, but not enough to kill.* Charlie defended herself in her head because she'd never had the opportunity in real life. She hadn't told anyone her views apart from Simon, knowing they were unfashionable and would be unpopular.

Ludicrously, most of the other members of the suicide prevention forum claimed to be supporters of the very thing they sought to prevent. In theory, they vigorously defended anyone's right to choose to die and make that choice a reality, while simultaneously working hard to bring down the suicide rate. Charlie found this laughable. Simon had stuck up for the hypocrites briefly, until Charlie had converted him to her way of thinking, but it hadn't felt like a true victory. Simon was a Catholic. He'd probably been persuaded by the ghost of childhood brainwashing as much as by Charlie. One of the few times she'd properly made him laugh, ever, was when she'd said, 'I know this sounds silly, but suicide doesn't do anybody any good.'

~

'Let's hear your excuses, then,' she said to Sam as they set off in his car. It was much brighter now. Even with the visors down, the glare of the sun made the road hard to see. Sam kept having to duck and lean to the side.

'I can't think who told you, but whoever it was . . . Proust didn't bargain for that,' he said. 'Do you know the Tim Breary story so far?'

'The Don't Know Why Killer.'

'Perfect name for him,' said Sam. 'Did Simon think of it?'

'No, I did. I was standing near Simon when it happened, though. Maybe his brain's like wireless internet: if you're near enough, you pick up the signal.'

Sam laughed. He was at peace with the idea that Simon was the source of all brilliance, and assumed Charlie was too. 'On Tuesday, Proust spent the morning digging about in the Tim Breary case, on his own, without telling any of us why. Late afternoon, he summoned Sellers and ordered him to alter the transcript of our first ever interview with Breary – to take part of it out.'

'You keep the recorded version too, though, right?'

'We do. Exactly.'

'Exactly, what?'

'Proust knew the recording would be put into evidence, to be whipped out later by anyone wanting to prove that Sellers' transcript wasn't quite right. Sellers was worried, understandably, about being asked to produce an incorrect transcript, about how easy it'd be to prove that he'd altered it. So he came to me, and I felt the same way: it was crazy.' Sam shook his head. 'And out of character for Proust to ask. Apart from the way he treats us, he doesn't bend the rules, and this was more than a bend he was asking for. I couldn't believe he'd risk his job and reputation—'

'He risks nothing,' Charlie cut in. 'Sellers is the one doing the deed, right? If it ever comes out, the Snowman denies all knowledge. You corroborate Sellers' version, Proust calls you both liars . . .'

'And it's two against one,' Sam hijacked the point Charlie was trying to make. 'He's universally hated at the nick. Sellers isn't; neither am I. Why would he take that risk, give Barrow and the Chief Constable an excuse to get rid of him early?'

'Did you ask him that?'

'I did. He said there was no risk: Simon wouldn't find out, and even if he did, he wouldn't do anything about it.'

'Probably true.' Charlie sighed. 'Is that it? Did he say anything else about Simon?'

'You don't want to know.' Sam's face had reddened. He twisted his head to the right and said something under his breath about driving blind. The car swerved.

Charlie shielded her eyes with her hand and waited for Sam to tell her the rest. She was pleased the sun was torturing him on her behalf.

'He said Simon was a masochist.'

'Oh, not that speech again!'

'You've heard it?'

'In full. Simon's upbringing was so warped that he learned to misinterpret pain as pleasure because it was all he had. That's why he wouldn't be any happier working for someone who treated him well and why the Snowman's the best possible boss for him, one who meets all his needs. Actually, I think there's a lot of truth in it,' Charlie said.

'It doesn't explain why the rest of us tolerate Proust's unacceptable behaviour: me, Gibbs, Sellers.'

They'd left Spilling behind and were heading out of town on the Silsford Road. Which meant that soon they'd see clouds, and visibility would no longer be an issue. Everyone in Spilling knew that the weather was worse in Silsford, always.

'The default setting of human beings is to put up with infinite shit,' said Charlie. 'Look at me, trundling along in the car of a turncoat. You conveniently missed off the end of the transcript story: you did it. Or you told Sellers to do it. And you agreed to keep it from Simon and Gibbs. Did Proust threaten you with the sack?'

'Yes, he did, but no, we didn't. I refused on behalf of us both, me and Sellers. Proust said nothing, just waved me out of his office. I assumed he knew he'd lost. I thought he'd sulk for a while and then forget about it – he never initiates the disciplinary proceedings he's forever promising. But then yesterday I checked the transcript and found that he'd done it himself. The part of the interview he'd wanted gone was gone, and so was the recording. There was nothing to prove anything had been removed, apart from mine and Sellers' memories of what Tim Breary had said that had disappeared from the record. The evidence log had been altered – no mention of the recording where previously there had been. I couldn't believe it. I didn't say anything to Sellers, to Proust, to anyone. I needed time to think it through.'

'You didn't tell Simon.' Charlie thought the point worth stressing. She lowered her window, pressing the button with her

Sophie Hannah

elbow as she lit a cigarette. 'You were at the Brown Cow with him after work last night for at least an hour, and you said nothing.'

'I was still thinking it over,' said Sam. 'Should I put in an official complaint, take it to Superintendent Barrow? Decisions that big can't be made quickly.'

'Yes. I can see how you'd need at least a week to decide whether to turn a blind eye to blatant corruption. It's one of those tricky ambiguous areas.'

'Charlie, I would never have gone along with it. It was a question of how not to, that's all. And it wasn't a week, it was less than twenty-four hours. I'm glad I didn't rush into anything.'

'When you next see Simon, ask him if he shares your gladness.'

Less than twenty-four hours. Simon needed to be made aware of that detail. Would it make a difference? To anyone reasonable, yes, but to someone as obsessive as Simon, who never questioned his right to invade the minds of others and know everything straight away?

'When I turned up this morning, it was to make us all happy,' Sam said. 'Me because I hate keeping anything about a case from Simon—'

'Sounds as if you've tried it more than once,' Charlie interrupted.

'I haven't,' said Sam solemnly. 'I hated it, Charlie. I wanted to spill the whole story last night in the Brown Cow, but I can't do anything without thinking first, and I know Simon *can* when he's in a rage. That's why I waited. And then last night, tossing and turning in bed and keeping Kate awake, I realised that by keeping quiet, I was doing the *opposite* of what Proust wanted.'

Charlie opened her mouth to argue, but found she couldn't. It made sense. There was no way Proust would take that big a gamble if the risk were genuine. 'He wanted you to tell Simon in a way that'd grab his full attention,' she said. 'Wrapped in a fake attempt to keep it from him. He was banking on Simon not reporting him, and even if he did, Proust could produce the missing recording of the Tim Breary interview and Sellers' original transcript, and claim the whole thing had been tactical. Temporary.' None of which he'd told his wife or daughter, assuming Regan Murray was a reliable witness. She'd been convinced his true aim was to keep Simon in the dark, so that he wouldn't question Tim Breary's guilt.

'Precisely.' Sam sounded relieved to have got his point across. They turned onto a single-track road, lined with tall trees on both sides. So they were going either to Lower Heckencott or Upper Heckencott, Charlie deduced. Very nice. Each hamlet had no more than five houses in it, and each one looked from the outside as if it was sure to have a grand piano in its forty-foot entrance hall, whether it was an eighteenth-century mansion or an ostentatious newbuild with one of those fat-pillared outdoor porches, or 'portes-cochères', as Liv pretentiously called them.

'So the deletion was . . . what?' Charlie asked Sam. 'Something that cast doubt on Tim Breary having done it?'

'How did you work that out?' This time Sam didn't suggest that her good idea must have originated with Simon.

'Proust doesn't think Tim Breary murdered his wife, but Breary's confessed.' Charlie flicked ash out of her open window. 'The Snowman needs Simon to challenge that confession, because he won't risk being visibly wrong himself. He knows Simon's likely to make more of something if he thinks he's uncovered it against someone's will, so he stages a cover-up, knowing you'll run bleating to Simon about misconduct. No offence.'

Sam was nodding. 'I go to Simon, bleat, Simon asks me what's missing, what was Proust so determined to strike from the record? I tell him, he latches onto it in a way that he might not have done if he'd just read it without knowing anyone had tried to hide it from him. He decides Breary can't have killed his wife—'

'Except that it wasn't you that told Simon,' Charlie reminded him. 'It was Proust's daughter.'

The car swerved to one side, then righted itself. 'Proust's *daughter*?'

Charlie decided she didn't owe Sam the full story. 'What did Tim Breary say that might or might not be suspicious?' she asked. Simon knew, but wouldn't tell her. Charlie had waited up for him until two thirty last night. He hadn't been with Regan Murray all that time; he'd been walking the streets, thinking about what she'd told him. He'd mumbled something to Charlie about not being ready to discuss it before getting into bed and falling asleep instantly, leaving her lying awake feeling as if she'd lost something important but couldn't work out what.

Sam opened his window: a silent rejection of the guilt-free nicotine hit Charlie was offering him. 'When Breary told us he'd killed his wife, obviously we asked him why. He said he didn't know. It wasn't planned – he was sitting beside her bed talking to her and, without knowing why, he picked up a pillow, pressed it down over her face and smothered her to death.'

'Did she fight back?' Charlie asked.

'She couldn't. Two years ago she had a stroke that left her hardly able to move and unable to speak.'

'How old?'

'Francine was forty when she died, thirty-eight when she had the stroke.'

'That's incredibly young.'

'It is,' said Sam. 'She was a clean-liver, too: exercised regularly, not overweight, didn't drink much, non-smoker, dedicated healthy eater.'

'There's your motive, then,' Charlie said. 'Dull as fuck to live with. Even more so post-stroke, presumably.'

'You're all heart,' Sam teased her. As a diplomatic way of concealing his shock, Charlie guessed. Sam never said any of the things that no one should ever say; he certainly didn't strive to extend the canon in the way that Charlie did.

'Seriously,' she said. 'How about that for motive: he didn't want to be saddled with a vegetable for a wife?'

'Francine wasn't . . .' Sam was stuck. Charlie made a silent vow: if the words 'a vegetable' were the next thing out of his mouth, she would give up smoking forever; this would be her last cigarette. 'Mentally, she was in possession of her faculties,' Sam said eventually.

'So she couldn't speak or move, but her mind was intact?' Charlie shuddered. 'Horrendous. Also, another possible motive: he was putting her out of her misery.' That must have been what Simon meant last night: if Tim Breary had killed his wife to spare her further suffering, if perhaps they had agreed, as some married couples did, that each would mercy-kill the other if necessary, then Francine Breary's death might not be murder. Her husband could plead guilty to aiding and abetting a suicide instead, and stay out of prison. And be given a bottle of wine by the Crown Prosecution Service and a box of chocolates too, probably; everyone was so perky about assisted suicide these days.

'Both motives suggested and rejected,' Sam said. 'Tim Breary denies the euthanasia angle vociferously, and almost as firmly – though not quite – denies wanting Francine out of the way because he was sick of being lumbered with her.'

'So he knew why not,' Charlie said thoughtfully. 'Two reasons why not. But he claims not to know why.'

'Right,' said Sam. 'No idea, he said in that first interview, and it's what he's been saying since. And here's the part Proust thought interesting enough to magic out of the file: when Sellers and I annoyed Breary by refusing to move on from motive as quickly as he wanted us to, when we asked him to have a good hard think and see if he could come up with anything, he said something odd.'

Here it comes, Charlie thought. *Occam's Beard: the weirdest explanation is always the correct one.*

'He said, "It's normal for a person to commit a murder without knowing why. Happens all the time. It's only in films and books that every killer has a cogent motive." He delivered that part with confidence, as if he knew what he was talking about, but then . . . it was as if he suddenly doubted it. He switched from telling us to asking us, said, "Isn't it common for someone to kill another person and then tell you they don't know why they did it? Something came over them, they acted on impulse – that sort of thing?" Sellers asked him if he knew anyone who worked for the police. He said no. "So where have you got that from?" Sellers asked. Breary snapped at him. "I don't know – Radio 4, probably," he said. "I have no original thoughts in my head. Please understand that, and save us all a lot of time and trouble." This guy, I swear, I've never met anyone like him before. He says the strangest things.'

'He sounds like an intelligent, articulate murderer who doesn't want his motive known,' Charlie said. 'Who imagines he can successfully pass himself off as the kind of incoherent skunked-up scrote who knifes someone and says, "It just happened. The knife was in my hand and I stuck him, dunno why."'

'He knows why,' said Sam. 'That's assuming he did it. I think he did, personally, but I'm a minority of one: Simon, Sellers and Gibbs all disagree, and if our theory's right, Proust does too.'

'What makes you think he's guilty?' Charlie asked.

'Tim Breary identified the pillow he used to smother his wife. She had four on her bed. They were all scattered on the floor when Lauren Cookson walked into the room and found Breary standing over Francine's body. Lauren was the care assistant who looked after Francine.'

'How anyone does that job is beyond me,' said Charlie.

'Breary told us he used the pillow with a paisley-patterned cover. Our lab tests proved him right: it was covered in saliva, mucus, oedema fluid – all Francine's. The others were clean.'

'So you're right,' Charlie said. 'He killed her, and doesn't want to say why.'

'I think so. Most of the time. I'd be more certain if it was only Breary saying he used the paisley pillow as a murder weapon and everyone else was saying they had no idea what happened, maybe doubting his word, saying they couldn't believe he'd do it.'

'What do you mean? Who's the everyone else?' Were there witnesses to the murder? How could Tim Breary's guilt be in doubt if there were?

'Kerry Jose. Dan Jose. Lauren Cookson. Jason Cookson.' Sam reeled off the names expressionlessly. 'All the inhabitants of the Dower House were home at the time of the murder. Apparently only Tim was in his wife's bedroom when the murder actually occurred – that's what they all say, Tim included – but they all seem to know what happened in that room as if they'd witnessed it first-hand. They're a small, unanimous community of five.'

Charlie heard frustration in Sam's voice and tried not to smile. He hated it when, despite his best efforts, he didn't feel able to believe witnesses.

'Of the four who aren't Tim Breary, none of them's saying, "Ask Tim what happened, he was the only one in the room when Francine died." They tell it as if they saw it, and their stories are identical. They all talk about the paisley pillow, they quote Tim without saying they're quoting him. It's as if they *were* all there in the room with him. Except they say they weren't, they say he told them what happened afterwards, but . . . I don't know. It feels wrong.'

'Are you thinking *Murder on the Orient Express*?' Charlie asked. 'Agatha Christie. Have you read it?'

'I haven't, but I've seen it on telly. They all did it, together – all the suspects.'

'And it's fiction,' Charlie said pointedly. 'And the reason for all doing it together was so that everyone could be alibied by a suppos-edly unrelated third party, so that it looks as if none of them can have done it. Brilliant idea, but there's only a point if no one wants to go down for murder. Your Tim Breary seems keen to do just that – in which case, why would they all need to . . .' Charlie stopped and laughed at herself. 'Of course they didn't all do it together. It doesn't take five people to hold a pillow over a semi-paralysed stroke victim's face.' In the Agatha Christie novel, the participation of all the conspirators wasn't necessary to ensure the death of the target, but was symbolically significant: everyone wanted to get revenge in person and at close range by inflicting his or her own knife wound. Pillow wound? *Stop it, Zailer.*

Sam pulled the car over by the grassy bank at the side of the road. Charlie tossed her cigarette butt out of the open window and listened to the kind of silence you only ever hear near the homes of the very rich. Ahead was a pair of grey stone gateposts topped by large stone balls. 'Welcome to Lower Heckencott Hall,' said Sam. 'The Dower House doesn't have separate access, so we have to go through the grounds of the big house.' He chuckled. 'That's what Kerry Jose calls the Hall. You should see the size of her place.'

Charlie couldn't take her eyes off the gateposts. On each one was a carved relief of what looked like a cake stand piled high with fruit. Odd choice, so far from a kitchen. Charlie pictured, instead of the fruit platters, an image on each post of a pillow, with a woman suffocating beneath it, a hand pressing the pillow down. Or perhaps several hands, each one pressing on the one beneath . . .

'What if Tim Breary did it, but they all wanted it done?' said Sam. 'I've no proof, but maybe that's where the group thing comes in – the conspiracy, if you want to call it that.'

'You obviously do.' Funny, he'd thought of the word too. Charlie reminded herself that she hadn't yet met any of these people. She was in no position to be theorising with Sam.

He turned to face her. 'Personally, I think Tim Breary killed his wife, but that doesn't mean he isn't lying. Whatever the story is, they all know it. They all know the word-perfect lie they've agreed to present for public consumption, and they all know the truth. And none of them's telling.'

7

Friday 11 March 2011

'So what did you do?' Detective Constable Chris Gibbs asks me. 'When you realised Lauren was talking about Tim Breary.'

I thought I'd finished the story I came here to tell. That's why I stopped talking.

Staying focused is hard. My eyes ache to close and won't stop watering. The left one twitches every few seconds; I've tried rubbing the skin around it, but the spasm is stubborn and won't be smoothed away. My hair is unbrushed and tangled, my trousers are streaked with mud and there are coffee stains on my top thanks to a bout of mid-flight turbulence. I must look repulsive. Poor DC Gibbs; I wouldn't want to be stuck in a too-small, too-warm interview room with me.

'Does it matter what I did?' I say. 'This is about Tim Breary, not me. He didn't kill his wife, so drop the charges and release him. You don't prosecute when there's no chance of a conviction, do you?'

'Not as simple as that, and not up to us,' says Gibbs. 'It's the CPS's call. Crown Prosecution Service.'

'You, them, whoever,' I say impatiently. 'What's a jury going to think when I stand up in court and quote Lauren Cookson on the subject of letting an innocent man go to prison for murder?'

'Your word against hers – that's what I'd think. I'd also wonder about your feelings for Tim Breary. I *do* wonder about them.' He stares at me. Am I supposed to feel guilty for having feelings? It would be so convenient to have none. I'd be able to sit here and concentrate on protecting my interests, and Tim's, with no red whirlwind raging inside me; police detectives would hear my rational arguments and not sense the havoc underneath.

'Whatever your relationship with Tim Breary is or was, at some stage someone's going to sniff it out,' Gibbs says. 'When and how did the two of you meet?'

I'm not ready for this. 'I'll save someone the effort by not hiding anything,' I say, hardly hearing myself. Reasonable speech is no competition for the roaring whirlwind. 'Tim and I were good friends at one time. It's no secret. I'll tell them that, and then I'll tell them what Lauren said about him being innocent of murder, and the jury will acquit him. Except there won't be a jury. It won't come to that. The CPS will drop the charge as soon as they've read my statement.'

Gibbs doesn't disagree as I expect him to. 'It wouldn't happen that quickly,' he says distractedly, as if something more interesting has drawn his attention away from me. 'A lot's going to depend on whether Lauren confirms or denies your account of last night.'

So Tim's freedom hinges on the testimony of an unstable tattooed moron. That's comforting to know. 'She'll deny it because she's scared shitless,' I say.

'You'd be surprised how many people cave in at the first challenge,' says Gibbs.

I want to tell him to stop wasting time speculating and get out there and find Lauren.

'Where's Tim?' I ask. 'Is he here, in a cell somewhere?' If the answer is yes, I'm going to find it hard to stay in my seat. 'Is he in prison? I need to see him.' I think of what Lauren said last night about smashing down doors.

'He's on the CPS's side.'

'What?'

'Who's a more reliable witness in your opinion, Tim Breary or Lauren Cookson?'

I can't give him the quick answer he wants. No question about Tim's character can be answered easily. He is both reliable and unreliable.

'Because they disagree,' Gibbs says. 'Assuming what you're telling me's the truth and she's claiming he's innocent.'

'Every word I've said is true.' Gibbs' words are the problem, not mine. I don't understand them. Who disagrees? With what? Is this how Lauren felt last night, trying to talk to me? 'In an ideal world, I'd be having this conversation after ten hours' sleep,' I say. 'I know you probably don't mean to, but . . . please, can you not mess me around?'

'Tim Breary's confessed to the murder of his wife.'

My stomach lurches. I swallow hard, do my best to breathe at the same time as keeping my throat shut tight. I compensated for lack of sleep with a big cooked breakfast at Cologne airport this morning. It looked and tasted disgusting, but will give me enough energy to get through the day, if it doesn't end up splashed all over the table in front of me.

'If he's confessed, he's lying,' I say once my stomach waves have subsided. *He can't have.* The article I read said nothing about a confession, only that Tim had been charged. 'Why would he confess? It must mean . . .' I fall silent, temporarily unable to locate the meaning. I didn't expect a police station to be so much like an airport: being here makes me feel grainy, undefined, simultaneously lost inside myself and trapped outside my life.

'You're too tired to work anything out,' Gibbs says. 'If you want to help Tim, answer my questions. You can think later.'

If I tell him that I can usually do both at the same time – thinking and answering – will I come over as big-headed?

You're pathetic. You want him to know that you're the great Gaby Struthers, but look at you. You can't keep a coherent idea in your brain for two seconds.

'What did you do after you Googled Lauren Cookson's name and found out about Tim?' Gibbs asks.

Fell apart. Am still falling. 'Tried to convince myself to believe it,' I say. 'I had no idea what I'd do when Lauren came out of the bathroom, what I'd say. I wanted to run away.'

'Why?'

'Isn't it obvious?'

'The obvious thing would be to talk to her, wouldn't it?' Gibbs says. 'Tell her that you know her innocent man and you don't think that can be a coincidence?'

'How can it *not* be a coincidence?' I wipe my runny eyes. 'I know it can't be, but if it isn't, that has to mean—'

'Gaby,' Gibbs interrupts me. 'You're exhausted.'

Why is he telling me things I ought to be telling him?

'Don't put yourself under pressure. It's my job to work out what's going on, not yours.' He smiles at me as if he wants to get his smiling practice over and done with for the day. Or maybe he wants to be warm and reassuring, but doesn't know how to go about it. 'Why did you want to run away from Lauren, once you found out her innocent man charged with murder was Tim Breary?' he asks.

'I wasn't thinking straight. I wanted to get back to the UK and the police as soon as I could. Not that tramping miles along a German dual carriageway at night would have made that happen – which is why I stayed put.'

'You said you wanted to run away. That suggests running from as well as running to.'

He's got me there. In exchange for his smile, I decide to tell him the truth. 'I'd mentioned Tim to Lauren already. Not by name, but I'd told her about a man who'd been important to me. Then to find out she must have meant Tim . . .' The red whirlwind roars louder.

'Take your time,' Gibbs says quietly.

There is no time. I have to see Tim now, help him now. 'I was scared she'd walk out of that bathroom and I'd grab hold of her and shake her till she told me everything: why she was letting Tim take the blame for a crime he didn't commit, how she knew he hadn't done it, who did it if not him. I didn't think I'd be able to restrain myself. She'd have seen how much it mattered to me. Even someone as stupid as Lauren would have guessed it was Tim, the man I'd been talking about.'

'If she didn't know already,' says Gibbs.

I nod. It's hard for me to keep this in mind: that Lauren might have had the upper hand all along. *Must* have had. 'I'd never have told her what I did if I'd known she knew him,' I say. The idea of her inaccurately reporting our conversation back to Tim makes my stomach churn with shame: *She says she'd ditch her bloke and pull you now, given half a chance.* Please don't let that happen, God-that-I-don't-believe-in.

I reach for the chain around my neck and press it between my fingertips, wondering if I'm desperate enough to start praying to a gold medallion. *Do I still count as a traveller, St Christopher, even though I'm back in the UK? Are you still the right person to be talking to, or did your shift end when I landed at Combingham? Is there a patron saint for women who love innocent men charged with murder?*

'I had to find out the truth, for Tim's sake,' I say. 'That mattered more than anything else.' He can't have confessed. Any second now, Gibbs will tell me it was a lie, a tactic to get a reaction out of me. 'The quickest way to do it was to stay and confront Lauren. Or so I thought.'

'Go on.'

'She was in the bathroom for ages. I was glad. It gave me a chance to get myself together. When she finally came out, everything was . . . too different, too quickly. I didn't have to say anything. As soon as she saw my face, and my phone in my hand, she knew. I've never seen anyone look so guilty. She stood there like a block of stone, waiting for me to accuse her. I said, "I know Tim Breary, Lauren. What the hell's going on?" She grabbed her jacket and her bag and ran.' I don't tell Gibbs, because it's too humiliating, that I was sitting cross-legged on the floor when Lauren darted out of the room, that in my shock it hadn't occurred to me that she might try to escape, even though she'd run away from me before.

'I went after her, but she was too fast – she was in the lift before I got to the door. I thought I might be able to catch her if I ran down the stairs, but there was no sign of her in the lobby. I went outside, shouted her name, ran up and down the dual carriageway like a lunatic. I even went back to the grotty petrol station, but she was nowhere.'

'So what did you do?'

It won't help him to know that I fell down in a heap on the wet, muddy forecourt in the pouring rain and howled at the top of my lungs, helpless with frustration and rage. 'I went back up to the room. Tried to work out what the hell was going on, tried to get some sleep. Failed at both. I ended up writing Lauren a long letter – begging her to tell me what was going on, basically.'

'What did you do with the letter?'

Nothing, yet. It's in my bag. 'I tore it up,' I lie. 'It was full of personal stuff about me and Tim. I read it through and decided I wasn't comfortable with the idea that it existed, let alone the thought of Lauren ever reading it. I just had to do something to calm myself down.'

'And in the morning? Lauren wasn't there for the coach at 7 a.m.?'

'No. Nor at the airport, nor on the flight home. We landed, and I came straight here.'

Gibbs writes something down on the notepad on the table between us. From where I'm sitting, it looks like a pattern of squiggles that wouldn't be improved by being turned the right way round. 'If her fear of being in a foreign country on her own was genuine . . .'

'It was,' I say.

'Then she was even more scared of answering your questions, once she knew you knew. She was willing to go it alone and miss her flight, get back to the UK later, increase the risk of her husband finding out she'd lied to him.'

'She knew I'd force the truth out of her,' I say, wondering if I'd have resorted to physical violence. Probably not, not then. I would today, now that I've had a chance to think about it:

I'd put my hands round her stupid throat and squeeze until she told me everything.

'She wouldn't have been able to sustain a lie over a long period, assuming she could come up with one in the first place,' I say. 'She hasn't got the psychological resources. When you find her, it won't be hard to get her to talk. You can speed things up by telling her what you've worked out. Then all she·has to do is agree.'

Gibbs looks up at me. 'What I've worked out?'

'She's lying to protect her husband. Jason Cookson killed Francine Breary. He must have.'

'For the sake of argument, why couldn't it have been Lauren herself?' Gibbs says. 'From your description, she sounds volatile – easily provoked.'

'According to the internet, Francine Breary had a stroke two years ago and couldn't move or speak. How do you provoke someone into committing murder when you're mute and immobile?'

Gibbs nods matter-of-factly. This is the second time I've made a good point and he's seemed bored. He's an odd man.

'Lauren isn't and couldn't be a killer,' I tell him. 'She'd think it was . . . unfair to murder someone, whatever they'd done.'

'Unfair?' His mouth twitches. He's mocking me.

I can't be bothered to explain what I mean. 'I know I've only met her once, but it was a very long once, and it felt even longer. She didn't do it. Can you say the same about her husband?'

'I can't, but Tim Breary can. He's pretty sure he killed his wife. He ought to know, don't you think? He's told us things that only the person responsible would know.'

'Unless the person responsible shared their knowledge with someone else, which you can't guarantee they didn't,' I snap. Why is everybody I meet so stupid? 'Why did he kill her? Was he trying to help her? Was it so she wouldn't suffer any more?'

Gibbs brushes my unentitled questions aside with an officially sanctioned one of his own. 'What does Tim Breary stand to gain by protecting Jason Cookson?'

Bringing Jason into it was a mistake. I can't be certain he's the killer

'If I had to pick, from everyone I've ever met, the one person who might confess to a murder he didn't commit for a reason that would make perfect sense to him and no sense at all to anybody else, I'd pick Tim Breary,' I say.

Something Gibbs said is brushing awkwardly against the back of my mind. Three words: *stand to gain.* 'Who benefits financially from Francine's death apart from Tim?' I ask.

'That's restricted information.'

'I'm guessing Tim's the main beneficiary, if not the only one. I know he and Francine both had life insurance policies.'

'How?' Gibbs pounces on this as if it's a revelation.

'He was my accountant for years.' So misleading, yet completely true. It makes my relationship with Tim sound safe and boring. 'When my partner Sean and I were buying our house, Tim shopped around for mortgages and life insurance for us.'

'That explains how he'd know *you* had life insurance,' said Gibbs. 'It doesn't explain your knowing the same about him and Francine.'

Smartarse. 'He told me,' I say irritably. 'I asked him. I wanted to check that what he was recommending for me was something he'd done himself. I always do that. Never spend money unless the person advising you thinks it's worth his money too, right?'

Gibbs isn't listening. Or rather, he's listening to the voice in his head that's whispering, 'She's in love with Tim Breary, and she knew his wife's death would be profitable.'

I refuse to think like a guilty person when I've got nothing to hide. I didn't murder Francine, and if anyone tries to suggest I did, I'll simply ask when she was killed and then direct DC Gibbs to whatever flight I was on at the time and the many airline operatives and passengers who will be able to confirm my whereabouts. One advantage of being a workaholic with a packed schedule is that alibis are easy to come by.

Under Gibbs' incisive gaze, my bravado wears off quickly. Have I put my foot in it and made things worse for Tim? How can I have, when he's confessed to Francine's murder? For all I know he's sitting in a prison cell right now, holding up a banner that says in capital letters, 'I DID IT FOR THE MONEY'.

Except that wouldn't have been his motive. Not in a million years.

I straighten up in my seat. 'If Tim were ever to commit murder, it would be for someone else's sake, not his own,' I say. 'He wouldn't be the beneficiary.'

'That's an unusual character trait to have,' Gibbs says woodenly. 'Most of the murderers I meet aren't so public-spirited.'

'It's true. Tim wouldn't think it was worth the fuss, just for him. Even for someone else, he wouldn't do it. It's too extreme. Tim hates extreme . . . expressions, extreme actions, more than anything, because they make people vulnerable. They allow others to control you and know you too intimately. Tim likes to glide along the surface. He likes controlled and ironic, letting things happen, pretending nothing matters even when it does.'

I see that I have lost Gibbs somewhere along the way. *Keep it simple.* 'Tim's no more a killer than Lauren is,' I say.

'Have you ever met Jason Cookson?'

'No. You're right. I know nothing about him. If I could take back what I said about him, I would.'

'It's always easier to believe that the people we don't know and don't care about are the evil ones,' says Gibbs.

'I don't *care* about Lauren,' I say indignantly. 'Saying she can't be a killer is hardly a declaration of undying love.'

'Undying love. That's an interesting phrase.' Gibbs leans back in his chair. 'What made you think of it?'

'My ambition to find new and inventive ways of being sarcastic,' I say flatly.

'Tell me about your relationship with Tim, aside from him being your accountant.'

i carry your heart with me, i carry it in my heart.

Tears flood my eyes, spill over. 'I can't,' I whisper.

'You said Lauren seemed frightened of you at Dusseldorf airport, when you first spoke to her.'

Did he mean to help me out with that swift change of subject? I'm grateful for it either way. 'Yes. I gave her a fairly ruthless pep talk at the boarding gate. She was yelling at the airport staff, yelling at other passengers, at anyone who told her something she didn't want to hear. Except me. Soon as I weighed in, the fight went out of her. It was instant. She just stood there and looked at me as if she couldn't believe I was talking to her. I don't know if it was surprise or horror or what, but direct contact with me was a problem for her. It makes sense now, but it didn't at the time. Then later, when I bumped into her in a corridor, after—' I break off.

'After what?'

He doesn't need to know about the pregnancy test. 'After we'd been told to go to Departures and wait for the coach. She ran away from me as if I was chasing her, which I then did.'

Gibbs frowns and looks at his notes again. 'She ran away, but then a few minutes later she threw herself into your arms, told you she'd helped to frame a man for murder, and ordered you to look after her all the way back to Combingham.'

'Yes. It makes no sense.'

'I wouldn't say that.' Gibbs stands, walks over to the window. He balls his hands into fists and presses them against the glass as if he's getting into position for smashing it. 'It makes sense if her feelings about you are mixed. She wants to get near you, or else why's she there?'

He must be right. But why? Why shadow me all the way to Dusseldorf and back? How did she know about me? Did she hear Tim mention my name?

'She's on that flight because of you, and frightened in case you find out her reason for being in Germany, which is that you're in Germany. Last thing she wants is a confrontation.'

'Then what does she want?'

'Let's stick to questions we can answer,' says Gibbs. 'Was she on your morning flight as well?'

'That was the impression I got. She had no suitcase with her, so she hadn't been away overnight, and she mentioned having seen me in the morning. There's only one Combingham to Dusseldorf flight on a weekday morning – the one I was on, the 7 a.m.'

'Can you think, off the top of your head, how she might have known you were planning to go to Germany yesterday, and your flight times?'

'I have a blog,' I say, embarrassed. *I can't communicate with the man I live with, so I compensate by over-sharing on the internet.* 'It's mainly about science-y tech-y stuff, but it has my schedule on it.' *So that Tim can keep track of what I'm doing. So that one day, if he ever wants to, he can be waiting for me at the airport when my plane lands.* 'It also has a lot of me exaggeratedly moaning about having to get up early in the morning to fly to various places. Including Dusseldorf.'

'Name?'

'You know my . . . oh, right, the blog. Gaby Struthers dot com forward slash blog.'

'What line of work are you in?' Gibbs asks.

I hate answering that question unless I can do it properly. It's difficult to summarise, and I'm too passionate about my work to skirt over any of the details. 'At the moment I'm part of a company called Rawndesley Technological Generics. We're working with a German company on a new product. Hence yesterday's trip.'

'New product as in something you've invented?'

'Something we're trying to invent.'

Gibbs walks back to the table and sits down. 'What?' he asks.

'Is it relevant?'

He shrugs. 'I'm interested in people who invent things. I've never had the urge myself. Everything I want exists already.' Something flickers across his face: a problematic or unhappy thought. His strained smile immediately afterwards convinces me that I didn't imagine it. 'I've always reckoned people who invent things are trying to make life too complicated, but that's probably just me.'

'Lucky the person who dreamed up the wheel didn't agree with you,' I say.

'That's different. I'm not saying nothing *ever* needed to be invented. It was different in the old days, before we had everything we needed.'

Is he being serious? 'So you wouldn't bother to invent intelligent string, then?' *As if you'd have a hope in hell of succeeding.*

'What's that?' Gibbs asks.

'What it sounds like. Imagine being able to wrap one piece of string around a box, say, and have the string measure the dimensions of the box.'

'Is that what your company makes? Intelligent string?'

'We're trying. We're not quite there yet.' *We need another twenty million pounds' worth of investment. Fancy chipping in?*

Gibbs looks annoyed. 'I've seen string,' he says. 'How d'you make it intelligent? It's just string.'

I'm too tired to explain that what my colleagues and I are struggling to create is not the kind of string he's picturing, that you buy in a ball from the hardware shop. If I did, he'd probably ask me why I call it string when it isn't. 'I need to sleep,' I say. 'Can I . . . how soon can I talk to Tim?'

'That's for HMP Combingham to decide,' says Gibbs. 'That's where he's remanded.'

The word makes my heart thud like a dropped lead ball.

Tim. In jail. Because Francine's dead. If I could get in, I would: live there with him forever if I had to.

Where are these thoughts coming from? Who is the person having them, this doormat who would sacrifice everything she's worked for to live in prison with a man who rejected her? I don't recognise myself at all.

Gibbs hands me a hanky from his trouser pocket. 'What are you thinking that's made you start crying?' he asks.

I was doing so well and now it's ruined. Lauren Cookson ruined it, and I hate her. I hate her for making me feel like this again, when I thought I'd beaten it.

I am not, in fact, thinking at all. Things are crashing through me: that would be a more accurate way to describe it. 'What's the nearest hotel to the prison?' I ask, standing up. I can't bear to be in this cramped room for another second.

'Aren't you going home?' Gibbs jolts to his feet. Is he about to grab me and force me down into my seat?

'Yes. Right.' I dab at my eyes with the hanky. 'I have to go home first.'

I have to go home so that I can tell Sean I'm leaving.

8

11/3/2011

'There's no need to visit me as often as you do,' Tim Breary said to Simon.

'From your point of view.'

'I wouldn't presume to speak from yours.' Breary smiled. He and Simon were in the room at HMP Combingham known unofficially as 'the parlour'. It was spacious, newly decorated, comfortably furnished, and only ever used by top-ranking prison staff for important meetings – apart from now. Simon had asked for it for this interview, and been surprised to get it. He was hoping that a change from the usual grey dingy backdrop to his stand-offs with Tim Breary would make all the difference.

Breary seemed not to have noticed the new setting. 'I'm not bored or lonely in here, and I won't be, however long I stay,' he said. 'I've made a couple of friends and I'm reading a lot, even for me. Dan and Kerry have very kindly donated more books to the library than the poor orderly in charge knows what to do with.' If Breary was trying for a neutral expression, he was failing. He looked pleased with himself. 'A handful of recidivist offenders have been introduced to the early works of Glyn Maxwell that otherwise might not have been,' he said.

Simon assumed Glyn Maxwell was a poet. Everyone Breary mentioned who wasn't his dead wife or Dan or Kerry Jose was a poet.

'"Don't forget,"' Breary said in his quoting voice, which was both louder and gentler in tone than the voice he used to admit to killing Francine. '"Nothing will start that hasn't started yet. / Don't forget / It, its friend, its foe and its opposite."'

'I'll bear it in mind.' Simon was determined not to get impatient. Suspects often talked nonsense as a way of warding off questions they didn't want to answer, but Breary didn't have the standard bad attitude. His manner towards Simon was almost . . . caring had to be the wrong word, but it was close to that. Simon was becoming increasingly convinced that Breary's aim was not to obstruct but to entertain and communicate – to make a connection of some kind. And his nonsense wasn't nonsense, though it risked sounding as if it was. Simon found he wanted to dismantle each interview once it was over, analyse it line by line. Was Breary's cryptic approach a way of denying or disguising the need to connect?

Don't forget / It, its friend, its foe and its opposite.

Everything about the man sitting opposite him puzzled Simon and had from the start. Breary was a comfortable actor, revelling in the ongoing performance that was his everyday behaviour, yet he seemed entirely genuine at the same time. How was that possible? His articulate charm wasn't smarmy in the way that it easily might have been. There was something restful about being in a room with him. Even when he was determinedly withholding information, there was still the sense that, in his presence, what you were hoping for might happen. *Totally false, based on nothing.* Simon could well believe that Breary had persuaded some of the more easily led scrotes that they were as interested in the early poems of Glyn Maxwell as they were in where their next skag fix was coming from.

Today, Breary's projected bonhomie was more palpable than usual. He seemed less guarded than when Simon had spoken to him previously. Was it the room, with its chairs arranged in a friendly semi-circle? Simon was glad he'd requested it. He wanted Breary relaxed and expansive, imagining he'd got away with pretending to be a murderer.

Simon was certain he was nothing of the sort, and he was prepared to sit here all day – all night too, if he had to – in order to hear Breary admit as much. He'd switched off his phone, and relished the idea that Sam Kombothekra would by now have contacted Charlie and discovered that, as far as Simon was concerned, Sam's perfidy had released him from his contractual obligations to Culver Valley Police for as long as he wanted that release to last. Proust wouldn't see it that way, but Simon had another trump card lined up for that round of the game.

'I've been doing a bit of writing myself,' Breary said. Then he smiled. 'Don't worry, I make sure to tear up all my creations once they're finished.'

When Simon didn't answer, Breary looked at the empty armchairs that dotted the space between them, as if he might get a reaction from them instead. Three empty green chairs. *Francine Breary, Dan Jose, Kerry Jose*. The other players, the absent ones. Simon wondered about the peripherals, Lauren and Jason Cookson. They lived with the Joses, had both been in the house when Francine was killed. *No empty chairs for them.*

All five – Breary, the Joses and the Cooksons – had separately said, when asked, that it was unusual for the five of them and Francine all to be at home at the same time. Tim Breary, by his own account, had chosen a moment when the house was at its fullest to murder his wife, except his story was that he hadn't chosen, hadn't thought about it at all; he'd found himself doing it, without warning or anticipation, for no reason he was aware of.

'What have we done to deserve so much extra visiting time?' he asked Simon. 'Is it you or me that's getting special treatment? Ah, that's your shy face. That means it must be you. Are you going to let me in on your secret?'

'If you let me in on yours,' Simon deflected. He hated the idea that he had a 'shy face', and that Breary recognised it. He was embarrassed by the preferential treatment he received from HMP Combingham, and a couple of other prisons too. When Charlie teased him about what she insisted on calling his celebrity status, he usually left the room. It didn't stop her. Next time she tried it, Simon would tell her Tim Breary had never heard of him, so his reputation couldn't be as powerful as she liked to pretend it was.

'Why did you kill your wife?'

'I've already told you: I don't know. I wish I did. I'd like to be able to help you, but I can't.'

Prison wasn't normally good for anybody, but Breary looked no more under-nourished or sunken-eyed in here than he had as a free man. *Odd.* Usually, the skanky estate lowlifes held up better; it was less of a change for them. Upper-middle-class professionals tended to deteriorate rapidly, mentally and physically.

Not Tim Breary. His eyes glowed with what Simon wanted to call anticipation, though he wasn't sure he could justify the choice of word; it was no more than a half-formed impression. Breary's skin, too, looked particularly buffed today, as if whatever gave skin its nourishment had spruced it up from within. It was frustrating not to be able to reach inside the man's head and uncover the cause of his wellbeing, drag it out into the light.

'Are you pleased Francine's dead?'

'A new question. Excellent.' Breary seemed to be giving the matter some thought. 'No,' he said eventually. 'No, I'm not pleased.'

'You seem it.'

'I know,' Breary agreed. His smile faded, as if the discrepancy bothered him as much as it did Simon. 'Maybe . . . Maybe one day I will be, but at the moment I'd rather . . .' His words tailed off.

'Rather someone hadn't killed her?'

'I'd rather *I* hadn't killed her. Death should happen naturally. And I say that as someone who once cut his wrists and ankles open.'

This was news to Simon. He made sure to show no shock. 'And as someone who, more recently, murdered his wife?'

'Yes. I didn't think that worth adding because you know about it already.' The first hint of irritation from Breary. 'There's no point trying to catch me out. You won't succeed.'

'You say death should happen naturally, yet you took a pillow, put it over your wife's face and smothered her.'

'No mystery there. I acted in a way that was out of kilter with my beliefs, as I've been doing for most of my life. I've always thought it polite: a way of showing courtesy towards the dearly held principles of others, if I deny my own. The spirit of family-hold-back, rolled out across the plain of ethics, if you like.'

Simon didn't. Was Breary crazy? No, that was too easy. 'Why did you cut your wrists and ankles open?'

Breary frowned. 'Do we need to talk about that?' He said it as if it was Simon rather than himself that he was tactfully trying to spare.

'I'd like to know.'

'I did it and shouldn't have done it for the same reason: the world is better off if I have no influence on anything or anybody in it. That's the dilemma of those of us who know we don't matter. Are we more influential if we commit an act of violence to remove ourselves once and for all, or if we do our best to fade into the background?'

Simon tried to picture the foreground capable of making Breary fade. He failed. There weren't many people whose conversation was so unpredictable, or so dramatic.

'"You send an image hurrying out of doors / When you depose a king and seize his throne,"' Breary said, proving Simon's point. '"You exile symbols when you take by force."'

'What's that?'

Breary held up a finger to indicate that he hadn't finished. '"And even if you say the power's your own, / That you are your own hero, your own king, / You will not wear the meaning of the crown."'

'Did you write that?'

'I don't have that kind of talent. A poet called Elizabeth Jennings wrote it.'

'What does it mean? Not about kings,' Simon clarified. 'About you. What made you think of it, in connection with cutting your wrists?' The suicide attempt was something new and solid, he told himself: consolation for the stalemate on Francine's murder. He made a mental note to ask Dan and Kerry Jose about it.

'It means what I said before,' said Breary. 'Let nature take its course. Take no lives – your own or anyone else's. Don't force the world to do your bidding, don't unseat a monarch and try to take his place. "You will not wear the meaning of the crown."'

'Like you aren't wearing the meaning of HMP Combingham?' said Simon. 'You've deposed a murderer and seized his throne. Or hers. Was that what you meant? That you might get a life sentence, but it'll be easy for you to serve the time, knowing that its meaning – the punishment aspect – doesn't apply to you?'

Breary threw back his head and laughed. 'Simon, that's brilliant. Wrong, but brilliant.'

Praise was the last thing Simon wanted, and he couldn't remember asking to be called by his Christian name in this interview or any of its predecessors. He was fighting the uncomfortable feeling that he and Tim Breary weren't part of the same reality and that there was nothing he could do to change that. 'When my colleague DC Sellers interviewed you, you said that people often don't know why they commit murder.' *That's what I've heard second-hand from a woman called Regan. Let's hope it's true.* 'Did you research what real murderers do and don't say? You must have wanted to make sure you got it right, not being a murderer yourself.'

'I didn't research anything,' said Breary. 'And if I had, would that prove I didn't kill Francine?'

Simon thought so, but sensed he was about to be told why he was wrong.

'Haven't you ever had an experience and wondered if anyone else has had the same experience? Looked into it, maybe, to see if you have company in your predicament?'

'No,' Simon said truthfully. 'Why would what's happening to me have anything to do with anyone else and their life?'

Breary sat forward. 'Are you being serious?'

A dangerous question when asked in that half-amused, half-shocked tone. Simon knew it well: less a genuine enquiry than a recommendation that you abandon your seriousness because the asker finds it inappropriate. The best answer, always, was 'no', unless you wanted to embarrass yourself, and Simon didn't. He let the silence run on.

'Sorry,' Breary said. 'I'm starting to want to work you out, just as you're probably about ready to give up on me. The question is, would I rather understand or be understood?'

'And the answer?'

'Understand.'

Same here. Every time.

'I'm not giving up on anything,' Simon told him, aware of a tightness in his chest that hadn't been there a few seconds earlier. Why was it so hard to keep people on the right side of the barrier? Strangers turning up at his door wanting to talk about shared bullying trauma, murder suspects wanting to solve him as if he were a puzzle . . . That was life, when you boiled it down: one human puzzle trying to solve another. Simon wished he could resign himself to not knowing, and that everyone he met would be content not to know him.

'You'll have to settle for second best and help me to understand you,' he said. 'You killed your wife, you tried to kill yourself. Yet you disapprove of killing.'

'Yes.'

'Except sometimes it's necessary, for the avoidance of pain, isn't it? Lying there in that bed was no kind of life for Francine, so you helped her end a life you knew she didn't want to live any more. A mercy killing.'

'How kind of me, if only it were true,' Breary said with sudden bitterness.

'Why not pretend it's true and maybe avoid jail?'

'Why plant the possibility in my head? Don't you think murderers deserve to be locked up?'

'Yeah. I do.'

'I want to be punished so that I can move on with a clean conscience.'

'The only place you'll be moving to if you keep pretending you murdered your wife is one prison cell after another.'

'Metaphorically, I meant.' Breary didn't challenge the part about pretence.

'I had an idea, on my way here,' Simon said. 'I kept thinking, why wouldn't he take the euthanasia lifeline I threw him?'

'You haven't been listening. There are other goals in life aside from getting away with as much as you can.'

Simon was uncomfortable with those thoughtful eyes on him. He stood up and walked over to the window. *Out of reach.* 'You're a good liar, but I don't believe you. All other things being equal, you don't want to be here, locked up.'

'I don't know why anyone bothers with that expression,' Breary said.

'Neither do I. All other things never are equal.'

'Agreed.'

'I've been trying to think of a motive for you,' said Simon. 'For a murder that wasn't a mercy killing.'

'Thank you, but I didn't have a motive. I didn't need one. I was able to kill my wife without one.'

'I've been thinking,' Simon pressed on in spite of Breary's courteous discouragement. 'One person's need or fear can turn into another person's obligation all too easily.' It might not have happened with Francine and Tim Breary, but it happened often, and it was wrong. All those people who'd give anything to turn and run in the opposite direction as they wheeled their sick husbands or wives through the doors of the Dignitas clinic, wishing for just one more month together, even in pain – one more week, one more day . . .

Simon was jumping ahead. He needed to create the scenario for Breary instead of reacting to it in his mind. As so often, he had to remind himself that he wasn't alone in the room. 'Plenty of couples have the conversation while both of them are fit and healthy,' he said. 'One of them says, "If I'm ever not able to look after myself, if my quality of life's shot to shit and I can't end it . . ." And so on.' Simon didn't like to think about the details of what might be said. It was too distressing. 'Did you and Francine have that discussion? Did she make you promise that if she were ever so incapacitated that she couldn't take her own life, you'd do it for her? Maybe she found a way to communicate with you, even though she couldn't speak.'

'Not possible,' said Breary. 'Francine had a left cerebral hemisphere stroke that left her with Broca's aphasia. She couldn't communicate at all. Before you ask the question everyone asks: no, she couldn't pick out letters on a board by blinking. Not all stroke victims can. Only the ones that make the headlines.'

'All right, so you talked about it before she had her stroke,' said Simon.

'Except we didn't.'

'Francine made you promise to kill her if the choice was to let her lie there like a vegetable day after day, year after year, with no self-control and no dignity. How did you feel when she made you promise to do that? Perhaps you said you weren't sure, but she wouldn't take no for an answer.'

'Which would mean what?' Breary asked.

'I know how I'd feel if my wife asked me. Not that she would. She wants the opposite: "Leave me to vegetate," she says. "Sit by my bed and read—"' Simon broke off. He'd been about to say *Moby-Dick*, and was glad he'd stopped himself. Tim Breary didn't need to know the name of his favourite book.

'Read . . . ?' Breary prompted.

'Read a book next to her, keep her company, but not kill her. She'd never ask me to do that. It wouldn't be fair. I wouldn't ask her, for the same reason.'

Breary nodded. 'You're well matched, then. Francine and I weren't so well matched, but we never had the discussion you're describing.'

Simon knew his favoured theory was crazy, but he wanted to

get it out there, see how Breary responded. 'Maybe Francine asked you to do it, and maybe you felt it was unfair. It's too much to ask of anybody, that they kill you – especially the one person who'd be lost without you, the person who'd want you to live no matter what. I'd want my wife alive whatever state she was in, even if she was brain-dead and machines were breathing for her and doing everything for her. Having her there'd still be better than not.'

It was only when Breary said, 'You obviously love her very much,' that Simon realised he'd let his focus slip and allowed his private business to get mixed up in what he was trying to achieve here. His satisfaction at having avoided mentioning *Moby-Dick* was cancelled out. 'She'd feel the same about me,' he said. 'It's not an unusual way to feel. Is it how you felt? Did you agree to kill Francine, or help her kill herself if that terrible moment ever came? Did you feel forced into agreeing? Because that's what it is, all that it's-your-duty-to-kill-me-and-end-my-suffering bullshit: blackmail, plain and simple. And blackmail's been known to trigger murder.'

'Never when I've been the murderer.' There was nothing flippant about Breary's delivery. He looked and sounded serious about making Simon understand. 'Others might, but I would never kill for that reason. I'd never kill for any reason. The minute a motive reared its head, I'd question it. I'd end up tearing it to pieces. I could only kill in the way that I killed Francine – for no reason, because it just happened, because I just *did*. I just did,' he repeated quietly.

What the fuck was going on here? Was Breary implying that only crass, inferior murderers would act on something as hackneyed as a motive, that he was somehow more organic and intellectually modest for letting it happen without knowing why? Confused, Simon returned to his far-fetched theory, which was less outlandish than the reality of Tim Breary and every state-ment that came out of his mouth. 'How hard was it, seeing Francine lying there, incapable of moving or speaking, knowing what you'd promised her – knowing she knew it too? She wasn't brain-damaged.'

'Of course she was.' Breary looked surprised. 'What do you think caused her Broca's aphasia and loss of mobility?'

Simon waved his words aside impatiently. 'I mean, she wasn't brain-*dead*. She could think, even though she couldn't speak.'

Breary ran his tongue back and forth along his lower lip. Eventually he said, 'If the experts and their endless tests can be trusted, Francine's brain still worked. She could listen, she could hear. I talked to her, played her music, read her poetry . . .' He blinked a couple of times, then looked straight at Simon, as if he'd said to himself, *That's enough of that.* 'And then, on 16 February, I killed her.'

'You read her poetry because you wanted her to want to live. Why else would you bother?' Simon snapped, annoyed in advance because Breary was going to shoot down his theory, and it was a good one. 'You didn't want to do what you'd sworn you'd do. You thought if Francine could listen and think, there was a point to her staying alive. But you knew she disagreed. She couldn't say so, but she didn't need to: she'd made her views clear in the past. You knew she'd hate to be helpless, and you knew she'd be remembering what she'd made you promise. Every time you read her a poem, you heard her unspoken accusation as loud as if she'd screamed it: "How can you let me down so badly? How can you betray me? You promised to kill me if I ever ended up like this."'

Breary cleared his throat. 'Go on,' he said quietly.

'Why, so you can tell me I'm wrong? Fine. I think maybe you started to feel some rage of your own. Defensive fury. Yeah, you were letting Francine down, but what about what she was doing to you? Lying there silently begging you to turn yourself into a killer, to do something that would haunt you forever – something illegal, apart from anything else. To risk your freedom. You couldn't stand it. Every time you went into her room, it was harder for you. Did you grow to hate her? Feel as if there was no way out?'

Silence from Breary. His eyes flitted about the room, as if trying to locate the source of the words he was hearing.

'If it was me in that situation, I'd have felt the pressure building,' said Simon. 'What can you do? You have to kill her. You've promised, you know she wants it. She's trapped. Relying on you. You can't handle the blame you're sure you can see in her eyes every time you look at her, but you're furious too: she's got no right to impose such a . . . destructive obligation on you, destructive not just of her, but of you too – you *more*. The duty to kill her, your wife, of all people. To rip up your own heart and soul, ignore what you know's right and do the worst thing a person can do. So you have an idea. It's nearly as bad as what you're trying to avoid – maybe it's worse, even – but it's all you can think of, the only escape route: you murder Francine.'

Simon was less convinced this was a possibility now that he was saying it out loud. It sounded deranged. It *was* deranged.

'You *want* to kill her for what she's forced you to agree to, so you do,' he said, feeling the desire to obliterate as he described it. Charlie had once accused him of saving all his passion for situations that existed only in his mind; was she right? 'Francine expected you to put your principles and your free will into cold storage and do her bidding – something no human being should ever ask of another. When you thought about that, you decided she deserved murder, not mercy. You were pleased to get one over on her. When she saw that pillow coming towards her, she misunderstood. She thought you were keeping your promise, for her sake. "At last," she thought. She had no idea you were murdering her – but you knew, and that was enough. You were taking your revenge.'

Simon wiped sweat from his upper lip. 'That's why I'd have done it if I were you,' he said, trying to find a way back to normal interview mode after his outburst 'You dealt with your obligation to your wife, your guilt and your anger in one easy action: a pillow over the face. That's why you'll never admit that what you did was assisting a suicide, no matter how it might help you – because if it was that, if you say *even once* that that's what it was, then Francine's won, hasn't she? She's the boss, even in death, and you're weak.'

Breary stood up and pulled something out of the elasticated waistband of his prison-issue trousers; the speed of the movement made Simon take a step back, but it was only a folded piece of paper, not a weapon. 'Take it,' Breary said.

'What is it?'

'Give it to Gaby – Gaby Struthers, Rawndesley Technological Generics. Don't do it when Sean's around, the man she lives with. Make sure she's alone.'

Simon unfolded the page and saw a handwritten poem, a sonnet. The words 'falling in love' leaped out at him; he was too distracted to take in any more. There was nothing to indicate who had written it.

'I'm sorry to ask a favour when I've given you nothing,' Breary said.

Was he serious? One look at his face told Simon he was: he wanted Simon to deliver a love poem to a woman. Was it his way of hinting at a motive that so far hadn't been suggested? The name Gaby was a new one to the investigation.

'She might be able to help you,' Breary murmured. Simon could only just hear him.

'How?'

'Your answer to that question will be better than any I could give.'

Except that Simon didn't have an answer. *Will be better*, future tense: once he'd met Gaby Struthers and found out . . . what? In the meantime, he would happily have settled for Breary's inferior explanation, the one he knew he wouldn't be getting.

'I haven't got much imagination, but I recognise and admire it in others,' Breary said. 'Yours is superhuman. I fooled Francine into believing I was helping her to die while privately, in my mind, I was murdering her? I wouldn't have thought of that if

I'd tried for a thousand years. And since you're no closer to knowing what I did or didn't do, or why, or why not, you'll need to come and see me again and think up more theories. Which will give me something to look forward to.' Breary looked away, sighed. 'Listen, I know this might be the last thing you want to hear and I'm sorry, but . . . I feel irrationally proud to be the subject of your brilliant ideas. And all the more guilty for not being able to help you.'

Simon didn't often find himself on the receiving end of overt, unqualified praise. When other people talked about his amazing theories – and, yes, he couldn't deny that he usually turned out to be right – they tended to load their voices with exasperation. Correct, inspired, but still a pain in the arse; would be more palatable if he were more ordinary and wrong more often. That was most people's take on Simon. It felt good to meet the exception.

Even if he's a killer?

Was Tim Breary's flattery, like his lack of motive, part of a carefully crafted campaign to avoid a murder conviction? Or to secure one?

Simon was having trouble thinking straight. Was he, for once, not the cleverest person in the room?

'Will you find Gaby and give her the poem?' Breary asked him.

'Why should I?'

'Should doesn't come into it. You'll give it to her because I need you to. Because you'd keep your wife alive, even if she was brain-dead. Because you can imagine.'

Simon waited for Breary to tell him what he could imagine. When no more details were forthcoming, he turned to leave.

'Simon, wait. When you give Gaby the poem . . .'

'I haven't said I will.' It was only at the beginnings and ends of his sessions with Breary that Simon was made vividly aware of their different circumstances: in a few minutes, he would step outside, gulp free air into his lungs and drive away, while whichever staffer was stationed outside the parlour would escort Breary back to his cell. The idea activated Simon's escape reflex every time. He only turned back because he'd heard more than words and didn't want to miss the visual clues.

Breary seemed to be chewing and swallowing air; his jaw and Adam's apple were working frenetically. It was a few seconds before he was able to speak. 'Don't mention my name. Don't tell Gaby the poem's from me.'

The request was so staggeringly inappropriate, Simon would have felt like a sadist if he'd pointed it out.

He was still wondering if and how he should respond when Tim Breary said, 'Tell her it's from The Carrier.'

POLICE EXHIBIT 1441B/SK – POEM 'SONNET' BY
LACHLAN MACKINNON.

A HANDWRITTEN COPY OF THIS POEM WAS GIVEN BY
TIMOTHY BREARY TO DC SIMON WATERHOUSE ON 11/3/2011 AT
HMP COMBINGHAM, WITH REQUEST FOR IT TO BE PASSED BY
DC WATERHOUSE TO GABRIELLE STRUTHERS

'Sonnet'

Suppose there was no great creating Word,
That time is infinite. Corollary?
The present moment gives infinity
An end, by coming after it. Absurd.

Say the beginning of the world occurred
In time, and call that moment moment T,
Everything needed for the world to be
Was, at the point T minus X. Absurd.

Falling in love's a paradox like this.
Either it happens like a thunderbolt,
So when it makes our lives make sense, it lies

Or we had long been hoping for the kiss
That changed us, and, aware how it would jolt
Our beings, we could suffer no surprise.

POLICE EXHIBIT 1433B/SK – TRANSCRIPT OF HANDWRITTEN
LETTER FROM TIMOTHY BREARY TO FRANCINE BREARY DATED
25 DECEMBER 2010

Dear Francine,

It is Christmas Day. If you are the same Francine you have
always been, then you will think that since I am your husband
and since you are not dead, I ought to give you a Christmas
present. I agree. In previous years I have not, but I have
changed my mind. The poem in this letter is your present from
me this year. It is one of my favourites.

The old Francine would have regarded a transcribed poem as an
inadequate gift. For all I know, New Francine might agree. All I
can offer in my defence is that, in making my choice, I gave no
thought to keeping cost or effort to a minimum. If the world
contains a better gift than poetry, I have yet to discover it. (I am
not talking about what passes for poetry these days – inert
chopped-up prose that has no obvious point or inherent music to
it. Not that you care about such distinctions, Francine.)

I am not going to stuff this letter under your mattress as Kerry
would like me to. I shall do what I have always done with the
Christmas gifts I have bought you: put it into your hand. I will
read it to you first, of course.

'In a Dark Wood' by C. H. Sisson

Now I am forty I must lick my bruises
What has been suffered cannot be repaired
I have chosen what whoever grows up chooses
A sickening garbage that could not be shared.

My errors have been written on my senses
The body is a record of the mind
My touch is crusted with my past defences
Because my wit was dull, my eye grows blind.

There is no credit in a long defection
And defect and defection are the same
I have no body fit for resurrection
Destroy then rather my half-eaten frame

But that you will not do, for that were pardon
The bodies that you pardon, you replace
And that you save for those whom you will harden
To suffer in the hard rule of your Grace.

Christians on earth may have their bodies mended
By premonition of a heavenly state
But I, by grosser flesh from Grace defended
Can never see, never communicate.

I have to go downstairs now for Christmas dinner, but I will be back later to read the poem to you again and tell you what I think it means. 'The body is a record of the mind'. Would you agree, Francine?

Kerry is calling me for dinner. Never fear – I shall be back.

Your husband, for worse and for worse, having given up all hope of better,

Tim

9

Friday 11 March 2011

I pull up on the grass verge where the narrow road comes to a stop. Tim's house is hiding from me: the Dower House, in the grounds of Lower Heckencott Hall. I can't see it, but I know it's behind these high wooden gates, thanks to a consensus of search results. The Hall is Grade I listed and features on websites called things like 'Architectural Treasures of the Culver Valley' and 'Britain's Finest Historical Houses'.

Tim's home, I correct myself. *Not his house.* One of my searches yielded a PDF of plans for an extension drawn up by Roger Staples Design Studios for Daniel and Kerensa Jose. That makes sense; Dan and Kerry are the ones with the money. Thanks to nethouseprices.com, I know they paid £875,000 for the Dower House in February 2009.

Kerry never told me her name was short for Kerensa. Tim would have known. I hate myself for hoping that Francine didn't. It makes no difference to anything, but I prefer to think of her as ignorant, an outsider.

The conviction Kerry planted in my mind six years ago is still stubbornly, crazily there: Francine might have been married to Tim, but she didn't belong in his life. 'You're the fourth quarter of our quartet,' Kerry told me once when Dan and Tim were late to meet us at Omar's Kitchen. The idea took root, fast and firm. I believed her because I needed it to be true.

I still need it to have been true when she said it. *If it was true once . . .* It must have been; Kerry told me about her dad – something she, Dan and Tim had agreed never to tell Francine.

Rain drums on the roof of my car like an angry reminder,

chastising me for letting down my guard and admitting to weakness. It doesn't matter that no one heard me apart from me. Life punishes the needy; admit you can't live without something and it's taken away.

I don't need Tim in the way that I used to. I've proved I can live without him. I want to help him, that's all.

If my scientist colleagues could hear me trying to talk Fate round, they'd think twice about ever working with me again.

I understand that whatever this is, it is not Tim being returned to me. No one has invited me back into anything. Look at those closed gates.

When I knew Kerry and Dan, they had no gates to hide behind. They lived on Burtmayne Road in Spilling, in a two-bedroom gardenless terrace that was all front; from the street it fooled you into thinking it was double its actual size, but it was only one room deep. Tim and Francine lived a two-minute walk away on Heron Close, in a three-bedroom detached newbuild with a garden so overlooked by other identical detached newbuilds that Tim referred to it as 'the theatre in the round', though never in Francine's presence according to Kerry.

And now Tim lives here, with Kerry and Dan. And I live with Sean.

DC Gibbs asked for my address; it was one of his first questions, a formality. 47 Horse Fair Lane, Silsford, I recited. It sounded like an address and nothing more. When I left the police station, I headed straight for the Dower House, uninvited and probably unwelcome. Coming here felt as accidental and incongruous as going home would have. I knew I needed to sleep, but couldn't imagine doing it in my own bed. The idea that I have a bed, a home, a boyfriend, strikes me as something I might have wanted to believe even though it's never been true: as if I found a collection of things all conveniently together in one place, pretended they were mine, and everyone else was too polite to object.

Stop driving yourself crazy. Do something useful.

I open the car door, close it again. The go-away gates are too off-putting. I tell myself that if Tim lives here then my feelings for him justify my being here. And there's no 'if' about it: the news websites all agree that this was where Tim and Francine were living at the time of Francine's death. Rent-free: that's the part I worked out on my own. Kerry and Dan would skip down the street naked before they'd charge Tim rent. He might have tried to insist on paying his way, but they wouldn't have let him.

The idea that I might see Kerry again – that she might be in her house now, behind these gates – makes my eyes water. I blink away the tears. I was so devastated when Tim walked out of my life, it was only months later that I was able to see past the loss of him to the smaller sadness of Kerry being gone too. I didn't know her for long, but I missed her more than I'd expected to. She'd helped me in the most important way I have ever been helped: she explained Tim to me. Not completely – that would be impossible, given that Tim is Tim – but enough. Kerry made sense of my life for me when I'd lost my grip.

I mustn't allow myself to hope that she can do it again.

The rain stops as suddenly as it started. I get out of the car, leaving my bag on the passenger seat but taking my switched-off phone with me. *A compromise.* If I suddenly decide I'm ready to talk to Sean, I can switch it on and lose no more time. Though before ringing him I'd probably want to listen to the eighteen angry messages he's left, to gauge his mood, and after listening to them I'd probably be even less keen to speak to him than I am now, so what's the point?

Which is also my gut reaction to the millionaire's fortress in front of me: what's the point of trying to get in, when so much design effort has gone into keeping people out? The sign says 'Lower Heckencott Hall', but it ought to say, 'Abandon hope all ye who want to enter here', a subtle but crucial variation on the well-known phrase. I try not to feel intimidated by the carved stone gateposts, the intercom system with its two buzzers, the high stone perimeter wall with even higher hedges forming an extra layer of protection above it. Now that I'm standing, I can see, in the distance, a repeating pattern of identical windows: the top two storeys of a vast square building that must be the Hall. The long, straight driveway makes its presence felt while hiding out of sight – longer than a street with thirty families living on either side, judging by the position of the house in relation to the gates.

Despite its trappings of privacy, Lower Heckencott Hall looks public and practical, with its rigid corners and inflexible lines. I picture a large dusty meeting room within its walls, full of men shouting and waving leaflets in the air. One of my search results described it as 'the grandest example of vernacular architecture in the south of England'. Another called it a mansion, which strikes me as way off the mark; 'mansion' implies a lavishness that's absent here. There are no flourishes, no softening details, no decorative touches, just a stone cube with nothing but windows to break up the monotony of the façade. Not even a sloped roof; the Hall is a flat-top.

The word jolts me back twelve years, to when I first met Sean in the gym at Waterfront Health Club. I don't want to think about him, but he keeps invading my mind. Is it a guilt reflex, because I know I'm probably going to leave him?

Not probably. Definitely.

Probably.

When he asked me out, instead of saying yes or no, I told him I had a confession to make and blurted out that for months I'd thought of him as Sexy Boiled Egg because his flat-top hairstyle created the illusion of someone having removed the dome of his skull. 'Obviously that's partly complimentary and partly not, and you might not want to have dinner with me now you know,' I said. Sean laughed politely. It was clear he found my admission neither funny nor charming nor offensive – merely an obstacle to him getting his question answered. When he saw that I was waiting for an answer too, he said, yes, he still wanted to take me out for dinner. He told me the venue, the date and the time as if it were a pre-existing arrangement: The Slack Captain in Silsford, the following Saturday; he'd pick me up at seven thirty.

He arrived with a brand new crew cut, looking a little thuggish and four hundred times sexier. I thanked him for coming to collect me and told him – in case it hadn't occurred to him, and for future reference – that we could have met at the restaurant. I didn't say that the Slack Captain wasn't my idea of a restaurant. 'We could have met there,' Sean agreed, 'except that I invited you.' I asked what that meant and he said, 'It means dinner's my treat and my responsibility. I pick you up, and I drive you home afterwards.' Still in the dark, I decided to drop it; his four-hundred-times-sexier appearance made perfect sense even if his words didn't.

I shunted aside my unease about his having fixed all the details of our date before I'd agreed to go out with him, decided his rapid hair response meant that he was flexible and open-minded, and told him so, making a joke about it being easy to keep an open mind if someone's sliced off the top of your head. Sean gave me a flattening look and I stopped laughing.

He asked for the bill while chewing his last mouthful of steak. I'd finished my main course a few minutes earlier, but I hadn't realised our dinner was over. It didn't occur to Sean that I might want pudding or coffee; he didn't, so why would I?

He doesn't want a career that involves getting stuck overnight in Dusseldorf; why do I?

I force the image of him out of my mind – horizontal on our sofa; gone – and am about to press the lower buzzer on the intercom, the one labelled 'The Dower House', when the gates start to open with what looks like great reluctance. I hear a car engine and picture a silver Mercedes, a chauffeur in uniform. He might die before there's a gap wide enough to drive through.

I stand to one side as a grubby blue Volvo S60 emerges. It stops at the gateposts. The driver's tinted window slides open and I see a skinny man of about my age with a goatee beard and straggly shoulder-length brown hair that has an indent, as if he's recently worn it in a ponytail. He stares at me. There's a dead Christmas tree lying across the back seat of his car and, on top of it, a bulging green garden refuse sack.

I smile at him to thank him for opening the gates, and walk past the Volvo into the grounds of Lower Heckencott Hall. Here's the long, ruler-straight driveway, exactly as I pictured it.

'Oy!' the man calls out.

Is he talking to me? I retrace my steps. He looks angry. 'Who said you could go in there?' His accent is roughest Culver Valley.

'I pressed the buzzer for the Dower House and they buzzed me in,' I lie.

'No, they didn't. I opened the gate. No one buzzed you in. They're busy at the Dower House. They don't want to be disturbed.'

'Kerry buzzed me in,' I say, determined to stand my ground. 'I'm an old friend. My name's—'

'Gaby Struthers.' He says it as if he's found me out, even though I was about to tell him.

'How did you know?'

'So it's Kerry you've come to see, is it? Not Lauren?'

'Lauren? Cookson?' We're never going to get anywhere if we keep answering questions with questions. 'Why would I come here to see Lauren? I know she used to work here, but . . .' I can't bring myself to say, *But Francine Breary's dead, and dead people don't need care assistants.*

He makes a noise that's halfway between a laugh and a jeer, and leans his arm out of the car window. The movement pushes up his shirt sleeve to reveal a tattoo that would have made me think of Lauren if we hadn't already been talking about her. Hardly anybody I know has a tattoo. Does she know anyone who isn't covered in them?

'Don't pretend you don't know Lauren lives here,' the man snaps, but I'm not listening. I stare at the blue words on his skinny arm: 'IRON MAN'.

Jason Cookson. Lauren's husband, three-time-survivor of the Iron Man Challenge. Gardener-cum-handyman-cum-remover-of-dead-Christmas-trees.

Murderer of Francine Breary? Maybe.

'Is Lauren back yet?' I ask. 'I'd like to see her too, if she's—'

'She's not.'

'How did you know who I was?'

'Lauren said you'd come looking for her.' He stares at the road ahead. The message is clear: he might have to speak to me, but he doesn't have to look at me. 'She doesn't want you meddling in her life, so you're wasting your time.'

'I'm here to see Kerry. I had no idea Lauren lived here until you told me.'

'You're bullshitting,' Jason says to his steering wheel. 'Word of advice: never bullshit a bullshitter. If I were you, I'd turn round and walk away.'

So he's a bullshitter, by his own admission. *Interesting.* 'You're not me,' I say.

'You'd better not still be here when Lauren gets back.'

'Off to pick her up at the airport, are you?'

'If she comes home and finds you here, she'll get herself in a right state. Stay away from her. She wants nothing to do with you. She's scared shitless of you.'

'Whatever she's said—'

'Forget what Lauren said, and listen to what I'm saying: get lost. No one wants you here.'

'Forget everything Lauren said?' I ask. 'Or just the part about Tim Breary being innocent of murder?'

'Cocky bitch!' He jabs the air with an angry finger. I preferred it when he wasn't looking at me. 'Why don't you fuck off back to your snooty yuppie house on Snob Street?'

He drives away before I can call him a hypocrite. Though it's likely to be stupidity rather than a double standard; to apply two different sets of rules to two similar situations would be beyond Jason Cookson's intellectual capabilities. He must have forgotten that he lives in the grounds of a stately home.

The gates have started to close. I sprint inside, then feel embarrassed, even though no one's watching me, because there was no need to run. To my left, a path wide enough for a car to drive down follows the line of the wall around the farthest edge of the garden and disappears behind the Hall. I take the most direct route instead: the grass. *Because it was grassy and wanted wear . . .*

One of Tim's favourite poems: Robert Frost's 'The Road Not Taken'. 'It's incredible how little people understand when the words and syntax couldn't be simpler,' he said during one of our lunches at the Proscenium. 'Everyone thinks the poem's a celebration of non-conformity, but it's nothing of the sort. The writer's tearing the narrator to shreds for his pompous self-deception, for being too vain to face the truth.' I asked what the truth was. 'That all our choices are insignificant,' Tim said, grinning.

Three quarters of the way across a lawn that's bigger than most crop-growing fields, I see a two-storey brick and stone building ahead and to the left. The Dower House; it has to be. It's easily large enough to accommodate twelve people, with a clock tower protruding from the middle of its sloping roof, square bay windows and a wisteria that must look beautiful in bloom covering most of its façade.

I can see why Dan and Kerry bought it. It's softer and more attractive than the Hall, and makes me think of a vicarage from a nineteenth-century novel. I bet Kerry fell in love with it before she'd crossed the threshold, when she first stood where I'm standing now. There's a generous gravelled parking area outside with three cars parked on it. Does that mean Kerry and Dan have a visitor? Was Jason telling the truth when he said they were busy and wouldn't want to be disturbed?

I don't care. I need to know why Tim's lying about killing Francine. Kerry will be able to tell me more than anyone else can.

The presence of so many cars on a weekday suggests that in their new life, Dan and Kerry don't have Monday-to-Friday nine-to-five jobs. Dan was an accountant when I knew him before. He worked with Tim at Dignam Peacock. Kerry was a care assistant, like Lauren. Perhaps they also met through work. And then one day Kerry said she was leaving. She wouldn't have said why, wouldn't have mentioned the money. How surprised must Lauren have been, however many months later, to be offered a job by her former colleague, better paid than any she'd had before and with accommodation in the grounds of Lower Heckencott Hall as a perk?

What will happen to Lauren now that Francine's dead? Will Kerry find other work at the Dower House for her to do? I shiver as I picture a grey-skinned faceless woman, a stroke victim like Francine, being wheeled in on a trolley as a substitute. To give Lauren someone new to look after.

Why Lauren, Kerry? Tim? Why choose thick, sweary Lauren?

Maybe Jason came first; Dan and Kerry hired him, then found out his wife was a care assistant . . .

Or . . .

I shake my head to banish the idea. And again, with no luck. It's determined to stick around until I acknowledge its presence, which I don't want to do because it frightens me.

What if Tim, or Kerry, wanted Francine's carer to be as stupid and vacant as possible? So that she wouldn't notice . . . what?

This is useless. I could speculate all day and I still wouldn't have a coherent theory at the end of it. I take a deep breath, march towards the Dower House's front door like someone who knows what she's doing, and ring the bell, hoping it will silence the voice in my head that's still murmuring all the worst possibilities.

What if Tim and Lauren were . . . ? No. No way.

But what if?

He's one of the few people who doesn't think he's better than her, she said. She sounded fond of him. What if she knows Tim's innocent not because she knows Jason's guilty but because she was with Tim in a hotel room nowhere near the Dower House when Francine was murdered? What if she's his alibi, and they can't tell the police because they're scared of what Jason would do if he found out?

I'd rather Tim were a murderer than sleeping with Lauren. It makes me feel sick to know this about myself.

There's a date carved into the Dower House's stone door-head: 1906. The tails of the 9 and the 6 are threaded through the 0. It makes me think of Lauren's 'Jason' tattoo: red hearts on green stalks wound around the vowels. Did he come up with the design? Did he put on a soppy face or a threatening one as he demanded hearts on stalks? What about her dad, when he asked for the 'FATHER' tattoo on Lauren's arm as his birthday present?

I ring the bell again, more insistently this time. I've been alone with my thoughts for too long; I'm starting to feel unreal.

Dan Jose opens the door. His fine fair hair is longer and more dishevelled than it used to be when he worked at Dignam Peacock. He's got new glasses: square black frames instead of his old silver wire ones. 'Gaby,' he announces, as if I might not know who I am.

'Is Tim sleeping with Lauren Cookson?' I ask him.

He leaves it a few seconds. Then says, 'Of course not. There's been nobody.'

This is more information than I hoped for. Even more surprisingly, it's good news. I start to cry. Dan steps forward, pulls me into a hug. 'It's good to see you, Gaby. Even . . . like this.'

I believe him; of course I believe him. All the same, I can't get the other, untrue story out of my head: that Tim is involved with Lauren, or was before he had himself sent to prison. Of all the women he's ever met, he wants her least, respects her least. That's why he chose her; she's what he thinks he deserves. He'd have been able to read her his favourite poems and smile to himself when she asked him to stop spouting a load of boring old shite. If he really wanted to prove that the choices we make couldn't matter less, Lauren would have been his perfect fling.

'Tim didn't notice Lauren at all,' Dan says. 'It was embarrassing.

Kerry tried to have a word with him about it but it had no effect. He didn't see her in rooms, didn't say hello to her when he passed her in the hall. I thought it was a snobbery thing, but it wasn't.'

'Then what was it?' I ask. Years since we've met, and not even two minutes of small talk. Good. It would be unbearable to have to go through the whole pointless 'So, what have you been up to?' charade.

'Kerry could tell you better than me,' Dan says. 'She reckons that after . . . well, after everything that happened, Tim deliberately shrunk his world, so that there was no one in it but him, me and Kerry. And Francine, obviously, after she had her stroke.'

'After?' What a strange thing to say. 'And before, presumably?'

Dan looks over his shoulder, into the house. I can't see much, only a mirror above a dark wood cabinet with drawers and legs. There are no lights on in the hall. Despite the reassuring hug, Dan hasn't invited me in.

What did he mean by 'everything that happened'? Tim's and my bust-up? More than that? Were we going to have to do the 'So, what have you been up to?' routine after all?

'There's a lot you don't know, Gaby. Tim left Francine shortly after he last saw you, then went back to her after the stroke. I'd . . . I know Kerry would love to talk to you, but now's not a good time. The police are here.'

Tim left Francine. Tim left Francine. The words reel in my brain.

Dan's right: there's a lot I don't know because he and Kerry didn't tell me. A year and two months after I saw Tim for the last time, Kerry wrote me a letter. I've still got it; I know it by heart. Tim had moved to the Cotswolds, she wrote. There was no mention of Francine, and I assumed that since she was his wife, she had moved with him. Kerry and Dan had, Kerry told me, since they no longer needed to be in the Culver Valley for work reasons. The letter contained some vague, small-talk-ish mentions of future work plans: Kerry had made a contact at a local nature reserve and hoped to be able to get more involved, Dan was thinking of doing a PhD on narratives of risk and how our attitudes to financial gambles are determined more by the stories we tell ourselves than by our chances of ending up richer or poorer. That part would have made me smile if it weren't for what followed immediately after it. Tim had asked Kerry to transmit a message to me: I was not to contact him again, ever.

Kerry also wanted me to know that she and I couldn't be friends any more. I wasn't surprised. I'd spoken to her only twice on the phone since Tim's decision to boycott me, and both times she'd sounded uncomfortable. In her letter, she explained how important it was for Tim to know that I was no longer part of her or Dan's life either, since they were the only two people he could rely on. 'We're his whole world now,' she wrote. I didn't suspect that this meant Francine was no longer on the scene; I assumed she was in the background, as restrictive and toxic as ever, but that Kerry didn't want to dwell on the negatives. I thought she meant that she and Dan were the only good things in Tim's life.

'Knowing I was meeting you for lunch or even just chatting to you on the phone would kill him,' the letter went on. 'You're his past, we're his present. If you appear in our present, you'll spill over into his, and he couldn't bear that. I really hope you understand. Tim adores you and he always will (no, he hasn't said so, but I KNOW!) and he can't cope with the feelings.'

Every night, as I lie beside Sean or on my own in a hotel bed somewhere in Europe or America trying to fall asleep, I write letters to Kerry in my mind, letters I never commit to paper or computer. *I've been nothing if not obedient, Kerry. Look how successfully I've disappeared: not only from Tim's life but from my own. I bury myself in the dazzling brilliance of my work and vanish from my home life more and more every day.*

'Which police?' I ask Dan. 'DC Gibbs?' I could have given him a lift from the police station.

'Have you been talking to Chris Gibbs?'

Sophie Hannah

I tell him I've seen Gibbs once. I explain about Dusseldorf, my delayed flight, meeting Lauren. I quote her on the subject of letting an innocent man go to jail for murder.

Dan's face drains of colour as I speak. 'Did you tell Gibbs that Lauren said that?' he asks.

Is he joking? 'Why do you think I went to see him, Dan?'

'Fuck.' He closes his eyes.

'What's going on?' Dan has the opposite of a poker face; always did.

'Now's not a good time, Gaby. You'll have to come back.'

'I'll wait till Kerry's free,' I say, forcing my way past him and into the house.

'Why was Lauren on your plane?' he calls after me.

Good question. Did Tim tell Lauren about me? Or maybe he tried not to mention me but couldn't help it, and Lauren guessed that I would always mean more to him than she ever could; maybe she caught him looking at my website or my blog once too often. Was she envious enough to want to see first-hand if she had anything to be jealous of?

No. They weren't having an affair. There's no reason to think that they were.

I picture Tim passing Lauren in the hall I'm standing in, avoiding her eye, pretending not to have noticed her presence . . .

If Dan's following me as I start to search his house, I'm not aware of it. I run past closed doors, lots of them in a row. Dan and Kerry should apply for change of use and rebrand this place as a door museum. Wrong turn. I go back the way I came, turn right where I turned left.

Two roads diverged in a yellow wood . . .

This looks more promising: a patch of light at the end of the hall that must mean an open door. I hear a voice that doesn't sound like Kerry's. A woman. As I get closer, she says, 'I'm interested in your and Dan's money. You're obviously not short. Sam says Tim hasn't worked for some time, so it can't have been him paying for all this, and a care assistant for Francine.'

Who's Sam?

'Where did the money come from? And how come you're so generous with it?'

I know the answer to that one. I swallow hard and walk into the room.

10

11/3/2011

'Shall I explain about the money?' the woman standing in the doorway asked Kerry Jose. To Charlie she said, 'Without me, there wouldn't be any – that's my excuse for butting in.' She had thick brown shoulder-length hair, this intruder; pale skin, large brown eyes, a scattering of freckles across the bridge of her nose. Charlie was puzzled by her clothes. They had the unmistakable gleam of designer-expensive, but were heavily creased and dirty in places: muddy, food-stained. The whites of her eyes were bloodshot.

'Sorry, I've come straight from an exhausting delayed-plane endurance test,' she explained, looking down at herself. She didn't sound sorry. Her tone would have been better suited to the words 'Tough shit'. 'No time to change,' she added, aiming a challenging stare in Charlie's direction.

All right, so she was clever; she'd known what Charlie was thinking. And confident: very few people walked into a murder investigation in progress and declared that money wouldn't exist if it weren't for them.

Charlie was about to ask the woman for her name when she was distracted by a yelp from Kerry Jose. She turned. Kerry, who was leaning against the Aga rail, had covered her mouth with her hands and was crying. She'd been dry-eyed and calm only seconds ago. 'Gaby! Oh, thank God!' Kerry flew across the room suddenly, making Charlie jump, and gripped the dishevelled visitor's body in a vice-like hug, pinning her arms to her sides.

Unambiguous, then: somehow, this woman was important. She

belonged here, though Kerry evidently hadn't known she was coming.

She even looked as if she belonged. Her appearance, simultaneously affluent and mud-smeared, worked perfectly with the vibe of Kerry and Dan Jose's sunflower-yellow-walled kitchen, which was a similarly bizarre mix of the aspirational and the shocking. It was a huge room that easily swallowed up two tables, six chairs around each one, and had amazing unframed oil paintings on the walls. It was also one of the messiest domestic spaces Charlie had ever seen. Not a single surface or part of a surface was visible; Charlie had had to balance the cup of tea Kerry Jose had made her on a pile of old Christmas cards, prompting Kerry to say, 'Yes, use those cards as a coaster, good idea!'

Every counter and tabletop was piled high with unstable towers of things that had nothing in common with each other and didn't belong together: a telephone directory on top of a board game on top of a box of cereal on top of a book of fabric samples balanced on a tennis racket. Next to that particular tower was a fruit bowl that contained a tape measure, a sheep brooch made mainly of pink wool, a packet of plasters, a rolled-up pair of socks, four old ice-lolly sticks with red and orange staining on their top halves, and a broken bra with the underwiring poking out of the black fabric. Between the two tables – one rustic, wooden and round, one with elegant dark wood legs and a veined white marble top – at least fifteen cardboard boxes were stacked in the middle of the floor. Charlie could only see the contents of the top layer: books, maps, a folded rug, a clock with cracked glass and a bent big hand.

How could anyone live like this? Had Kerry and Dan Jose trained themselves to look only at the paintings when they came in here? Charlie had to admit they were stunning, though she couldn't work out if they were abstract or not. They seemed to depict women's bodies merging into mainly blue and green landscapes in a way that made their elbows and knees look like mountains. No faces. No heads, in fact. Sinister but beautiful.

If this were my kitchen, Charlie thought, I'd keep the art and chuck everything else. She and Simon were the opposite of hoarders, she realised. They bought as little as possible, threw away as much of it as they could as soon as they'd eaten or drunk the contents. Charlie could easily see how Kerry Jose might think differently; she could imagine Kerry coming up with what she considered to be a good reason to keep an old ice-lolly stick. Kerry focused on the positive whenever she could; that had been obvious from the brief conversation Charlie had managed to have with her before this Gaby woman interrupted. Also obvious was the almost total absence of a desire to control or steer the conversation; Kerry had seemed happy to let Charlie take their dialogue wherever she'd wanted to, and had answered every question willingly and almost . . . gratefully couldn't be the right word, could it? That was how Kerry had sounded: appreciative of Charlie's prompts. The dynamic between Kerry and Dan, her husband, had seemed rather odd too, but Charlie knew it was too early to reach a verdict about that: the three of them had sat at the kitchen table together for less than a minute before the phone had rung and Dan had gone to answer it, and then the doorbell had rung several times – overbearingly, Charlie had thought. That must have been Gaby, that insistent ringing with its air of 'Is any fucker going to let me in?'

And yet Kerry was delighted to see her. Her arrival had elicited a 'Thank God'. The two of them were obviously friends of some description, though they looked as if they would have nothing in common: the tassel-skirted, fluffy-jumpered Bohemian and the glossy, assertive businesswoman. Not so glossy today, perhaps, but Charlie could imagine how intimidatingly stunning Gaby would look after a good night's sleep.

Gaby's expression was more agonised than delighted. She was trying to shake herself free of Kerry's embrace. 'Kerry, don't. You'll start me off. I don't want to waste my limited time with the police crying.' Kerry backed off, nodding, and wiped her eyes, visibly comfortable with being ordered around.

That's what's odd: she and her husband both like to be told what to do. They glance at each other hesitantly, hoping for a cue of some kind, unsure who's in charge. Weird marriage.

Black kettle. Black pot.

'You are the police, right?' Gaby's confident voice broke into Charlie's thoughts.

'Sergeant Charlie Zailer.' She stood up, held out her hand.

Gaby shook it. 'Gabrielle Struthers, only ever known as Gaby. I'm a friend of Kerry and Dan's from years ago. Also a good friend of Tim Breary's.'

'What you said about not wanting to waste your limited time with the police . . .' Charlie began, not really knowing where she was going with this, or, come to think of it, what she was doing here without Sam. He'd stuck his head in to say something had come up and he had to nip back into town, told Charlie to text him when she wanted picking up. An obvious ruse. He was hoping she'd be able to connect with Kerry Jose more successfully than he had, get something out of her that he'd failed to extract. She planned to tell him later, proudly, that she'd bypassed the empathetic-emotional route altogether and asked about the household finances instead. As far as she could see, it was the most interesting aspect of the set-up at the Dower House, as well as the most suspicious. Not with regard to Francine's murder, perhaps, but strange nonetheless, and therefore worth investigating. Fair enough, Tim and Francine Breary were close friends of the Joses, but most close friends weren't willing to support each other financially till death did them part. A lot of parents wouldn't even do that for their kids.

Charlie became aware that Gaby Struthers was staring at her, eyebrows raised expectantly. Waiting for her to finish the question she'd started asking.

'Most people aren't that keen to talk to us,' she said. 'Guilty or innocent, they avoid us if they can.'

'Guilty or innocent, most people are cowardly and superstitious,' Gaby said, pulling a chair out from beneath the table so that she could sit down. There was something round and silver on the seat. A napkin ring? No, too big, too sharp edges. A pastry cutter. Charlie knew people owned them – people whose lifestyles were very different from hers. She'd have had more use for a fat giant's wedding ring, which the silver thing also might have been.

Gaby picked it up, tossed it into a Pyrex oven dish on the table that was full of shells, stones, elastic bands and packets of aspirin.

'Why's your time limited?' Charlie asked her as she sat down. 'Do you have to be somewhere?'

'No. I assumed you did. Look, what I've got to say won't take long. Why don't I just say it and then you can get on with dismissing it, like DC Gibbs did, and talking to the people who'll tell you what you want to hear instead?'

'You should know . . . I'm not actually directly involved in the Francine Breary investigation. I used to be CID but I'm not any more. So I don't know what Gibbs said or did to annoy you, but if there's a party line on this, I'm not party to it.'

'You're not directly involved in Tim's case?' Gaby looked at Kerry, who shrugged helplessly.

'I didn't have a chance to explain that to Kerry before you arrived,' Charlie said. *A good friend of Tim Breary's. Tim's case.* It was clear what Gaby Struthers cared and didn't care about here. Was she at all disturbed by Francine Breary's murder, or was Tim's welfare her only concern?

'Then, if it's not your case, if you don't work for CID, what are you doing here?'

'I'm not sure. Sam Kombothekra was coming and he asked me to come with him – he's the DS in charge.' Charlie shrugged. 'Maybe he thinks a woman's touch is needed.' She allowed Gaby and Kerry to hear her sarcasm.

'Needed for what?' Gaby asked. 'Is the case still open? Does that mean DS Kombothekra doesn't believe Tim killed Francine?' Her pronunciation of Sam's surname was perfect after only one hearing.

Charlie had to be careful. One option was to answer honestly: 'Sam thinks everyone in this house is lying about something. The word conspiracy's been mentioned.' A line like that, with its shock value, might have a productive effect on Gaby Struthers, but would obliterate the rapport Charlie had been building with Kerry Jose, out of whom the truth, assuming she was withholding it, would have to be coaxed gently.

'Because he didn't kill her,' Gaby said with certainty.

'Gaby,' Kerry murmured, closing her eyes. 'I wish he hadn't done it as much as y—'

'He *didn't* do it, Kerry. On Thursday, I flew to—'

'Dusseldorf. I know,' Kerry said, as if it was causing her pain to utter each word. Her eyes were still half closed.

'You *know* Lauren was on my flight?' Gaby snapped.

'I booked her flights for her. She told me she was going to visit friends, that Jason mustn't know anything about it.' Kerry sighed. 'Well, he knows now. He's on his way to the airport to collect her. She's not in good shape, apparently. To be honest, I don't know what's going on with Lauren.'

'Dan didn't know Lauren was on my flight,' said Gaby pointedly. 'When I told him a few minutes ago.'

'I haven't had a chance to tell him,' Kerry said. 'He was in London this morning, only got back about half an hour ago. I've been busy talking to Sergeant Zailer.'

'Please, call me, Charlie.'

'Do you know *why* Lauren decided to stalk me all the way to Germany?' Gaby asked. Her manner reminded Charlie of Simon in interview mode. *You'll tell me what I want to know, or you'll regret it.* 'How did she even know about me?'

Kerry shook her head. She was hiding behind her long ginger-blonde hair, holding it like a shield in front of her face. With her other hand, she picked at it, made a show of flicking something on to the floor. Charlie didn't believe there had been anything in her hair that had needed removing; it was an act, to avoid meeting Gaby's eye.

Interesting. Kerry hadn't been afraid when she'd been talking to Charlie alone. And yet she'd been genuinely delighted when her friend had walked into the room; that wasn't an act.

'She didn't tell me anything, ask me for anything,' Gaby spoke to Kerry as if she'd forgotten Charlie was there. 'Apart from what she let slip out by accident . . .'

'Could someone please fill me in?' Charlie asked, worried she'd fall hopelessly behind if she allowed the two women any more private communion time.

'I told DC Chris Gibbs the full story this morning,' Gaby said. 'He can fill you in on the details. Short version? I went to Dusseldorf yesterday. Lauren Cookson, the care assistant who looked after Francine, followed me there. She blurted out something about letting an innocent man go to jail for a murder he didn't commit.'

'What?' Kerry dropped her hair.

'She was talking about Tim,' said Gaby. 'Somehow she knows he didn't do it, and since she must have been around Francine every day, since she *lives* here, I believe her a hundred per cent. I also know Tim's not a killer and never could be. What's going on, Kerry? Why's he saying he killed Francine when he didn't? You must know the truth.'

'He killed her, Gaby.' The muscles in Kerry's face were tight with anxiety. 'I'm so sorry, but we were all here. Dan and I—'

'And Lauren?' Gaby demanded.

Kerry nodded. 'Lauren knows . . . what we all know,' she said almost inaudibly, looking down at the floor. 'I can't think why she'd say otherwise.'

'Gaby, is it okay if I ask you a couple of questions?' said Charlie.

'Ask away.'

'Where were you on 16 February?'

'The day Francine was murdered?' Gaby reached into her bag, pulled out a dark brown leather diary with 'Coutts 2011' embossed on its front cover.

'How do you know that's when Francine was killed?' Charlie asked.

'How does anyone know anything? Google. 16 February: I was in Harston, a village near Cambridge.'

'All day?'

Gaby nodded. 'Got up at 5 a.m., got there for 7, was in meetings all day.'

'Meetings?' All day, in a village? First the church hall about the flower arrangements, then the post office to discuss the padded envelope window display?

As if she could read Charlie's mind, Gaby said impatiently, 'Sagentia's UK head office is in Harston – they're a product development company. We've outsourced a small but crucial part of our work to them. Google my name if you want to know more about what that work is, and ring Luke Hares at Sagentia if you want confirmation that I was there all day on 16 February.' After a pause, Gaby added, 'I didn't kill Francine Breary any more than Tim did. Christ, if he was going to kill her he'd have done it years ago.'

Charlie saw Kerry Jose stiffen. She decided not to pursue it for the time being and mentally filed Gaby's comment for future reference.

'You said you were going to tell me everything I needed to know about the money.'

'Happy to,' said Gaby. 'In a nutshell, Kerry and Dan have got plenty and Tim's got none.' Kerry had put the kettle on and was putting a teabag into a mug. 'What's happened with the Heron Close house?' Gaby asked her.

'It was repossessed. Tim hasn't worked since he left Francine, which wasn't long after you last saw him. He didn't have hardly any money saved. Couldn't make the mortgage payments.'

Gaby laughed. 'Did he care? He hated that house.'

Charlie watched Kerry's features jerk and reset themselves. It would be useful if this could continue to happen every time Gaby revealed a detail that Kerry had hoped to keep secret; for

Charlie, it was like having a yellow brick road of significance to follow.

'After Francine had her stroke, she couldn't make the payments either. I'm . . .' Kerry made a choking noise, gagging on her own words. She tried again. 'I'm sorry I didn't get in touch, Gaby. I wanted to tell you everything – about Tim leaving his job, leaving Francine, but . . .' She shrugged. 'Well, I explained in the letter I wrote you. Did you get it?'

Gaby nodded.

'I just couldn't,' Kerry said, her eyes filling with tears.

'Can we come back to the money,' Charlie prompted. 'So Tim and Francine had a house on Heron Close that was repossessed . . .'

'Yes. Dan and I support – supported – Francine, still support Tim,' said Kerry. 'Always will.'

'That's extremely generous,' Charlie said.

'We're family,' Kerry said firmly. 'Not literally, but we're all he's got and he's all we've got. And it's not as if Dan and I are going to have children.' Her face reddened as she realised what she'd said. 'There are . . . pathologies in my biological family that I don't want to risk passing on,' she explained.

'Kerry and Dan wouldn't be wealthy if it weren't for Tim,' said Gaby, as Kerry brought her mug of tea over to the table. 'Have you heard of Taction?'

Charlie shook her head.

'The Da Vinci surgical robot?' Gaby said it as if it were the most ordinary thing in the world. 'At the moment, the Da Vinci's the only one on the market, but there are a couple of companies working on new robot models that'll be cheaper to manufacture and less invasive than the Da Vinci if they can be made to work. That's a big "if". There are no guarantees, but if the front-runner competitor makes the killing it hopes to make, it'll be partly thanks to me. My first company, the one I created and sold, invented a tactile fabric.'

'Taction?' Charlie guessed.

Gaby nodded. 'We designed it specifically to be used in the

manufacture of tactile feedback gloves. We also designed a proto-
type glove that doesn't work with the Da Vinci, but another
company's incorporated it into the design of a rival surgical plat-
form they're working on. The glove provides whoever's operating
the robot with data that closely simulates what she'd feel with the
five fingers of her own hand if she were performing manual lapa-
roscopic surgery.'

*So . . . I'm sitting here talking to some kind of cutting-edge
technological genius superstar.* Charlie kept the thought to herself;
Gaby Struthers didn't appear to be in need of a boost to her
confidence.

'In order to fund our development and trialling, we needed
money.' she said. 'Tim advised me on where to get it from. He
brought me investors – all the investors I needed.'

'So Tim was your . . . what, your business partner? Your
accountant?' Charlie asked.

'My accountant, eventually. At first, though, he just saw exactly
what my business needed, and he got it for me.'

'You mean the money to make your product?' Charlie
asked.

'Yes, but not only that. I could have gone to any number of
venture capital firms with my business plan and they'd have fallen
into my lap,' said Gaby, with what Charlie was starting to recognise as her characteristic modesty and self-effacement. 'They'd
also have wanted control, and they'd have tried to squeeze me
out. That's what these people do. I wasn't having that. It was *my*
company, my expertise going into the product. I knew that if we
succeeded, the investors would get the lion's share of the money
– that was fine, I had no problem with that. But I had a huge
problem with the idea of big slick bastards in suits wading in and
telling me how to run the show because – at the risk of sounding
big-headed – I knew what I was doing, better than they ever
could.'

'Gaby's company sold for nearly fifty million dollars,' said
Kerry. 'To Keegan Luxford.'

Charlie nodded. She knew she should say, 'Wow,' or something like that. She wondered if Keegan Luxford would be interested in buying anything of hers for fifty million dollars. Simon's brain, perhaps. Even that was a non-starter. Removal and delivery would be too complicated. 'So Tim found you investors who'd hand over the money but let you do what you wanted with it?'

'Exactly,' said Gaby. 'He only asked people he knew well, who trusted him. He had unwavering confidence in me.' She looked uncertain for a second. 'I never really understood why. *I* knew I could make it work, as much as you can ever know with something so high-risk and speculative, but Tim can't have known. He just . . . believed in me, the way devoutly religious people believe in God. Faith. Somehow, Tim managed to convey that faith to enough of his clients and acquaintances, who all invested. He told them the best thing they could do was let me get on with things in my own way.'

'He knew it was true, and it was,' said Kerry.

'Or he was in love with me and that was all he cared about,' Gaby fired back at her. 'Maybe he didn't care if his clients and friends lost all their money as long as he got to impress me and be the one who solved all my problems.'

'Gaby, stop.' Charlie heard authority in Kerry's voice for the first time since she'd arrived at the Dower House. 'Poor Tim. You're not being fair and you know it.'

Poor Tim? Poor wife-smothering Tim? Charlie felt as if she'd been cast adrift on waves of oddness, without a map or a pair of oars. Or even a boat.

'I'm sorry.' Gaby sounded as if she meant it. She covered her face with her hands for a few seconds. 'Ignore me. I had no sleep last night. You're right, Tim would never have advised his clients to act against their own best interests. I don't know why I said that.' She sighed. 'All along, he claimed to know I'd succeed, that there was no risk at all, only an enormous profit to be made by all involved. I knew no such thing, but he *knew*. I just find it hard to believe sometimes, that's all. How can he have known?'

'We knew too,' Kerry told her, squeezing her arm. 'Tim's confidence in you was so powerful, we didn't doubt him for a second, him or you. And you *did* pretty much know, Gaby – you're being modest. Why else would you have spent all that money on the whole Swiss—'

'That's nothing to do with anything,' Gaby cut her off abruptly.

Charlie felt her inner antennae twitch as the mood in the room changed.

'I'm just saying, you must have known there was a very good chance—'

'Kerry, for fuck's sake, can we drop it?'

This role reversal was unexpected: suddenly Gaby was the cagey one and Kerry the big-mouth. *The whole Swiss . . .* what? Tax avoidance was all Charlie could think of.

'Tim wasn't as honest with you and Dan about your investment as you think he was,' Gaby muttered into her cup of tea.

'You and Dan invested in Gaby's business?' Charlie asked Kerry.

'Three hundred thousand pounds,' said Gaby.

'Everything we had,' Kerry confirmed. 'Aside from our earnings from work, which weren't much. Dan was an accountant, so he had what seemed like a decent salary at the time. I was earning peanuts as a care assistant.'

'You invested all your savings, the lot?' Charlie allowed her incredulity to be obvious.

Kerry looked at Gaby as if she wanted her to take over the telling of the story.

'Dan's mother died, left him the money,' Gaby said. 'He didn't want it. He and his mother hadn't spoken for years before she died. She was a bitch – always threatening to cut him out of her will.'

'She threatened to do it when he wanted to marry me,' Kerry contributed. 'We both thought she had. That's the last time Dan spoke to her, just before we got engaged. She refused to come to the wedding. I wasn't good enough for her precious son, I was *just* a home carer. From tainted stock.' Kerry started to cry, wiping the tears away discreetly as if she imagined she could hide them.

A look from Gaby warned Charlie not to ask. 'Nice woman,' Charlie said. To say nothing would have seemed heartless.

'So then she dies, and Dan finds out he's got all this money,' Gaby picked up the story again. 'But it's hers, the same money that was used to bribe and blackmail him for most of his life, so he doesn't want it. Kerry didn't see it that way.'

'No, I didn't. What kind of fool gives away three hundred thousand pounds on principle? We argued about it. Endlessly.' Kerry shuddered. 'It's the only time we've ever come to blows about anything. I couldn't bear for Dan to give the money away, wherever it came from, but he wouldn't listen. He said we were fine as we were, and how could he live with himself if he accepted an inheritance from Pu—' A deep flush spread across Kerry's face. 'From his mother,' she corrected herself.

Gaby grinned. 'I forgot you used to call her Pue. PUE,' she told Charlie. 'Pure Undiluted Evil. Didn't Tim coin that one?'

Kerry nodded.

Charlie sipped her tea. 'So when Tim came along suggesting you invest the three hundred thousand in Gaby's company . . .'

'It was the perfect solution.' Kerry's eyes lit up, as if she'd just this second worked it out. 'We could give away the money – all of it – and the money we'd get back wouldn't be *hers*. It'd be different money, money from whichever company bought up Gaby's. Keegan Luxford, as it turned out.'

Inheritance laundering, Charlie thought.

'Different money, and a hell of a lot more, if things went according to plan – which, thankfully for all of us, they did,' Gaby said. 'Meanwhile I'd have spent Dan's mum's money getting my product to trial stage – about which I had no moral qualms, I have to say. She wasn't *my* bitch of a mother.' Gaby and Kerry exchanged a smile; they'd clearly had a version of this conversation before, probably many times.

'Tim and Francine couldn't invest,' Kerry told Charlie. 'They didn't have a lump sum like we did, so Tim couldn't benefit from his own brilliant life-changing advice. That's another reason why Dan and I will always look after him.'

'They could have had lump sums coming out of their ears,' Gaby said quietly. 'Francine wouldn't have let Tim invest a tenner in GST. Not even a fiver.'

Kerry's mouth twitched. She tensed in her chair. What was it that she didn't want Charlie to know? That Francine and Tim hadn't had the best marriage in the world? That Francine had been a controlling cow who'd made Tim's life a misery? If it were true, Charlie couldn't work out why it should be such a big secret, when Tim Breary had confessed to killing his wife weeks ago and confirmed his guilt in every conversation he'd had with the police ever since.

'What's GST?' she asked. *Guilty Smothering Tim?*

'The company I sold: Gaby Struthers Technologies.'

Charlie said to Kerry, 'So you moved Tim and Francine in with you, paid for full-time care for Francine . . .' She lost her thread. Gaby had pushed back her chair and stood up suddenly, as if she'd remembered something urgent.

'Gaby?' Kerry stood too. *Follow the leader*. 'Are you okay?'

'I want to see Tim's room. His room here. I need to see it.'

Kerry stared at her, blinking as if she hadn't understood the words. Charlie waited.

'I'm not sure I should let you. God, Gaby, I hate saying no, but without Tim's permission . . .'

'You'll have to physically stop me,' said Gaby, halfway to the door.

Kerry made as if to follow, then hesitated. She looked at Charlie, a plea in her eyes. 'Is there something in Tim's room that you don't want Gaby to see?' Charlie asked.

Friday 11 March 2011

I run upstairs and nearly crash into Dan on the landing. I'd completely forgotten about him. He doesn't seem to be on his way anywhere; he's just standing there. His guilty eyes tell me everything I need to know. 'So, you're up here skulking, are you? Avoiding the cosy chat with the cops? You're not a natural liar, Dan. You must be sick of lying about Francine's death.'

'You don't know what you're saying, Gaby.'

'Don't you trust yourself not to blurt out the truth?'

He turns away from me, takes a couple of steps towards the top of the stairs.

'Go on, then, down you go,' I say. 'Except you won't, will you? You don't want to end up in the kitchen with Sergeant Zailer. Has Kerry told you to stay out of sight in case you give something away?' As soon as I've said it, I have a better idea. 'She's playing the martyr, isn't she? You both hate lying, but Kerry would rather put herself through it than you. You're being spared the ordeal.'

'Gaby, please stop and think,' Dan whispers forcefully.

'About what?'

He looks past me. I turn. There's nothing there apart from a long corridor with five doors on either side and another one at the end. *Upstairs at the Culver Valley Door Museum.* A window somewhere would have been a good idea. Is everything grey-brown up here, or is it the lack of natural light that makes it appear that way?

When I turn to face Dan again, he still isn't looking at me. 'I'd love to stop and think,' I tell him. 'I'd love to think about exactly what you're thinking about right now, but I can't, can I, unless you tell me what the fuck's going on?'

'Gaby.' He places his hands gently on my arms. 'I'm not your enemy.'

'Great. Now tell me who is.'

'I'm Tim's friend. His best friend. Remember that.'

I'd like to scream the roof off this house that my work made it possible for him to buy, but it wouldn't do any good.

'Do you know what, Dan? I'd rather you told me nothing at all than things I already know. The meaningful look on your face isn't adding an extra layer of significance, not for me – it just makes you look stupid. Yes, you're Tim's best friend. I know that. But in this context, the way you said it just then, I have no idea what you mean. Whatever I'm supposed to be getting, I'm not getting. Tim's your best friend, so . . . what? That makes it okay for you to lie about him killing Francine?'

'Tim's confessed, Gaby.' Another meaningful look. 'He's confessed.'

'All right, so you and Kerry aren't plotting to send Tim to prison for a crime he didn't commit. Or, rather, you *are*, but he is too. He's plotting against himself, and you and Kerry are supporting him. Right?'

Dan says nothing. He's switched off his intense stare.

'Tim's never had his own best interests at heart,' I say quietly. 'You know that as well as I do. Has it occurred to you that backing up his false confession might not be the right thing to do? How can it be good or right for him to go to prison for the rest of his life if he's innocent? Lauren doesn't think it's such a great idea. How come she feels worse about it than you do? Because her husband killed Francine? Is that why? *Tell* me, Dan. If we all have to lie for Tim's sake, explain to me why and I'll lie too! I'd do anything for him – you know that!'

Dan's breathing as if he's been running, sweating from the effort of saying nothing.

'You won't tell me because you know I wouldn't go along with it,' I say. 'Tim's taking the blame for Francine's death for some stupid, crazy reason, and you're letting him. And you know I wouldn't. You know how much I love him. Or maybe you don't – in which case, you do now!'

Does Dan think it strange that I still love Tim? Yes, it's been years, but it's excessive proximity, not separation, that wears love away. And I never really had Tim; he wasn't mine. My craving for him was never satisfied.

That's not love. That's need. Addiction.

I push the thought away. Moving will help.

'Where are you going?' Dan calls after me as I run along the corridor of doors.

'Which room is Tim's?'

'Gaby, you can't just—'

'Stop me, then. This must be Lauren and Jason's room.' I stand in the doorway and stare at the pictures on the wall opposite the bed: two framed black and white photographs of Lauren glammed up: full make-up, a clumpy retro hairstyle like a forties film star, a floaty evening dress and a fur wrap over her shoulders. This must be Jason's idea of tasteful. 'Lucky she's got the wrap to cover her "FATHER" tattoo,' I say to Dan, blinking away tears. *Have you lost it, Struthers? Getting sentimental over a couple of pictures of Lauren Cookson, the thickest care assistant in the western hemisphere?*

The only one brave enough to speak up. Even if she changed her mind as soon as she'd said it.

'Gaby? You okay?'

I tell Dan I'm fine and focus on the physical details of the room. I don't expect it to tell me anything helpful, but I look anyway. A wall of built-in wardrobes, two bedside tables, a lamp on one of them. No books. A pine bed with a pale pink flowery bedspread; drawers underneath, built into its frame, all open. Three cuddly toys – a bear with a red heart for a nose, a duck and an owl – are sitting on the pillows, leaning against the head-board. There are clothes scattered on the floor on both sides of the bed, mainly thongs in various colours on what must be Lauren's side. On Jason's, there's a white T-shirt, a pair of jeans, a few socks and a ripped silver condom packet.

'I don't think Lauren and Jason would want you in here, Gaby.' Dan approaches me tentatively, as if we're at the zoo and I'm a lion on the loose.

'You all sleep within a few feet of one another? How cosy: you, Kerry, Tim, Lauren and Jason, all sleeping symmetrically behind your symmetrical closed doors. And Francine, before she died.'

'Francine had a room on the ground floor,' says Dan. 'Not that it matters. What do you care where we all sleep?'

'I don't,' I tell him. 'Convenient for you, though. Do you all meet on the landing at midnight every night, make sure you know all your lies by heart?'

'I think you should leave if you're going to be like this.'

'I'm not leaving until I've seen Tim's room. Where is it?'

'No.'

I assume that the door Dan has hurried over to block with his body is the one I want.

'Kerry and I don't go in there and it's our house. Our cleaners don't even go in there. Tim prefers to clean it himself. That's how much he values his privacy.'

'Sometimes,' I say. 'Other times, he's happy to sign up for a lifetime of shitting in front of his cellmate in a shared toilet with o door, and having prison warders stare at him through bars as if he's a monkey in a cage.'

I see the effect my words are having on Dan and press home my advantage. 'I'd say I value Tim's privacy a whole lot more than he does at the moment – and his happiness, and his freedom. How many times have the police been in his room since Francine died?'

Dan sighs and stands to one side. 'Don't touch anything,' he says.

I swear under my breath and open the door. Soon as I'm in, I pick up a book from one of the piles on the floor beside the bed and wave it in the air, to show Dan that I intend to ignore his no-touching rule. Having made my point, I'm about to put the book back when I notice what it is: e. e. cummings' *Selected Poems 1923–1958*. A strong jerk-back sensation takes hold of my body, as if my blood vessels are reins and someone's tugged them taut, pulling me away from the brink.

i carry your heart with me (i carry it in my heart)

Did Tim first read the poem in this book? If I look at the index of first lines, will I find it?

I mustn't look. If I read that poem now, in front of Dan, I'll fall apart.

'Are you okay, Gaby?' His voice seems to come from a million miles away.

Why do people ask that? It's such a pointless question. What's 'okay'? I'm still able to stand up and breathe; I think that's pretty good going. I think I'm doing better than okay.

'I need to take this book,' I tell Dan.

'No!'

I recoil at the sound of his raised voice. Dan Jose doesn't yell. Ever. Then I realise it's himself he's angry with, not me. He's embarrassed by his inability to take control of the situation. He has given an inch, several inches, and now I want to take a poetry book.

'It's Tim's book,' he says.

'I'm taking it. Tim wouldn't mind. You know he wouldn't.'

Dan stares out at the view that was Tim's before he had himself moved to HMP Combingham: a vast expanse of green and then Lower Heckencott Hall beyond, in the distance. Having used up all his energy, Dan's decided the best thing he can do is avert his eyes and let me get on with it.

Good.

I am in Tim's bedroom for the first time. Only Tim's; nothing to do with Francine. I want to stay in here forever. I want to examine each of his possessions in detail, but I've frozen. This is too important. I'm looking but not seeing; my mind's too jittery to process the visual data.

Calm down, for fuck's sake.

It's smaller than Lauren and Jason's bedroom, though still a large room. There's a single bed pushed up against one wall. The sight of it makes me angry. 'Single beds are for children,' I say. 'Tim's a grown man in his mid-forties.'

'His choice,' says Dan. 'Kerry tried to persuade him to get a double, but he insisted.'

The pillow and duvet are white. There's no headboard, no bedside table, two tall piles of books by the side of the bed. A wardrobe, a desk and office-style swivel chair, a leather armchair in the corner. I walk over to the desk and look at the spotless stack of notepaper, the pile of matching envelopes, three pens that look expensive. It all looks brand new and untouched. I flinch, thinking that Tim might have bought these things because he wanted to write to people who aren't me.

Or he bought them because he wanted to write to me. Desperately. But didn't know how, or what to say, and so never did.

My scientist's mind points out that there is no evidence to support my preferred theory, so I mustn't allow myself to believe it.

On the wall there are poems – unframed, Blu-Tacked – that look as if they've been cut out of magazines: George Herbert, W.B. Yeats, Robert Frost, Wendy Cope, someone called Nic Aubury. His poem – or hers, if Nic is short for Nicola – is only four lines long.

'The Somelier and Some Liar'

Knowledgeable-nonchalant,
I tell the waiter, 'Fine,'
When really what I'm thinking is,
'I'm fairly sure it's wine.'

I smile. Tears snake down my cheeks from the outer corners of my eyes.

What's going to happen to me without Tim? With Tim in prison for . . . how long?

'Dan,' I whisper.

'What?'

'I need Tim not to be locked up. You have to help me.'

'Gaby, I . . . Jesus!' Dan leans his forehead against the window-pane. He might be crying too. 'I've done everything I can, trust me.'

'Before, when Tim and I were apart, it was okay, I could live with it . . .'

'You live with someone else,' Dan says accusingly.

'Sean. Yes. Is that supposed to be proof of my disloyalty to Tim? You know what happened. I'd have left Sean like a shot.'

'I know.' Dan holds up his hands. 'I didn't mean it to come out like that.'

'I always knew that if I wanted to find Tim, I could. He didn't want me, he'd made that clear, and I could live with it, as long as I knew that he was *there*, out there, reachable when I was ready to try again. To persuade him he'd made a mistake. I hadn't given up, Dan. I was . . . waiting.' *Procrastinating. Treading water in my relationship with Sean until I felt the time was right to approach Tim again.*

If I'd been pregnant, I'd have done it. It would have been the perfect excuse to contact him: *Look, I've got exciting news! I'm having Sean's baby, I'm no threat to your marriage any more, please can we be friends?*

I'd have lied through my teeth to trick my way back into Tim's life. He's not the kind of man who would tell a pregnant woman to fuck off and leave him alone.

And you knew that when you came off the pill, didn't you?

'Dan, if Tim's convicted of murder—'

'What? It'll ruin your happy-ending fantasy?'

'Fuck you!' Did Lauren feel the way I feel now when she laid into Bodo Neudorf at Dusseldorf airport? Desperate, out of control?

'I'm sorry,' Dan murmurs. 'I really am, Gaby. You're not the only one, you know. We all . . .' He can't finish his sentence.

I aim a brittle smile in his direction. 'Things seem to go wrong when we try to talk, so let's not bother.'

Dan shrugs: *whatever you want*. The easy way out. 'You all done in here?' he asks.

Panic starts to build inside me. *All done*. I've seen what there is to see. I want to linger, but how can I justify it? What else is there for me to do in this room? Dan is plainly eager to get me out.

'Tim wouldn't treat me like this if he were here,' I say. I am not someone who gives up. At work, I have a reputation for laying waste to every problem that crosses my path. 'He'd welcome me in, show me his books, read me extracts from his favourite poems.'

'I think you were right before, Gaby. We shouldn't talk about this, and I'm not comfortable that we're still in Tim's bedroom. Shall we—'

'No! Wait.' I kneel down beside the two piles of books. How could I have forgotten to look at Tim's twin poetry towers? Poetry is all he's ever been interested in reading. 'The second most important thing in my world, after you,' he once said to me. I laughed and asked him if he'd really said it or if I'd imagined it. 'You imagined it,' he told me with a smile. 'But that's okay. It's what I would have said, if I were the sort to get carried away. And I've made nearly a whole personality out of your imaginings of me.' For the forty-three thousandth time since we'd met, I asked him what he meant. 'You're an inventor,' he said, as if it should be obvious. 'You've invented me.'

Wrong, Tim. It was the other way round. Why can you never take credit for anything?

Unless it's something you haven't done, something horrific like murder. Then you can.

I lift a book off the top of one of the piles. *Selected Poems* by James Fenton.

'Gaby . . .' Dan tries to pull me away.

I shake him off. My eyes make their way down the tower, spine by spine, title by title. Minus the e. e. cummings that I've taken, there are only four collections of poetry here. There's a voice in my head that's whispering in protest before I've worked out what's wrong; it takes me a few seconds to catch up with it. 'What are all these?' I ask Dan. 'Where did they come from?'

The rest of the books are about monsters: Myra Hindley, General Augusto Pinochet, a Nazi war criminal called Demjanjuk. There's one about the Libyan Lockerbie bomber.

This isn't right. I've never felt as strange as I do at this moment: as if I pulled on my mind in a hurry this morning, and I've only just realised I've been wearing it inside out all this time.

I look up at Dan. 'Tim doesn't read books like this. What are they doing in his room?'

'Are you accusing me of planting them to make him look like a killer?'

Dan's one of the most intelligent people I've ever met. He knows the difference between an accusation and a simple question. Has he forgotten that I'm clever too?

'Instead of falling into your distraction trap and wasting my time denying a phony charge, I'll ask again: why is Tim's bedroom full of books about murderers?'

Dan's the one who looks trapped: desperate to turn his back on me and make his escape but unwilling to relinquish any territory.

Is there something else in here that I'm not supposed to see, something besides the books? Is that why I must be supervised for as long as I'm in here?

The kernel of resolve inside me is growing bigger and harder, colonising more and more of me, leaving hardly any space for breathing or rational thought. I'll ask the questions I need to ask, all of them, whether I'm rewarded with answers or not. 'Are these books part of Tim's I'm-a-murderer act, for the benefit of the police?' Even as I'm suggesting it, I don't believe it. If Tim wanted to make himself look guilty, all he'd have needed to do was type the words 'Best way to kill wife' into Google. Why buy books about Chilean dictators and Nazi death-camp guards? What connection could they possibly have with something as domestic as putting a pillow over your wife's face and smothering her?

I pick up the book about the Lockerbie bomber. It's called *You Are My Jury.*

'Gaby, put that down, please.'

'What's going on, Dan? What does Tim having these books in his bedroom mean?'

Dan shakes his head as if to say, *Sorry, no answer.*

But there is an answer, here, now, in the room with us, though I have no idea what it is. I can feel its presence in Dan's mind – silent, stationary, ready to go; wondering how long the wait will be. Like a passenger trapped at a boarding gate with no plane to board.

I can't bear it. Have to escape.

I do my best to look as if I'm not running away as I leave the room, walk down the stairs and out of the house, into an external world of unexpected and implausible sunlight.

12

11/3/2011

'That's it.' Kerry Jose rested her elbows on the mess on the table, held her neck between the palms of her hands and rubbed the back of her bowed head with her fingertips. 'That's all I can tell you. The only person who can fill in the blanks is Tim, and I'm not sure even he can.'

'Not knowing why he killed Francine, you mean?' said Charlie.

Kerry nodded.

'You believe that?'

'How long will he have to stay in prison?'

Charlie smiled. 'You dodged my question. And I can't answer yours, I'm afraid. I don't know.'

'What's the average? For people who confess and help the police, like Tim?' Kerry stumbled over her words in her haste to get them out. 'He's never done anything wrong before, never been in any trouble of any kind until now.'

Like many people Charlie had interviewed, Kerry didn't seem to realise that loading the how-long-behind-bars question with bias and hope would make zero difference to the answer.

'Murdering your wife's a big thing to do wrong, even if you've never previously been nabbed for illegal parking. If you care about Tim's freedom, you could always tell me the truth. I know it's hard, Kerry, but—'

'Would you like another cup of tea?'

'No, thanks.' Two was more than enough. Charlie's brain felt jumpy and swollen. 'I'll have a glass of water,' she said, sensing that Kerry would find it easier to talk if she had a practical task to occupy her at the same time. Easier, also, to avoid talking while fussing over a guest: the hospitality of desperation. Charlie waited until Kerry was at the sink with her back turned to say, 'I wasn't expecting you to tell me the story of Francine's death in the way that you did.'

'What do you mean?'

'You told it from Tim's point of view. You left yourself out.'

'I thought you meant . . . I wasn't directly involved in Francine's death, so I—'

'But you were in the house,' Charlie raised her voice to be heard over the sound of the running cold tap and juddering pipes. 'You were here the whole time, weren't you?'

I wasn't directly involved. Was that a peculiar thing to say, or was Charlie reading too much into it?

The noise stopped abruptly as Kerry turned off the tap. She came back to the table with a large wet patch in the centre of her shirt. *So nervous that she can't fill two glasses with water without spilling nearly as much again.* 'Kerry, can I give you some advice? Thanks.' Charlie rescued her drink from a shaking hand. 'If you're committed to lying about Francine's death, you're going to have to lie better. This is a murder case.'

'I know that,' Kerry said quietly. She sat sideways on her chair with her arm round its back, clinging on. With her other hand, she grabbed the soaked part of her shirt and held it in her clenched fist.

'Avoiding the questions you don't want to answer by offering cups of tea . . . it's not going to fool anyone. I'm sensing you want to help here, Kerry. You're not the kind of person who obstructs a police investigation. Which is why you're doing every-thing you can to avoid having to tell outright lies, sitting on the fence so that you can kid yourself you're not doing anything wrong.'

Charlie watched as the red blotches on Kerry's cheeks grew and changed shape. If only guilty hot flushes could be translated into words. Still, Charlie was encouraged by all the body language she'd seen so far. This level of stress wasn't sustainable. Lying required stamina. Kerry's energy levels would at some point hit a dangerous low, worn down by the slow, insistent rattle of imaginary bars. Melodramatic, perhaps, but Charlie knew from countless witness interviews that this was how bad liars felt when they lied: as if they'd put the poor, victimised truth in a cage against its will. Good liars – like Charlie when she needed to be – were able to make their lies last because they didn't believe truth always had right on its side.

'You'll get a sore bum if you stay on that fence for much longer,' she told Kerry. 'If I were you, I'd jump off: one side or the other. Either tell me the real story or work on your act. And make sure it's airtight because believe me, if it isn't, someone cleverer and closer to this case than I am will soon be along to blast a big hole in it.'

Kerry said nothing. She was busy scrunching and unscrunching her shirt. Was she wondering if she could make the coherent lie option work for her? Charlie's best chance was to deprive her of thinking time by piling on the questions.

'You were in better shape before Gaby turned up,' she said. 'What was it about Gaby's arrival that threw you? Actually, it wasn't her arrival, was it? You gave her a saviour's welcome when she first walked in. "Thank God," you said.'

'It was a figure of speech. I didn't mean . . . I meant I was glad she was here, that's all.'

'No, it was more than that. You were relieved to see she was safe, was that it? Or you thought she'd be able to keep *you* safe? Or Tim?'

'No.'

'What can Gaby do to help Tim?'

'You're twisting my words!' Kerry blinked away tears.

'Sorry. I don't mean to.' Charlie was trying to pick out a middle path between going easy and applying too much pressure. 'You know what it is? I forget that I'm "the police" sometimes.' She mimed quotation marks, taking care to keep her voice matter-of-fact and friendly. 'Especially when I'm not on duty, like today. But, generally, most of the time. In my head I'm just a regular person like you, not some scary authority figure. You've got all the power here, Kerry. You know and I don't, whatever the secret is. In my position, you'd probably also feel frustrated and make wildly inaccurate guesses.'

'You wouldn't understand.'

'Try me.'

Kerry nodded. 'Gaby loves Tim. As much as I do. She knows how special he is. That's why I said, "Thank God". I've been having a rough time since Francine died. I've been desperate for someone to talk to, someone who'll understand. I've got Dan, but he's not coping well. I don't want to add to his worries. Gaby's stronger. Than any of us, than all of us put together.'

Arse still firmly on fence. Charlie felt a flash of impatience. She had no trouble believing that Kerry was keen to talk to someone who would understand, but understand what? Why it was so crucial to pretend that Tim Breary had murdered his wife, and protect the real murderer?

'Gaby made a few comments you didn't seem comfortable with. Do you remember? I suppose you could hardly brief her, with me here. That's why she mentioned what she wasn't supposed to mention, why you went from thanking God to tense-as-a-tight-rope-walker's-calf-muscle in such a short space of time.'

Kerry shook her head: more automatic self-defence than a specific denial.

'She said that if Tim had wanted to kill Francine he'd have done it years ago. Also that he'd hated his and Francine's house on . . . Heron Road, was it?'

'Heron Close.'

'Why didn't you like Gaby mentioning those things?'

'Tim's a private person,' said Kerry. 'There's no reason for anyone to be discussing the details of his relationship with Francine.'

'If I were desperate to preserve my privacy and keep all noses out of my marriage, the last thing I'd do is make headlines by smothering my spouse,' Charlie said. 'Is that why Tim's claiming he doesn't know why he did it, to avoid sharing things he'd find too personal to talk about?'

'No,' Kerry said flatly.

Charlie grinned as if none of it mattered. 'That's not a clever answer. You almost, but not quite, admitted that he's lying.'

'Is that what you think I'm doing – trying to be clever?'

Charlie leaned forward. 'The opposite, actually. I think you're trying *not* to be clever in order to feel less guilty. Bare minimum deceit, that's what you're aiming for. Know how many Brownie points it's going to earn you? None. Not enjoying lying doesn't count as mitigation in a conspiracy to pervert the course of justice charge.'

Kerry pulled her long hair taut as if it were an alarm cord, and made a noise that was easy enough to interpret: raw fear. Was this the first she'd heard about how the law might be used against her if she kept up her pretence? Had Sam Kombothekra been too polite to mention it? Another reason why he ought to hand the job back to Charlie.

'Gaby doesn't share your concern for Tim's privacy, clearly,' she said. 'She's more interested in getting him out of prison. I think you underestimated her.'

'Gaby's brilliant,' Kerry murmured. She stared at the door as if willing her friend to walk through it again.

'She seems pretty keen on uncovering the truth. Are you confident you can talk her into keeping quiet about whatever she finds out? I wouldn't be.'

Kerry turned her stare on Charlie, making real eye contact for the first time. The intensity was alarming, invasive, as if her eyes were reaching inside for something that wasn't hers to take. 'My brain's a pea compared to Gaby's,' she said fiercely. 'So's yours, so are most people's. Whatever Gaby does, whatever she wants, I trust her absolutely.'

'Right. But you don't trust yourself,' Charlie deduced aloud. 'Or Dan, or Tim – not in the way you trust Gaby. You didn't like her saying those things because—' She broke off. The idea was too complex to be easily put into words.

'I told you,' said Kerry. 'Tim's a very private—'

'Yeah, I know. Sorry, that wasn't a question. My pea-brain was busy assembling the rest of what I was trying to say.' Charlie grinned and made a cross-eyed face. Kerry didn't reciprocate the smile. 'You want brilliant Gaby to take charge, but only once she's been fully briefed. Right? What about Lauren Cookson?'

'What about her?' Kerry asked.

'She lives here, was here the day Francine died. She presumably *has* been briefed, yet she seems to have blurted out the truth in Germany yesterday: that Tim didn't do it.' The longer she spent in this house, the more convinced Charlie was of Tim's innocence. Hard as she'd tried to come down on Sam's side and prove that she wasn't unduly influenced by Simon, she couldn't shake the feeling that she'd walked onto a carefully arranged stage set.

'How bad was Tim and Francine's relationship? I know Francine had been out of action for a couple of years,' Charlie qualified. 'I'm talking about before that.'

Kerry chewed the inside of her lip. 'I'm not sure Francine thought it was bad at all. She arranged it exactly as she wanted it.'

'Didn't she confide in you? Sam said she and Tim were your best friends, yours and Dan's.'

'Tim was our best friend. Is. Francine was his wife, so we pretended.'

'To like her?'

Kerry nodded.

'Like me with my sister's fiancé, the smug tosser,' Charlie said. 'I've hated him from the first time we met, but when they got engaged I pretended to change my mind to make life easier for everyone.'

'Did your sister believe you?' Kerry asked.

Charlie nodded. 'It's her greatest talent: an ability to believe whatever will make her happy, however ridiculous.' Seeing that Kerry looked interested, she added, 'It's infuriating. You try to force her to confront something and she frowns and looks solemn for a bit, as if she's taking it seriously, and then it's like she just forgets and reverts to her impenetrable jolly self. Hah! Impenetrable's *so* the wrong word. She's currently involved with two men, her fiancé and . . .' Charlie stopped herself in time. Gibbs' and Kerry's paths were bound to cross soon if they hadn't already. 'Sorry. Over-sharing.' *And now I'd be grateful if you could do the same.*

'Pretending to like Francine wasn't enough,' Kerry said slowly. 'Dan and I had to pretend to be as close to her as we were to Tim. She demanded equal status, superior status. Not directly, but Tim made it clear what was expected: could we talk more to her than to him when they came round, ask her more questions, put her name before his on Christmas cards? Could I invite her for girls' nights out, just the two of us, tell her things about my relationship with Dan – made-up things if necessary – and ask her not to tell Tim?'

'Don't tell me you agreed,' said Charlie. 'That's crazy. No one would expect to be instantly as important to their boyfriend's best mates as he was. That kind of thing takes time. Sometimes it never happens. Normally the original friend stays the closest, and if you break up, both parties get to keep the friends they brought to the table, pretty much, and lose the rest.'

'Normally, yes,' Kerry agreed. 'Francine wasn't normal.'

'This might be a stupid question, but why didn't you tell her to eff off?'

'It would have seemed unprovoked. She hardly ever said anything to us directly. It was usually Tim who asked us to pander to her in all these ludicrous ways. It was clear from the first time we saw them together that his plan was to placate her rather than stand up to her. He didn't want to lose me and Dan, we couldn't bear the thought of losing him . . .' Kerry shrugged. 'It was obvious to all three of us that our lives would be easier if we toed Francine's line. So we did.'

'Did it start to feel natural after a while?' Charlie asked.

Kerry laughed. 'Nothing about Francine felt natural, nothing within a hundred-mile radius of her. Ever. What made it easier was that we didn't have to pretend with Tim. He knew how we felt about her. He felt it too. Our connection with him was strengthened, if anything, by the need for secrecy. Believe me, Dan's and my pretence was nothing compared with what Tim put himself through every day of his married life, trying to please someone who'd find fault if you plonked her down in the middle of paradise. All Dan and I had to do was make sure not to do or say the wrong thing. Things, plural – there were so many of them.'

'Such as?'

'Disagreeing with her. Mentioning any incident from the time before she came on the scene, when it was just the three of us. Oh – choosing the wrong restaurant, if Francine's meal turned out to be in any way disappointing. Seriously,' Kerry said in response to Charlie's raised eyebrows. 'We kept thinking we had a full list of all the faux pas to avoid and then we'd find ourselves in a new situation, and make her angry in a way we hadn't fore-seen – like when we went to the pictures together for the first time, all four of us. We only did it once. Francine wouldn't go again after what happened, not even on her own with Tim.' Kerry frowned. 'I think she thought it was a waste of money when you could stay in and watch films on telly for free, but Tim was led to believe that he'd spoiled the cinema for her forever with his thoughtlessness.'

'What did he do?' Charlie asked.

Kerry appeared to have forgotten about her wish to protect Tim's privacy. 'None of us realised anything was wrong until we left the cinema,' she said. 'Francine wouldn't say a single word to any of us. She gave us a chance, she told Tim later. The length of the film, some clichéd bank heist nonsense, I can't even remember its name – that was the window of opportunity she so generously allowed us to see the error of our ways, and we'd missed it. Another black mark against us. We had to beg to be told, as always: "Please, Francine, enlighten us. Let us know what our sin was so that we can atone for it." She'd tell you eventually, in her tight-lipped, grudging way, or a message would come second-hand from Tim. Then you had to grovel until she felt like forgiving you.'

'What was the cinema sin?' Charlie asked.

'Prepare to be disappointed,' said Kerry. 'The four of us sat side by side in a row: Dan and Tim in the middle, me and Francine on the two ends. None of us cared that Francine was at the end of the row. That's it.'

Charlie didn't understand.

'We should have made sure she sat in one of the two middle seats. According to her, that's what we'd have done if we gave a damn about her. We should have realised she might feel left out and made sure she got a seat that didn't reinforce her sense of isolation.'

'That is fucking insane,' said Charlie. She covered her mouth with her hand. 'Sorry, but . . .'

'No need to apologise. That was Francine. Not insane – fully functional, held down a high-pressure job as a partner in a law firm until she had the stroke – just congenitally insecure and dissatisfied. Emotionally, she was like a two-year-old, required everyone to tie themselves in knots to make her feel better. Which she never did, and it was always our fault, mainly Tim's. If he didn't cancel his plans when she had a headache to prove he cared, if he didn't spend an outrageous amount of money on her birthday present when she'd *specifically told him* not to spend too much money . . .' Kerry sighed. 'The cinema debacle wasn't even a stand-out incident. I wish it were. I could tell you hundreds of stories like that one.'

'Why didn't Tim leave her?'

Kerry smiled sadly. 'I could keep you here all day answering that question. He did leave eventually, after . . . Later.' She rubbed her mouth with her index and middle fingers. She'd been at ease, and now suddenly she wasn't.

Charlie's inner antennae were twitching. 'After' and 'later' were not interchangeable. And now Kerry was looking at the door again and quickly looking away, as if she'd been ordered to look anywhere but there. Charlie thought about Gaby Struthers' sudden need to see Tim Breary's bedroom, and decided to risk jumping to the obvious conclusion. 'Tim had an affair with Gaby, didn't he?' she said.

~

Gibbs had nearly finished his first pint by the time Simon arrived at the Brown Cow. 'I'll have another,' he said, without making eye contact.

'You will if you go to the bar and give them some money.'

Gibbs grinned but didn't look up. He was busy with his new favourite hobby: adding more bands to the red elastic-band ball he was making. He'd started shortly after his twins were born. Asked why – which he was a lot, at first – he said, 'Why not? The postman drops them all over the pavement. It's something to do.' So was helping your wife look after two babies, Simon had heard many people point out. Gibbs was disciplined about refusing to be drawn. 'It's something relaxing to do,' he clarified occasionally, though more often he shrugged and said nothing. There had been speculation at work about how long Debbie was likely to put up with him, mutterings about the red elastic-band ball being the least of her worries.

Simon doubted there was anyone working for Spilling police who didn't know about Gibbs' long-running affair with Charlie's sister Olivia. Last year, Simon had told Proust, Sam and Sellers. He'd had to; Charlie's diary, in which she'd written angrily about Liv's enduring fling, had found its way into a murder investigation. Simon felt guilty about the secret having spread further than CID, though Gibbs didn't seem to mind or to hold him responsible – him or anyone else. Recently, Simon had wondered if the leak could have been Gibbs himself.

'Another pint, yeah?' He pulled out his wallet. 'When I get back from the bar, I'll need the attention you're giving that ball.'

The room was too full; it always was at the Brown Cow. Simon hated packed pubs – packed anything. Silent, empty environments suited him better, whether they were pubs, restaurants, parks, houses. There was a place on the other side of town, the Pocket and Pound: an end terrace adjoining the Culver Valley Museum, and possibly the thinnest pub in England. For a narrow strip of ale-soaked dinginess, it didn't have too bad an atmosphere. Or rather, it was one Simon liked and could relate to: understated failure accepted but never remarked upon, the suspicion that success, never sought, would have disappointed – worlds away from the Brown Cow's aura of manic hedonism.

Simon only ever went to the Pocket and Pound with Charlie. She thought it was possibly the worst pub in the world, and enjoyed going there for precisely that reason. 'It's hilarious – much more fun than going to a good pub,' she'd said once. 'In good pubs, I spend all evening watching you sulk. Here you feel at home, so you're in a good mood, and I get to sit and laugh at you and think, "This is my husband. This is his favourite pub. This is where we're spending our Saturday night."' They'd both laughed at that.

'Know what I've learned since I started this?' Gibbs held his red elastic-band ball in the air. 'How insecure people are. No one'll talk to me if I've got it in my hand – as if I can't listen and stretch rubber bands round a ball at the same time. It helps me to concentrate.'

'Not when you're walking down the road, it doesn't,' said Simon. 'Looking behind you in case you've missed any, banging into bins.'

'That happened once.' Gibbs made a dismissive noise. 'Not you too with the snippy comments. Looks like it's me and my little red friend against the world.'

'Big red friend.' The ball was approaching obesity. Simon wondered how Liv felt about it. Did Gibbs put it to one side for her, but for no one else? Would he need it, and call it a friend, if Liv were marrying him and not Dom?

Very psychological, Waterhouse, Proust would have said.

Simon pulled the poem Tim Breary had given him out of his pocket. 'Read this while I get the drinks in,' he said. 'Read it more than once.'

Instead of holding the poem in front of his eyes as he once would have, Gibbs put down his ball and draped the paper over it so that he had to hunch over the table to read it. It looked like the preamble to a magician's trick.

Simon turned to go to the bar. Gibbs called him back. He held out the sheet of paper. 'Forget it,' he said. When Simon didn't immediately respond, Gibbs threw the poem at him. Simon tried to catch it but it float-fell out of reach, landed on the floor. He bent to pick it up.

'Forget what?' he said.

'Poem means fuck all to me. There's no way. What's it even saying?'

An extreme response to a neutral stimulus: interesting. Simon pocketed his wallet, sat down. 'No way what? What do you think I'm asking you?'

'I know what you're asking. It's not happening.'

'I went to see Tim Breary this morning,' Simon said. 'He gave me the poem at the end of our interview. Have you heard of a woman called Gaby Struthers?'

Gibbs' face changed. 'Gaby Struthers? She came to see me today.'

'Today? When?'

'This morning.'

'Why didn't you fucking tell me?' Simon snapped.

'I just did. Are you serious? I said on the phone I had something to tell you, when I said meet me here.'

'Fair point,' Simon muttered. *More than fair: obvious.* His self-righteous fury, so strong only seconds ago, had evaporated. It was Sam he was angry with, not Gibbs.

'Tell me about this poem, then.' Gibbs addressed the request to his rubber-band ball. Embarrassed about his outburst, Simon suspected. *Which was nothing to do with Tim Breary, nothing to do with work*. Had Gibbs thought the poem had come from Liv, via Charlie?

It was none of Simon's business. If Gibbs wanted him to know, he'd tell him. Simon was itching to ask about Gaby Struthers, but he owed Gibbs an answer first. 'Breary asked me – kind of begged me, really – to give the poem to Gaby Struthers. When the bloke she lives with isn't around.'

'Reasonable enough,' said Gibbs. 'I would say that, wouldn't I? Sympathy for the underdog in any love triangle.'

It was a throwaway comment, but telling nonetheless. Assuming Gaby Struthers and Tim Breary were having or had had some kind of illicit relationship, surely the man Gaby lived with was the love triangle underdog? 'Breary asked me not to tell Struthers the poem came from him,' Simon said. 'He wanted me to say it was from The Carrier.'

Gibbs rolled his ball back and forth across the table's surface using only his index finger.

'The Carrier? What does that mean?'

'No idea.'

'An illness, a baby,' Gibbs speculated. 'What else is carried?'

'I was wondering about an illness,' said Simon. 'Carriers often don't have the disease themselves – they just pass it on to others.'

'Breary can't seriously think you'd keep his secret and get involved in whatever game he's playing with Struthers. You're not going to, are you?'

'I don't know. What do you make of it – the sonnet?'

'Don't understand what it's trying to say.' Gibbs finished off his beer. 'I could probably work it out, but I can't be arsed.'

'It's a love poem, though,' said Simon. It was half a statement and half a question. He had read it more than ten times and still wasn't sure.

'Isn't it some kind of puzzle?'

'Puzzle?'

'Yeah – isn't the word "paradox" in there somewhere? I suppose love is a paradox, since it makes no sense. Maybe that's what it's saying.'

'What brought Gaby Struthers to the nick this morning?' Simon asked. There was a limit to how long he could spend discussing love with Chris Gibbs. *Or anyone.*

'It looks as if Lauren Cookson followed Gaby Struthers to Germany yesterday,' said Gibbs. 'The "followed", I mean – that's the part I'm not sure about. Lauren definitely went to Germany on the same day Gaby did. She booked the same outgoing and return flights, though she didn't end up flying back with Gaby. I haven't had time yet to track down the flight she got instead, assuming she's not still wandering the streets of Cologne.'

'Wait, rewind.' Simon held up his hand. 'Lauren Cookson – Francine Breary's care assistant? Does she know Gaby Struthers?'

'She does now,' said Gibbs. 'They got talking at the airport, not in the most friendly of circumstances. Lauren kicked off when the flight was delayed, Gaby told her to stop whining. Then Lauren said something about an innocent man going down for murder.'

'I need to talk to Gaby Struthers,' said Simon, tapping his foot on the floor. 'Tell me everything she told you.'

Gibbs passed his red ball from one hand to the other as he spoke. He was good at detail, better than Sellers or Sam. Forty minutes later, when Simon was confident he knew as much as Gibbs did, he finally went to the bar. He tried not to mind the buffeting back and forth while he waited, the bodies pressing against him, like on the tube in London. Why weren't they all in their offices? Simon distracted himself with thoughts of intelligent string. Wondered how it might work.

He arrived back at the table in a worse mood. A full pint in front of him didn't lift his spirits in the way it did Gibbs'. 'Have you got Gaby Struthers' number on you?' he asked.

'Not on me, no.'

'Find it, ring her, tell her I need to see her. Who else knows she came in and what she said?'

'No one but you,' said Gibbs. 'I haven't seen Stepford and Sellers since I saw her.'

'Listen, I found something out last night,' Simon told him. 'Something you're not going to like any more than I did.' He relayed the story about the doctored interview transcript, leaving out only one detail: Regan Murray.

Predictably, Gibbs' first question was, 'Who told you?'

'I don't want to say, for the moment. I'll tell you, but not yet. I have to tell someone else first.' The notion of being fair to Proust was a new one for Simon. He didn't know where it had come from, this idea that the Snowman had a right to hear the truth about his daughter first. Did he fear that the wound he was about to inflict might be too severe, that consideration around the edges would be needed to soften the blow?

It wasn't guilt. Telling someone the truth meant doing them a favour. Always.

'Sam turned up at the house this morning, after I'd left,' Simon said. 'If I'd been in, he'd have told me then, if I hadn't known already. Charlie thinks that's a point in his favour.'

'You don't?' Gibbs asked.

'He should have told both of us, soon as he knew.' So what if he'd kept it quiet for less than twenty-four hours? Charlie had offered this as mitigation when she and Simon had spoken on the phone half an hour ago, as if it ought to count in Sam's favour. It didn't. 'What if he'd rushed to tell you the second he found out?' she'd said. 'It would have taken him at least forty seconds to get from the Snowman's office to your desk. Would that have been forty seconds too long, in your book? Forty seconds of betrayal?' Simon didn't like being mocked; he'd cut her off.

'Where have Sam and Sellers been all day, apart from avoiding having to look the mates they've shafted in the eye?' he asked Gibbs.

'Stepford's at the Joses', I think. Sellers is doing the rounds of Francine's former colleagues and then Breary's at Dignam Peacock, seeing if he can turn up anything worth looking into.' Gibbs smiled. 'Let's see if Breary's colleagues describe him as quiet and normal, the only two adjectives anyone ever uses to describe their friend who went on to become a murderer.'

'Breary's neither,' said Simon. 'Certainly not normal, whatever that is.'

'It's the way he talks that gets me. When you listen to the recorded interviews, he sounds . . . I don't even know how to describe it. Scripted. Like his lines were written by someone. Like he's starring in a film.'

'Yeah, he's got some kind of weird . . .' Simon stopped short of saying 'star quality'. That would have sounded odd. 'Listen, do us a favour, Chris. Only if you want to, if you don't think I'm out of line to ask. Can you keep this quiet?' Simon hoped he'd got the tone right. He didn't want it to sound like an order, or like begging. He'd never called Gibbs 'Chris' before. 'Gaby Struthers, the poem, The Carrier. Don't tell the rest of the team.'

Gibbs laughed. 'You're not serious? Tit for tat? They kept something from us, we keep something from them? In a murder inquiry?'

'What if Proust was okay with it? What if he told you to report to me on the Breary case, not to Sam?'

'Why would he do that? You're not skipper. Stepford is.'

'Stuff why up its own arse. What if he did?'

Gibbs tapped the top of his red elastic-band ball with his finger. 'I'd tell him I'd rather report to Stepford, who never says, "Stuff why up its own arse" when I ask him a question.'

Simon sighed and rubbed his forehead with his thumb and index finger, a pincer movement. Surprisingly, it helped: smoothed the tension away. 'When they chose to keep quiet, Sam and Sellers declared war.'

'That's one way to look at it.'

Simon was glad he wasn't a politician. Speeches like this were hard – ones designed to win people over. 'I didn't start the war, but I can win it,' he said. 'Gaby Struthers and Lauren Cookson, their connection, that poem – they're going to lead us to the answer, and soon. I can feel it. I want Sam and Sellers to look like dicks when we sort this, dicks who knew fuck all. I'm going to fucking show them. Sorry if you think that should be beneath me. It's not.'

'Liv hasn't asked you yet, has she?'

Of all the things he might have said . . .

'Liv?' Simon injected his voice with as much incredulousness as possible. *You're thinking about your love life, in the middle of the most important conversation we've ever had?*

'About reading at her wedding,' said Gibbs.

'Charlie mentioned it. I said I'd read a passage from *Moby-Dick*. Apparently that wasn't good enough.'

'It's not about good enough, it's about right for the occasion. *Moby-Dick* isn't.'

Neither was Tim Breary's sonnet that might or might not be about love. That was why Gibbs had reacted badly to the poem. His first thought had been Liv's wedding, not Francine Breary's murder, and he'd attributed the same order of priorities to Simon.

'What are you and Charlie doing tomorrow night?' he asked.

'Nothing, far as I know,' Simon told him.

'Have dinner with me and Liv – tomorrow's one of our nights. There's something we need to ask you together. Our treat.'

One of their nights. While Debbie stayed in and looked after the twins alone? And what did 'our treat' mean? They couldn't have a joint bank account, surely. Simon and Charlie didn't; Charlie had told him while they were engaged that he could bog off if he thought she was going to fuse her finances with his.

'You do me this favour, I'll do whatever you want about work,' Gibbs said. 'Tell, not tell, I don't give a fuck – whatever you say.'

'Deal.' Simon held out his hand for Gibbs to shake. Gibbs threw him the red ball instead.

~

'Hello, have I got the right number for the Incredible Sulk? It's me. Can you stop being a baby and ring me? Thanks. Bye.' Charlie pressed the 'end call' button and balanced her phone across the top of her empty mug. 'Voicemail,' she said. 'Which means I'm being ignored. He'd have picked up if he'd forgiven me.' She shook her head. 'Husbands – don't they drive you mad?'

'Mine doesn't,' said Kerry. Her body had assumed the defensive hunch position.

'You're lucky, then. Mine's in a strop. When I nipped out for a fag before, I dared to ring him and tell him that someone he's furious with has put things right and is champing at the bit to apologise.' Charlie waited to be asked why any wronged person would object to the contrition of the offending party.

Silence from Kerry.

'There's nothing my husband hates more than an instant apology,' said Charlie, annoyed not to be able to mention Simon by name; it would serve him right if the key witnesses in his case found out what a petty git he was. 'He likes to indulge his anger, can't stand to have his wallowing cut short by his enemy turning out not to be against him after all.' She smiled. 'Relationships are weird, aren't they? So, tell me about Tim Breary's affair with Gaby. Or would you rather leave it till another time, when she's not upstairs?'

'She's not any more,' Kerry said. 'Didn't you hear the front door slam? That was Gaby leaving. Angrily, or in a hurry. Or both.'

Charlie waited.

Eventually Kerry said, 'It wasn't an affair, not in the usual way. Tim and Gaby never slept together as far as I know, and I think I *would* know. Gaby would have told me.'

'Why didn't they?'

'Tim wouldn't. He wouldn't explain why, either to me or to Gaby, but I think I know: fear of Francine. He didn't want there to be any evidence of his infidelity, which, if he hadn't been unfaithful physically, there couldn't be.'

'Francine could have found evidence of a platonic relationship, couldn't she?' Charlie asked.

'Absolutely. I was surprised she didn't, to be honest, the amount of time Tim spent with Gaby. I suppose he could always have said, "I'm not sleeping with her", and it would have been true. I reckon a lot of people salve their consciences in that way.'

And a confident, successful woman like Gaby Struthers had put up with this non-physical affair, aka total waste of time? Charlie tried to suppress her irritation. Why couldn't someone tell men like Simon and Tim Breary that blokes were supposed to want sex? All the time, with anyone, irrespective of the consequences. What was the point of being a man if you couldn't comply with that basic rule? Traitors to their gender, that's what they were.

'It was a weird time, and for sure the happiest Tim's ever been,' Kerry said. 'Gaby was like his parallel-track wife. For more than a year, Dan and I were part of two foursomes.'

'Meaning?'

'We still had our stilted, shoeless evenings with Tim and Francine, but we also went out with Tim and Gaby and had fun – even more fun because we were so aware of the contrast.'

Shoeless? Charlie decided to let it pass.

'The first time Tim invited us for dinner to meet his new friend, as he called her, I couldn't work out what he was playing at. He was obviously head over heels, though he'd have died sooner than admit it, and I thought, why's he involving me and Dan? I didn't mind; I was glad he felt able to share it with us, but . . . most people planning an affair don't invite their friends along to participate in the deception. They keep it as quiet as possible.'

'Tim sounds unusual in lots of ways,' Charlie said.

Kerry nodded. 'Tim's unique. I mean, everyone is, supposedly, but with Tim, you never know what he'll say or do next. It's . . . well, it's exciting. Everyone he meets adores him – you can see it. You see them not being able to work out why they're so drawn to him, and then they realise: they don't know anyone else who can make a conversation so much like a . . . roller-coaster ride. Sorry, it sounds stupid, I know, but . . . It's not just the unpredictability. Tim has a way of focusing all his attention on you when he's talking to you – attention and admiration. He makes people feel as if he really *sees* them. Hears them. Every word you say matters when you're talking to Tim. That's so rare, isn't it? And, if you've seen him . . . well, he's incredibly good-looking.'

'You'd better stop before I fall in love with a man I've never met,' Charlie interrupted the adoring monologue. 'So why didn't Tim mind you and Dan being party to his not-quite-affair with Gaby?'

'I think he'd decided he could never allow himself to leave Francine, but he wanted to try out the other option,' Kerry said. 'Dinners with me, Dan and Gaby – a simulation of the life he couldn't have. That's why it was important to him to have a little taste of it, more important than being discreet and keeping Gaby secret from us.'

'But he left Francine eventually, you said?'

'Yes. Shortly after things went wrong for him and Gaby. I don't know what happened, before you ask. Neither of them would say a word about it. It nearly destroyed Tim. I think, at that point, he was so miserable, he couldn't pretend with Francine any more. He left me and Dan too, and his job – literally, walked out of his life, left it all behind. I don't think he'd have left *only* Francine, if you see what I mean. It had to be everything, so that she didn't take it too personally. And, oddly, she didn't – oddly for someone accustomed to thinking everything was all about her. She told me Tim must have had a breakdown: if he'd been in his right mind, he'd never have left her.'

'Did she try and contact him?' Charlie asked. 'I bet she wrote him off as damaged goods soon as he was out the door, didn't she?'

Kerry looked surprised. 'How did you know? Dan and I were stunned by her reaction. It seemed so . . . not her. I still don't get it.'

'You've just described the most manipulative woman in the world,' Charlie told her. 'Manipulators are as sensitive to their own fluctuating power levels as brokers are to the markets. They use that knowledge to ensure that they never look like losers. Once Tim did the unthinkable – threw off his chains and walked out – Francine would have known her spell was broken and there was nothing she could do to bring him back. It would have annoyed her massively, but her pride would have kicked in to conceal the defeat.'

'So she set about portraying herself as the winner,' said Kerry, frowning. 'The strong woman, better off without her mentally ill husband. Wow. I think you might be on to something there.'

Charlie smiled. Would she repeat her insight to Simon later? It was always hard to predict what would impress him. Sometimes she shared details of what she imagined to be an achievement and he launched into a lecture about how wrong she was.

'I said to Dan at the time, it's lucky Tim broke off contact with us too when he disappeared. What if he hadn't, and he'd asked how Francine was taking it?'

Charlie waited, unsure where this was going.

'We'd have had to lie. If I'd said, "She's totally fine: going to work as usual, not falling apart at all, not asking after you—"'

'He'd have kicked himself for not having left her sooner?'

'Hard to say, Tim being Tim. I certainly would have, in his position. All those years, wasted.' Kerry shuddered. 'Course, Francine couldn't have been fine deep down, whatever gloss she may have put on it. And everything I heard was second-hand anyway, via our only mutual acquaintance, and she didn't know Francine *that* well. I preferred to think of Francine as secretly falling apart. She deserved to be.'

'Kerry, what happened here on 16 February?' Charlie asked, as if it were a natural continuation of what they'd been discussing. 'From your point of view, not Tim's. Tell me how it was. Everything you can remember. If you don't mind, that is.' She made a point of looking at her watch. 'And then I'll have to go. Let me just . . .' – she pulled her phone out of her bag and started to key in a text to Sam – '. . . summon my chauffeur, DS Kombothekra.' That should be enough to put Kerry at her ease; if Charlie was making plans to leave, they couldn't be about to have the most important part of the conversation. 'Right. Done. Sorry, go on.'

'I was in here cooking supper,' Kerry said. 'It was a recipe I hadn't tried before: spinach and asparagus crepes, béchamel sauce. I was excited. That must sound stupid.'

'Not at all.' *Rather a lot.* Nothing bored Charlie more than people pontificating about food.

'Tim was in Francine's room. I knew that. He'd come in to tell me he was going to see her. He always told me and Dan beforehand, so that we wouldn't come in and interrupt him. We'd tell Lauren, make sure she didn't barge in either.'

'Tim wouldn't tell Lauren himself, then?' Charlie barged in verbally.

Kerry shook her head. 'No. We were his conduit. He'd talk to Jason, but not to Lauren if he could avoid it.'

'Why?'

'He found her irritating in all kinds of ways: mainly her lack of intelligence, I think. Also . . .'

'What?' Charlie watched as Kerry silently debated whether or not to answer the question.

'Tim and Lauren had a bit of a power struggle going on. Both wanted to be . . . sort of in charge of Francine.'

'Did they share the day-to-day care?'

'No, Lauren did all the intimate care. And any moving and lifting – with Jason's help, usually, mine once or twice. Tim went in every day, though, to talk to Francine or to read to her.' Kerry looked up at Charlie suddenly. 'Make sure everyone knows that, will you? The police, the press. The judgers and the haters. Whatever the problems in their marriage, even though he'd left her and thought he'd left for good, when Francine had her stroke, Tim was straight back here to look after her. That's why we all came back.'

From where? Charlie would ask later. 'Going back to Tim and Lauren's power struggle . . .' she prompted.

'It wasn't really a struggle.' Kerry shifted in her chair. 'Nothing was ever said. It was a territorial thing more than anything. Dan and I hardly ever went into Francine's room. Jason never did, unless he was looking for Lauren, or she needed him to help lift Francine. Lauren and Tim both did, and each found it annoying when the other was in there. It wasn't much more than that, really. One of them always seemed to be waiting outside the door, impatient for the other to come out so they could go in for a chat. Well, not a two-way chat, but . . . you know what I mean.'

'So Tim still cared about Francine?' Charlie asked.

Kerry looked distracted, as if she was thinking about something else. 'No. Not in the way you mean, not at all. But . . . It's hard to explain. Francine was his wife. He'd come back to look after her, and I don't think he wanted Lauren taking her over.'

Why not? Kerry's explanation almost made sense, but not quite.

'Going back to 16 February,' said Charlie. 'You were here in the kitchen. Alone?'

'Yes.'

'And?'

Kerry's eyes glazed over. 'I heard Lauren scream,' she said in a monotone. 'It . . . it didn't stop, the screaming. I ran to where the noise was coming from.'

'Which was?'

'Francine's room. Jason was with me. He came out of the lounge as I came out of the kitchen. The doors are opposite each other. We nearly collided. We ran to Francine's room together and, well, we saw her. She looked . . .' Kerry stopped, pressed her eyes shut. 'We could tell straight away.'

'Go on,' said Charlie.

'There were pillows on the floor. Tim was standing by the window, looking out, and Lauren was screaming, holding a pile of clean washing, clutching it against herself. Some had fallen on the floor. She'd been in the utility room when it happened, next door to Francine's room. Tim went in there and told her what he'd done, and then—'

'Kerry, sorry,' Charlie cut her off. 'Just tell me what you saw and heard. Francine's room: you, Jason, Tim, Lauren, clean washing. Pillows on the floor.'

Kerry nodded. 'Dan came in then, wet, with a towel wrapped round his waist. He'd been in the bath upstairs. I hugged Lauren until she stopped making a noise. Tim said, "I've killed Francine. I smothered her with this." He lifted up one of the pillows.'

'How long did he hold it for?' Charlie asked. 'Or did he drop it, once he'd shown you which one he used?'

'I . . .' Kerry swallowed and looked away. 'I don't remember. I think he . . . no, I don't remember, sorry.'

A lie. 'When you say he lifted up the pillow, you mean he lifted it over his head? Or did he hold it at chest level?'

'He . . . he held it at chest level?'

Charlie had met plenty of people – usually younger than Kerry Jose – who made everything sound like a question. Something very different was going on here, something that felt a bit like: *I haven't thought about this part of my story and I'm not sure what I ought to say. I know you're the person I'm lying to, but please can you help me?*

'What was Jason doing in the lounge?' Charlie asked, picturing the collision as he and Kerry had rushed out into the hall at the same time. She wasn't sure why this detail had snagged in her mind. And then she had it. 'Lauren was in the utility room sorting out the washing,' she said. 'Was that one of her normal jobs?'

Kerry nodded. She was pulling her hair again, yanking her head to one side. It looked painful.

'Dan was in the bath, you were cooking,' said Charlie. 'Tim was busy with Francine. I know what everyone was doing except Jason. DS Kombothekra told me he's the handyman here as well as the gardener. Is that right?'

'Yes.'

'Well, there's no garden in the lounge. Was he fixing something?'

'Yes,' Kerry said breathlessly. Too quickly.

'What was he fixing?' Something in this house needed fixing, that was for sure; Charlie thought it was unlikely to be anything a handyman and his tool-box could easily resolve.

Silence from Kerry.

'You're sure Jason hadn't finished work for the day?' A lifeline or a trap; Charlie was interested to see how it would be received.

'No, he . . . I'm wrong, sorry. I must have . . .' Kerry inhaled unevenly. 'He was *outside* the lounge, at the front of the house.'

'What? But you said he came out of the lounge as you came out of the kitchen. You nearly collided, spilling out of your opposite doors – that's what's you said.'

'We *did* nearly collide. In the hall, as Jason came inside after cleaning the outsides of the lounge windows. I was running from the kitchen and—'

'Was Jason also running?'

'Yes. We both panicked. Lauren was screaming.'

'Sorry, Kerry, let me get this straight.' Charlie feigned confusion. 'A minute ago, I asked you if Jason was fixing something in the lounge. You said yes.'

'Sorry, I got confused. No, Jason was *outside* cleaning the lounge windows when Tim killed Francine.'

'And then when Lauren screamed, he ran inside and nearly bumped into you in the hall?'

Kerry nodded.

'Where, exactly?'

'At the foot of the stairs.'

Charlie picked up her phone and her bag and stood up. She felt dizzy after sitting in the same position for too long. 'Would you mind participating in an experiment?' she asked Kerry. 'I'm going to go and stand at the front of the house, outside – by the lounge windows. Can you go to Francine's room and scream at the top of your lungs for about ten, twenty seconds? I want to see if I can hear you. I'm assuming the lounge windows were closed while Jason was cleaning them. What about the front door – was that closed too? It'd be good to reproduce the conditions as closely as we can.'

Kerry's mouth hung open. Her face had drained of all colour.

'It might help you as much as it helps me,' Charlie told her. 'Nothing releases tension like a good screaming session.'

Seated at the kitchen table, Kerry opened her mouth and screamed her husband's name.

Hello, Francine.

This is the first chance I've had to write to you since Christmas
Eve. I've been wanting to say that I'm sorry I had to take away the
Christmas present Tim gave you. He left it in your hand, but I had
to put it where it wasn't visible. I had no choice. Hopefully you
didn't mind. It was only a poem. A mightily depressing one, too.
You hate poetry and can't see the point of it, right? Anyway, I
didn't destroy it. It's under your mattress, with Dan's and my
letters to you, so it's safe and still yours as far as I'm concerned.

Did you have a wretched Christmas, stuck in here with no company
apart from Lauren's fleeting practical visits? I imagine the festive
season must be unbearable when you're bedridden and incapable
of enjoying life. I can't bring myself to feel sympathy for you,
Francine – for which I'm sorry, believe it or not – but I can
sympathise with your situation when I remove you from it. Maybe
that counts a bit. I'm not sure it does.

Did I have a good Christmas? Not especially. I was tense the whole
time. My shoulders are so rigid, they're like a concrete vice round
my neck. Which is pretty stiff and sore too, come to think of it.
It's true what that poet wrote in the poem Tim gave you: 'the body
is a record of the mind'. Dan thinks a deep tissue massage will
sort me out, but there's only one thing now that can make me feel

any better and that's for this horrible situation we're all in to end. And, at the risk of being greedy and asking for too much, I would so love it to end in a way that doesn't involve anyone going to prison for murder. So, once again, Francine: are you sure you still want and need to be here? If you don't, please can you switch yourself off somehow?

Lauren spent the whole of Christmas Day telling us all rather frantically what a fantastic and lovely time we were all having, in between popping into your room to see you. She seemed on the edge of hysteria, to me at least. I suspect she was thinking, and trying not to think, about the contrast between your miserable experience of Christmas and our designed-to-look-jolly one, with its crackers, Port, music and board games. You know she and Jason only spent Christmas with us because of you, Francine? She told me she could see her family any time, but she couldn't bear to leave you, not on Christmas Day. She'd asked me at the beginning of November if you could be part of the festivities. I had to tell her no. Tim insisted: no to your bed being brought into the lounge, no to us moving several chairs and all the Christmas paraphernalia into your room so that you could be included in that way.

Were you confused in the run-up to Christmas? Lauren put decorations up in your room, only for Tim to rip them down as soon as he saw them. He was outraged, and wondered why Lauren was suddenly making an effort this year. I told him that she had probably wanted to make you part of Christmas last year too, but hadn't dared ask. 'It's none of her business,' Tim said. 'Explain to her what we know and she doesn't: there was never any point trying to make Francine happy, and there's even less point now. Do you know what she'd say if she could speak, if we included her in Christmas? She'd accuse us of rubbing it in: parading our fun in front of her, with the sole aim of making her feel worse!'

I didn't need to explain anything to Lauren. She was standing behind Tim, listening to every word he said.

I'd love to know how you feel about Lauren, Francine, assuming you feel anything for her. I wish I could make her life and role here easier for her, but what can I do? She's a kind-hearted girl, but Tim's right: she's an employee. I hired her to look after you, so that neither Tim nor I would have to do the hands-on stuff. I can't take her side against him. I don't want to. I hate to sound as if I'm pulling rank but I suppose I am: Lauren didn't know you before the stroke, and Tim, Dan and I did. That matters.

So, we didn't 'parade our Christmas fun' in front of you, as Tim put it. If we had, would you have been sensitive enough to spot that it wasn't fun at all, not for any of us? Or, post-stroke, are you still only sensitive to your own feelings? Perhaps that's a sensible way to be. I'd certainly have had a more relaxing Christmas if I hadn't been acutely aware of everyone else's emotional agitation. Jason was in a bad mood because Lauren was so hyper. He spent most of the day giving her foul looks that had the opposite of a calming effect on her. Tim stiffened with irritation every time Lauren announced what a wonderful Christmas we were all having. He has always treated her as if she were invisible ('and, more importantly, inaudible,' as he might say), but recently he's seemed less able to block her out. That reached its peak on Christmas Day. Dan and I were terrified all the way through dinner that he might explode and say something horrendous to her, and then Jason would punch him. Unlike Dan or Tim, Jason is the sort of man who would punch anyone who insulted his wife in his presence.

Lauren couldn't have known or anticipated the effect it would have on Tim every time she told us all that our Christmas was one we'd remember forever as having been perfect (clue: nails scraped down a blackboard). Lauren doesn't know about Making Memories Night, does she, Francine? You're not in a position to tell her anything, are you? That's assuming you even remember (oh, the irony!).

Seriously, though: even before the stroke, your memory had

something wrong with it. So often you said, 'No, that didn't happen,' about things that had unquestionably happened, and in front of reliable witnesses. After a while, Dan and I started to collect the didn't-happens. Here are some of my favourites:

1. 'I didn't ask for a dry white wine. I asked for a Bacardi and Coke. You could try listening to what I say for once in your life.' (You asked Tim to get you a dry white wine. We all heard you.)

2. 'Tim, why's the heating on? It's boiling. What? No, I didn't. Why would I turn the heating on when I'm boiling?' (Dan, Tim and I had all seen you adjust the thermostat, turning it up from 20 to 25.)

3. 'I didn't say that Valentine's Day was a meaningless commercial waste of time. I was probably being tactful, so that you wouldn't feel you had to go to great trouble and expense to surprise me – which you clearly had no intention of doing anyway, because you don't give a toss about me, obviously.' (When were you probably being tactful, Francine? When you didn't say the thing we all heard you say?)

Dan reckons you're not so much dishonest as unable to think clearly when you're angry or hurt, which I refuse to accept. If everything that was wrong with you pre-stroke was the result of a psychological flaw that you couldn't help, I would have to make allowances, and I can't. I want to hate you, awful though that sounds.

That's why I always found it so unsettling when something happened that seemed to support Dan's theory. Remember when you went apoplectic at Tim over the twist at the end of that film? I can't remember its name – it was a schlocky TV movie, your favourite kind. For a technically bright person, you had such stupid taste in everything, Francine. Favourite TV programme: *Hollyoaks*. Books: you only ever read fantasy goblin nonsense – you weren't interested in reading about human beings, were you? Favourite song: 'That Don't Impress Me Much' by Shania Twain. I suppose it was apt, at least. Nothing impressed you. Do you know, I don't think I ever heard you say in a restaurant that your food was nice, or lovely, or even okay. Tim always asked you, 'How's yours, darling?', afraid of being accused later of failing to care about the quality of your dining experience, and the answer was always pursed lips and a disgusted shake of the head: the pizza base was too thin, the curry too spicy, the beef too underdone, the vegetables too soggy or too dry.

When the schlocky film finished, we turned off the telly and had the discussion that everyone who watched it had: did we guess the twist or not? 'I guessed,' you said proudly, expecting our admiration. 'Did you?' Tim asked. 'How early on?' Poor sod, he thought it would be an opportunity to praise your intuition, boost your ego. 'I guessed as soon as she opened the filing cabinet in the garage and saw what was in there,' you said. 'It was so obvious.'

Dan, Tim and I looked at each other, baffled. If only we hadn't. You caught the look and demanded to know what it meant. Dan made things worse by denying there had been a look. Tim decided to cut his losses and be honest, hoping to win points for full disclosure. 'I don't think that counts as guessing the twist, darling,' he said as mildly and good-naturedly as he could. 'That was the moment of official revelation, when she opened the filing cabinet.' 'What do you mean?' you snapped at him. '"Official revelation" – what are you talking about?' Tim went on as if he hadn't noticed your sneery mimicry of him. 'That's when the film-makers showed the viewer the truth.' He stressed the word 'showed'. 'You know: the "ta-da!" moment.'

You'd think Dan and I would have been laughing by now, wouldn't you? We weren't. We were perched tensely on the edges of our chairs, awaiting social Armageddon. 'No,' you said indignantly. 'No one revealed anything! No one said anything. It just showed her opening the drawer of the cabinet and seeing what was inside.'

Sophie Hannah

'That was the reveal,' I told you, thinking Tim shouldn't have to carry the burden alone. 'Everyone watching the film knew the twist at that point.' Yes, I'll admit it: as I aimed those words at your utterly uncomprehending face, Francine, I wondered if Dan might be right and there might be something structurally wrong with your brain – something a neurologist could point to on an X-ray and say, 'You see that knobbly nodule there with an impossibly long Latin name? That's what's been causing all the problems.'

I've never seen anyone storm out of a room so quickly. Tim, Dan and I didn't have a chance to exchange any words before you marched back in with a hammer and stood with it beside the TV, gripping it so hard that I could see a muscular bulge in the sleeve of your top. 'Francine, please don't—' Tim started to say. You interrupted him, jabbering too fast, as if you'd necked a bottle of speed: 'Please don't what? Please don't put up the picture I've been meaning to put up for ages? Why not?' You then insisted Tim get up and hunt everywhere for a hideous painting of two sheep in a field, which you'd bought from a craft fair for thirty pounds nearly a year earlier, I later found out from Tim; this was the artwork you suddenly, urgently needed to put up, despite having completely forgotten where you'd put it. While Tim searched, you stood next to the TV, staring at the screen, swinging the hammer dangerously close to it. You wanted us all to be scared of what you might do, didn't you – to the TV, to us? You wanted us to fear what might happen if Tim didn't find the painting, and the tin with the nails in it. Luckily, he did. I remember thinking, 'For God's sake, get the hammer off her.'

That painting's up on the wall just outside your room, in the hall. Shame you can't see it.

I wish I'd kept a diary, Francine. Perhaps one day I'll collate all the letters Dan and I are writing to you and make them into something – I don't know what. I am growing increasingly certain that it's important to remember the bad things that happen as well

196

as the good. You inflicted suffering on a scale that ought to be remembered, Francine. I truly believe that. It bothers me that I can't remember when the hammer horror evening was, chronologically. Six months after Making Memories Night? No, later. You and Tim were living in the Heron Close house by then.

And now I don't have time to write about Making Memories Night because I've got to drive to the tip with all the empty Christmas bottles. Which, having written this, I feel more like smashing over your head, Francine.

13

Friday 11 March 2011

I stand in front of my house and stare at the key in my hand. It proves that my life must be inside this building – my real life. Sometimes I feel as if it isn't firmly located anywhere, but constantly sliding out of sight as I race to catch it up.

After everything I've been through to get back, I wish I felt happier about being here. The sound of football rushes out from the single-glazed windows to greet me; the ever-present backing track to my evenings at home. West Ham could play Liverpool in my lounge and invite all their fans and I don't think I'd notice; I'd walk straight past the closed door on my way to the kitchen, assuming it was the TV making the god-awful noise as usual.

I take off my St Christopher and slip it into my jacket pocket before letting myself in. Sean hasn't seen it since I first unwrapped it, when it provoked a row that ruined Christmas Day. Correction: when *Sean* provoked a row that ruined Christmas Day. He accused me of buying the medallion for effect, to make a point: that I planned to do even more travelling in the coming year and he'd better get used to it. It's one of the few times I've burst into tears instead of fighting back. I couldn't bear to explain that I'd bought it for my sake – that I was someone who had a sake all of my own; Sean clearly wasn't thinking of me and didn't plan to any time soon.

I forget the details of most of our rows soon after they happen, but that non-row was a landmark that led to the introduction of new policies: I decided that St Christopher and I would only get together when Sean wasn't looking, and that in future it would be sensible to keep my soul safely out of reach.

I open the front door, feeling like a teenager who's ignored her curfew and must now face the consequences. Sean's standing in the hall with a bowl of something in one hand and a fork in the other. Steam from the food rises in the air between us. I smile at the man I have lived with for eight years. If I want this conversation to surprise me by not instantly degenerating into acrimony, smiling is a sensible first step.

Sean's response is discouraging. As welcoming committees go, this one errs on the side of scowling like a self-centred tosser.

'So,' he says. 'You decided to come back, then.'

Tell him. Tell him you've only come back to explain that you have to leave.

I don't know how to say it. It's easier to fall into the familiar groove of petty point-scoring, at which I happen to excel. I have no experience of abandoning a partner and a shared home. Sean's the only man I've ever lived with. 'Yesterday evening I decided to come back,' I say in my best upbeat voice, looking at my watch. 'I checked in for my flight home at six o'clock, twenty-three hours ago. It's taken that long. Rubbish, isn't it?' I am still smiling, skin stretched tight. 'I was furious with the German weather at first, but I got over it.'

I force myself to look at Sean's face as a way to avoid seeing his feet. I keep noticing new things about him that grate, and today it's his socks – the same kind he's worn since I met him, but they've never bothered me before: woolly, bulky as shoes, with things like 'Extreme Precipice Crater Climbing' emblazoned across them. Which would be fine if he wore them for more adventurous missions than padding to the kitchen to get another beer.

'I haven't made you any supper.' He lifts his bowl. 'If you'd rung to tell me what time you'd be back . . .'

'I'm not hungry. Sleep's what I need. I didn't get any last night.' Why did I say that? I don't want to go upstairs and get into a bed that smells of Sean; I want to pack a suitcase and leave. Except I might have to lie down and close my eyes for an hour first. The way I feel now, I'm not sure I'm fit to drive.

Sean knows I'm a for-better-or-for-worse sleeper. He's watched me sleep on airport floors, in loud train carriages, in nightclubs with deafeningly loud music blaring out. I wait for him to ask me what happened last night to keep me awake, but all I get is a mumbled 'Sorry if I'm keeping you up.' It isn't a genuine apology; its sole purpose is to draw attention to the apology I'm not offering him, the one he's convinced he deserves. He turns his back on me and heads for the lounge. There's a lager can protruding from each of his back trouser pockets.

No. Not today. Not the beer and football routine.

I beat him to the remote control and mute the sound. 'I got no sleep because I nearly had to share a tiny double bed with a weirdo who ended up running away in the middle of the night, but not before she'd confessed to framing an innocent man for murder.'

Sean puts his bowl and fork on the floor, pulls the two beer cans out of his pockets and stands them on the arm of the sofa. He sits down and devotes his silent attention to the equally silent television, as if he and it have arranged to meditate together.

Nothing. No response whatsoever. Unbelievable.

I shouldn't have agreed to such a huge TV. Even switched off, it would be the most commanding presence in any room. I regret all the arguments I let Sean win in the early days of our relationship: the too-soft mattress, the wet room he's always just had a shower in, so that the loo seat needs to be patted down with paper before I can sit on it. And last but not least, our picture-hanging policy. As a result of my lust-induced weakness when Sean and I first bought this house, each of our paintings and prints hangs from a triangle of cord that in turn hangs from a picture rail. It looks fussy and old-fashioned, and I hate it nearly as much as I hate the fact that one of the pictures, framed for a mere £56, is a poster of some guy who used to play for Chelsea that anyone with a brain would see was hideous and chuck in the nearest skip.

'Is there no part of what I've just said that you'd like to explore further?' I ask Sean. 'Murder, et cetera? I can elaborate if you want. That was my concise introduction, not the full story.'

'Your plane landed at Combingham at eleven o'clock this morning,' he says.

'Yeah, I know. I was on it.'

It's Sean's turn to look at his watch. 'It's five o'clock. It doesn't take six hours to get from Combingham airport to Spilling.'

'No. It takes an hour and a half. Oh, hang on!' I fake a moment of enlightenment. Acting plays a central part in my relationship with Sean, in so many ways. 'You're angry that I didn't rush home straight away, even though you were at work.'

He's communing with the mute television again, blocking me out. If he looked up, if he expressed even minimal concern for my wellbeing, I might tell him everything. *The love of my life is in prison, charged with a murder he didn't commit. I thought I'd be able to rely on Kerry and Dan's help in getting him out, but they're lying too. All of which has brought home to me that if I've only got you, Sean, then I've got nothing. There's a book of poems by e. e. cummings in my bag that means more to me than you do.*

It's probably best if I keep quiet about all the important stuff.

'You got back when?' I say. 'Ten minutes ago? Five? And you found the house empty. You'd looked on the internet, found out when my plane landed, and you were expecting me to be home before you. But I wasn't here. Which means . . . what? I'm a heartless bitch who doesn't love you?' Is that what I am? Am I floating that description of myself to see if he'll recognise it and identify me?

'I rang here, rang your work,' he says, tight-lipped. 'No sign of you.'

'For God's sake, Sean! I was out of touch for a while – it's not a crime. I told you when we spoke yesterday I'd be home as soon as I could. I needed to go to the police, so this is it, now: the soonest I could get back.'

'I rang your mobile – no answer.'

I can't take my eyes off his face. If he isn't embarrassed to be wearing that expression then he ought to be. It's redolent of hopes cruelly dashed. I want to scream, 'Nothing bad has happened to you! At all!'

'You didn't think to ring Spilling police station?' I say instead. There is no trace of mockery in my voice; I wouldn't be so careless. I am a master of domestic passive-aggressive warfare techniques.

'*Police* station?' Sean says in a put-upon voice, as if it's a huge inconvenience for him to have to hear about it. At times like this, I feel the presence of his selfishness as if it were a third person in the room with us, hulking and invisible: twice Sean's size, sitting next to him on the sofa, refusing to budge.

Some people might expect a reference to murder to be followed by a reference to the police. If I relayed this conversation to an impartial witness, I'm fairly sure he or she would be astonished to hear that Sean asked no questions about the violent crime I'd referred to in passing. 'None at *all*?' they would say, and I'd have to explain that Sean walks around – or, rather, lies around – wrapped in a thick cloak of No Concern Of Mine. It repels any kind of experience that isn't the sort of thing that happens to sensible people like him, or that doesn't affect him personally.

Except this murder does. If Francine Breary were still alive, Lauren Cookson wouldn't have followed me to Germany. If I hadn't met Lauren, I wouldn't know that Tim was in trouble and I wouldn't be thinking about leaving home.

'That's right,' I say breezily, taking off my coat. 'I've been *daahn the nick*,' I put on a cockney accent. 'Where else would I go to sort out the whole innocent-man-charged-with-murder palaver?' I drop my bag on the floor by mistake and find I'm too wiped out to bend and pick it up.

There's no way I can get out of here tonight. Sean would find me in the morning collapsed on the doorstep, comatose. My eyelids start to slide closed as I imagine my blacked-out self.

'That's it, pretend you're too tired to talk,' he says bitterly. I forgot: I'm not allowed to be too tired when I get home from a business trip – for anything. It's the price I pay for having been away. Sean expects me to come back full of energy for reunion sex and fighting, one after the other. I never know what the order will be.

'You couldn't have made a quick phone call, let me know you were okay?' he persists.

My fingers itch to dig into him and gouge out chunks of flesh. I sink down into an armchair. 'You don't care if I'm okay, so why would I bother?'

'I don't *care*?' Sean holds up his hands as if to say, *Then why am I sulking and yelling?*

'You care about a malfunction in your remote surveillance system, and you confuse that with caring about me,' I tell him.

'What the *fuck* are you talking about?'

I'm experimenting with telling you how I really feel. I'll probably regret it. I should stop.

'Remote surveillance system?' He shakes his head. At least he doesn't mind that his food's going cold – that's a point in his favour. 'Put yourself in my position for two seconds, Gaby.'

'If you want me to do that, you'll have to shift your arse off the sofa.'

'I miss you when you're away,' he says quietly. 'I look forward to you coming back. Is that so terrible?'

I should tell him not to waste his time, that it's impossible for the Affectionate Pitch Antidote to work at this late stage; my resentment is too far gone. The way I feel at the moment, I'd prefer almost any other man to Sean. A stranger would be nice – he wouldn't expect too much in the way of conversation. I wouldn't care what characteristics he had as long as the first thing he always said when I got in from a gruelling work trip was, 'You look shattered. I'll stick the kettle on. Earl Grey with milk?'

Perhaps my next work project should be inventing my ideal man. I'd make sure every last design flaw was eliminated before

I let him move in. If I hadn't been so obsessed with work when I met Sean, I'd have noticed that physical attraction wasn't a good enough reason to get stuck in a long-term relationship with someone.

And Tim? What about the design flaws there? A man who wouldn't leave the wife he didn't love for you, even though you begged him to? I force the thought from my mind.

'We've been through this before,' I say to Sean. 'The me you miss isn't real. It's a different me from the one that has to travel a lot for work – you don't like that me at all, do you? If you did, you'd be nicer to her.'

'Gaby, there's travelling a lot and there's being a fanatical workaholic who allows no room for a personal life. Even when you're here, you're planning your next foreign jolly: looking at hotel websites, booking plane tickets . . .'

Foreign jolly. That's a new one.

'I've been away an average of three nights a week for the past six months,' I trot out. I did my diary statistics on the plane on the way home, anticipating that I'd need to have them to hand. 'That means an average of four nights a week at home in the same period.' I rub the back of my neck, which aches from the strain of holding my head up. 'What else can I do, Sean?'

Why do I never point out to him that my work-related gallivanting – and he's right, I do a lot of it – led to the creation of a company that eventually sold for 48.3 million dollars and enabled us to buy this house outright as well as a house for my parents, one for my brother and his family, and a flat in London for Sean's sister?

Sean never mentions it either. When I told him that my new company might end up selling for as much or more if all goes according to plan, he said, 'If it does, will you stop starting businesses and spend more time at home?'

Sean's work doesn't involve any out-of-hours swanning. He adheres to a classic routine: leaves the house at seven thirty every morning, spends the day teaching secondary school pupils in Rawndesley how to play football and tennis and hockey, and returns home between four thirty and five. His job has the good manners to confine itself to regular working hours; he doesn't see why mine can't do the same.

'Meanwhile, I'm missing the football,' he says, holding out his hand for the remote control.

I think of the choirgirl who sat behind me on the coach, the one with a brother called Silas. 'Let's say I'd been pregnant, and it was a boy,' I say to Sean. 'Let's say he grew up to be a famous footballer.'

'Are you going to give me the remote?'

If Silas played for Manchester United, would you support them, or would you still support Stoke City? I never heard what Silas's dad said in response; Lauren distracted me.

'If he played for Liverpool, would you still support Chelsea?' I ask Sean. 'Or would you support the team your son played for, because he'd matter more to you than football?'

'Don't be stupid.' Sean opens a beer and his mouth and pours. I've seen petrol pumps approach the transfer of liquid with more finesse. 'You know the answer.'

'The answer being . . .?'

'Are you winding me up? No one who cares about football stops supporting his team just because his son ends up playing for a different one.'

'That can't be true,' I say, but Sean's scornful laughter makes me doubt myself mid-sentence. Could he be right? Is the world really so crazy that millions of men would prioritise . . . what? A shirt and shorts in a particular combination of colours over their own sons? Female football fans wouldn't, surely. I like to think women are saner.

'If we had a son and he played for Liverpool, or for anyone, I'd support Chelsea, till I drew my last breath.'

'Right.' *How pathetic.* 'So, it's Chelsea v Liverpool in the FA Cup Final and your son's about to take a penalty kick for Liverpool and possibly score the winning goal. You'd know it was one of the most important moments of his life . . .'

'I'd support my team. Chelsea. More to the point, so would he,' Sean adds as an afterthought.

What? I must have misheard, or misunderstood. I'm Lauren-lagged, that's my problem. 'So would who?' I ask.

Sean rolls his eyes. 'My son. Plenty of players play for one team and support another – it's no big deal, just . . . your team's your team. Once a Chelsea fan, always a Chelsea fan.'

I can't believe what I'm hearing. 'Your son, the famous foot-baller, taking a penalty kick for Liverpool, would want to *miss*?'

'Much as his professional pride would want to score the winning goal, Chelsea winning'd mean more to him,' Sean says with authority.

'Because . . . he'll be such a devoted Chelsea supporter?' I think I'm up to speed, but I'd better check.

Sean's nodding.

'How do you know?' I ask. 'What if he supports Arsenal?'

'For fuck's sake! What's the point of all this? Give me the remote. He'll support Chelsea because he'll be my son, and I'll bring him up to support Chelsea.'

Thank you for telling me everything I need to know. This might be the most useful conversation I've ever had in my life. 'Sean,' I say. 'I don't want to be with you any more. Sorry to spring this on you with no warning.' I stand up and nearly lose my balance, lightheaded with fatigue. 'I don't love you any more. I don't want to live with you, or have children with you, and even if I did, I wouldn't stand by and let you tell those children what they are and what they'd better turn out to be.' I pick up my bag and hold it against my body, forgetting for a second that it isn't a baby I'm protecting from its father's mind control. 'I'm going upstairs to pack some things,' I say. 'Don't follow me.'

That's when my life explodes in tears and swearing, and I realise that, having done nothing about my relationship crisis for years, I now have to move fast. Very. Seconds later we're both running up the stairs, Sean reaching out to grab hold of my hair and my clothes. I sting and burn in different places; it's hard to predict where the next pain will come from and whether it will throb or pierce, especially against a soundtrack of bitch and whore and evil and monster. I keep my mouth shut so that I can concentrate on moving, slip out of Sean's grasp twice on the landing and manage to get to the bedroom. He's too close behind for me to slam the door, and then I'm not in our room any more because he's pulled me back onto the landing, and the only way I can think to stop him from really hurting me is to surprise him with words. 'There's someone else,' I scream into the arm that's pressing against my face. 'I'm leaving you because of another man.'

It works.

Sean slumps in a heap outside the bathroom door. He's crying. Irrelevantly, I notice that it's not sad crying; it's angry, like Lauren's at Dusseldorf airport. Like all the moisture being squeezed out of a bloated grudge.

I sink down to my haunches, panting. I need to explain properly. Once Sean understands, he might not be so upset – once he realises I'm going mad and screwing up my life rather than riding off into the sunset with a new soul mate. 'Do you remember Tim Breary?'

'Who?'

'He used to be my accountant, years ago. You never met him.' *And I didn't mention him unless I absolutely had to.* 'Nothing happened between us, nothing physical, but—'

'So something did happen!'

'I fell in love with him. I think he fell in love with me too. Maybe he didn't, but at the time that was the impression I had. But . . . he ended it. Not that there was anything to end, really.'

'He dumped you?'

I nod.

'Good.' Sean spits the word in my face. 'I hope you suffered.'

'I did.'

I want to tell him more about my suffering. I'll try taking all the blame and judgement out of it, as I was once taught to do on a course for company directors that one of my investors suggested I attend, one whose suggestions I couldn't afford to ignore. 'You didn't notice that I was discreetly falling apart. I hid it as best I could, but I couldn't hide all of it. I worked out that I was safe as long as there was football on telly. I could sit across the room from you, lean my elbow on the arm of the blue chair and cry behind my hand.' *And you never noticed.*

Sean wipes his eyes. 'I don't need to listen to this shit,' he says.

The course didn't cover what to do if you attempt non-judgemental communication and get an abusive response. Or perhaps it did after lunch; I had to leave at midday to fly to San Diego.

'Why don't you go, if you're going?' Sean says. 'I doubt I'll notice the difference – you're never here anyway. Sex is a joke these days. You lie there like a dead woman, wishing I was him, probably.'

'Silently going over my to-do list for work the next day, more likely. Sean, I'm not leaving you to start a relationship with Tim.'

Hope flares in his eyes. 'You just said . . .'

'Yes, it's because of him that I'm going, but it's not how it sounds. I love him, yes, but I've no reason to think he's interested in a relationship with me. He didn't want me before, so why should he want me now?'

'Then what the fuck . . . ?'

'He's in prison. He's confessed to the murder of his wife.'

'The murder of his wife,' Sean repeats quietly. 'Have you gone mad, Gaby?' I've not heard this tone before. Ever. For the first time in eight years, is he genuinely concerned for me?

'He didn't do it. Tim's not a murderer. I don't understand it, but . . . all I know is, until he's free and everyone knows he's innocent, this is what my life's going to be about: helping him, doing everything I can for him. Until I know he's safe, I can't think about anything else, I can't *be* with anyone else. I can't even work. I know that probably makes no sense . . .'

Sean laughs. 'You're a fucking crackpot. I've no idea who you are, do you know that?'

I nod. Of course he doesn't know me; I've been hiding from him for years – me and my St Christopher together.

'Good riddance to you.' He hauls himself to his feet. 'Get out of my life, sooner the better, and stay away, because I can promise you one thing: I won't be having you back when it all goes tits-up for you.'

'It already has,' I say. 'Tim behind bars for a murder he didn't commit is the worst thing that could happen to me, so there's no need to put your gloating on hold. You can start now.'

'Go and waste the rest of your life on a murderer, be my guest! You and this Tim guy sound perfectly matched. Every killer deserves a callous bitch like you! Hoping you can persuade him he wants you this time round, are you?'

'I'm hoping to save his life.' As I hear myself say it, my mission suddenly becomes real, a tangible thing in my mind. I've made my first official statement, declared my aim. I feel better for it. 'I don't trust anyone else to get it right.'

'Arrogant bitch,' Sean sneers. 'You can't bear to fail. That's what this is about. A man turned you down once, and you have to make him want you – that's all this is, nothing to do with *love*.'

I swallow hard. I'd like to scrape his words out of my mind, but it's too late. 'Make up your mind,' I say. 'Either you know me or you don't.'

'I don't want to know you! I wish I'd never met you!'

Sean hauls himself up off the floor, pushes past me on his way downstairs. A few seconds later I hear a loud slam, then the wretched football, noisier than usual. In the bedroom, I shake as I throw things into a suitcase: pyjamas, toothbrush, hairbrush, disposable contact lenses, some clothes.

I'm never coming back here. I don't want to see any of it again. Sean can keep everything.

I creep downstairs and out of the house, closing the front door gently behind me.

Free.

I run to my car, fumbling with the keys. *Nearly there, nearly gone.* I push the button on the key fob, hear the lock spring open. *Thank God.*

'Gaby,' a voice behind me whispers. Not Sean, not a voice I recognise. I try to turn, but before I can move, there's an arm around my neck, squeezing, and I feel my mind slide out of reach to a pinpoint of bright black.

14

11/3/2011

Proust was in his office: good. And no one else was around. This was going to be easy.

From the CID room door, unseen, Simon watched the inspector's motionless bald head in its glass-sided booth, noticed the way light from the tall lamp in the corner fell on it, as if to draw it to an audience's attention. Silent, unaware of your presence and facing in the opposite direction, Proust still managed to project an aura of 'Cross me and your fate will be one of unimaginable horror'. *Bullshit*. Only things that didn't exist managed to achieve this level of unimaginability.

Simon stood out of sight, not yet ready to change his relationship with his boss in a way that might prove irreversible, and stared at the dome of shiny pink skin. *An ordinary bald head. No one can tell what's inside just from looking.* Simon knew what was in there: the world's largest and most remarkable collection of self-serving strategies. No special powers. Proust might not like what he was about to hear, but there would be nothing he could do apart from sulk and snarl, and he did that anyway. He could try to get Simon fired, but he wouldn't risk losing his greatest asset.

'If there's something you'd like to say, Waterhouse, I suggest you get in here, be a man and say it. The taxpayer doesn't pay you to lurk in doorways eyeing me up.'

Simon walked into the inspector's small corner office and closed the door behind him. He decided to get the work conversation over with first. It would help him to gauge Proust's mood before he raised the subject of Regan.

'I know what Tim Breary said in his first interview with Sellers, and I know you committed fraud in order to hide it from me,' he told the Snowman. 'I could go straight to Superintendent Barrow.'

'Oh, get off your high horse, Waterhouse! I feel sorry for the poor, exhausted creature.' Proust was stacking his papers in neat rectangular piles. 'Racehorses that trip over Grand National fences and get shot have an easier time of it. And next time, check the evidence before you accuse me.'

'Oh, I'm sure you've replaced the original interview transcript by now,' Simon said. 'Doesn't make it okay that you substituted another version and ordered Sam and Sellers not to tell me.'

'I agree. That would be unacceptable. It would also be your word against mine that I'd done any such thing. If you imagine that Sergeant Kombothekra and DC Sellers would back you up, you're more deluded than I thought. Those two haven't got a backbone between them. As for the buffoon Barrow, I could tell him as many illuminating stories about your code of professional conduct as you could about mine.'

True enough.

'I'll be honest with you, Waterhouse: my mentoring of you is mainly self-centred. I only care about keeping you in your job for as long as I'm in mine. The results you get, as a member of my team, reflect well on me.'

'You wanted Sam to tell me,' Simon said.

'Which he evidently did.'

'No. He said nothing.' Simon had reached the point where he no longer agreed with his own unreasonable assessment of Sam's conduct, but he wasn't yet ready to relinquish it altogether.

'Then who did? Sellers wouldn't have dared, and no one else—' Proust broke off, visibly angry with himself for having allowed an admission to slip out.

'No one else knew? Are you sure?'

'Who?' Proust spat the word at Simon. The phone on his desk started to ring. He switched off his full-beam glare as he answered it, harrumphing at whichever masochist had dialled his direct line. He kept his eyes on Simon and made notes on an inconveniently positioned pad without looking at what he was writing. Rather than move the pad, he crossed his right arm over his chest awkwardly, as if trying to straitjacket himself.

Simon recognised a perfect opportunity when one came along. Proust wasn't solely focused on him. This was his moment; it would never be easier to say than now. 'Your daughter knew,' he said. 'Amanda. She told me.'

~

'Gibbs! Been looking for you everywhere.' Having found him, PC Robbie Meakin had blocked Gibbs' path, an acne-spattered obstruction with an annoying grin. Coming back to work after an afternoon spent skiving in the Brown Cow was always a mistake, one Gibbs had only made because if he'd turned up at home before seven, he'd have been unable to avoid his twins' bedtime or the post-bedtime tidying of the house. He wanted to avoid both those things more than he wanted to avoid work or his colleagues – even Meakin, the nick's very own happy and proud Super-Dad. Meakin had three kids. Gibbs had heard him . . . what was that word Liv liked? Pontificating. He'd heard Meakin pontificating in the canteen about how the whole kids thing was such hard work, oh yes, but so worth it. *Fucking creep.* Gibbs wouldn't have objected if he'd been talking only about himself and his own experience of being a parent, but it was clear he wasn't; there was nothing Meakin enjoyed more than telling new dads how they should feel and soon would, if they didn't already.

'Got a second?' Meakin asked.

'Not really,' Gibbs said curtly.

'Believe me, you'll want to see this. It involves Tim Breary.'

Gibbs held out his hand for the papers that were in Meakin's. He knew without looking that they were all he'd need, as surely as he knew that Meakin would insist on taking up more of his time than was necessary.

'Shall we grab a cup of tea and then I'll talk you through it?' Meakin suggested.

There was probably a way of getting the information while simultaneously denying Super-Dad his moment of glory, but Gibbs couldn't be bothered to manipulate the situation. 'All right,' he said. 'You're buying.'

'Saving the pennies, are we?' Meakin laughed as they walked along the corridor towards the smell of lamb and cabbage left over from lunchtime. 'Shocking how expensive kids are, isn't it?'

Don't say it. Don't fucking say it.

'Worth every penny, though, right?'

'Too early to tell.' Gibbs didn't see why he should have to lie to suit Meakin. By the time his twins grew up, Debbie would have kicked him out for sure, and she and her mother would have turned them against him. However hard he tried, Gibbs couldn't persuade himself that fatherhood was a sensible investment, financially or emotionally.

'You don't mean it.' Meakin laughed again. 'Don't worry, you can admit you love 'em to bits. I won't tell anyone.'

They'd arrived at the canteen. 'Why don't I look at what you've got there while you get the teas in?' said Gibbs, holding out his hand a second time. There was a long queue at the serving hatch; it'd be good to have something to do while he waited.

'I'll only be a sec.' Meakin clung to the bundle of papers that made him temporarily more important and interesting than he normally was. 'Why don't you have a seat? I'll push in and grab the teas.'

Gibbs sat at the only empty table in the room and took his red ball out of his coat pocket, along with some new bands he'd picked up on the walk back from the Brown Cow. He stretched them around the ball. Meakin had joined the back of the queue. Why say he was going to push in and then not do it? Who was that likely to impress? *Idiot.*

'Gibbs.' Sergeant Jack Zlosnik appeared beside him. 'Robbie Meakin's looking for you.'

'He's found me.' Gibbs nodded towards the serving hatch.

'And you're still sitting here? He hasn't told you, then?'

'No, he hasn't. Any chance you can tell me while I wait for him?' Gibbs glanced over at Meakin, who was busy staring straight ahead and had no idea that Zlosnik was about to make all his careful foreplay redundant.

'It seems your murderer Tim Breary's been tweeting on Twitter from prison.'

'Possible, but highly unlikely,' said Gibbs. 'Unless he's over-powered a guard and nicked his iPhone, and that's not Breary's style.' Thanks to Liv, Gibbs knew all about Twitter. He knew that no one who used it would say, 'tweeting on Twitter'. Liv had been determined to sign him up, insisting that he'd miss out otherwise. He'd chosen an alias – @boringbastardcg – and hadn't added a picture of himself to his profile to replace the anonymous white egg image. He'd tweeted once so far, to Liv, to say that he was missing her. She'd told him off. Had he forgotten Twitter was public? No, he hadn't; he didn't give a shit.

When he couldn't see Liv in person and his frustration was making him want to head-butt a hole in a wall, he read her Twitter timeline. She mainly tweeted about books and publishing, back and forth with a load of people who did the same. There was often an issue under discussion that Gibbs couldn't imagine ever giving a toss about: were literary agents becoming super-fluous? Were publishers becoming superfluous? Authors? Readers? High street bookshops? Physical books? Apostrophes?

Gibbs thought Liv's fiancé Dominic Lund was superfluous. Occasionally he wondered if any of Liv's publisher or journalist Twitter cronies would care to discuss that with his white egg alter ego.

'All right, then, someone's been tweeting under Breary's name,' said Zlosnik. 'Someone rang it in because of the nature of what was being said.'

'Which was?'

'An SOS, basically. Something about a woman being attacked outside her house. An address in Silsford – Silsford nick spotted the Tim Breary connection and—'

'What woman? Was there an address?' Gibbs was on his feet. 'Have Silsford sent a car? They're fucking useless, that lot.'

'I don't know. Horse Fair Lane, Silsford. Course, the tweeter could be messing about, mistaken . . .'

Gibbs was halfway to the canteen door.

'Victim's name's Gaby Struthers,' Zlosnik called after him.

~

Proust slammed down the phone, having contributed no more than the occasional affirmative grunt to the final ten minutes of the conversation. Come to think of it, perhaps the call had ended much earlier, and those last ten minutes had been a sham for Simon's benefit; Proust wasn't that good a listener.

'You were saying, Waterhouse? I told Sergeant Kombothekra and DC Sellers not to tell you, but really I wanted them to tell you? Why would I do that?'

Why this question instead of the one you should be asking? Hadn't he heard Simon say, 'Your daughter told me'? He'd even said her name. Her old name: Amanda. Could Proust have missed it?

'This might come as a surprise to you, but we don't all ask for the opposite of what we want. That's one of the many differences between you and me, Waterhouse. That's why, when the prospect of marriage to Sergeant Zailer – she of the many careless owners – filled us both with horror, you proposed to her and I didn't.'

Simon wished that someone would murder Proust. He wished he had the mental strength to do it and take the consequences. The world would be a better place.

'It wasn't about making me doubt Tim Breary's story, was it?' he said. 'Drawing my attention to something he said that probably means he didn't kill his wife – trying to look as if you're hiding it from me, so that when I find out, it seems more significant than it is. It wasn't about any of that.'

Proust groaned, leaned back in his chair and folded his arms behind his head. 'You've lost me, Waterhouse. This happens every time we speak: you beat a path to your special private land at the top of the lunacy tree, and I don't understand a word you say from that point on.'

'You don't believe Breary's a murderer.'

'In fact, I do.'

'No, you don't. I don't either. But if he's confessed, if everyone else in the house that day backs him up, if all the forensic evidence falls into line and supports his story, what have I got to work with? You know I'm stubborn, but maybe this time that's not going to be enough to break through the wall of lies. So you decided to give me an extra incentive.'

'Wall of lies?' Proust muttered. 'Is that the one that borders the orchard of obsession that contains the tree of lunacy?'

'Breary's been charged. That worries you. Never happened before, has it – that I've failed to get to the truth in time to stop the CPS charging an innocent man? You must have worried I was losing my touch.'

'Do you want to start race riots in the Culver Valley, Waterhouse? Is that what you're trying to do?'

What did race have to do with it? Simon said nothing. He'd fallen into enough of Proust's traps in the past to know the warning signs. An obtrusive non sequitur was the verbal equivalent of flashing neon.

'Because if you carry on in this vein, I'm going to pitch myself out of the window. People will film me on their mobile phones, and the local news will get hold of the story, and then the national news, and everyone will think Spilling police station has been attacked by a jihadi-hijacked plane, which will fuel both Islamophobia and Islamic extremism. All that will be your fault, Waterhouse.'

'Did you think I'd work better if I felt everyone was against me?' Simon asked. 'Maybe you're right: set me against Sam and

Sellers and I'll need to prove myself all over again, like I used to have to when no one gave a fuck what I said about anything.'

'"Not leaping flames, not a falling ceiling, not colleagues screaming in agony,"' Proust spoke into his empty World's Greatest Grandad mug as if it were a microphone. '"Our information suggests that poor DI Giles Proust leaped to his death in order to put an end to his conversation with DC Waterhouse, because it was the only way."'

Simon ignored the show. 'You decided I needed a new enemy to bring out the best in me. That I'd work better against Sam than with him.'

'Perhaps you're right. I can't say for certain. I remember none of my thoughts beyond "Please make this stop, oh Lord."'

'You knew Sam would tell me. You also knew he wouldn't tell me straight away, and you knew how I'd react when I found out he hadn't. And you were right. You wanted this reaction from me and you've got it. I'm not working with Sam any more, not on this case. I'm not telling him fuck all: not where I am, not what I'm doing, nothing. He won't know what I'm thinking, what my plans are . . .'

'You're not going to tell him what you're thinking?' Proust snapped. 'My white-hot envy of the man is indistinguishable from hatred. If the invertebrate sergeant were here now, I'd end up doing something to him that I wouldn't regret.'

'Everything I've said applies to Gibbs too,' Simon told him. 'He's working with me.'

'I wondered when the ventriloquist would mention his dummy. That red ball your dummy's so fond of – gift from you, was it?'

'I should be thanking you,' Simon said. 'Without Sam and Sellers' mediocrity dragging us down, we'll get there faster. You're right to be in a good mood. Your plan's going to pay dividends. If I've lost a friend because of it . . .' Simon shrugged. 'You don't care about that, and neither do I. Sam can't have been as good a friend as I thought he was.'

The harder he was on Sam now, the easier it would be for

Simon to make peace with him at some point in the future. It was important that the worse behaviour should be his, Simon's. It was the only way he'd ever managed to forgive anyone. He didn't expect Proust to understand. Or Charlie, for that matter.

'There's no denying that Sergeant Kombothekra is sub-prime on almost every level,' the Snowman agreed. 'Though you might hold him in higher esteem when you reach the purge stage of your cycle. In case you haven't worked it out, Waterhouse, you have a bulimic ego. It binges on self-regard until it becomes so bloated it can't take any more. At which point it spews up all the self-esteem it's spent the last however long gobbling up, leaving you feeling like the lowest of the low.' Proust stood up, stretched, and walked over to the window. 'Tell me I'm wrong,' he said.

Simon would have loved to. The words weren't there.

'It won't be long before you decide that you and Sergeant Kombothekra are about as worthless and immoral as each other. You'll soon be propping him up again, helping him to pretend he's a fully fledged person, and he'll be doing the same for you. One setback – that's all it'll take to set your next ego purge in motion.'

'I'll be able to tell you who killed Francine Breary in one week's time, maximum, and I'll be able to prove it,' Simon heard himself say. He didn't care that he'd backed himself into a corner; he was about to do it again. 'You asked me who told me about the interview transcript – your little conspiracy. I had a visitor last night. She told me.'

'*She?*'

Had Proust still not worked it out? Had he really not heard Simon say 'Amanda' before?

'Does the name Regan Murray mean anything to you?'

The inspector frowned. 'Murray's my daughter's surname. I don't know any Regans.'

'Regan Murray's your daughter. She's changed her name. Legally. She couldn't stand to keep the name you chose for her.'

Simon watched the Snowman's Adam's apple do a jerky under-skin dance. 'She's too scared to tell you she's not Amanda any more. Regan's a character from *King Lear*, by the way: Lear's daughter who doesn't give a shit about him but pretends she does. Sound familiar? She's also too scared to tell you about the psychotherapist she's seeing.'

'No member of my family would waste money on psychotherapy,' said Proust. 'Your need to invent such a story says more about you than it does about my daughter.'

'She came to see me to compare notes. I'm her hero, for standing up to you. I said she should tell you how she really feels. She looked terrified. When I said I'd tell you the truth if she didn't, do you know what she did? Burst into tears, begged me not to say anything. Know what her worst fear is? That you'll stop Lizzie seeing her. She's furious with Lizzie for not protecting her from you when she was a kid. Same time, she sees her as a fellow victim, too scared to acknowledge what was going on.'

The Snowman didn't look like a person listening to another person – more like a stake with a vein-ringed head that had been driven into the floor of his office. Simon couldn't shake off the sensation of having drifted into a horror film against his will. His heart was pounding; sweat dripped down his sides from under his arms.

'I know lies when I hear them,' said Proust.

'You think I'm making it up?'

'My daughter wouldn't discuss family business with a stranger.'

'Wouldn't she? So how do I know about her friend Nirmal's eighteenth? Amanda's taxi broke down. She had to get out and flag down another one, and got home ten minutes late. Ten minutes, that's all. Lizzie was relieved she was safe, but that wasn't enough for you. How many hours did you make her stand outside in the rain, with Lizzie cringing in the background, too scared to tell you you were being unreasonable?'

No response.

'I know the answer,' Simon said, in case Proust had thought the question was rhetorical. 'I know how many hours it was, because Regan remembers. Do you?'

The Snowman walked indirectly back to his desk, stopping in front of his filing cabinet on the way for no reason that Simon could work out. He pulled his jacket off the back of his chair, took his keys from the pocket and, jangling them in one hand, headed out of his office. He was going to lock the door behind him. Simon saw what was about to happen, and did nothing to prevent it.

Had Proust locked him in deliberately? More likely he'd done it automatically. Was he in shock? He wasn't the only one, if so.

The conversation Simon knew he needed to have with reception in order to be set free was the kind he most dreaded: awkward, absurd, humiliating. Charlie could take care of it for him; she'd make it feel manageable and harmless. He pulled his phone out of his pocket and rang her. When she answered, he said, 'It's me. The Snowman's locked me in his office. I need you to come in and get me out.'

'So you're talking to me, are you? Now that you need something.' She sounded upbeat.

'Is that a yes?'

'It's my day off.'

'That why you've been at the Dower House all day, doing Sam's job for him?'

'You don't know the half of it. I don't want to boast, but there's been an interesting development, thanks to my efforts.'

'I suppose Buzz Lightweight's already heard all about this development.'

'Oh, *God*! *Swear* to me that you'll stop blathering on about traitors and treachery like some fucking neurotic medieval monarch, or I'm going to leave you locked in there!'

Simon listened to Charlie lighting a cigarette. It was one of his favourite sounds, especially over the phone. He found it comforting:

the crackle of cellophane, the metal scratch-crunch of the lighter's wheel, the deep inhalation.

He walked over to the desk and sat on it, resting his feet on Proust's chair. 'I told the Snowman about Regan,' he said.

'Uh-huh. I knew you would.'

Simon listened for clues. That was either a smoke-ring or a sigh of desolation.

'You told me not to.'

'That's how I knew you would. Is that why Proust locked you in?'

'Telling him was the right thing to . . .' The words evaporated in Simon's mouth as he noticed Proust's notepad, the one he'd scribbled on while on the phone. The handwriting looked more like germs under a microscope than letters of the alphabet, but Simon could make out a few words. 'Attack' was one of them. And the name Gaby Struthers.

'Get me the fuck out of the Snowman's office,' he said to Charlie. 'Now!' By the time he remembered to add a 'Please', she'd already gone.

15

Friday 11 March 2011

Can't see. *Wrong, achingly wrong, don't understand.* This can't be me, can't be about me, must stop soon. There's something covering my face and head. *Plastic.* When I breathe in, it touches my mouth, smells like a cheap cagoule I had as a child. I try to breathe it away, but the wind blows it back, pressing it against my face. *Wind.* I'm still outside, then. Outside my house. My arms are behind my back, held together. By him?

Heavy-set, short hair. I saw him. His neck . . .

I want to be unconscious again. That's where I'm going.

My mind scatters its pieces. Flooding panic as I come to, washed in terror. I'm upright. I must be standing, though my legs feel shaky and hollow, not solid enough to hold me up.

Don't overreact. Don't react at all.

I struggle to pull my hands apart. Something peels away, leaves a small patch of skin on my wrist stinging, but the movement is minimal. *Try again.* No difference at all the second time. *Tape. He's taped my wrists together.* Something's putting pressure on my windpipe. Not crushing it – it's uncomfortable, but there's no pain. Neck-brace tight, but not getting tighter.

This must mean I'm calm: I'm able to distinguish between inconvenient and life-threatening.

I can control this fear if I focus. It's an opportunity to be good at something. I mustn't fail.

A ripping sound: tape tearing off a roll. *Tighter. Pain.* He's winding tape round my neck to keep whatever he's got over my head in place.

My brain caves in on itself. I'm going to suffocate and I don't know why. I can't die without knowing why and who.

A man with short hair and things on his neck. I saw him.

'Gaby, Gaby, Gaby. You've well and truly overstepped the mark, haven't you?'

The sound of his voice sends my body into spasm. This is real. This is happening. I try to run, blind, and hit a barrier – his body? – which throws me back against a harder, more even surface. My car. I was standing by my car. Leaving Sean.

He's going to kill me. Because I overstepped the mark. What mark?

I can't give up. No reward, ever, for those who give up. There must be a way out that involves thinking; I just have to find it. I'm good at thinking, better than most.

'I wish I didn't have to do this to you,' he says, sending another wave of revulsion rolling through me. 'I'm not going to enjoy it.' His talking is the worst thing, worse than the bag over my head: hearing that he thinks he is justified, being too weak with fear to argue.

He sounds so ordinary. I try to fit his face to a peripheral man in my life: the heating engineer who came to service the boiler last week and made it worse, the parcel man, the takeaway delivery driver. No, he is none of those. I've never seen him before. He's nobody from my world. How can I be the person he means to harm? I've never done anything to hurt him. I know life isn't fair, but it's fairer than this, fairer to me.

'All this is for me, it's a job that needs doing,' he says. 'Get things sorted. It gives me no pleasure whatsoever, but you have to learn.'

I need to be telling him to let me go, but I can't mould my fear into words he'd recognise.

Learn what?

He is going to enjoy it. That's why he keeps saying he won't. Dread has siphoned all the strength out of my muscles. A few seconds ago, I ran. I couldn't now. My oxygen's running out, and I can't have any more once it's used up. *Not fair.* The harder I try not to breathe too fast, the faster I breathe: wasteful and helpless, buried alive above ground. He's made a plastic coffin for my head and wrapped me in it.

I suck in, feel fingers in my mouth. Then something bumps against my nose and there's a ripping sound, a gust of wind in my face. I can see my car window and smell a cigarette. It takes me a few seconds to realise he's torn a hole in the plastic.

'Please let me go,' I manage to say. He's given me air. He doesn't want me to suffocate. *Hold on to that.*

'Have you learned, though?' he asks, close to my ear, through the plastic. 'I don't think you have.'

I tell him I've learned. Over and over, gibbering. My stomach is coming apart inside itself.

'Oh, yeah? What have you learned? Let's hear it.'

Nothing to offer him. Nothing at all. I'd pretend if I knew how. *Not Jason Cookson, not Sean. I saw him.*

I can't think of anyone else who hates me enough to do this.

'You've learned nothing because I haven't taught you yet, but I will.' He presses his disgusting body against mine, wedging me against my car. 'Looks like I'll have to teach you not to lie as well. Open your mouth and stick your tongue out.'

'No.'

'Don't say no.'

Shuddering with terror, I obey the order.

'Further. What do you think I'm going to do, cut it off?' He sniggers. If I'd heard only the laugh and no words, I'd think he was younger: a teenager, not a man in his late thirties or early forties.

I saw him. Does that mean he'll have to kill me? If he doesn't, I'll go to the police. He'll be punished. He must know that.

'Tongue out.'

'I can't!' Cold tremors rack my body. If I'm going to die, I'd rather it happened immediately. *Can't say so. He might kill me.*

'You're not trying, Gaby.'

I try. Whatever's covering my face has shifted downward, the torn edge touching my upper lip. I can't see anything any more.

'What do you think a liar deserves to have her mouth washed out with?' he asks me.

I slump. Am falling in a narrow gap, sliding down the sides. He hauls me up by my arms. Any second now, someone will walk past, see us, rush over to help me. Any second. A couple out walking their dog will notice . . .

No, they won't. I parked in front of the garage round the back, not at the road end of the driveway where I normally park. *So that it would take me longer to walk to the front door, so that I could put off facing Sean for a few more precious seconds.*

Whatever this monster does to me, no one will see.

'I can think of a few things I could wash your mouth out with,' he says. 'Spoilt for choice, really.'

I try not to listen to the pitiful noises I'm making, or to him telling me that I won't need any more lessons after this one, because he's such a good teacher. The best.

I don't know how much time passes before he says, 'You can put your tongue away. And you can thank me for giving you a chance.' He grabs me by the face, his thumb and finger pressing into the bone of my chin through the plastic. 'I'm warning you, though: lie to me again and you'll get your mouth washed out with something you won't like the taste of.'

More humiliating than thanking him is meaning it. He's giving me a chance. He won't kill me. All he wants is to teach me something. I'm a good learner. *Thank you, thank you.*

He turns me round, pushes me against the car. Leaning into me, he circles my waist with his arms, takes hold of my belt. *Only to scare me. He won't undo it.* It's an empty threat, like the plastic over my face. See? He hasn't undone it. I can still feel the belt around me . . . and then I can't. He must have unbuckled it. I tense, wait for the sound of him pulling it out of its loops. He could strangle me with it. No, he's tugging my trousers down. He has a different horror in mind.

I scream. He hits me in the side of the head, hard. 'Please don't do this, please,' I sob. He can't rape me outside my house. It's not properly dark yet. Things like this only happen when it's dark.

'I don't want to do it,' he says. 'Like I said: gives me no pleasure.'
Then why?
Because I have to learn.

'What? Please, just tell me. Tell me what I need to learn. I'll do whatever you want.' I'd like to say more to convince him, but there's a blockage in my throat and mouth, a current. I choke, cough, spray the inside of the plastic with bile.

'I've never been as frightened as you are now,' the monster says matter-of-factly. 'Can't imagine what it's like to be so frightened that you're sick on yourself. Is it embarrassing? Or just disgusting? How does it feel?'

What will he do if I ignore the question? I don't want to find out. I give him an answer, not daring to lie in case he can read my mind.

'You're not going to tell the police about this, are you? That'd be the stupidest thing you could do. It'd show you'd learned nothing.' He yanks my underwear down. *No, he doesn't. No, he doesn't. That's not what's happening. This is a passing nightmare. Not real.*

I think about Tim's recurring dream. 'Recurring' means it goes away in between. I would gladly make that deal if I could, if it were the only way out. *Let this stop now and happen to me tomorrow instead – next week, next month. Just not now.*

'No fun, this, is it?' my attacker says. 'Not at all fun – not for you and certainly not for me. Think about that. Do I want to force myself on you? No, I don't.'

I hold the idea of Tim in my mind. He is suffering more: in prison, charged with murder. He must be frightened.

Cold air on my bare skin. *Too much skin.* I am all surface, no self. Disintegrating, losing too much too quickly.

Don't feel it. Think about Tim. Think of his nightmare, not mine. The first time he told me, the conversation we had . . .

It takes all my mental energy to set the scene: Passaparola, the table in the bay window. Can I will myself into the picture, forget where I am? Lunchtime, three weeks before Tim checked out of my life. 'I think Francine might once have tried to kill me,' he said. 'But that's impossible, isn't it? If I'm not sure?' On his plate, black linguine with squid: his favourite.

My safe place breaks up as vile words pour into my ear: 'Are you ashamed? I feel sorry for you. I really do. I'm not as hard-hearted as I seem, not once you know me.'

Don't feel it.

'It's not impossible, no. People do try to kill people, often their husbands and wives. Though it's odd that you don't know for sure.'

'I'd be ashamed if I were you. Would you say you're a coward, Gaby? People like you often are. I would, by the way – I'd say you're a coward.'

No. Cowards don't escape. Only the bravest escape, like me, back to Tim.

'I have this recurring dream. It's set in Switzerland, appropriately enough.'

'That's lucky. If you had a recurring dream set in the UK, think of the tax you'd have to pay on it. The rate'd probably go up with each repeat.'

'Repeated with cold sweat side effects on average three times a week. Keep this to yourself, okay? I haven't told Dan and Kerry. It's not easy to admit to being bullied by a dream. If you want to retain any dignity, that is.'

'Has this happened to you before, when you've been scared?' asks the monster. My skin burns as if it's caught fire. 'Well? When I ask questions, I expect answers, Gaby.'

I don't hear my answers, only Tim's questions: 'Why would

Francine have tried to kill me in Switzerland? I know dreams aren't reliable, but the setting's always the same.'

'Have the two of you ever been to Switzerland together?'

'Once – to Leukerbad, on holiday. It's where she proposed to me.'

'*She* proposed?'

'Yes. It was 29 February, a leap year. Women are allowed to propose, and men have to say yes.'

I fell into his trap. 'Men don't *have* to say yes,' I said.

Tim feigned shock. 'Really? Francine told me they did.'

I waited.

'It was probably the easiest stretch I've ever had with her, that holiday. She was happy – for Francine. Why would she try to kill me when I'd just said I'd marry her?' I watched as he lost patience with himself. 'For God's sake, if my wife tried to kill me, in Switzerland or anywhere, why don't I remember it when I'm awake? If it weren't for the dream, I wouldn't have this absurd idea in my head.'

'What happens in the dream?' I asked.

No answer. No Tim. I'm the one expected to answer: which is worse, the shame or the fear? What exactly is going through my mind? What's the worst thing the monster could do to me now? The worst three things? Will I try to forget this as soon as it's over? Because that would be against the spirit of the lesson; I must remember it every day, so I don't slip up again.

I am streamed into two separate zones: in a restaurant in Spilling, and in hell.

'Tell me about the dream,' I say in my head, to make hell disappear.

Tim is back. *Thank God.* 'There's not much to it,' he says. 'I'm in a small room – our Leukerbad hotel room, I think, except in the dream it's much smaller, the size of a bathroom. Square. Francine's walking towards me, diagonally across the room. A diagonal line, definitely. She's walking very slowly. I can't see her, only her shadow against the white wall, coming closer and closer. Carrying her handbag – not in her hand, draped over her arm.

It's the bag that I'm most scared of. Whatever she's going to use to kill me is in that bag. I stare at the triangle of white wall between the bag and its strap. I can't bring myself to look at the bag directly.'

'It's lucky you've got a bag over your head,' the monster says. 'Lucky you can't see how pathetic you look with your hands taped behind your back: like an animal with a tail, a squirming pink tail.' I stop moving my fingers. They stiffen. My cutlery falls to the floor with a clatter.

No, it didn't. I'm not in the restaurant now. It was my St Christopher that fell, from my jacket pocket.

'Francine's arm looks as if it's broken, the arm her bag's hanging from as she moves towards me,' Tim says. 'Something about the angle of it . . .'

'Did you break her arm? Did the two of you have a physical fight?'

'Gaby!' A sharp jab of fingers to the side of my head. 'You're not paying attention. When I talk to you, I expect you to listen. When I ask you a question, I expect you to answer.'

'I've never broken a bone,' says the shadow of Tim. 'Neither one of my own nor anyone else's. In my nightmare, I'm the prey, not the predator. I'm petrified, crouched in a corner, trying to keep completely still and not give myself away, but I can't. My body's shaking, jerking in odd directions. I can't control it. I know Francine's never going to stop sliding towards me. Oh, she's sliding, not walking – did I mention that? When she reaches me, I'll be snuffed out, forever. And there's nothing I can do to stop it – it's going to happen. All I can do is stare at the shadow gliding along the white wall, getting closer. Francine's twisted arm, the white triangle between the bag and its strap.'

'Do you know what the word "humiliate" means? "To make humble". That's what I'm doing to you, I'm making you humble. Humility's a virtue, isn't it? Not one that comes easily to you, from what I've heard.'

Tim? Where have you gone? Where has the table gone?

'Come on, don't cry. Stop snivelling like a baby. You don't know you're born.'

I can do this alone, without Tim. I can speak for us both.

The twisted arm has to be significant.

It's too thin, way too thin, like a starving person's. And . . . there's something sticking out, a lump of bone jutting out of the flesh.

Or an elbow?

No. I don't think so. Wrong place.

Has Francine ever broken her arm?

Not that I know of.

'Stay away from Lauren Cookson and we won't have a problem in future.'

What about Francine's other arm? Is that normal in the dream?

I don't know. That's a good question. I don't think I can see it. Don't notice it, anyway. I just see the too-thin arm and the bag. It was real, the bag – expensive. She bought it specially for our trip. I never saw it once we got back. When I asked her about it, she said the strap broke so she took it back to the shop.

Do you ever get to the part in the dream where Francine murders you? Do you know how she does it?

'There's no need for you to cross paths with Lauren in the future. Make sure you don't.'

No. To both.

Did the dream start while you were still in Switzerland?

I had it for the first time two days after we got back. Something happened there, Gaby. I just wish I knew what. Most men, if their fiancées tried to kill them, would review their options. If they weren't scared of being killed, that is. Kind of Catch-22, isn't it?

'Keep away from Lauren and I'll stay away from you. You don't always want to be looking over your shoulder, do you? Forget Lauren, and you won't have to worry, this will be over.'

Have you told Francine about your recurring dream?

Are you joking? What if I'm going mad, imagining the whole thing? What if knowing I know makes her try again?

'Lauren should never have gone looking for you in the first place. You're not the only one with a lesson to learn.'

How would you feel, Francine, if I told you that when you married
Tim, you took the surname of his secondary school English teacher?
Would you keep an open mind for his sake, because you care about
him, or would you bypass curious in your haste to get to furious? I
asked Dan about this this morning. He nearly spat out his cereal.
'Francine, open-minded?' he said. 'She'd be incandescent.' We
started to giggle over our Weetabix like hyped-up kids. The idea of
someone whose anger is frightening getting really, really angry is
funny as long as it's not actually happening.

I'd like to tell you – not the full story, just a teaser. You'd be
desperate to get your hands on all the details, but since you can't
speak, you wouldn't be able to demand them. Maybe I'd adopt the
morally superior tone that used to be your trademark and ask you a
test question: 'Do you want to know for the right reason,' I'd say, 'or
only so that you can assemble your Yet Another Terrible Thing That
Was Done To Me narrative? The Truth My Husband Withheld That I
Had A Right To Know?' If I felt really vindictive, I might then make
a show of waiting for the answer you'd be incapable of giving me.
How you'd hate me for using your beloved 'right reason' line against
you, for knowing something about Tim that you don't. How dare he
tell me and Dan and not you?

In case you haven't worked it out yet, Tim dares to tell me and
Dan things because he knows we'll accept his decisions, even the

---

Sophie Hannah

bad ones. Like marrying you. Like moving back in with you after the stroke. Though, actually, that's done him good. I was certain any contact with you would be dangerous for him, but I was wrong. (That's why you should never attack another person's autonomy, Francine – because what if you're wrong? What if you emotionally blackmail them into doing what you 'know' is right, and it turns out not to be? And isn't it kind of unbelievable that there are people like you who need this spelling out for them?)

Watching Tim lose his fear and start to be more natural around you convinced me that I'd miscalculated. I've stopped worrying that he'll try to kill himself again; now I worry instead that he'll kill you, which might bring him psychological closure but would also land him in prison. Having said that, I think Tim could live quite happily in prison – more so than most people. He doesn't give two hoots about his physical surroundings as long as there are books there. He'd have a prescribed routine, plenty of time to read, lots of people to charm and impress and, crucially, proof that he's a bad guy. I think he'd find that comforting.

Thank God prison is the worst-case scenario for him. Recently I've been thinking a lot about our capital punishment argument – remember that horrendous evening, Francine? If words could leave scars, yours would have. It started off as a discussion, but you quickly turned it nasty and personal. You were (are?) in favour of the death penalty, and Dan and I were (are?) against, and when we tried to explain why, you couldn't handle it, could you? You started yelling at us, saying that it was thanks to people like us that multiple murderers killed again and again. You told us there was blood on our hands. I remember, Dan and I laughed afterwards about how we'd both looked down at our hands at that moment. We examined them, found them unbloodied, then did what we always did when you made a scene: pretended you weren't behaving badly, upped our own politeness levels to counteract your self-righteous hostility. Anyone watching us would have found the scene surreal, as if you and we were participating in two wholly separate dialogues: a hissy, red-faced 'All I know is, I've got no child deaths on *my* conscience!' followed by a silky-smooth 'Absolutely, and your sense of justice is really admirable, and I can totally see why you feel the way you do, but . . .' And then a self-effacing shrug, because it would have been too incendiary to say, 'But we believe it's wrong to kill people, even if it's legal and those people are violent criminals.'

Tim rang us three days later to apologise for your aggression. Being Tim, he didn't use the word 'aggression' or say, 'I'm sorry' at any point in the conversation. I answered the phone and he chuckled and said, 'You two got off lightly the other night.' My heart plunged to my guts. I'd have preferred it if Tim had got off lightly, since he was the one who'd been unable to leave at the end of the evening, or at the end of any evening with you. Tim was the one who had to sleep next to you, wake up with you. Unlike me and Dan, he didn't get to escape with someone who loved him unconditionally and approved of him; he didn't get to laugh cathartically and compare notes about your insane need to create misery for yourself and everyone around you.

It surprised me to hear that he hadn't got off lightly, naïve fool that I was. Even then, well into his marriage to you, I hadn't got to grips with the full extent of your corrosiveness. By your standards, I thought, Tim had surely behaved better than Dan and I had. Insofar as it's possible for anyone to have done nothing wrong in Francine World, he had done nothing wrong. He hadn't disagreed with you about the death penalty, hadn't spoken a single word until the conversation had moved on to a less contentious subject. 'Did you say something to wind her up after we'd left?' I asked him, thinking it incredibly unlikely. Tim always took care to say as little in your presence as he could get away with.

'It's what I didn't say that was the problem,' he explained. 'My silence was disloyal, apparently. I should have made it clear I was on her side.' 'You're pro-death penalty?' I said, surprised. It's probably wrong of me, but I naturally assume everyone I like is anti. Tim said, 'If I'm only executing in the abstract, then I'll hang, guillotine and crucify all the livelong day to get my own sentence down.' Two days in the dark cloud for the minor disloyalty of failing to defend Francine's point of view. I'd get at least a fortnight for the major disloyalty of not agreeing with it. And she's quite right: she'd never be disloyal to me, minorly or majorly. When I start to defend state-sanctioned murder in public – and quite frankly, what's holding me up? – she'll be front and centre cheering me on, even after my unforgivable behaviour of the other night.'

I was stunned. 'She actually said that? That she'd defend you if you were spouting *her* opinions?' I resisted the urge to say 'bigoted, barbaric opinions'. 'Yup,' said Tim cheerfully. 'She meant it, too. My wife's a better person than I am: she never says things she doesn't mean. I do it all the time. And, to be fair to her, she thinks our opinions are interchangeable. She's far better at being married than I am.' God, he could be infuriating: the deadpan way he'd describe your outrageous attitudes and behaviour towards him as if he didn't disapprove of them himself, purely to wind me up.

What would the penalty be for lying about his name and his family, if you were in a position to hand out punishments, Francine? Would Tim's sentence be harsh or lenient? How long in the dark cloud for telling you his parents were dead and he had no siblings, when in fact he has two brothers – one older, one younger – and his parents are alive and well and living in Rickmansworth? Their surname isn't Breary, it's Singleton. That's what Tim used to be called. Breary came from his fourth year English teacher, Padraig Breary – housemaster at Gowchester School by day, poet by night, died of a brain tumour in 2007, aged sixty-three. Tim read about his death in one of the poetry magazines at his local library: if it weren't for the library, he told me and Dan, he wouldn't have made the effort to leave his Bath bedsit to buy food. He'd have starved to death and saved himself the bother of having to do melodramatic things with a knife.

It was exactly a month after Padraig Breary died that Tim tried to follow his example: same date the next month. Tim didn't tell me that. I found out by accident months later, when I read an obituary of Padraig Breary from *The Times* that Tim had cut out and kept. I never mentioned to him that I'd made the connection between the dates.

I don't think you'd be all that interested in Padraig Breary, would you, Francine, even if I told you what a brilliant poet he was? You were proud of your belief that poetry was a waste of everyone's time. You'd want to know all about the Singletons, though: the in-laws Tim denied you that were yours by right – his parents, Veronica and Trevor, both now retired, and his two brothers, Stuart and Andrew. Veronica used to be a solicitor like you, though her field was employment law, not pensions, so not too spookily similar. Trevor was something senior and managerish at British Airways. Stuart sort of followed his dad's example and is a pilot, and Andrew runs a gourmet pizza takeaway and delivery company. They're both married, with a child each.

Tim didn't tell me about his brothers' careers or families because he doesn't know. Shortly after his suicide attempt, I paid a private investigator for information about Stuart and Andrew Singleton. In case Tim ever wants to trace them, I've saved him the trouble. Though, truthfully, that's not why I did it: it had more to do with wanting to be able to get in touch with them quickly and easily if anything were to happen to Tim. He has no relationship with them now, but I'd want to let them know, and I'd want to know if I were them.

I don't think there's any circumstance that could make me want to contact Veronica and Trevor Singleton, who never spoke to their children apart from about the practicalities of day-to-day life, never kissed or cuddled or said they loved them, never took them anywhere a child might want to go more than an adult would. From all the stories Tim told me and Dan (as if they were hilarious and had happened to someone else) what most sticks in my mind is his description of family mealtimes: Veronica and Trevor reading in silence while shovelling in each day's identical food – porridge for breakfast, salad and tinned fish for lunch, stew for supper – with their books held up close so that their sons couldn't see their faces. They bought no books for their sons, ever, though they didn't mind if Tim read the paperback novels they'd finished with, which he did as soon as he was old enough. Stuart and Andrew never showed an interest, and read only at school when they had to.

The Singleton boys weren't allowed to be upset or to cry, weren't allowed to get angry or argue or make any kind of mess, weren't allowed to have problems of any kind, couldn't have friends round to play in case those friends created inconvenience, weren't allowed pets. It was made clear to Tim, Stuart and Andrew every day that their presence would only be tolerated by Trevor and Veronica if it mimicked an absence. They were expected to be hassle-free shadow children.

For the eighteen years that Tim lived in his parents' house, he was uncomplaining and compliant – the good son whose needs never inconvenienced his parents because he appeared to have none. Stuart suffered from all kinds of strange eating disorders as a child and was hospitalised several times with malnutrition because he couldn't keep food down. When they visited him, Veronica and Trevor took with them files full of paperwork and whatever books they were reading, and looked up from their printed pages only occasionally, to tell Stuart he had to get better quickly because it was yet another problem for them when he wasn't well.

The doctors could never find anything wrong with him. 'That's because membership of the Singleton family doesn't show up on X-rays,' Tim told me and Dan. The three of us laughed about our appalling families quite often. What else could we do? I never told you, Francine, but my father is a convicted paedophile. He's been to prison twice. My mother's still with him, unbelievably. She stood by him, and now lives as the wife of a known sex offender. Last I heard, my sisters were still in touch with him intermittently, trying to make the best of a bad situation. I haven't spoken to any of them for nearly ten years. It's the only way I can cope, by shutting it out, getting on with my life, trying very hard to be the best person I can be. (Which you make difficult, Francine.)

I'm supposed to be telling you about Tim, not about me. His dreadful parents, not mine. His brother Andrew got heavily involved in the local drug scene as a teenager and ended up in a young offenders' institute. Veronica and Trevor didn't visit him, not once. Andrew's attention-seeking criminal behaviour mustn't be rewarded, they said. Stuart visited once and was ignored by Trevor and Veronica for nearly six months as punishment, but Tim was unwilling to go against the parental line. 'I couldn't risk it,' he said. 'Mum and Dad were forever debating whether it was worth stumping up the school fees for Stuart and Andrew, given that they were such pains in the arse. They never said that about me, but I knew they'd start if I put a foot wrong. School was the only place I liked.'

Tim did brilliantly at Gowchester and got a first in English from Rawndesley University. Then came the accountancy training, the good job, the rented flat overlooking the river – all part of his escape plan from the start. Finally, he had a home and an income of his own and no longer needed his parents for anything. He'd already changed his surname to Breary by this point, though his family didn't know it. He also hadn't told them about the flat, and he'd lied about which firm he'd be working for. He moved out without giving notice to the Singletons, and he's had no contact with any of them since. As far as he knows, none of them has ever tried to find him.

How would you use that knowledge, Francine? If I told you the story I've just written down, and if you were fit and healthy, what would you do? Or perhaps I should ask instead: what would you make Tim do? Would it be all right with you that he'd opted out of the family and name he was born into? I don't think it would be. Would you criticise him for abandoning his brothers? Most people would. Tim's suffering as a child wasn't Andrew's fault, or Stuart's. True, Francine, but they're in touch with Trevor and Veronica, and that's unlikely to change, Tim thinks – that's why he can't allow their presence in his life.

I don't think you'd trust him to have made the right decision. You'd insist on meeting them all. That's why Tim would never have risked telling you – you'd have tried to seize control.

This is why your helplessness is hard to regret, Francine. You can't defend yourself, which means that, finally, Tim can. I hope he doesn't kill you for his sake, but if he does, it'll be the clearest case of self-defence there's ever been. I don't care if the law says otherwise.

16

12/3/2011

'Gaby wrote those tweets herself, about being attacked,' said Sean Hamer. He looked all wrong in relation to the room that contained him, which, Gibbs guessed, had had its colour scheme and furnishings chosen by Gaby. There was a lot of pale pink and pale green, silk curtains, expensive-looking Chinese vases dotted about on the various flat surfaces. Or maybe Japanese. A tiny silk handbag with a long strap and a pattern of embroidered dragons hung from the doorknob that faced into the room. The odd ones out here were the TV in the corner that was transmitting silent football, and Sean Hamer in his shiny football shirt, faded jeans and battered trainers. And Gibbs, who had been wondering since he arrived if this lounge was anything like the way Liv would have a room done out. He knew he'd never ask her; she'd tease him. It'd be too depressing, anyway, since the two of them would never share any kind of living space.

Gibbs waited in case Hamer had anything to add. Was he aware of having left any gaps? No, it seemed not. His tone couldn't have been more reasonable; he believed he was helping. His manner made Gibbs feel awkward about asking him for evidence to back up his claim. More than awkward; implicated. At first he couldn't work out why, then he realised: Hamer was behaving as if he and Gibbs had jointly proved, to their mutual satisfaction, that Gaby was behind the tweets from Tim Breary's Twitter account. There had been an unspoken 'We've established that . . .' about what he'd said.

As far as Gibbs could see, nothing had been established.

'What makes you so sure it was Gaby?' he asked.

'Because I know she wasn't attacked, and no one else would make-up something like that,' said Hamer – again, as if they'd already covered all the ground necessary in order to reach this conclusion.

Strange.

'How do you know she wasn't attacked, Mr Hamer? How do you know no one else would make it up?' *Do you know everybody on the planet?*

'Seriously, wherever Gaby is, she's absolutely fine. Gaby's always fine. She makes sure of that.'

'Do you have any proof that Gaby sent those tweets?' Gibbs persisted.

Hamer nodded. 'She'd have known this Tim Breary guy's password for Twitter. Definitely. She's probably been having an affair with him behind my back for years.'

'She *would have* known his password? Or she did?'

'Course she did.' Hamer glanced over his shoulder at the silent football on the television, then turned back to face Gibbs in slow motion, as if it required superhuman effort to twist his head back in that direction.

'How do you know Gaby knew Tim Breary's Twitter password? How do you know that she wasn't attacked?'

'I've told you.' Hamer's voice was a blend of impatience and confusion.

Gibbs could imagine it would be very confusing if you were logic-impaired and genuinely believed you'd offered ample proof, when in fact you'd provided none. 'You've told me what you believe to be true, but you haven't offered any evidence to back it up,' he said. 'So I'm not sure why you think what you think.'

Hamer sighed. 'Look, I'm the victim here, not Gaby.'

'Victim of what?'

'She left me. Just walked out – no notice, no trying to salvage anything. Nothing.'

'So you're the victim of her leaving you,' said Gibbs. 'Doesn't mean she wasn't the victim of an attack last night.'

'Nothing happened to Gaby last night. I've said that.'

Jesus fucking Christ. 'Yes, Mr Hamer, you've *said* it. But without knowing what you've based your opinion on, I can't agree or disagree with you. All I can say is, "Oh, yes, something *did* happen to Gaby last night." And then you'd say, "Oh, no, it didn't." That'd be a pointless conversation for us to have, wouldn't it? We'd make no progress.'

'Nothing happened to her,' Hamer insisted. 'Gaby looks after number one, always. She never slips up. She's . . . what's the word?'

Gibbs was tempted to say something random – 'wheelbarrow' – in order to hear Hamer say, 'No, that's not the word I was looking for.'

Yes, it is. And let me 'prove' it by saying once more: yes, it is.

'To be honest, I'll be happy if I never hear the name Gaby Struthers again,' Hamer said.

'You'll be deaf if you never hear the name Gaby Struthers again,' Gibbs told him. 'You're sure she's not made contact since she left here yesterday evening?'

'We barely had contact before she left.' Hamer craned his neck again to check on the muted footballers. This time he didn't turn back, but carried on talking with the back of his head facing Gibbs. 'That's why I'm not going to miss her. She was never here, and even when she was, her mind was on her next work trip, or . . . *him*, probably. Tim Breary. She's only done this to worry me: faking this attack, making me think she's been kidnapped or something.'

'Kidnapped?' The word leaped out at Gibbs. 'Why do you say that?'

'That's what she wants me to think, probably. Or worse: raped, murdered, chopped up into little pieces.' Reluctantly, Hamer turned back to Gibbs. He shrugged. 'Who knows?'

Sophie Hannah

'You don't seem worried,' said Gibbs.

'I'm not. From now on, I'll be worrying about number one. I've been all about Gaby for too long. Not any more.'

Gibbs didn't believe for a second that Hamer's air of 'Why should I care about anyone but me?' was less than twenty-four hours old. If he'd been devoted to Gaby as recently as yesterday, he wouldn't be casually talking about her being chopped up into little pieces today.

'Did you follow her when she left?' Gibbs asked him. 'In your car, or on foot? Or maybe you phoned her.'

'No, I let her go.'

'Really? Your live-in girlfriend walks out on the relationship after years and years, and you don't run after her?'

'I'd had lots of practice,' said Hamer. 'I've been letting Gaby walk out on me since we first got together. She was always going away. I was used to it.'

'For work, you mean?'

Hamer nodded. 'I don't know many blokes that'd put up with it, to be honest.'

Gibbs found this idea interesting, being a bloke who both would and wouldn't put up with it. From Debbie: no chance, but if he were married to Liv, or if they lived together . . . The way Gibbs felt at the moment, he'd willingly have accepted Liv being away six nights a week if he could spend one out of seven in the same bed as her. He wondered if he was only feeling this way because her wedding was coming up.

'Where were you when Gaby left the house?' he asked Hamer.

'I was in here. I told you, we'd had words. It was all over between us. I left her upstairs, came in here, shut the door, watched the footie. When I heard the front door close, I knew what it meant and I thought, "Good riddance".'

'You didn't go out into the hall and look to see where she was going, then?'

'No. I stayed in here.'

Gibbs eyed the silky dragons on the bag that dangled from the doorknob. Shame they couldn't corroborate.

'So you didn't see if she had a suitcase with her?'

'No, but she's taken a lot of her clothes. I had a look when I went up to bed last night.'

'You didn't see if she did or didn't drive off in her car?'

'I didn't care.'

Gibbs was becoming increasingly convinced that Hamer cared about Gaby a lot, albeit in a sullen and counter-productive way. The way lots of men cared about women. Including him? No, he hadn't been sullen with Liv for a long time. He spared her that side of himself, took it home to Debbie instead. It wasn't fair, he knew that, but it was simpler for him to keep the light and dark separate; a relief, in an odd sort of way, to be two completely different people sharing a body instead of what he'd been for so long before he met Liv: a dickhead on permanent autopilot who never considered how he felt and wouldn't have been able to work it out even if he had thought about it.

Liv had saved him. His biggest fear was that her marriage would change things between them, throw him back to where he'd been before.

'Did you hear Gaby's car at all?' he asked Hamer. 'Or any cars?'

'Nope. I turned the volume up and concentrated on the footie. Tried to, anyway. Your lot made that a bit difficult.'

'According to PC Joseph and PC Chase, you were the one who made things difficult for them,' said Gibbs. 'They said you refused to answer their questions and wouldn't let them in without a warrant. Both described your behaviour and attitude as suspicious.'

Hamer shook his head as if he couldn't believe it. 'Look, I just wanted rid of them as soon as possible, so I kept them on the doorstep.'

'That's the part they found suspicious, given that they were trying to find your missing girlfriend.'

'Ex,' Hamer said.

'Know what PC Joseph said to me? I shouldn't tell you, but I will. He said you were acting like you had a dead body propped up behind the door and couldn't wait to get rid of him so that you could bury it in the garden.'

Hamer smiled. Then he chuckled. 'That's funny,' he said.

'We'll be applying for the warrant as soon as Gaby's been missing twenty-four hours.'

'Search the house now if you like,' said Hamer. 'And the garden. Be my guest. I didn't have a dead body propped anywhere. I just didn't want to miss any more of the football. That's why I sent your copper mates packing. I've wasted enough of my life on Gaby – I didn't want to waste any more. I'd have told them that, but . . . well, it sounds a bit harsh, doesn't it? If you don't know the context.'

Gibbs would have enjoyed updating Hamer's definition of the word 'harsh', but that would have been unprofessional. He hoped that, wherever Gaby Struthers was and whatever had happened to her, she was at least able to appreciate not being here any more.

He stood up. 'I'll start upstairs, then,' he told Hamer.

～

'We all knew Tim's ID: @mildcitizen,' Kerry Jose told Sam. 'It's the title of one of his favourite poems, by a poet called Glyn Maxwell. His password's "dowerhousetim". We all knew that too. Actually, we suggested it, when he was having trouble thinking of anything.'

'Who suggested it?' Charlie asked.

Kerry's face reddened. 'I can't remember,' she said. 'We were all here, together. In this room. Tim was sitting here, where I'm sitting now, with his laptop on his knees.'

Lauren Cookson – skinny, pale as a hologram and wrapped in a fluffy brown dressing gown – nodded along to Kerry's words as if urging them on.

'Here?' Charlie made no attempt to hide her sarcasm. 'Clustered round the fire, glasses of wine in hand, all discussing what Tim should call himself on a social media site, and what his password should be?'

'Yes,' Kerry half whispered.

'Was Jason here too?'

'Yes.'

Again, Lauren nodded vigorously in support of Kerry's answer.

'How sociable that all of you were involved,' Charlie said in a flat voice. 'How inclusive. Definitely not just *one* of you who knew Tim's details, then.'

'So, any of you could have tweeted three times from his account last night,' said Sam. 'We know he didn't; we have a prison librarian's witness statement telling us that. So which one of you did it?'

'None of us.' Kerry's voice shook. 'We were here all evening, together. From when Jason brought Lauren back from the airport at four thirty until we went to bed. At eleven.'

'Safety in numbers,' Charlie muttered. 'Okay, let's try this: Kerry, you've proved you've learned all your lines – well done. You've had your turn as spokesperson. Lauren, why don't you take over for a bit? Where's Jason this morning?'

Sam was trying not to think about Agatha Christie's *Murder on the Orient Express*, in which all the suspects had committed the murder together. It was hard. The Dower House was exactly the sort of house that might turn up in an ITV Poirot adaptation, and, though Kerry and Dan Jose called the room they were sitting in 'the lounge', Sam couldn't think of it as anything but a drawing room, with its ornately carved stone fireplace, shutters, deep wooden window seats and decoratively plastered ceiling. It was immaculately tidy, in startling contrast to the kitchen, which was the messiest room Sam had ever seen. It was rare to encounter the two extremes in the same house.

Charlie had walked over to the window, and stood facing the greenery beyond and the drizzle-greyed air. Was she also thinking about *Murder on the Orient Express*?

Tim Breary, Kerry Jose, Dan Jose, Lauren Cookson, Jason Cookson. Perhaps they weren't jointly responsible for Francine's murder, or for the attack on Gaby last night. In which case, why did they tell each new lie as a perfectly coordinated group? They also stared and turned away in unison, Sam had noticed. When he looked at them – at any of them – they all lowered their eyes, but whenever he averted his, he could feel three pairs boring into him. Two of them, Kerry's and Lauren's, had been red and swollen when Sam and Charlie had arrived this morning, and, though Dan Jose didn't look as if he'd been crying, he seemed even more embedded in despair than the women. He'd hardly spoken, but Sam had noticed a stunned heaviness to his words and movements that suggested he couldn't quite believe where he'd ended up and couldn't see a way to get himself out. Like Lauren, he was wearing pyjamas and a dressing gown; Kerry was the only one of the three who'd managed to get dressed, though Sam had given them an hour and a half's notice.

'Lauren?' Charlie prompted.

Lauren burst into tears and buried her face in the brown collar of her dressing gown. 'Why can't you lot fucking leave us alone?' she said through its material.

'Jason's working on a friend's house renovations today,' said Kerry. 'He'll be out all day.'

'Doesn't matter,' said Charlie. 'You can just tell us what he would have said if he'd been here. Or is there a script somewhere, with his lines highlighted?'

'No, there isn't,' Kerry answered as if it had been a serious question.

'Any questions you'd like to ask us?' Sam said, looking at Dan.

'I thought you were here to ask us stuff, not the other way round!' Lauren snapped. Sam was swiftly coming to the conclusion that she wasn't as helpless as he'd assumed when he'd first seen her.

'I'm just wondering why none of you's asked what was in the tweets sent from Tim's Twitter account last night,' he said. 'Unless you already know?'

Dan gripped the thin upholstered arms of his chair. Kerry recovered quickest. 'I would have asked, but I didn't think you'd be willing to tell us,' she said.

Sam produced a folded piece of paper from his pocket, spread it open on his lap. 'Tim's only tweeted six times, and three of them weren't him. Numbers one to three were from May last year. The first two were a quote from a poem that wouldn't fit into one tweet. No mention of the title or who wrote it: "I have portrayed temptation as amusing. / Now he can either waver or abstain. / His is a superior kind of losing / And mine is an inferior brand of gain." The third one's also a quote. No title this time, but the poet's C. H. Sisson: "The best thing to say is nothing / And that I do not say / But I will say it, when I lie / In silence all the day."'

'Tim loved that poem,' Kerry said. She and Dan looked at one another, exchanged a silent message that Sam couldn't interpret. He caught the emotional charge, though: pain.

'Tweets four to six are from last night,' he said. 'They're a bit less poetic. "Call police urgent women being attacked outside her house horse fair lane spilling dont no number please dont ignore" – that's the first one. Then "URGENT women Gaby Struthers being attacked in drive back of house he will rape kill her if someone doesnt call police". And the last one: "help Gaby Struthers ring police NOW I cant do anything freekin out THIS NOT A WIND UP!!!"'

'Any of you know anything about those last three tweets?' Charlie asked.

Lauren and Kerry shook their heads. Dan stared down at his lap.

'Dan?' Sam asked.

'No. Nothing.' He couldn't have sounded more defeated.

'Is that true?' Sam asked. 'Because we don't know where Gaby is. Anything you can tell us might help us find her.'

'You don't know where she *is*?' Lauren erupted, flying up out of her chair like a wild animal. 'What the fuck's that supposed to mean?' She stood in front of Sam, shaking with rage, as if it was his fault – as if he'd deliberately mislaid Gaby Struthers out of spite.

'Lauren, calm down,' Kerry warned.

'She means "Be quiet", Lauren,' said Charlie. 'She's worried you're going to say something by mistake that isn't a lie.'

'Why aren't you out looking for her?' Lauren sobbed. 'Why are you pissing about here when you should be out finding Gaby?' She turned to Kerry. 'What if she's done something stupid? She wouldn't, would she? Gaby's the last person to do anything stupid, someone as clever as her?'

Kerry closed her eyes.

'We're doing everything we can to find her,' Sam said.

'No, you're not! You're sitting in a fucking chair, doing fuck all!'

'We're not the only two police officers in the Culver Valley,' said Charlie.

'I never said you were, did I?'

'Other detectives are looking for Gaby,' Sam explained. 'The hotels nearest to HMP Combingham are the first port of call. If we have no luck there, we'll contact her family, friends—'

'*You* could you be doing that now,' Lauren said accusingly. 'Instead of sitting on your arse in a big posh house!'

'Sam isn't here to improve his social standing,' Charlie told her.

'I've already spoken to some of Gaby's closest colleagues this morning, including the one who rang in about the tweets, Xavier Salvat.' Sam had been suspicious of Salvat's explanation at first – that he'd found the tweets while searching for Gaby's name on Twitter for no particular reason. He'd claimed he did it often, out of curiosity, to see if there was any mention of Gaby, Rawndesley Technological Generics, the work they were doing. Sam had found the randomness of this rather implausible, but he knew Charlie disagreed. Her sister, she'd told him, was always searching Twitter for mentions of her own name and the names of people she knew, to 'keep up with the gossip', apparently.

Lauren had appeared right in front of Sam's face. She jabbed her finger at him. 'Stop *talking* and start *doing*,' she snarled at him. 'If Gaby's done something stupid . . .'

'Just hold on a second, Lauren,' said Charlie. 'However convenient it might be to blame us, what about your own role in this? If Gaby's in danger – any kind of danger, from herself or anyone else – do you really think you're helping her by lying to us? I know you *want* to help her, and I understand that you're scared—'

'I'm not!'

'You are. You're terrified of the truth, whatever it is.' Charlie started to walk towards her. 'That's why you went all the way to Germany to talk to Gaby, isn't it? You wanted to tell her what was happening to Tim – you wanted to tell her he was innocent, so she could do something about it – and you knew the only way you could bring yourself to go through with it was in another country, thousands of miles from home. A different world, nothing to do with the rest of your life. Even then, you couldn't do it, could you? You ran away.'

Lauren was biting her nails, staring down at the polished wooden floorboards.

'If you care so much about Gaby—'

'I do!'

'Then why did you only get upset when you heard she was missing?' Charlie asked. 'Why didn't you get upset when Sam read you three tweets about her being attacked, maybe raped and killed? Do you want me to tell you why you didn't?'

'I want you to fuck off!' Lauren yelled in her face.

Sam jumped. He wished he could emulate Charlie's composure in the face of aggression.

'You didn't get upset by the tweets because you already knew about the attack on Gaby, didn't you?' Charlie turned to Kerry and Dan. 'You all knew – that's why the red eyes this morning. But you thought Gaby was all right after the attack: alive, in one piece, not too badly harmed. How do I know that? Because when you heard she was missing, Lauren, you asked Kerry if she might have done something stupid. Even though you knew from the tweets that there was a good chance Gaby had been attacked outside her house, you knew her attacker wasn't responsible for her going missing, didn't you? Maybe you were there, watching – one or all of you. Maybe one of you was the attacker. Maybe all of you were.'

'How can you think that?' Kerry's voice shook. 'That's . . . disgusting. I love Gaby. I'd never hurt her.'

'So was it Jason who hurt her, then: the one you're covering for by pretending he was here when she was attacked? By the way, before we leave we're going to need the name and address of the friend whose house he's helping to renovate today. Will that be a problem?'

'I don't know the name!' Lauren stared at Charlie, wide-eyed. 'Jason doesn't tell me stuff like that. He just said a friend, a house. That's all I know.'

Convenient, thought Sam.

Kerry started to weep. Dan looked away.

'Was the attack to warn Gaby off investigating Tim's possible innocence?' Charlie asked, looking around the room. 'In which case, you wouldn't have needed to hurt her that badly, or Jason wouldn't have. Scaring her might have been enough. Was that what you all agreed, since you love Gaby so much? Just a little attack, nothing too serious? And then someone broke ranks, someone watching the attack thought it was getting out of hand, didn't know where it might end. That someone panicked. Was it you, Lauren? Couldn't say anything, couldn't risk running or screaming in case Jason turned on you, so you used your phone to tweet for help, while he was busy attacking Gaby?'

Lauren was shaking her head.

'Detectives are working on tracing the three tweets,' said Sam. 'We'll find out which of your phones or computers they came from within a day or two, so you might as well tell us now.'

Lauren let out a loud wail. 'Are you fucking stupid?' she yelled at him, nearly stopping his heart. 'I don't give a fuck what you do with my phone, you can stick it up your scabby arse for all I care! Just find Gaby!' She rummaged in her dressing gown pocket, pulled something out of it. Sam saw a flash of silver.

'Put that down!' shouted Charlie.

'It's okay.' Sam could see now: it wasn't a knife, it was only Lauren's phone. She threw it into his lap and ran from the room.

17

Saturday 12 March 2011

The woman in front of me in the queue has dandruff on the shoulders of her black jacket. She is more upset than I am. *Like Lauren at the airport.* The name Lauren in my head makes it harder for me to stay here where I need to be, though logically I know it's not possible for me to attract another attack simply by thinking about her.

I can be rational, still. I'll prove it by staying put. If I run away, my thoughts will come with me. If I run from a man who's not here, how will I know I'm not running towards him? He could be anywhere.

Like Lauren at the airport, the woman in front of me is shouting. I can't see the face of the man she's yelling at, only part of his body in its police uniform behind the glass barrier. I picture Bodo Neudorf's face; he is safely far away from this tirade, in Germany. 'Tell you what, don't bother having my driving licence sent back to me this time. Keep it! Save me the trouble of having to bring it in every five minutes!'

I fix my eyes on a large grey sticker on the wall and try not to listen. The palms of my hands are damp and itchy. The sticker has curved corners and says, 'An induction loop system is available on these premises'.

'Would I have been pulled over if I'd been consulting a map?' the woman demands to know. 'I don't have a SatNav – I would do, except I've got no time to buy one or even think about buying one. I *do* have a knackered, torn road atlas, but for the past year it's been in the boot, covered in mud from my sons' football boots! I use my phone while I'm driving *only* to read the

The Carrier

directions I've emailed to myself. I wouldn't get done for looking at a map, would I, so I shouldn't be fined for looking at directions on my phone!'

She is the victim of an imaginary injustice, envious of phantoms: those who cruise along the M25 leafing through their untorn mud-free road atlases, cheered on by the police.

You're supposed to look at the road and your mirrors and nothing else.

I don't tell the angry woman this because I'm scared of her – also of the man she's haranguing and the two women sitting behind me in the waiting area. I'm frightened of them all. I've been monitoring my feelings carefully since yesterday and the one blocking out all the others is fear. Of everything: my surroundings, myself, noise, silence, any person I see or hear or pass on the street. Predictably, I'm scared of the man who terrorised me, because I can't see him and so don't know where he is, how close he is, but I seem to be equally scared of everybody who isn't him, which I wouldn't have expected. Alone and locked in my car, I'm afraid I won't be able to unlock the doors and get out if I need to; outside, I fear that something horrible is about to happen, something even worse.

I thought my panic would start to die away once the attack was over. When that didn't happen, I assumed I'd misjudged how long it would take. That could still be true, I suppose. It's less than twenty-four hours later, too early to decide that I will feel as I do now.

That's what I dread most: that I will be stuck like this, in a silent scream of horror. He untied my wrists before he walked away – slowly, complacently, not even bothering to run – but he didn't release my mind. That's the part I really needed him to free; I can still feel his plastic wrapped tight around it.

Should I give myself more time? Do I have a choice?

I refuse to sacrifice the rest of my life to this. If I thought I could get away with it, I'd refuse to sacrifice the rest of the day. There are important decisions and negotiations looming at work:

we have to refine our value proposition, convince Sagentia that the significant mark-up has to be on the disposables, which must be kept as simple as possible. I have to take care of all that and appear normal, make sure no one can see what's going on underneath.

I have to get Tim out of prison.

The woman in front of me turns away from the reception desk in disgust. Our eyes meet. 'Sorry for the hold-up,' she says. 'I should be embarrassed, but I'm too angry. '"I was at the end of my tether," said mother of two" – that'll be the headline if I end up strangling this guy.'

She's only talking. She won't do anything to you here, in front of witnesses. 'Don't worry,' I tell her, closing my hand around my St Christopher in my jacket pocket. It's all I can think of to say.

'My relationship with the UK traffic police isn't a happy one,' the woman explains. When she isn't yelling, she has a nice voice. What would I have thought of her if I'd met her before? What if I tell myself there's no reason to be scared of her and I turn out to be wrong? She was yelling at someone who didn't deserve it. If I blame what happened yesterday every time I feel fear, how will I be able to differentiate between harmful and harmless? If I can't make that basic distinction, how will I manage in the world?

More than anything, I would like to know if my reaction is normal. I don't think it can be. I wonder if it's happened to anyone else. I've heard of post-traumatic stress, but never of the terror not subsiding at all, even long after whatever caused it has finished.

'Gaby?'

It's Charlie Zailer. Next to me. Where did she come from?

I order myself not to turn and run. When I met Charlie yesterday, before I was attacked, I wasn't scared of her. I remember not being scared of her. I approved of her; she wanted to find out the truth and so did I. She listened to me.

'Gaby, are you okay? You don't look as if you are.'

'Yes, I do. I look fine.' I've washed every inch of myself and put on clean clothes. I'm able to speak and say what I mean. I'm not falling apart, not drawing attention to myself by shouting in public like the woman in front of me. I am looking better than okay, given the circumstances. 'Can I talk to you as soon as you're free?' I say.

'I can be free now.'

Lucky you.

'Gaby, do you know there are teams of police out looking for you?'

'No. Why? I'm here.'

Charlie Zailer smiles. 'You do seem to be,' she says. 'What have you got in your pocket?'

'You're not taking it.' I no longer have a home. I need it wherever I go.

'I'm only asking what it is. I'm sure it's fine. What is it?'

Inside my pocket, I unclench my fist. 'It's a St Christopher medal on a chain.'

'Can I see? I won't take it away. I just want to look at it.'

I show it to her.

'It's beautiful,' she says. 'Shall we go somewhere private where we can talk properly?'

'No.' What does she mean, 'somewhere private'? Why?

'You'd rather talk here?' She looks over at the chairs in the waiting area. The man on reception is telling the shouter to go and sit there.

'No,' I say. 'Not here.'

'We have a very nice private consultation room,' says Charlie. 'We can leave the door open if you'd like.'

The idea of an open door bothers me. And a closed one. I say nothing.

'Gaby? I'm happy to do whatever you'd like to do. Where shall we talk?'

Somewhere I've been before. A place I know I'm not scared of.

I'll be okay away from the police station if I have Charlie with me.

'The Proscenium.'

'What's that?' she asks.

'No, it's too far.' I'm not thinking straight. 'It's a private subscription library in Rawndesley. Where I met Tim. It's got the best collection of poetry books anywhere in the country. All first editions, some signed by the author.'

'I'll drive us to Rawndesley if that's where you want to go to talk.'

'They do lunches for members. Tim's a member. So am I. I could take you in as a guest, but I'm not hungry.' I am taking too long to make up my mind. If yesterday hadn't happened, I would know what I wanted to do by now.

I look at the doors I walked in through ten minutes ago. I'm not brave enough to walk out onto the street again, not yet.

'Let's stay here,' I say to Charlie Zailer. 'The private consultation room sounds all right. With the door closed.'

'Good idea,' she says. 'Shall we go via the tea and coffee machine? I wouldn't recommend the coffee but there's a decent range of teas – might help to keep you awake. You still haven't slept, have you?'

'I don't feel tired,' I tell her. *Sleep*. How will that ever happen again? I'll have to see my GP, get some strong pills to knock me out. Without sleep, I'll be no help to Tim. I only just had the energy this morning to cancel the three meetings I'd scheduled for today because the working week no longer adequately accommodates everything I need to do. As lies go, mine were hardly inspired: 'I'm ill. Can we rearrange? I'll be in touch as soon as I'm better.' I knew no one would doubt me. I wouldn't cancel a meeting unless I was half dead.

I follow Charlie Zailer along a brick-walled corridor, the brick broken up by thin floor-to-ceiling opaque glass windows on one side. She keeps slowing down so that I can catch her up, but I don't want to be level with her. I want to be able to see her and for her not to see me, especially knowing that soon I'll be facing her across a table and there will be no escape. Trying to keep my facial expressions and breathing under control has been the hardest part of today. One man I passed on the way from the car park to the police station stopped me and asked if I was all right. I hadn't said anything to him or looked at him; all I'd done was walk past him.

At the drinks machine, I choose Earl Grey tea because it's what I normally prefer, even though for once I would rather have ordinary. Isn't that what you're supposed to drink to help you through an ordeal: plain builders' tea? Is an ordeal any excuse for allowing myself to become a cliché?

The private consultation room is small and warm with two pictures on the walls, framed but not behind glass. They must be oils. You don't need to put oils behind glass, only police receptionists. One of the paintings is of a small building at the entrance to a park – a lodge house, with red leaves on its roof. It looks familiar; Blantyre Park, maybe. The other is of a man playing a piano. No, tuning a piano. Same artist. I walk over to look at the signature: Aidan Seed.

At the centre of the room are two blue-fabric armchairs, each one next to a small wooden coffee table, two tall pot plants and a view from the only window of a line-up of ventilation units embedded in a damp wall. The sight of them makes me feel immediately claustrophobic. I want to go somewhere else now that I've seen this, but I'm too embarrassed to ask. There's a blind, though – a plain white roller. I walk over to the window and lower it. It'll be better if I can't see the grilles of the ventilation units. I'll be able to imagine the view from a different bit of the police station. At the back of the building there must be rooms that overlook the river and the red bridge. I'll picture that instead.

In the far corner, there's a plastic-topped metal table with four metal-legged chairs. I would like it if Charlie Zailer would sit over there with her back to me and write down what I say, but she'll want to discuss everything with me and look at me, and probably ask questions, even though there's no need. All I need is for her to listen. I've been rehearsing my speech all the way here.

'The furniture in here changes from day to day,' she says. 'Shall we sit in the comfy chairs?'

I sit down. The worst thing I can do is leave it to her to steer things. I have to run this show; I took the lead by coming in, and I can't lose it. 'Did you get the truth out of Kerry and Dan?' I ask her. 'You know they're lying, right?'

She looks surprised. After a few seconds, she says, 'Gaby, if it's okay, I'd rather talk about you first. A lot of my colleagues have been very worried about you.'

'Me?' I'm fine, or I will be soon. Tim's the one in prison. 'No. I don't want to talk about me first. I want you to answer my questions.'

'All right. Yes, we all think Kerry and Dan haven't been straight with us. But I think and hope that we're getting closer to where we need to be. You seem to care about the truth as much as we do, which is . . . great. We don't often meet people like you. Most people either only care about keeping them and theirs out of trouble, or they don't care at all.'

'I only care about keeping Tim out of trouble,' I tell her. 'I know he didn't kill Francine, but if he had, I'd lie and say he hadn't. I'm not a good person.'

Charlie seems to find this acceptable. 'Who is?' she asks.

'Tim. Good and stupid. He's covering for Jason Cookson for some reason. I don't know why specifically but I can give you a wider explanation: Tim believes his own suffering matters less than anyone and everyone else's. Look at his marriage to Francine if you want proof that he's capable of long-term self-sacrifice.'

'You're saying Jason Cookson killed Francine Breary?'

'Yes.'

Charlie nods. I was expecting a barrage of questions. Instead, she's waiting for me to go on in my own time.

'You heard me tell Kerry yesterday about meeting Lauren

Cookson at Dusseldorf airport.' This part is easy; I've been going over it in my mind for most of the night, the exact words I'll use. 'So you know that's how I found out about Tim being charged with Francine's murder – from Lauren. "An innocent man" she called him. I couldn't persuade her to tell me any more. She was terrified: ran away, missed her flight home. That was how much she didn't want to talk to me about it. From her many references to her husband Jason – other stuff she said, nothing to do with murder – I decided he had to be the one she was scared of. Yesterday morning when I got back from Germany, I came here and told DC Gibbs that Jason Cookson must have killed Francine. Why else would Lauren keep quiet if she knew Tim was innocent?'

'Gaby . . .'

'No, wait. I don't know for sure that Jason bullies Lauren, but when I left here yesterday and went to the Dower House, guess who I met driving out of the gates? The bully himself. He was rude and threatening, warned me to leave Lauren alone and forget what she'd told me. He might as well have had "Thug" tattooed on his forehead, to add to his collection. He knew who I was before I told him. Lauren must have phoned him from Germany in a panic. She'd compromised security, hadn't she? She was probably scared I'd turn up at the Dower House asking questions, and wanted to warn Jason in advance.'

Charlie's expression hasn't changed since I started talking.

'Don't you get it?' I ask her. Am I not making sense apart from in my own head?

'Get what?'

'Why would Jason threaten me and warn me to keep away if it wasn't him that killed Francine?'

'Let's assume he did, then,' Charlie says. 'How does that fit with Kerry and Dan lying? Are they protecting him too?'

'Him or themselves. I'm not sure which. You need to find out if Jason's got some kind of hold over them. Lauren's his bullied wife, but I can't think of any reason why the rest of them would rather Tim went down for Francine's murder than Jason, unless they're scared he'll physically attack them. Which they might well be. Jason has henchmen: people to do the dirty work he'd rather not do himself.'

'How do you know that, Gaby?'

I've rehearsed this bit too: tell without telling. The bare minimum, then move on. 'One of them paid me a visit at home last night. To warn me. Same warning as Jason's: keep away from Lauren. Not surprising, since it was Jason who sent it.'

'How do you know Jason sent this man to your house?' Charlie asks.

'I can't prove it. That's your job. So is protecting vulnerable women. If I've been warned by Jason, and then again on Jason's orders, what do you think's happening to Lauren, who dragged me into it? Worse than warnings, for sure. You need to get her out of that house.'

That last part had an effect. *Good.*

'I take your point, Gaby, but I saw Lauren this morning. Sam Kombothekra and I spoke to her.'

'Did she seem terrified?'

'Everyone seemed . . . unsettled,' says Charlie. 'Not only Lauren. If she's part of a conspiracy to obstruct, as we're both saying we think she is, that'd be enough to explain her nerves, wouldn't it? And if it's more than that, if she's scared of her husband—'

'It is. You need to get her away from him!'

'I can't, Gaby. We don't have the power to separate women from their husbands against their will. What I *can* do is go to the house again, have another chat with her . . .'

'If Jason's anywhere in the vicinity, she won't tell you a thing. Even if he isn't, she probably won't.' I close my eyes. 'You don't get it, do you?'

'Actually, I do,' says Charlie. I hear defensiveness in her voice. 'I'm trying to explain that my powers are limited, but I'll do what I can. In the meantime, I'm more concerned about you.'

'Don't be. I can look after myself. Lauren can't.'

'This . . . warning, from Jason's henchman – what happened? You say he came to your house? Did he warn you verbally?'

I nod.

'Was that all he did?'

'Why do you ask?'

'You seem very distressed. And we were alerted to a possible attack. Someone posted an urgent appeal for help on Twitter.'

On Twitter. Where things can be retweeted dozens, hundreds of times.

So it's out there, in the world. People know. I dig my fingernails into my palms as the horror in my mind pulls the plastic covering off its head and swings round to face me. I couldn't see while it was happening; now it's everywhere I look.

'Whoever it was, they used Tim Breary's Twitter ID and urged anyone reading to contact the police. They said you were being attacked in your driveway. Behind your house.'

Someone wanted to help me. I can't dwell on that; it would involve seeing myself from the outside, as they saw me. Self-pity won't achieve anything.

Smoke. I smelled smoke.

'Gaby? What is it?'

'The tweets saying . . . were they . . . How badly written were they?'

'What do you mean?' Charlie asks.

'Grammar, spelling, punctuation.'

'Lots of spelling mistakes. Grammar and punctuation pretty much non-existent.'

'Lauren,' I say. 'She smokes. She was there. Watching.' My vision warps. I am looking at the room through a layer of oil, a wobbly film that coats my eyes. I can see things on its surface: lines, dark blots swimming diagonally downwards. 'Someone was smoking. I assumed it was the man who attacked me, but he didn't smell of smoke. I smelled his breath: no smoke. It was Lauren smoking. Whoever he was, he brought her with him. She'll have wanted to stop him but been too scared and too weak. He needs her to stay scared. Look, please, can you check she's all right? Now?'

'She was all right two hours ago, but I'll have someone check again,' Charlie says, pulling her mobile phone out of her pocket. She jabs at it with her thumb, swearing under her breath when she hits the wrong letter. 'Did this man attack you physically?' she asks me, her eyes on the message she's composing.

'Is this off the record?'

Charlie looks up. 'I'm sorry, but I don't think it can be. Anything you tell me that I think might be relevant to the Francine Breary case, I'll have to pass on.'

'In that case, let's move on.'

'Gaby, I understand that you might feel frightened or ashamed . . .'

'It's not that,' I tell her. 'I want to talk to Tim first. Until I know what's going on in his mind, why he's saying he killed Francine . . .' I know what I mean, but it's hard to put into words on no sleep. 'I'm not prepared to add any extra pressure to the situation until I understand all the permutations of what I'm adding to. Does that make sense?'

Charlie nods slowly.

'How soon can I see Tim? Today?'

'That's unlikely. Tomorrow, maybe, if the prison's favourite detective DC Waterhouse waves his magic wand.'

'Then make him wave it.' *Tomorrow.* The thought dissolves all others. Sitting opposite Tim, seeing him smile . . . What if he doesn't smile? What will be the first thing he says to me? What will he secretly be thinking?

I've never liked surprises. Tim is surprising enough for me in ordinary circumstances, everyday surroundings. Though when we were together it was never ordinary.

He'll try not to let you help him. As always.

'I want to go into that prison knowing as much as I can,' I tell Charlie. 'The more you can find out and tell me before I go, the better. I know you don't have to tell me anything, but . . .'

'Gaby, I can't—' she starts to say.

I cut her off. 'Have you searched Kerry and Dan's house? You need to search Tim's room. I don't know what you'll find, but there's something. There must be. Dan was on his guard the whole time we were in there yesterday, keen to usher me out as soon as possible. I don't think it was just that he didn't want me to notice the books.'

'Books?'

'True crime books, biographies of murderers, terrorists, dictators – Tim would never buy or read anything like that. Someone's put them there to make it look more like a killer's bedroom.'

'Maybe Tim himself,' Charlie suggests.

'I don't think so. He might want to pretend to be a murderer, but he wouldn't use props. He's cleverer than that.' I lose patience with the sound of my own voice. Charlie and I could waste hours speculating when there are people who know for sure.

I root in my bag, pull out the creased envelope and pass it to Charlie. 'Please could you give this to Lauren? Make sure Jason's not around when you do. It's a letter I wrote her in Germany, after she'd run away.'

'Do you mind if I read it first?' Charlie asks.

Can it do any harm if the police know Tim's and my history, such as it is? It can't be an invasion of my privacy if I'm the one handing her the envelope. She wouldn't know anything about the letter if I hadn't told her.

Still, I can't bring myself to give her permission. 'You'll read it anyway, whatever I say. Just don't read it in front of me. And when you've read it, don't ask me about it.' I don't know how to warn her about its contents, or if I need to. Wouldn't that be like warning a burglar that the sharp corners of your TV might damage his jacket? 'It's more of a love story than a letter,' I say in the end. 'I just thought . . . if it doesn't make Lauren want to tell the truth, nothing will, and something has to.'

'Gaby, I need to ask you a question. You might find it distressing but I have to ask. Have you been sexually assaulted?'

'No.' It's not a lie. He didn't touch me, not in that way. Only my wrists and neck, and leaning against me, crushing me against my car. I realise I have no idea whether the removal of clothes counts as a sexual assault, and I can't ask without revealing more than I'm willing to at this stage.

'Are you sure?'

'Yes.'

'Have you sustained any physical injuries? Do you need me to take you to a hospital?'

'No.' Two men have physically attacked me in the last twenty-four hours – Sean and the monster – and I have no marks to show for it. I choose to take this as proof of my resilience.

Charlie sighs. 'All right. If you ever decide you want to say more about what happened, you can. Whenever you're ready.'

'Thanks.' If I do, it'll be a strategic decision. I wish she'd stop talking to me as if I'm a volatile bundle of emotions.

'You need sleep,' she says. 'Is it true you've left your partner, Sean?'

I nod. *Partner.* That's a joke; Sean was never that.

'So we need to sort you out with somewhere to stay. Do you have a friend you can go to?'

'I have plenty of friends that I don't need to stay with. I've booked myself a room at the Best Western in Combingham. You need to sort yourself out with another visit to the Dower House,' I tell her. In case she has forgotten the to-do list I gave her or thinks it doesn't matter, I decide to go through the action points again as I would at the end of a meeting. In my work, I'm known for being either very or too thorough, depending on your point of view. Some CEOs won't work with me because of it. My companies consistently out-perform theirs. 'Go back to the Dower House,' I say to Charlie. 'Give Lauren my letter. Get her out of there and away from Jason – that's a priority. Whatever it takes, do it. And tell Kerry . . .' I hesitate. Am I certain? I could wait and ask Tim. Or talk to Kerry first. If she admits it, Tim won't be able to deny it.

Great idea: go back to two people who have lied to you and give them the opportunity to lie again.

'Tell Kerry I know that Tim has a history of taking credit for things he had nothing to do with.'

'Meaning?'

'I know who The Carrier is – tell her that. It wasn't Tim. It was her.'

POLICE EXHIBIT 1442B/SK – TRANSCRIPT OF HANDWRITTEN
LETTER FROM GABY STRUTHERS TO LAUREN COOKSON,
UNDATED, WRITTEN FRIDAY 11 MARCH 2011

Dear Lauren,

Well, I can't find you, and I can't think where else to look. And I
can't sleep because I'm too shaken by what I've found out, so I
thought I'd write to you. I hope you'll calm down and get yourself
to the airport in time for our flight in the morning. If not, I'll track
you down at home. Shouldn't be too hard.

Lauren, I don't know you at all, but I do know that you seemed
interested when I was telling you about my feelings for Tim. Really
interested. And you seem to care that he's been charged with a
crime he didn't commit. I think you're a good person (I'm sorry if I
didn't make that clear in the brief period we spent together) and
I hope that you'll care even more if I tell you what Tim means and
has meant to me. I need to make him matter to you as much as
he does to me, so that you'll do the right thing and tell the truth.

You've known Tim more recently than I have, and you might well
know him better than I ever did, but do you like him? Tim's not
always uncomplicatedly likeable. He's not uncomplicatedly
anything. I sometimes think he's the human equivalent of a
question with no answer, and that's why I'm so drawn to him. I've
never met anyone more unresolved than Tim, or more contradictory.
He makes me want to formulate theories, prove certain things
about his character are true. I've never felt that way about anyone

else. I should point out that this reaction is not unique to me. People want to solve Tim, cure him, define him, but no one ever can. Everybody tells themselves they will be the one to do it. If you know Tim well, Lauren, you'll hopefully understand what I mean. You'll know that every bit of time you spend with him makes you less certain of who he is, and more certain of who you are. He has a rare talent, but I couldn't begin to describe what it is. As someone who can easily solve most analytical and practical problems, I have always found this annoying and irresistible.

Are you still reading, or have you given up? I should try not to make this too complicated.

I first met Tim in a library in Rawndesley called the Proscenium. It's not an ordinary library. It's also a private club that you can join, and anyone who isn't a member or a guest of a member can't go in at all, unless it's to make an enquiry about joining. Among other things, the library has a large collection of very old, rare poetry books, mainly first editions, as well as lots of modern poetry – that's its specialism. There's also a restaurant where members and guests can have lunch, a drawing room where people can talk, though only quietly, and a reading room where if you talk AT ALL the librarian will descend on you in a fury and threaten to turf you out, member or not.

Remember I told you I had my own company and sold it for millions? Well, when I was first thinking of starting up that company, I needed to find money to fund it. A lot of money. I'd done some research, and I had my eye on Sir Milton Oetzmann as a possible key investor. You've probably heard his name on the local news, but in case you haven't: he's a philanthropist (that means someone whose hobby is to give away huge amounts of money to worthy causes) and I knew he was a member of the Proscenium. I met him in person shortly after I joined the library. I was upfront with him about what I hoped he might be able to do for me, and he was keen. He saw there was a good chance he'd end up making a shedload of money.

When Tim first approached me, I hadn't seen him before at the Proscenium. I must have been blind, because he told me later that he'd seen me several times. But I didn't notice him at all until he plonked himself down in a chair that had been vacated ten minutes earlier by Sir Milton after one of our long chats. I was packing away my paperwork, looked up and saw a face that shocked me (warning: this is going to sound very weird and corny) by being the face I'd been craving a glimpse of all my life, even though I hadn't known that until I saw Tim. I didn't even fancy him, not at first sight or for quite a while afterwards. It was more a feeling of 'That's him', accompanied by this craving for proximity that had nothing to do with sexual attraction, initially. It was far stranger than just fancying someone, nothing like the way I fancied Sean when I first met him. (Sean's my partner, remember?)

Does that make any sense at all? I couldn't look away, and Tim didn't seem to be able to either. We both understood that there didn't need to be a reason why he'd come over and sat down next to me. The reason couldn't have been more starkly obvious. After a few seconds, embarrassment set in. We realised that, as strangers, we would have to go through the motions of pretending we didn't know what we knew, so Tim introduced himself and said he hoped I didn't mind his accosting me, but he feared I was about to make a serious mistake. He was an accountant, he told me, specialising in tax planning, and one of his clients had had extensive dealings with Sir Milton that had made him want nothing more to do with him, even if that meant losing a substantial chunk of his funding stream.

I'm sure you're not interested in the finer details, Lauren, but in a nutshell: Tim said, yes, Sir Milton might be keen to invest in my company, but he'd also want to micro-manage everything (be involved in every aspect of my business rather than just letting me get on with it), and I'd end up wishing I'd never gone to him. I was on the point of asking Tim if he was perhaps a bit biased because of his client's negative experience when he said, 'I'll get you the money you need.' It was so outrageous, it made me laugh. I needed serious money from a venture capitalist (a person or firm worth several hundred million whose sole purpose and function is to fund start-up companies), and here was a local accountant offering to drum up a bit of cash for me. I asked Tim what he had in mind. Was he going to organise a raffle? Sell tickets to a karaoke night at his local pub?

I stopped laughing when he told me he dealt with the tax affairs of the Lammonby Foundation, and that Peter Lammonby tended to follow his advice to the letter. I'd thought about approaching Lammonby instead of Sir Milton, and only hadn't for a ridiculous reason: Lammonby's daughter had just made a fortune (one she didn't deserve, in my not at all humble opinion) from some new-age you-can-reinvent-your-life-type book. Not that that was her father's fault, but still. Milton Oetzmann had no connection with any personal growth nonsense as far as I knew, so I decided to focus on him.

'I think I know nearly as much about your business as Sir Milton does by now,' Tim told me presumptuously. 'I've listened in on at least two of your conversations with him. I'm confident I could get Peter Lammonby on board, and he really would be hands-off – he's your dream investor. My friend Dan might be interested too.' 'Your friend Dan?' I said scathingly. 'What, you think he'd want to bung in twenty quid or so?' 'Maybe three hundred thousand quid or so,' Tim corrected me. 'Gaby,' he said, sending a shiver of recognition through my body by saying my name, as if I'd heard him say it thousands of times before, 'I know nothing about scientific innovations, but if what I've heard you tell Milton Oetzmann is true, I can't see how your company can fail.' I told him any company can fail, but he waved it aside. 'Give me a month to get you the funds you need to make a start. If I let you down, go back to Sir Milton and write me off as a deluded idiot.'

I agreed on the spot. I'd have agreed to anything he suggested on the spot, I think. Tim was thrilled. We couldn't stop talking, asking each other hundreds of questions, wanting to know everything about one another. Anyone listening might conceivably have thought nothing more was going on than two Proscenium members enthusiastically getting to know each other.

We arranged to meet again. We had a lot to talk about, so we had to meet often – oh, what a shame! (That's me being sarcastic.) We didn't only talk about my work and the need to fund it. We talked about poetry. Tim was obsessed with poetry, and I soon was too, though I'd never given it a second thought before I met him. We had lunch whenever we could. We never mentioned how we felt about each other – that was taken as read, we didn't need to discuss it, and it would have been awkward if we had. Tim had told me early on that he was married and that his wife would have been beside herself with fury if she'd known he was meeting another woman for cosy lunches. He also said that knowing this wasn't enough to stop him, that he preferred my company to hers and there had been nothing in his marriage vows to say he couldn't eat with or talk to another woman.

I got the message: he wasn't ready to do anything that was against the rules. He didn't want to have an affair. Or, rather, he did, but he wasn't going to. At that point, I thought I could live with it if things never went any further. Just being with him and knowing how we felt about each other was enough for me at first. Just looking at his face, hearing his voice, reading his text messages and emails, made me feel as if something was grabbing hold of my body from the inside and shaking it. As if I'd swallowed an earthquake.

If you were here now, Lauren, I suspect you'd ask at this point how Sean fitted into all this. I can't imagine you'd ever be a self-serving two-timing hypocrite in the way that I was. Sean and I were already living together, and, yes, I was betraying him, emotionally if not physically. What's more, I was loving it – loving the idea that I was treating him badly. I had no moral problem with it whatsoever. When I tried to tell myself that I ought to feel guilty, I thought about how Sean complained whenever I had to spend a night away from home because of work and how he expected me to sit and watch him watch football whenever I wasn't away, and I thought, 'Sorry, but I'm putting my own needs first, and you won't be able to complain about it because you won't know.' My relationship with Sean is not ideal, Lauren, as I told you before. I've always known it wasn't ideal, but it took a weird night in a shitty hotel with you to make me realise quite how hopeless it is.

As promised, Tim got both Peter Lammonby and his friend Dan (Jose, of course) on board to the tune of nearly three million pounds, initially, with a guarantee of more from Lammonby if things went according to plan. Tim thought it would be a good idea to spread the opportunity around a bit, to which end he came up with a genius idea that made me fall even more deeply in love with him, if I'm honest. He told me he was sure several of his high net worth clients would be interested, but many would be nervous about something so risky. My company hadn't actually done anything yet, so people would literally have been chucking their money at a hope and a prayer. Tim asked me if I'd be willing to spend fifty thousand pounds of the company's money (which would have meant borrowing it from the bank at that point) in order to finance what he at first obliquely referred to as 'a show of confidence'.

I asked him what he meant. Tim outlined a plan that was as neat and perfect as a Shakespeare sonnet: I would spend fifty thousand pounds on his professional services and the services of a Geneva-based firm called Dombeck Zurbrugg. I don't want to bog you down in details, Lauren, so I'll explain this as simply as I can. Dombeck Zurbrugg is a company that helps UK high net worths (HNWs basically means very rich people) avoid tax by setting up trusts and parent companies that allow them to have their businesses based in Switzerland, for official purposes. They provide company director and company secretary services and a fiendishly complicated layered structure that makes it look as if it's a Swiss company when it isn't, apart from on paper. This enables the UK HNWs to pay much less tax. It's not foolproof, and the UK tax authorities could certainly unravel it if they were willing to devote huge amounts of time to doing so, but many, many people have got away with it and saved millions.

I told Tim straight out that I wasn't prepared to do it. Not because I'm a fan of paying lots of tax (I'm the opposite: I think there should be a fixed, low rate of tax, the same for everyone) but because I didn't want to have to be looking over my shoulder the whole time, wondering if the Inland Revenue was going to come after me. Tim nodded when I said this, as if he'd anticipated it. 'No one's going to come after you because you're not going to do it. You're not going to actually put any money into the vehicle DZ will set up for you. It'd be tricky anyway, unless you were prepared to relocate to Switzerland – you wouldn't be, would you?' I asked him flirtatiously if he would relocate with me, then wondered what I'd said that was so wrong. Tim looked as if I'd punched him in the stomach. For an awful second, I panicked in case I'd misread the dynamic between us: maybe his interest in me was solely professional, maybe he stared deep into the eyes of all the technological entrepreneurs he met.

'Gaby, I need to be honest with you about something,' he said. 'I don't think I have it in me to do . . . anything like that. Leave my wife or even . . . well, anything. I hope that isn't going to ruin our friendship.' A fortnight earlier, I might have nodded and said, 'Fine,' but I'd been falling more irreversibly in love with him every day, and his declaration of unavailability sounded so horribly final. He was telling me that, on a fundamental level, I had to give up on him. The disappointment was crushing. It was nearly a minute before I could get any words out. 'Moral scruples or fear?' I asked him. 'The latter,' he said, then qualified it. 'No, both. I fear that if

I do something that's generally agreed to be wrong . . .' He left the sentence unfinished. I was furious, though I tried not to show it. What was he so scared of? Couldn't he ignore the general agreement and think for himself? How could he think that us being together could be wrong on any level?

I said none of these things. His ethical qualms made me feel ruthless. Actually, I've always kind of known I'm ruthless, Lauren, but, truth be told, I've always quite liked that about myself. I thought I was ruthless in a refreshing, healthy way, but suddenly Tim had made me feel like a callous husband-thief.

None of this made me love him any less, unfortunately for me. If a sexually frustrated friendship was all that was on offer, I was too much in love with him to turn it down. Keeping my tone light, I asked, 'Does the ninety midnights rule still apply?' Tim told me it did. (If you don't want to pay UK tax, you can't spend more than ninety midnights in the UK.) 'So we could spend two hundred and seventy-five midnights in Switzerland together, and then for ninety midnights every year we'd come back to the UK, you'd live with Francine and I'd live with Sean. Who, frankly, gets more of my midnights than he deserves at the moment.' I often made barbed comments about Sean to Tim. He mentioned Francine as infrequently as possible. I thought it was an attempt to be gentlemanly at first, until I realised he couldn't bear to say her name.

Tim was keen to turn the conversation back to business planning. He told me it didn't matter that I wasn't prepared to become a tax exile and move to Switzerland. I only needed to be willing to waste fifty thousand pounds. He and Dombeck Zurbrugg would then do the work and set up a labyrinthine scheme that I would never use. The important thing was that Tim would be able to tell his clients that I was so confident of making a fortune, I was willing to spend a fortune on tax planning. 'A lot of companies in Switzerland and the Isle of Man offer similar services, but DZ are the best and the most expensive,' he said. 'If I tell my high net worths you're spending fifty grand with DZ at this stage, believe me, they'll be queuing up to invest. They'll think, this woman knows she's going to make hundreds of millions.'

He turned out to be right. My wasting fifty grand on the Swiss set-up that I never used brought in all the investors I needed, and all of them were Tim's clients apart from Dan Jose, who was Tim's best friend. But that's jumping ahead. That night, after Tim told me he would never leave Francine, I told Sean I wasn't feeling well and was going to sleep in the spare room. I stayed up all night, weeping – with frustration as much as sadness, to be honest. How could Tim accept so readily that what he wanted wasn't possible? I'm the sort of person who believes that anything and everything is possible. Anyone who doesn't believe that makes me angry.

By morning, my optimism had returned and I'd decided that it was up to me to show Tim that there was a brave man inside him, waiting to be let out. I drew up the romantic equivalent of a business plan and made a concerted effort to make him love me more – so much that he would soon be thinking, 'Who's Francine, anyway?', as willing to discard her as if she were a used paper napkin. (Are you disapproving of this, Lauren? If you are, then perhaps you've not yet met a man you love as much as I love Tim. I needed him. For me, Tim was the difference between feeling a hundred per cent alive and feeling one per cent alive. It's easy to abide by a principle when you aren't in the grip of a blazing need that won't be denied.)

My campaign worked. One day, in the Proscenium's restaurant while we were having lunch, Tim reached for my hand under the table. It was the first time we'd touched, apart from brushing against each other by-accident-on-purpose. Other people were there who might have seen. Tim knew he was being indiscreet, but was willing to take the risk. I thought to myself, 'No matter what happens from now on, even if my heart ends up in pieces, this makes it all worth it, this moment.'

From then on we held hands regularly, under as many of the Proscenium's tables as we could: in the restaurant, the reading room, the drawing room. People must have noticed, but everyone pretended not to. One day, Tim asked me if I'd be willing to have dinner with him. I was over the moon, then puzzled when he told me that Dan Jose and his wife Kerry would be there too. 'They're eager to meet the genius who's going to make them rich,' he said. I was confused. The way he'd started the conversation – 'Will you have dinner with me, Gaby?' – had sounded like a different proposition. 'So this is a business dinner?' I asked. 'Nope,' Tim said cheerfully. 'Dan and Kerry are my closest friends. It's about time they met you. If they don't know you, and know you and me together, then they don't know me, and I think they ought to, since they're my elective family. Is that okay with you?' I told him it was more than okay. Only a matter of time until Francine's history, I thought.

Tim and I never had dinner alone, but the dinners with Kerry and Dan (our chaperones, as Tim called them) became a regular thing. So did kissing. I was blissfully happy for a few months, thinking things were going my way. Then I started to get angry. Tim's love for me was plain to see, but he hadn't said he loved me, not once. I hadn't said it either, and at a certain point I decided I wouldn't, not unless he said it first.

We went to Switzerland together to meet the Dombeck Zurbrugg people. Same hotel, separate rooms. It killed me, Lauren: the sheer, outrageous waste of it. Tim mumbled something about it not being easy for him. That was on our first night there. I hoped he might see sense in time for us to spend the second and last night of the trip together. It didn't happen. On the way to the airport for the flight home, I lightheartedly mentioned the ninety midnights plan again, and Tim turned to me in the back of our taxi and said, 'Gaby, what we've got now . . . I really don't think I'll ever be able to offer you any more. Francine would know if anything happened. She'd sense it, I'm sure she would. I just . . . it's a line I can't cross. Do you understand what I'm saying?' I understood. No sex, ever: that was what he was telling me. He asked if it was okay with me, if I could handle it. Every cell of my body was wailing, 'No!' and 'You fucking hypocrite! "Francine would know if anything happened"? But so much *is* happening, all the time – we stand on the street kissing passionately, our bodies locked together, and Francine doesn't know anything about it! At least if we had sex we'd be likely to do it more discreetly, in a room with the curtains shut!' I didn't say any of that to Tim, Lauren. Instead, I said, 'Yes, of course.' I said it because a) if you want to tempt a man to leave or cheat on his wife, turning into a wailing harpy isn't the best approach, and b) I finally woke up and realised I might have to accept Tim's limits. If he could never leave Francine or be properly unfaithful to her, I faced a stark choice: either lose him altogether or live with the best he could do.

It wasn't a choice, Lauren. I couldn't lose him. I resigned myself to a tortured existence. And then, to my astonishment, less than two weeks later, something momentous happened. On Valentine's Day. Sean didn't get me anything, not even a card. He and I had never bothered with Valentine's Day. I'm so not a Valentine's kind of person that I didn't think to send Tim a card either, but a card for me arrived at my work that morning. There was a poem in it by a poet called e. e. cummings, a passionately romantic poem. You'll find it on the internet if you Google 'i carry your heart with me, i carry it in my heart'. The card contained the words 'I love you' and was signed 'The Carrier'. It could only be from Tim, I thought. Tim was the carrier of my heart, and he knew it.

I left work immediately and went to his work, where I'd never been before. We always met at The Proscenium. I walked into his office, sat on his desk and said, 'I love you too, Tim. I'm sorry I didn't send you a card, but yours has made not only my day but my entire life.' He looked terrified. Instantly, I felt stupid and crass and insensitive. I realised that Tim had signed his card 'The Carrier' for a reason. To write the words 'I love you' and sign the card in his own name would have been too much for him, given his fear of Francine. He'd have been paranoid that any such card with his signature at the bottom might fall into her hands. He needed to hide behind the safety of a pseudonym. Feeling clumsy and painfully exposed, I started to apologise, but Tim interrupted me and said, 'Do you really love me, Gaby?' He looked so wary, it made me laugh. I told him I adored him and had from the second I'd met him. I told him I felt as if there was a magnet in my gut, pulling me towards him, every moment of every day. He said, 'That's it. That's how I feel about you too. We need to try and work something out, don't we?' I didn't dare say a word, couldn't believe he meant what I thought he meant. But he did. I think hearing me say I loved him made a difference.

The next time we had lunch together, Tim told me about his recurring nightmare. Did he think that was the first step towards us 'working something out'? I don't know. I also don't know what would have happened if he hadn't mustered the courage to tell me about the dream. Maybe we'd still be having lunch together at the Proscenium twice a week, and dinner with Kerry and Dan once a month. Maybe we'd still be kissing passionately in doorways and car parks. Or perhaps I'd have grown tired of the hypocrisy and demanded to know how Tim was able to tell himself that he wasn't being unfaithful to Francine when any fool could see that he was. If he'd got drunk every Friday night and screwed a different nameless woman he picked up in a nightclub, that would have been less of a betrayal of his marriage than what he was doing with me. How could he not see that? Even now, years later, the irrationality of it makes me want to howl with rage.

Tim had (has?) a recurring nightmare in which Francine tries to kill him. Or is about to try to kill him: he always wakes up before it happens. In the dream, he's trapped in a small room with her, the hotel room they stayed in when they went on holiday to Leukerbad in Switzerland. She proposed to him on that trip, and he's convinced that she also tried to kill him, because ever since they got back he's been woken regularly by this nightmare. Francine is crossing the room diagonally, walking towards him. Tim's cowering in a corner, shaking, unable to keep still. He can't actually see Francine, only her shadow against the white wall, moving closer. Her arm looks funny, thin as string and with a kink in it, as if it's been broken and healed badly. She's carrying a handbag. In the bag is something she's going to use to murder Tim; he doesn't know what. He always wakes up before she reaches him.

After he'd told me about the dream, I understood a bit better why he was so scared of Francine. If he honestly believed she'd made an attempt on his life and might do so again, then, yes, I could see why he wouldn't risk leaving her. What I didn't understand was how it was possible for her to have tried to kill him and him not remember. I know people occasionally talk about trauma and memory loss, but I just didn't buy it. If your partner tries to kill you, generally you know about it consciously. You don't rely on hints in dreams.

I went to Switzerland, Lauren. A bit like you following me to Dusseldorf, I followed Tim's nightmare. I didn't think it would do me or him any good necessarily, but I was in love with him and obsessed with trying to help him. I thought the hotel staff might remember something. Maybe if I asked the right questions, one of them would say, 'Oh, yes, Tim Breary – he stayed here with his girlfriend and she plunged a screwdriver into his carotid artery in the middle of the night.' I booked myself into the hotel they'd stayed in: Les Sources des Alpes in Leukerbad. Same room. I had to bribe the hotel staff to trawl through old files to find out which room had been theirs.

Would you believe me if I told you I solved the mystery, Lauren? Well, I did. There were no clues in the room or in the hotel, but one day I went for a walk and I saw the answer. I saw that nothing was what Tim thought it was, and I realised his nightmare wasn't a memory. It was a metaphor (something that represents something else). Which meant that, in all probability, Francine hadn't tried to kill him, which explained why he had no conscious memory of her doing so.

Thrilled and proud of my discovery, I couldn't wait to tell Tim. Now my biggest regret is that I didn't keep my mouth shut. As soon as he heard that I'd been to Leukerbad, his behaviour towards me changed completely. I should have spotted it instantly and started to backtrack, but I was too full of myself and my great discovery. I told him I thought I knew what his dream meant, at least in part, and he completely freaked out. He wouldn't let me tell him, said I should leave him alone, get away from him and stay away, or he might say something he'd regret, which of course was worse than if he'd actually said whatever it was that was in his mind. I imagined the worst possible thing: 'I don't love you and I never have. This was all a terrible mistake. I'll hate you until the day I die.'

You'll have noticed I haven't told you what I found out in Leukerbad, about Tim's dream. Since he refused to be told, and felt so strongly that I had no business knowing, it would hardly be fair for me to tell anyone else.

So, there you have it: my relationship with Tim and how it ended. Since then, my life's been monochrome. Diminished. I didn't realise quite how much until I met you and suddenly my past was dragged into my present.

I'll be honest with you, Lauren: I'm devastated to think of Tim in prison for a murder he didn't commit. But at the same time, I'm excited, because it's an opportunity for me. For me and him, for us. Years have passed, Francine is dead, and Tim needs my help. I have hope burning inside me again. It's agony, but I prefer it to the numb detached feeling I had before when I thought all I had to look forward to was a life spent watching Sean watch football.

In order to help Tim and save both our lives (yes, that really is how it feels) I first need your help, Lauren. I don't know who killed Francine. You do, I think. Please, please, tell me what's going on. Or tell the police. Please be brave. Do the right thing. Don't let Tim pay the price for someone else's wrongdoing. I know you're too good a person to let that happen. I know you'll read this and decide that the man I've described in this letter – the Tim I know, with all his mysteries and flaws, all his fears and hypocrisies, all the love he feels that he can't express – deserves better than to be framed for a crime he didn't commit.

Yours sincerely,

Gaby x (07711 687825)

18

12/3/2011

'You've never seen *West Side Story*?' Liv squealed at Simon across the arm of the waiter who was scraping breadcrumbs off the white paper tablecloth with something that looked like the blade of an ice-skate. 'I can't decide if that's touchingly quaint or just culturally impoverished. Chris *loves* it. You *have* to see it.'

'He's not interested,' said Gibbs.

'"One Hand, One Heart",' Simon practised saying the song's title, tried to imagine himself reading out the lyrics to more than a hundred wedding guests.

'It's the song Tony and Maria sing when they're imagining getting married,' Charlie told him. 'They know it can't happen for real, so they stage an imaginary wedding in her bedroom and sing their tragic duet. It's a bit much to make Simon read both parts,' she told Liv. 'Is there a reason why I haven't been asked to sing Maria's part, or am I being paranoid?'

'You're tone deaf, and I'm not *singing* anything,' said Simon self-consciously. Theirs was the only occupied table, and the room was small enough for the waiters to overhear them.

In her message this morning, Liv had described the restaurant as casual and intimate – two words that, for Simon, didn't belong together at all, though he could see that they might if you were the sort of person who slept with other women's husbands. 'Like dining in your own home, almost!' Liv's text had promised. Simon strongly disagreed. His home wasn't a cellar, didn't have a low dome-shaped ceiling of roughly spiked white plaster, and didn't contain men in suits who asked him if everything was all right every twenty seconds.

'We don't want it sung, we want it tastefully read aloud,' said Liv. 'By your delightful husband.' She beamed at Simon.

'"We"?' said Charlie. 'You mean you and Dom?'

'No. Me and Chris. Chris and I.' Liv reached for Gibbs' hand. Charlie kicked Simon under the table. He kicked back, knowing she'd misinterpret it. Her kick, at a rough guess, had meant, 'Look at them squeezing hands in public as if they're a proper couple'. His meant, 'Stop staring, for fuck's sake.'

He wondered about Gibbs' elastic-band ball. It hadn't made an appearance so far this evening. Was it at home with Debbie?

A waiter moved towards them, holding aloft the widest tray Simon had ever seen. More food he had no appetite for. What had Charlie ordered for his main course? He couldn't remember. He hadn't enjoyed the starter she'd chosen for him: slices of mozzarella with very thin, dark, strong-tasting ham, all covered in yellow-green oil and flecks of something.

'Dom's happy for me to sort out the finer points of the cere-mony,' said Liv. 'He's up to his eyes in work as usual. I've chosen all the other readings with him in mind, and I've chosen this one for me and Chris. *We've* chosen it.'

'But you're not even going to be there,' Charlie said to Gibbs.

'Aren't I?'

The waiter set down their plates in front of them. Simon was relieved to see a steak on his. He'd have liked chips with it. Instead, he had what looked like a varnished clump of potatoes in a small cylindrical ornament.

'You and Debbie are coming to Liv's wedding?' Charlie's voice radiated disbelief. She kicked Simon's leg again.

'Kick Gibbs,' he told her. 'He's the one you're talking to.'

'Not Debbie,' said Gibbs. 'Just me.'

'I know what you're thinking, Char,' Liv said. 'Obviously it's not going to be easy for Chris, but at the same time, how can he not be there? That'd be worse, for both of us. It'd be like . . . look, this is a bit of a horrid analogy, I know, but if I were in hospital, dying, I'd want Chris there.'

'A *bit* of a horrible analogy? Liv, it's a double helping of horrible with a side dish of grim as fuck.'

'You can say no,' Gibbs told Simon.

'It isn't grim, any more than "One Hand, One Heart" is tragic,' Liv said indignantly. 'How can a death-defying love song be tragic? We don't all choose to look at the world through Charlie-Zailer-tinted glasses.'

'You said you wouldn't lose it, whatever happened,' Gibbs reminded her.

Simon wondered what they'd expected to happen.

'I haven't lost anything,' said Liv. 'I've *found* a useful metaphor: glasses with lenses that enable the wearer to see only . . . dead bodies and misery!'

'Not everyone's willing to blind themselves in order to be happy,' Charlie said.

'This isn't getting us anywhere,' said Gibbs. 'Look, Charlie, nobody here's blind. We all know the score. We see things differently, that's all.'

'I can't see me reading this.' Simon handed the printed lyrics back to Liv. 'Sorry. I'm willing to read something else, if it matters that much to you. Something that makes the same point, give or take.'

'Really?' Liv bounced up and down in her seat. 'Heaven on a stick! You'll really do it?'

'It can't just be anything,' said Gibbs. 'It has to mean something.'

Charlie laughed. 'Has my sister taught you nothing, Gibbs? You pretend it means whatever you need it to mean. The exact words might be "Call me Ishmael", but we can all tell ourselves that means, "This is secretly the wedding of Liv and Gibbs, even though it looks like the wedding of Liv and Dom."'

'"Call me Ishmael"?' Liv looked worried.

'Simon's only going to agree if he can read a passage from *Moby-Dick*.'

'I can speak for myself, Charlie.'

'I'm just trying to save us some time.'

'You can get someone else to read "One Hand, One Heart" - anyone,' Simon said. 'If you want me . . . Look, I've never read at a wedding before. I'd feel more comfortable reading something I'm used to.'

'Such as?' said Gibbs.

'"Rainbows do not visit the clear air; they only irradiate vapour,"' Simon quoted. '"And so, through all the thick mists of the dim doubts in my mind, divine intuitions now and then shoot, enkindling my fog with a heavenly ray. And for this I thank God; for all have doubts; many deny; but doubts or denials, few along with them, have intuitions. Doubts of all things earthly, and intuitions of some things heavenly; this combination makes neither believer nor infidel, but makes a man who regards them both with equal eye."'

'That's beautiful.' Liv sniffed and blinked. She looked at Gibbs. 'What do you think?'

He shrugged. 'Up to you.'

'Don't *say* that! I hate it when you say that, as if your opinion doesn't matter.'

'In no way does that passage make the same point as "One Hand, One Heart",' said Charlie, annoyed that they were considering it. Did it matter that much to them to have Simon read at their fake-wedding-within-a-real-wedding? 'What about me?' she heard herself say. 'Seriously: I'll read "One Hand, One Heart".'

'You will?' Liv cupped her hands over her nose and mouth and pressed the tips of her index fingers into the corners of her wet eyes. Simon looked away. Nothing made him feel more uncomfortable than people crying near him.

'You're not just pretending to make me happy, so that I'll be even sadder when I realise it's a big lie?' Liv asked through her hands.

Charlie sighed. 'Yes, that's what I'm doing, because I'm the dictionary definition of evil. Are you sure you want me on the guest list at all?'

'Not evil, just against me and Chris.'

'Once, maybe. Now the only thing I'm against is both of you staying with people you don't love any more.'

'I think we should have both,' said Gibbs.

'Evidently,' Charlie quipped. 'You've got Debbie and Liv, Liv's got you and Dom.'

'I meant both readings: "One Hand, One Heart" and *Moby-Dick*.'

'Yes!' Liv yelped. 'I actually love that quote from *Moby-Dick*: earthly doubts and heavenly intuitions. Perfect!'

A waiter was approaching. Simon looked down at his plate. None of them had eaten anything. 'Is everything all right? There is a problem with the food?'

'We're wonderful, thank you.' Liv's smile faded as he walked away. 'I've never tried to explain to you before, Char, but we do have our reasons. I didn't think you'd be interested.'

'They don't need to know our reasons,' Gibbs muttered.

'They don't *need* to, but I think they deserve to.'

A statement that could be taken in two ways, Simon thought. He wondered if Charlie was thinking the same thing, or if he was spotting things that weren't there to be spotted. Like whatever had been removed from Tim Breary's bedroom at the Dower House before Simon and Charlie had searched it late this afternoon. Simon had felt its absence. Had Dan Jose worked out on Friday that Gaby Struthers would have been suspicious of his eagerness to evict her from Breary's bedroom? Had he disposed of something incriminating as soon as she'd left? If it was that incriminating, wouldn't he have got rid of it on or shortly after 16 February, the day Francine was killed?

Simon had nearly said to Charlie on the way to the restaurant that this was the most puzzling and frustrating case he'd ever worked on, but he'd held back, knowing she'd have laughed and called him a drama queen. This was his boy-who-cried-wolf moment, Simon acknowledged to himself. He'd complained before to Charlie, countless times, about cases that were so unfathomable they made his brain hurt. He should have kept quiet, saved his hyperbole for Tim and Francine Breary, the couple that made no sense at any point in their story.

He hates her, so he stays. He leaves her, then, finally free, attempts suicide. He tells Dan and Kerry Jose he can't ever go back to the Culver Valley because Francine's there, then goes back to look after her when he hears she's had a stroke. He smothers her, admits it, and expects everyone to believe he had no reason for doing so.

Beside him, Liv was saying, 'Dom's happy at the moment, because he has no idea. In a way I do still love him, Char – in the way that I love you, or Mum, or Dad. Gibbs loves Debbie in the same way, probably.'

'I don't love your parents at all, or Charlie, so . . . yeah,' Gibbs agreed. 'In the same way.'

'What, not even in a close-friendy ex-skipper kind of way?' Charlie pretended to be hurt. 'Thanks a lot!'

'I'm not allowed to walk out on my kids.' Gibbs stared down at his sea bass fillet.

'Not allowed by who?' Simon asked.

'Olivia.'

'I just don't want to hurt anyone,' said Liv. 'This way, we fulfil our obligations to the people who depend on us, and pain is kept to a minimum.'

'Unless Debbie or Dom finds out,' Charlie said. 'In which case, there might be a bit of a max-out on the pain front, mightn't there?'

'Yes,' Liv said defiantly. 'But I can't make important life decisions based on fear and worst-case scenarios.'

I could give you lessons, thought Simon.

'No one ever finds out the complete truth, in a nice convenient package, Char. Not even you, Simon, with your luminescent brain. Even if someone walked in now and saw me and Chris together, that's all they'd see: one instance of us being together. Would it really devastate Debbie or Dom to hear we'd been together in a restaurant *once*? It's impossible for them to find out the emotional truth, or any more than whatever one thing they happen to witness, unless we tell them. Which we never will.'

'I recognise that!' Charlie announced triumphantly. 'The recycled wisdom of Colin Sellers. His influential treatise: How To Get Away With Screwing Around. Gibbs? Anything to declare?'

'Sellers is right,' said Gibbs. 'Unless you let someone film you in bed, you're not going to get caught in a way you can't talk your way out of. Most cheaters crack at the first challenge from a suspicious partner.'

'It's the feelings that hurt in these situations, not the catching in bed,' said Liv. 'And you can't prove feelings. No one can film another person's emotional landscape.'

Simon pushed away his plate and stood up. The beginning of an idea was gathering in the lower reaches of his mind, so provisional that it was trying not to be noticed. 'Every cheater's different, right?' he said. 'Some crack, some don't. Some hope for the best, some fear the worst.'

'I could stop cheating on Dom, quite easily,' Liv said. 'But then I'd feel as if I was cheating myself, and Chris, and . . . life's generosity towards me.'

'I sense we're leaving,' said Charlie, stuffing a forkful of lasagne into her mouth. 'Simon's not thinking about you any more, Liv. Sorry. Good line, though.'

A new waiter came over. 'Sir, is everything all right?'

'It's not random. They were chosen for a reason.'

'Sir?'

'What reason?'

'I'm not sure what you're asking me, sir,' said the waiter.

Simon wasn't asking him and wasn't interested in discussing. He needed to get out of the restaurant so that he could think. As he unlocked his car, he heard Charlie call out to Liv, something about practising her Puerto Rican accent. He had no idea what she was talking about.

~

'You're still here,' Sam said to Proust, who was sitting in his dark office with the door ajar. Sam hadn't seen him; he'd sensed the presence.

'I'm like a small boy with a gap in his teeth.' The Snowman's voice emerged from the shadows. 'Hoping to catch a glimpse of the tooth fairy bringing a shiny new pound coin.'

'Prepare to be disappointed,' said Sam. 'I've got nothing new and shiny for you. I've got the same Dower House liars I've had from the start, all still lying, sticking to the new story: Jason Cookson was outside cleaning the lounge windows when Francine Breary was killed, and they all somehow forgot to tell us originally. Oh, and they all got confused in exactly the same way, too – all mistakenly telling us he was *in* the lounge the first time we interviewed them. And they're all echoing what Kerry told Charlie yesterday, about Tim Breary picking up the pillow he used to smother Francine and holding it at chest level – suddenly, that detail's part of each of their stories and they all express it in exactly the same way: "chest level". Before you say separate them and twirl them, we've tried. No luck so far.'

'Luck?'

'Sir, we've talked and threatened and sweetened and done everything. If you think you could do better, go ahead and try.'

'Are those the only two options, then? You doing badly or me doing better? How about you doing better? Or Sergeant Zailer, since I notice she's involved herself: CID's very own Woman in Black, whose spirit we can't seem to lay to rest.' A strange noise emerged from the darkness: a sigh-groan hybrid. 'Switch on the light, Sergeant. Or shall we have a séance? If there's a chance your initiative might try to make contact . . .'

'My initiative's been at it all day and can't think of anything else.' That sounded too final. 'I'm sure I'll feel differently in the morning,' Sam qualified, turning on the light. The Snowman was pinch-rubbing his chin between his thumb and forefinger as if he'd invented a new obscene gesture.

'We shouldn't neglect the possibility that Tim Breary killed his wife, sir. He says he did, and Charlie could be right: it might be a double bluff. Breary knows suspicion's going to fall on him, so he pre-empts, confesses, gets his disciples on board. Between them, they make the whole thing feel so shaky that we assume there can't be any truth in their lies.'

'Disciples?'

'I'm fairly sure Breary's the mastermind of whatever's going on,' Sam said. 'For what it's worth, I still think he's our man. He had no money of his own, no income. Francine's death meant he could cash in her life insurance policy. No one else had a motive as far as I can see.'

'The Joses?' Proust suggested. 'Francine was a drain on their resources. Do you enjoy having friends to stay for the weekend, Sergeant?'

'I do, yes.'

'No, you don't. Think how pleased you are when they leave. Now imagine they've brought their vegetative former partners with them and intend to stay not for a weekend but for the rest of their lives.'

Sam would have bet his own life insurance policy that neither Dan nor Kerry Jose had smothered Francine Breary with a pillow. 'If Tim Breary didn't kill his wife, my second choice would be Jason Cookson,' he told the Snowman. 'He's got a history of violence. I had Sellers do a bit of digging around.'

'And?'

'Two dropped GBH charges – one from 1998, the other in 2008. Second victim lost an eye. Sellers is chasing the details of the first, but the second charge fell apart because the vic changed his tune at the last minute, pronounced himself unable to ID Cookson as the man who went for him with a knife in a care-home car park.'

'So Cookson got to him somehow,' said Proust.

'Cookson wasn't around today. He's working on a friend's house renovation, apparently. They all alibied him for last night, but I'm sure they're lying. I think he did it.' Sam held up his hands, seeing the disbelief on the Snowman's face. 'I know Gaby Struthers says the man that attacked her wasn't Jason Cookson. I think she could be lying too. For the same reason: fear. Cookson took a man's eye out, sir. Dan, Kerry and Lauren, they're all frightened—'

'Not necessarily of Cookson,' said Proust. 'Perhaps they're scared because they know they're lying to the police in a murder inquiry and will soon have to face the consequences. And if Gaby's so scared of Cookson after he attacked her, why report the attack at all?'

'I don't know.' Sam had wondered that himself. Jason Cookson seemed by far the most obvious contender; if not him, then who? Dan Jose? No, no way. 'Let's say Gaby's right and Cookson sent an associate of his to scare the living daylights out of her, because he doesn't want her getting any more information out of Lauren. Let's say we even find this thug – where does that get us? We still won't know what it is that the Dower House lot are hiding.' Sam sighed. 'I think we've got a problem we can't easily solve, sir.'

'Could that be because we're a major crimes investigation unit, not the Brownies?' Proust snapped. 'You're right: this isn't going to be fixed by DC Gibbs leaping over a toadstool, chanting, "We are the gnomes, we help in the homes". Not that Gibbs *does* help in any homes, his own least of all.' The Snowman chuckled. 'Ah, look, the thunderer returns,' he said as Sellers walked in. 'The weighty wanderer.'

'First GBH charge went the same way as the second, Sarge,' Sellers addressed Sam and ignored Proust. He was out of breath. He needed to lose a few pounds, that was for sure. 'Victim and two witnesses went from being a hundred per cent certain Jason Cookson was the assailant to having seen nothing at all. The first GBH wasn't just a drunken brawl, either. It was a bloke who made the mistake of chatting to Cookson's then girlfriend, Becky Grafham, in a Chinese takeaway. Ended up in hospital with multiple broken bones. When I heard that, I thought it might be worth asking about motive for the second.'

'And?' said Proust.

'Same. Cookson was married to Lauren by then. The man he

stabbed in the eye was the son of one of the . . . inmates at the care home where Lauren worked, if that's what you call them. Poor bloke made the mistake of exchanging a bit of harmless friendly banter with Lauren when he came in to visit his mother. One day Jason was there picking Lauren up from work and overheard it.'

'That's a mistake you often make, isn't it, Sellers?' said Proust. 'Exchanging harmless banter with other men's womenfolk, as a prelude to other exchanges. I suppose you'd weigh less if you lost an eye, on the plus side.'

'Sir, I've tried to contact this Becky Grafham—'

'Why?' Proust barked.

'Maybe I'm being daft, but I couldn't square the GBH temper stories about Cookson with what happened to Gaby Struthers yesterday. I know Charlie said she hadn't got anything like the full story out of Struthers, but she's seen her, spoken to her. There's no broken bones, no missing eyes or other body parts, no serious physical injuries. I suppose I just wondered if Jason Cookson's in the habit of attacking both men and women, or arranging for them to be attacked and if so, does he adapt the method depending on the sex of the victim?'

'And?' said Proust impatiently.

'I spoke to Becky Grafham's mum, who said it was Cookson who dumped Becky for another girl, which I don't suppose means anything necessarily, but she also mentioned that she'd told Becky at the start that Cookson would dump her. It was only a matter of time, she said, and she was right. Before he met and married Lauren, Jason Cookson had a reputation for not sticking around. He might stay a week, a year, two years, but he'd be off to pastures new in due course. He left every girlfriend he ever had.'

'Someone who stays in a relationship for two years can hardly be described as flighty,' said Proust. 'That's a significant time investment, two years.'

'Right.' Sellers looked pleased. 'That's what I thought too. So I wondered: how come a guy who has a series of normal, varied-length relationships ends up with a rep as a leaver?'

Proust held up his hands in an exaggerated gesture of bored and irritated confusion. His body language had always been fuller and more complex than that of anyone else Sam had ever known.

'What if it was because no one ever left him – ever?' Sellers persisted. 'What if not a single girlfriend left, because they felt as if they couldn't? Either they'd been told they weren't allowed, or they were too scared.'

Proust drummed the flats of his hands on his desk. 'I don't see where that gets us, even if it's true,' he said eventually.

'We'll only see where it gets us if we pursue it,' said Sam. 'Track down Cookson's exes,' he told Sellers. 'Let's see how many of them are still too scared of him to talk openly, even at a distance of several years.'

~

Simon pulled up outside the house and switched off the engine. He made no move to get out of the car. He was always slower to emerge than Charlie, as if driving had sent him into a trance from which he couldn't easily extricate himself. Sometimes she lost patience and went inside alone. Tonight she didn't move. 'Are you going to tell me?' she asked.

'No Harold Shipman, no Fred and Rosemary West. No Saddam Hussein or Osama Bin Laden.'

'True,' said Charlie. 'It's a big plus that none of those guys will be there.'

'What?'

'At Liv and Dom's wedding.'

'That wasn't what I meant.' Simon slid his seat further back to give himself more legroom.

'We'll have a better time without them than we would with. If only because they're nearly all dead.'

'What the fuck are you talking about?'

Charlie cheered silently and tried not to laugh. Why hadn't she thought to use this tactic before? She blamed excessive sobriety; tonight she'd had three large glasses of wine and felt inspired. Normally she was ineffectually straightforward when she didn't have a clue what Simon was mumbling about: telling him she didn't understand, asking him every five seconds to explain, until eventually he did – when it suited him and not one second sooner. This new technique was more fun: for every baffling statement he made, she would fire one back at him. Why should she be the only one unable to follow the thread of the conversation?

'Think about Tim Breary's room,' said Simon. 'The books by his bed.'

'The ones about murderers?'

'I need strong black tea,' Simon said suddenly.

'Traditionally, that would involve going into the house.'

'I can think better out here.'

'You're insane. Oh . . . bloody hell! Fine.' Charlie got out of the car and slammed the door. 'I can practically *feel* a massive rod growing very near my own back,' she muttered, pulling her keys out of her bag. The phone was ringing as she let herself in. She ignored it and headed for the kitchen, thinking it could only be Liv. It rang five more times while she made Simon's tea. Each time sounded more urgent somehow, though the ringing sound was exactly the same.

Charlie's curiosity got the better of her. 'What?'

'Charlie? It's Lizzie Proust.'

'Oh. Hi, Lizzie. Everything okay?' *Or has my husband trashed your entire family dynamic?*

'Yes, fine. I'm sorry to phone so late.'

'It's okay. It's not late.'

'Oh, good.' Lizzie sounded surprised. 'Charlie, this is a bit awkward. I assume you know about Amanda – Regan, as she is now. You know Simon had a word with Giles and . . . explained the situation to him?'

'I tried to stop him.'

'But you didn't succeed?'

'Well, obviously not.' If she'd succeeded, Lizzie wouldn't be ringing her at nine forty-five on a Saturday night. Nor would she know that her daughter had changed her name to Regan.

'It's just that . . . well, Ama— Regan and I are somewhat baffled.'

'Shall I ask Simon to ring you?' Charlie was keen to stay out of it. She didn't feel up to the task of unbaffling anybody; that was Simon's department.

'Giles hasn't said anything, you see. Nothing. He's behaving exactly as if nothing's changed. I only know about it because Simon rang Amanda earlier and . . . Sorry.' Lizzie laughed nervously. 'I'm not sure I'll ever get used to the new name but I've promised her I'll try, as long as Giles isn't around. Simon rang *Regan* earlier and told her what he'd done, and she rang me in a terrible flap. She was beside herself – talking about having to move abroad, coming out with all kinds of hysterical nonsense. She said Simon had told Giles everything, and how could she ever face him again, knowing he knew?'

'I hope Simon apologised to Regan for having landed her in the shit,' said Charlie. 'I told him to.'

'I said on no account must she run away – she should come home with me and we'd face him together. I thought the best thing would be if she denied it all, said it was a lie from start to finish, but she didn't think Giles would believe that, and since Regan's now her legal name . . .'

'Wait a second.' Charlie took a sip of Simon's tea. It confirmed her suspicion that no one who preferred tea without milk could be entirely sane. 'You want to get yourself and Regan out of trouble by portraying Simon as a liar when he's telling the truth? I know he's an annoying arse, but that doesn't seem very fair.'

'No.' Lizzie sighed. 'Of course it isn't. I'm not proud of any of this, but I'm afraid panic did rather set in. You know what Giles can be like. It wasn't just me and Amanda in a tizz. You should have seen my son-in-law, he was white as a sheet. Anyway, as I say, Amanda – *Regan* – didn't think Giles would believe her if she denied it outright—'

'Lizzie, for fuck's sake!' Charlie blurted out. 'This is all totally mental.'

'I know,' Lizzie said mournfully. 'I do know, Charlie, really. And I'm so sorry to involve you in it.'

'Forget *me*. Think about yourself, and Regan. Tell Proust the truth, let him see the situation as it really is: his daughter's got a problem with him. A big one.'

'I can't do that. Giles has always relied on his family. More than most people, perhaps. We're his rock.'

Why was it always a rock, Charlie wondered? Were rocks particularly helpful to ordinary people in urban and suburban settings? Why did no one say, 'He's my central heating' or 'He's my fitted carpet'?

'If Giles thought his loyal wife and his only daughter had anything but love and respect for him, he'd be devastated.'

'Do you love and respect him?' Charlie asked.

'Of course I do!'

'Why "of course"? Regan doesn't.'

'Oh, I can sort her out,' said Lizzie impatiently, as if it were as easy as doing the weekly shop. 'It's this therapist she's been seeing. These people are wicked, Charlie. Wicked. They help themselves to your hard-earned money and fill you so full of grudges and grievances that you're worse off than when you started, and not only financially. Honestly, they do more harm than good. Some of them implant false memories of abuse. I read an article—'

'Lizzie,' Charlie cut her off. 'I have to go. If you want to bury your head in the sand, that's up to you, but I think you should listen to Regan. She's right about Proust: he's a bully. Has been for as long as I've known him. I'm sure he has redeeming features, but . . . well, I've only ever seen the tiniest glimpse.'

'Why are you saying that?' Lizzie's voice shook. She'd dropped the world-weary organiser persona and sounded about eight years old. 'Giles is immensely fond of you, and Simon. He thinks the world of both of you. "Redeeming features" implies there's some terrible . . . *sin* or something that's been committed. If you'd said "sterling qualities", you'd have been closer to the mark! You're the one who should listen to Amanda – now, I mean. She's dreadfully embarrassed by her outpouring to Simon. She admits she went way over the top.'

'Because she's frightened,' said Charlie.

'Of what, exactly? Giles is devoted to her, and to her children. She knows that perfectly well.' Lizzie's tone was clamping down again: zero tolerance. *She's imitating Proust,* Charlie thought with a shudder. That had to be it: she alternated, in her mind, between her voice and his, her own thoughts and her master's. *Like a schizophrenic.* 'Giles has never laid a finger on Amanda, and he never would.'

'Fingers aren't the only thing to fear. Psychological cruelty can hurt more, and it's easier to get away with. No visible scars.' *Keep going, Zailer. If anyone can undo the brainwashing of a forty-year marriage in one telephone conversation, you can't. Don't let that put you off, though.* 'If Giles is so jam-packed with sterling qualities, why do you think Regan felt the need to create a new identity? And why are you willing to call her Regan? Aren't you buying into her disloyalty every time you do?'

'Probably,' said Lizzie defiantly. 'It's all a bloody stupid charade, Charlie. If you want to know how I really feel, I think Amanda's wallowing in negativity and blowing every tiny thing that's ever happened out of proportion – but, of course, I can't tell her that. I have to placate her and call her by her silly new name so that she'll smooth things over with Giles, or else I might end up not being able to see my grandchildren, which is, frankly, unthinkable. If Giles decides we can't see Amanda any more . . .'

'Tell him to fuck off. Go and see the grandchildren on your own.'

Was Lizzie blowing up a balloon on the other end of the line? Didn't people give her this sort of advice all the time: her female friends, acquaintances, neighbours?

'Charlie, you're not making this easy for me. I didn't ring to talk about my high-maintenance daughter.'

'Stop talking about her, then, before I start leafing through the *Yellow Pages* to see if there's such a thing as a Barnardo's for grown-ups.' Adoption for the over-18s: why had no one invented it? It was a brilliant idea: new parents for adults.

'Giles has said *nothing*.'

'What do you mean?'

'He's behaving as if nothing's happened, nothing's changed,' said Lizzie. 'Regan and I have been waiting for the explosion, but . . . nothing. It's as if he doesn't know, Charlie. Are you absolutely sure Simon told him?'

'I can't see why he'd lie about it.'

'Then why hasn't Giles brought it up?'

'Why don't you bring it up?' Charlie asked.

'I'm clinging to the hope that Simon didn't tell him.'

'Lizzie, if he told Regan he did, then he did. I know why Proust's not saying anything, and so would you, if you thought about it. Like all despots, he didn't get where he is today by giving away any power. Think about it: the minute he reacts, he's a bomb that's gone off. You're all busy dealing with the wreckage. No one's scared of what's already happened, are they? By not reacting, he can keep you suspended in a state of fear, waiting for what's coming. Wondering why it never arrives, too scared to ask. You're not even sure he *knows*. That's even better – he's depriving you of certainty as well as acknowledgement. He gets to keep all the power.'

'What kind of monster do you think my husband is, exactly?' Lizzie snapped.

Saddam Hussein, Harold Shipman, Osama Bin Laden. Giles Proust.

Charlie had it, suddenly: the answer to the question Simon hadn't got as far as asking. 'I've got to go, Lizzie.'

'Wait! I'm sorry I raised my voice. Look, I do take your point. You're probably right, in the main.'

Would this ever end?

'I need to ask you a favour, Charlie. That's why I rang. Could you . . . would you mind asking Simon if he could have another go, try to talk to Giles about it again? Maybe pop round one evening, so that they wouldn't have to have the conversation at work? I could arrange to be out, that's no problem. I just . . . I'd be able to deal with this so much better if I knew what Giles was—'

Thinking. Charlie didn't hear the last word; she'd pressed the 'end call' button and put the phone back on its base. It started to ring again. She unplugged it, went back to the kitchen, poured Simon's tea away and made him a new cup.

Lizzie would never have let her go.

Simon hadn't moved, and didn't look up when she got back into the car. There was no point telling him now about the most dysfunctional telephone conversation in human history; he had fallen into a deep, dark pocket of obsession and would be there for a while yet.

'Ask me,' Charlie said, handing him his drink.

'Hm?'

'The question in your head. No Harold Shipman, no Fred and Rose West . . . I think I might have the answer.'

'Why those murderers? The books in Tim Breary's room: why Pinochet, that old Nazi, the Lockerbie bomber, Myra Hindley? Why the mixture of political and non-political murder?'

'Coincidence? Random?'

'That's your answer?'

'It's *an* answer. Probably the one most people would come up with.'

'You're not most people. You're better than most people.'

'Then let me hasten to prove my worth,' Charlie said sarcastically. 'Hindley, the concentration camp guard, all the killers in Tim Breary's books – they're all distanced from their crimes in a significant way, either by time, or contrition, alleged contrition . . .'

'Which doesn't apply to the killers Tim Breary *wasn't* reading about.' Charlie heard the excitement in Simon's voice. 'Harold Shipman, the Wests, Saddam Hussein, Bin Laden. Shipman was still at it, wasn't he? Only stopped killing when he was caught. Fred West: the same. He and Rose would have carried on, probably, if the police hadn't stopped them.'

'Do we know enough about any of these people to be able to say that for sure?' asked Charlie.

'I think so,' said Simon. 'Bin Laden and Saddam Hussein were both still openly proud of their murderous achievements when they carked it, weren't they? They might have found time to fit in a few more murders if they'd lived.'

So you don't know for sure, then. Charlie was sensible enough to keep her mouth shut.

'Some murderers will always be murderers,' Simon said. 'It's how they are. Others you know won't do it again. Pinochet and that Nazi guy – didn't people say about both of them that there was no point making them stand trial now that they were old and infirm?'

'I've no idea,' said Charlie.

'They'd both been free for years, decades, and not clocked up any new victims,' Simon said. 'Same with the Lockerbie bomber. He's been sick and dying and claiming he's innocent for as long as I can remember. His killing days were over long ago, assuming he ever was a killer.'

'Myra Hindley,' Charlie put her doubts to the back of her mind and joined in. 'Contrite, BA Hons, claiming to be a whole new shiny person, that idiot Lord Whatsit lobbying to let her out.' She took Simon's tea from him and sipped it. He didn't seem to notice. 'So . . . what? Tim Breary wanted to kill Francine, but he didn't want to be saddled with the guilt and the blame forever? He wanted to know if it was possible to shake off the taint of evil, once you've done something terrible?'

'No, not the taint of evil, not in himself,' said Simon. 'This is about trying to detect the *presence* of evil. Or guilt.'

'In who?' Charlie could think of only one possible candidate. 'Francine?'

'Hold on. Let's be sure we're right about this. Hindley's different from the others in Tim Breary's collection. She never had the chance to prove she wouldn't reoffend if released.'

'But . . .'

'But she wouldn't have, would she? No one believed she'd have killed or tortured again.'

'No. It was the combination of her and Ian Brady that was lethal,' said Charlie. 'Without him, she'd never have done it. Wait, is that another thing they've got in common, the monsters in Breary's books? The Nazi – did he come out with the old excuse about having to obey orders?'

'What, you mean without Hitler he wouldn't have done it? Probably. Most Nazis who weren't ringleaders said afterwards that they were just following orders. Pinochet's defenders certainly claimed he'd never known about the murder and torture his minions had been involved in. The Lockerbie bomber – some people, including him, seem to think he isn't guilty.'

Simon turned to face Charlie. 'This is about the presence of guilt,' he said. 'Or the absence of it. Breary's collection of murderers – they're all people you might argue about: to what extent can they still be blamed? Were they ever evil? Are they still evil now, and just hiding it more successfully than people like Harold Shipman and the Wests?'

'So . . . before Francine had the stroke, she made Tim's and everyone else's life a misery,' said Charlie.

'But she couldn't have done it without his willing participation, to go back to your point about it taking two to tango.' Simon sounded excited again. 'He stayed with her, so how far could she be held individually responsible for whatever happened between them?'

'He was just obeying orders, if we believe Kerry Jose,' said Charlie. 'Orders he could and should have disobeyed.'

'After the stroke, Francine was harmless, powerless, almost

unrecognisable, but she was still Francine,' Simon said. 'Her mind was at least partly intact. Perhaps she was sorry and couldn't say so.'

'There's no reason to assume she was sorry, is there? Apart from for herself.'

'No,' said Simon. 'That's the point: Breary didn't know what to think, and he wanted to know. Needed to. The stroke put Francine at a distance from the person she used to be. Breary had no idea if it was still acceptable to have all the same feelings about her that he'd had before.'

'To want to kill her, you mean?'

'Maybe. Think about it: imagine he *had* wanted to kill her, before. In his position, could you have done it once she'd had the stroke, and been sure you were killing the same person? What if she didn't remember anything from when she and Breary lived together? What if the stroke had affected her mind as radically as it had her body, and she was desperately sorry, but couldn't say so?'

'And you think Breary was looking for answers in his books about monsters who might have stopped being monsters, or who might never have been monsters in the first place?'

'If I had to guess – and this *is* just a total guess . . .' Simon drummed his fingers on the steering wheel. 'He couldn't forgive Francine. He read those books to see if they could help him decide who was more guilty, him or her. Him for being unable to forgive her even in her weakened, altered state, or her for having been the person she was before the stroke – and maybe *still* was, until her death. Most people feel their feelings and leave it at that. Not Breary – he analyses them right down to their tiniest components. That sonnet he gave me for Gaby Struthers, it's all about love being a paradox. The poet's trying to work out what love is.'

'Isn't it freezing your arse off in a cold car?' said Charlie. 'That's what I heard.'

'Tim Breary's obsessed with love, and with guilt. He wants to understand them both better: his love for Gaby and his blaming of Francine. Big question is: which matters more to him, the love or the hate?'

'Explain?' said Charlie hopefully.

'When he left the Culver Valley and moved west, was it his love for Gaby that drove him away or his hatred of Francine?'

'Dunno. I couldn't have less of a clue if I tried.'

'He left them both: love and hate. Then when Francine had her stroke, he moved back to the Culver Valley. Was it his love for Gaby that brought him back, or his loathing of Francine?'

'That's . . . easier?' said Charlie doubtfully. 'Had to be the love, surely? Though Gaby says he didn't contact her at any point. But why come back and look after your invalid wife if you loathe her and you're not even together any more?'

'Because you can see how easy it would be to kill her,' said Simon, as if it were the most obvious thing in the world. 'Then, once she's dead and you're unencumbered, that's when you think about getting in touch with the woman you really love.'

'But Tim Breary *didn't* get in touch with Gaby even after Francine's death. And you don't think he killed Francine,' Charlie reminded him.

'I *didn't*,' Simon conceded. 'I don't know what I think any more, except that whatever the fuck's going on, it's stranger and more complicated than anything I've come across before.'

'Well, that's lucky,' said Charlie, swallowing a sigh. 'Stranger and more complicated is exactly what you need. Virtually everyone I meet comments on the disappointing lack of strangeness and complication in your professional life.'

'Do they? No, they don't.'

'No. They don't.'

'This case is all about feelings, Charlie.'

You'd better ask to be taken off it, then. She didn't say it; it would have been cruel. Wasn't every case about feelings? Did he mean romantic feelings, specifically? He seemed to have latched onto the idea of Gaby Struthers and Tim Breary as the hero and heroine of a doomed love story; so far, Charlie hadn't had the heart to point out that Breary might want Simon to think precisely that, or to tell him to stop staring at that sodding sonnet as if it was suddenly going to offer up an ingenious solution. She'd been woken at three this morning by Simon switching on his bedside lamp, and had opened her unwilling eyes to find him lying flat on his back and pillowless, holding the poem directly above his face as if to fend off non-existent rain.

Charlie hadn't been able to get back to sleep. She'd been hoping for an earlyish night tonight to compensate. Who am I to judge Lizzie Proust? she thought. Would Lizzie be able to understand Charlie not daring to say, 'I'm going inside now – I refuse to spend the whole night in the car,' in case it broke some kind of spell?

'I should be able to make sense of this case,' Simon said. 'I'm exactly like Breary. I put every emotion under the microscope.'

'Even your passionate love for me?' Charlie asked, having first put all the usual low expectations in place.

'No. Too big. Wouldn't fit under the lens.' Simon smiled at her.

'Excuse me? Could you say that again?'

He turned away. 'One day we'll never see each other again. Do you ever think about that?'

'No. What do you mean?'

'When one of us dies.'

'I never, ever think about that.'

'I do. All the time. I try not to let it ruin everything,' Simon added in a more upbeat tone.'

'Well, that's . . . good. I think.' Charlie wished she'd brought the vodka out to the car. Her heart was doing athletics inside her chest.

'It's not true, is it? Those stupid *West Side Story* lyrics: "Even death won't part us now". Yes, it will. It has to. You're going to be reading out a lie.' Simon pushed his seat further back, put his feet up on the dashboard on either side of the wheel. 'Why don't they care about *living* a lie? Do you think Liv pretends when she's with Dom? Pretends he's Gibbs?'

'In what context?' Charlie asked mock innocently. 'You mean when they're in the supermarket? Or when they're in a restaurant?' She grinned to herself. She wasn't going to worry about death. At some point – when she was in her late fifties, maybe – she would find a way round it, even if that meant making herself believe in something preposterous.

'You know what I mean,' said Simon. 'In bed.'

There was a time not all that long ago when he wouldn't have been willing to utter those words. As a couple, they were making progress. Amazing progress, actually. Charlie knew she ought to appreciate every step in the right direction, instead of wanting more from him than he could give. 'I wish I could tell you I've no idea, but sadly I know the answer,' she said. 'Liv's tried pretending, but it doesn't work. Dom and Gibbs are too different, technique-wise. I can provide more detail if you'd like me to, but I'd advise against. Spare yourself. It's too late for me, but you can still escape.'

'I pretend,' Simon said almost inaudibly.

Charlie was in no doubt about what she'd heard. 'Is that why we're sitting in a dark car?' she asked evenly. She was getting good at keeping her feelings out of her voice. 'So you can't see me? Will that make the pretence easier, when we get into bed?'

'Don't be stupid. I didn't mean that. It came out wrong.'

Ah. My entire life knows how that feels.

'I don't mean I pretend you're someone else. Why would I? There's no one else I want to be with.'

Charlie waited. Was this going to be another brilliant/shit thing, in the tradition of 'I love you but we're both doomed to die'?

'I'm talking about me,' he said.

'You mean . . .' Charlie stopped to check: implausible, yes, but there were no other possibilities. 'You mean you pretend *you're* someone else?'

Simon said nothing.

'Who?' *Fucking fuck fuck.* Was that a crass question? Charlie knew Simon well enough to know that no name would be forthcoming.

Gordon Ramsay? Nick Clegg? Colin Sellers? Ugh, please not.

'No one real, just . . . I don't know. A physical manifestation of no one or nothing. A symbolic figure without an appearance, standing in for me. I can only carry on if I never think about it being me. If I let myself see it as a scene I'm part of, that's when it doesn't go well.'

This is where you tell him that a shrink he once met has a theory that neatly explains everything that's wrong with him: it's the perfect opportunity.

'Do you think that makes me a freak?' Simon asked.

'No.' *I think it makes you someone with a common but rarely diagnosed psychological condition. If I tell you its name, you'll never be able to get it out of your mind. Trust me, I know. Emotional Incest Syndrome. You can call it EIS if you prefer, or CIS: Covert Incest Syndrome. Can you cure it, though? If not, what's the point of knowing you suffer from it? What if it only makes you feel more like a freak?*

So much easier to change the subject.

To prove to herself that she was nothing like Lizzie Proust, Charlie said, 'You need to tell Sam everything you haven't told him. The sonnet, everything Gaby Struthers told Gibbs, the lot.' *There, see? I'm not scared of telling my husband things he doesn't want to hear if I'm sure he needs to hear them.*

'What?' Simon sounded surprised. Not angry, thankfully. 'Where's that come from?'

'I'm not preaching forgiveness,' said Charlie. 'This is about the proper rules of competition. Getting there first only counts for something if you're both starting from the same point. Why don't you blindfold Sam and lock him in a cupboard? That way you'll definitely find the answer before he does.'

'That's how you see it?'

'It's how it might look to others, definitely.'

Simon swore under his breath. Then some more. It was what he always did when he realised he was wrong and Charlie was right.

∼

It might as well be the middle of the night, Sam thought as he walked out through the double doors of the police station into the car park. Spilling was well known for being silent and deserted even on weekend evenings; people who wanted nightlife went to Rawndesley. And tended not to live in staid, respectable Spilling in the first place.

Sam loved the silence and the calm, though in certain company he pretended to find it stifling. He looked at his watch: ten o'clock. His wife Kate would be pleased to see him home before eleven, when he'd told her to expect him. Privately, he had hoped to be home by ten and therefore assumed he'd never manage it. 'Rounding up to the nearest disappointment,' Kate called it.

Exchanges like the one he'd just had with Proust were eroding Sam's spirit. He would hand in his notice as soon as he'd sorted things out with Simon. He couldn't leave with the situation as it was between them. He hadn't admitted to Kate how bad he felt about Simon's unsubtle and wholehearted rejection of him as a friend and colleague. How could he explain it? It was as if his heart had something heavy pressing on it. Kate would laugh at him if he told her how empty and insubstantial Simon's disdain made him feel – that's if he was lucky. The scarier possibility was that Kate would ring Simon and yell at him, which Sam couldn't risk. If that happened, he'd have to resign from the planet Earth, not merely from Culver Valley Police.

'Resignation season again, is it?' Kate had been saying lately, as if it were all a big joke. Sam didn't mind her teasing him. He found it comforting; how bad could things be if she was giggling about it? She didn't believe he'd ever hand in his notice; soon she would see that she was wrong. Sam resolved never to tell her that it was a helpful hint from Charlie this afternoon that had finally made up his mind.

He knew what she'd say: 'For God's sake, Sam, you're playing right into her hands. She wasn't trying to help you at all. She's done this deliberately to undermine your confidence and make you think you need to slink off in disgrace because you're such a rubbish detective. You're not, by the way, and I can't believe you'd trust Charlie's motives further than you can throw them. Yesterday she told you she regretted walking out of her job and leaving it open for you; now she's hoping you'll be good enough and spineless enough to return the favour. Which is exactly what you mustn't do. You don't even know she's right. It's a hunch, that's all. Like all hunches, it's more likely to be wrong.'

Sam felt his face heat up as he realised he'd been talking to himself inside his head, writing Kate's lines in their imaginary dialogue, the words he desperately wanted and needed to hear. *Pathetic.* And unfair to Charlie, who, Sam believed, had genuinely been trying to help him: not to rescue his lacklustre career as an also-ran, but to heal the rift with Simon. 'I shouldn't be giving you this,' she'd said, pressing a folded sheet of white A4 paper into Sam's hand. 'I'm on a mission to persuade Simon to stop being a knob and start talking to you again, but in the meantime . . .'

'What is it?' Sam had asked.

'A poem. Simon went to Combingham to see Tim Breary yesterday. Breary gave it to him, asked him to pass it on to Gaby Struthers. Breary and Struthers are both members of the Proscenium Library in Rawndesley – a library that has the biggest and best collection of poetry books, past and present, in the western hemisphere. Apparently.'

Sam had wondered why Charlie was staring at him in a peculiar way, as if waiting for him to realise something.

'That poem might be in a book in the Proscenium, don't you think?' she'd said eventually. 'Given their exhaustive collection.'

'I suppose so. What are you getting at?'

'Read the poem,' she said. 'It's very ambiguous – no clear message. I can't see why Breary would want it passed on to Gaby Struthers. On the surface, it reads like a love poem, but it's not, not really. So maybe it's not about the poem itself and what it's saying – maybe that's not the intended message. What if Breary wants Gaby to go to the library and find the relevant page of the relevant book? Obviously it's a long shot, but—'

'You think he's left a message for her in the book?' Sam asked.

'Not really,' said Charlie cheerfully. 'But if you have that idea in front of Simon, he'll be impressed, and more likely to forgive you. Just don't tell him I gave you the poem, if you can possibly avoid it, or he'll have my head on a spike.'

Sam had been excited until he'd realised how utterly humiliating it was: Charlie giving him ideas that he could pretend were his own. It had been the signal he couldn't ignore that it was time for him to move on.

Before he went, he would do a version of what she'd suggested: he would have her idea in front of Simon if and only if he could prove it to be worth having. First thing Monday, he would go to the Proscenium and see if he could track down the sonnet, even though he was certain that the successful closing of this case wasn't going to depend on clues hidden in books, but, rather, on successfully interpreting the complex web of relationships and secrets at the Dower House.

Sam would have loved to hear Simon's angle on it. Alone, he couldn't work it out. No, it was more than that: he couldn't work out whether there was anything *to* work out. Maybe the story of the Brearys, the Joses and Gaby Struthers was no more abnormal than most people's life stories. Look at Gibbs and Olivia Zailer; look at Sellers and his one-hour stands in cheap B&Bs with any woman under the age of sixty who'd have him. And Simon, who'd asked Charlie to marry him when they were no more than colleagues – ones who had never dated, never slept together. And Charlie had said yes. Crazy, all of it.

So perhaps it wasn't so remarkable that Tim Breary had been unhappy with his wife, and in love with Gaby Struthers, but had decided to stay in his miserable marriage despite there being no children to keep him there. Sam reminded himself that he only knew what Dan and Kerry Jose had told him. Mainly Kerry; she did most of the talking for the two of them. Knowing first-hand how bad a liar she was, Sam had believed her on this occasion. She'd told the story naturally and effortlessly.

After ordering Gaby to give up on him, Tim Breary did exactly what he'd insisted he never would or could: he left Francine, didn't tell Gaby, jacked in his job, abandoned the Joses and the Culver Valley, and moved to a squalid bedsit in Bath. Several months later he tried to kill himself, except he undermined his suicide attempt by summoning Dan and Kerry to rescue him. Which they did, both locally and more generally: they rang an ambulance and got Tim the medical attention he needed, and shortly afterwards they abandoned their jobs in order to look after him practically, emotionally and financially. They were happy to do it, Kerry said – all of it. They no longer needed their salaries; thanks to Tim, and to Gaby Struthers, they had recently become extremely wealthy.

Tim was adamant that he wouldn't go back to the Culver Valley because it contained Francine, so Kerry and Dan bought a barn conversion near Kemble, in the Cotswolds. Kerry had shown Sam photos, pressing her hand against her heart and becoming tearful as she talked about her former home and how she'd hated having to leave it.

So why had she? Sam had asked and she'd answered, but he hadn't understood, and had been too polite to tell her that her explanation clarified nothing. Why were the Joses so willing to relocate every time Tim Breary changed his mind about where he needed to be? Kerry had found work in the Cotswolds, helping out on a nature reserve – 'the only genuinely fulfilling job I've ever had', she'd called it – and Dan had been in the middle of a PhD which required him to go to London once a week during term time. By car or by train, Kemble was half an hour nearer to London than Spilling was. This was the part Sam didn't get: having moved once for Tim's sake, why did the Joses agree to do it again? When Francine had her stroke and Tim decided he wanted to go back to the Culver Valley to look after her, why didn't Kerry and Dan say, 'Sorry, but we can't come with you this time'? Instead, Kerry gave up her dream job and the home that she loved, and uprooted herself a second time.

Did she think that Tim wouldn't survive without her and Dan close by? Was it as simple as that? That was the only explanation that satisfied Sam, who knew he would willingly move to somewhere inconvenient, dragging his complaining family behind him, to save Simon's life. Or he would have.

No, he still would. Another thing never to mention to Kate, who was a firm believer in the rule of reciprocity, and took great pleasure in deleting from her Christmas card list the name of any friend or acquaintance who dared to send an e-card instead of a real one. 'It's worse than sending nothing at all,' she'd said when Sam had challenged her.

For many aspects of Tim Breary's behaviour, Sam could imagine no possible explanation: why did he tell Gaby he would never leave Francine, then change his mind almost immediately afterwards and leave her? Why, having done so, did he not contact Gaby to tell her things had changed and he was available? And why, suddenly, after her stroke, was Tim prepared once again to share a home with Francine, when previously he'd been unwilling to share a county with her?

Actually, Sam could see himself doing that: if he'd left a wife – any wife, however ill-suited and unappealing – he would return and do his husbandly duty in the event of illness or disaster. And he could all too easily imagine himself married to a woman he didn't love, but too scared of change to leave her.

He sighed, and wished not for the first time that he had less self-knowledge. It was depressing to be so aware of his own short-comings. He'd rather be clueless like Sellers, who believed he was a sex god poised for the greatest adventure of his life every time he checked into the Fairview Lodge B&B with a woman too drunk to know who he was or feel much of what he did to her.

Sam unlocked his car, shielding his eyes as another car turned into the police station car park, its headlights on full beam. In spite of the glare, Sam could see that there was no registration plate at the front; someone had removed it. Before coming to the nick? Most scrotes in the Culver Valley weren't quite so brazen.

Nothing happened, for too long. Sam felt a tightening in his gut. He could think only of guns, and took a step back as one of the car's back doors opened. Something started to come out horizontally. A person, climbing out? No, no feet touched the floor. More like . . . a big parcel, inclining downwards as more of it emerged.

It fell to the ground with a thud. Once it was out, the door slammed shut and the car reversed out of the car park and screeched away at speed. No number plate on the back either.

Sam was aware of how still he was standing, holding his breath. No more than a second had passed between the shutting of the back door and the car swerving out onto the street again: not enough time for one person to jump from the back seat to the front. So, a driver and at least one passenger.

It couldn't be what it looked like from where Sam was standing. Not delivered to the police station. Who would do that?

What else could it be? Just because it had never happened before didn't mean it wasn't happening now.

Sam walked over to where the large, heavy thing had landed. *Oh, Jesus Christ.* It was; there was a foot sticking out of the end of the wrapping. Bubble-wrap, lots of it, around a bulky, unevenly covered tubular package.

A whole human body. A dead one.

POLICE EXHIBIT 1436B/SK – TRANSCRIPT OF HANDWRITTEN
LETTER FROM KERRY JOSE TO FRANCINE BREARY DATED 10
FEBRUARY 2011

Hello, Francine,

Do you know what day it is? Probably not. You don't need to know
about dates and times any more, so why would you? I don't need
to as much as I used to either. When I was a full-time care-worker,
I was constantly looking at my watch. Now I tend to judge the
passing of time by how hungry I am. Which isn't always reliable –
I'm not exactly known for my tiny appetite!

Anyway. It's Dan's birthday, and the anniversary of Making Memories
Night. I've been meaning to write to you about this for a while, and
what better day than today? You'll have to pardon my tipsiness.
Dan, Tim and I went out for lunch at Passaparola and I had two Kir
Royales – and that was before we got started on the wine.

Does the name mean anything to you, Francine? Obviously, you've
never heard it described as Making Memories Night. Do you even
remember what happened? If your reactions seemed reasonable
and ordinary to you, perhaps the evening didn't stick in your mind.
It certainly stuck in mine. Over the years, I missed many chances
to make clear to Tim how urgently I thought he needed saving from
you, but that night was the first time. It only takes one incident to
start a pattern, and Making Memories Night set the tone.

It was a few months before your and Tim's wedding. You were still
living in your separate flats, house-hunting, bound together by

neither marriage nor mortgage. If I'd waved a metaphorical red flag that night, Tim might have listened. He might have escaped your clutches.

Regrets are pointless, I know, but facing up to mistakes you've made is a valuable use of anyone's time. I was weak and indecisive that evening, and on many subsequent occasions. I allowed you to storm to power, Francine. You were better prepared than I was, with your detailed plan for every aspect of Tim's life, and your manifesto-like birthday and Christmas card messages: 'Happy birthday, darling Tim. No one in this world could love you more than I do.' 'I will love you come what may, until my dying day.' You had a knack for picking endearments that sounded like threats.

Dan and I loved Tim too, but we couldn't marry him. We were married to each other. And Tim needed someone in his bed every night to prove to the world that he'd been chosen, that he wasn't a reject. It's common for the children of severely neglectful parents to mistake a desire to control for love.

That's what I should have told him on Making Memories Night, after you'd stormed upstairs in a rage. I've always wanted to ask you, Francine: at what point did you decide to turn Dan's and my bedroom into your tantrum headquarters? Halfway up the stairs? Did you stop and think about it? The bathroom or the spare room would have been a more appropriate choice. We heard the door slam, and Dan mouthed, 'Our bedroom?' at me.

Wherever you'd chosen to locate your protest, it would have been inappropriate. All Tim did was criticise a hotel you'd asked him to look at in a brochure – possible honeymoon accommodation. It wasn't as if your parents were the owners, or the place meant something to you sentimentally. Your only connection to the Baigley Falls Hotel (I will never forget its name) was that you had seen a picture of its swimming pool and terrace and thought it looked nice.

The blurb beneath the picture said, 'The minute you arrive at Baigley Falls, you'll start making memories.' 'What if we don't?' Tim asked. 'Do you think they'll throw us out? What if they insist we bring each new memory we make down to reception, so that they can inspect it?' Dan and I laughed, but you didn't get the joke, did you, Francine? 'Why would they do that?' you asked. 'How could they? You can't see a memory.' I wondered how you managed to hold down a job as a lawyer, deaf to nuance as you so manifestly were. Tim ditched the lighthearted approach and explained that memories, if they happened, ought to come into being without any strain or effort on anyone's part, or else there was something false about it. You stood your ground, determined to misunderstand. 'So you don't want to try to remember any part of our honeymoon,' you said quietly. 'I won't need to try,' Tim said. 'Trying to remember is for shopping lists and exam crib sheets, not honeymoons.' Dan and I made things worse by joining in. I said, 'They probably take photos of you when you arrive to sell you when you leave.' Dan said, 'The blurb might as well say, "Don't live in the moment; do everything you do in order to look back on it later."'

You shut down at that point, Francine. Shut us all out. You got up, left the room, marched upstairs. The next thing we heard was the slamming of our bedroom door, so loud it shook the house. Tim ran up after you. I should have tried to stop him, but I didn't. Dan and I heard him saying your name over and over again, trying to reason with you. We heard what sounded like him straining, pushing against the door. Ten minutes later he came back down and stood in the middle of the lounge, looking more bewildered than I've ever seen anyone look. 'What's going on?' Dan asked. Since nothing had happened to warrant your storming off, he assumed he'd missed something. Tim shrugged, a defeated gesture that said, 'You know as much as I do'. I told Tim there was no lock on our bedroom door, and he mouthed, 'She's leaning against it.' 'Did she think we were taking the mickey out of her?' I asked, going over the conversation again in my mind, feeling guilty before I'd even worked out what I'd done wrong, if anything. 'She can't have. We weren't.'

Tim's mobile phone buzzed in his pocket. He read the message, and, with both hands, started to key in his reply. I turned to Dan, incredulous; Francine had sealed herself away in our bedroom, and Tim was replying to a random text message? The look Dan gave me, casting his eyes upward, set me straight: of course the message wasn't random. It was from on high. That much was obvious from the expression of intense concentration on Tim's face as he jabbed away with his thumbs. You'd refused to open the door and talk to him face to face, Francine, but you'd sent him a communication from upstairs. Even though I knew it had to be true, I couldn't believe it. 'Tim?' I said. 'Are you replying to a message from Francine?' He nodded. 'What's she said?' I asked. He wouldn't tell me, just moved further away with his phone to the other side of the room, as if he thought I might snatch it from his hands. That was the first time he protected you, the first of hundreds.

Did you appreciate his trying to shield you from the condemnation you deserved, Francine? Long after there was any point, he still made the effort. He knew that Dan and I knew exactly how unreasonable and vicious you were, yet he hid as much of your atrocious behaviour as he could, from everybody. To spare himself the public humiliation, yes, but it wasn't only that. My theory, for what it's worth, is that he never stopped believing you had a good side to your character, Francine. I think he thought that to tell us about all the awful things you'd done would actually be misleading – it would make us latch on to the badly behaved you and imagine that was all there was to you.

How many messages did you and Tim send each other while you

were shut in Dan's and my bedroom? Ten? Fifteen? There was quite a bit of to-ing and fro-ing by text before you deigned to emerge. You didn't come back into the lounge to say goodbye or sorry. Dan and I didn't figure in your calculations at all: we were the suckers who'd provided the stage for your scene, nothing more. Not people with feelings who mattered, not Tim's friends who had been looking forward to spending a fun evening with him. On Dan's birthday, too – not just any old evening.

You waited for Tim outside the house. Having spent a good hour and a half standing in our lounge jabbing at his phone, he was suddenly in a desperate hurry to leave, on your orders. He apologised to us – not on your behalf, but as if he was the one who'd ruined the evening. I said, 'No need to apologise,' then regretted it once he'd left, in case he thought I'd meant no need on anyone's part rather than no need on his.

I never found out what was in those messages, Francine. I'd still love to know. Was it out-and-out sweary aggression and accusations from you, and fawning contrition from Tim for having offended you? I bet it was more subtle and passive-aggressive: 'You claim you love me, but then you mock me in front of your friends. I'm sure you're having more fun laughing at me amongst yourselves than you would if I were there.'

Once you and Tim had gone, Dan turned to me and said, 'What was that all about? Pre-wedding nerves, do you think?' It was such an absurd and inadequate justification that I burst out laughing and started crying at the same time. You'll probably think me a wimp for crying, Francine. All I can say in my defence is that until you embedded yourself in my life, I wasn't used to having my evenings wrecked by random acts of emotional violence. (I never saw you cry, not once, no matter how allegedly upset you were.)

Dan's 'pre-wedding nerves' comment quickly became one of our regular jokes. It's still one that never fails to make us laugh, even now, years later. Whenever someone's reported on the news as having done something unspeakable, Dan and I turn to one another and say, 'Pre-wedding nerves, do you think?' and laugh uproariously.

If I could turn back the clock to Making Memories Night, I would say, 'Tim, you can't marry her. She's twisted. Her reactions and her behaviour are too abnormal to brush aside. If you stay with her, she'll make you suffer every day. She'll start by cancelling the honeymoon – to punish you for questioning her choice of hotel.'

Okay, I admit it: I'm cheating. Shocked as I was by your behaviour that night, Francine, even I wouldn't have predicted that you'd take it out on your honeymoon. Tim was back at the office two days after the wedding, trying to pretend it was actually quite useful not to have to go away when he had such a backlog of work.

I said nothing. I let him believe that I still liked you, understood that you were sensitive and prone to stress, could see what he saw in you. I consolidated my cowardice into a position, which I laid out for Dan. 'We have to be clever here,' I explained. 'Tim's inviting us to join him in the lie he's choosing to live. If we make an issue about Francine, we'll draw his pretence to his attention in a way that'll make him too uncomfortable. He'll feel ashamed for staying with her, guilty for inflicting her on us. We'll drive him away. We have to pretend we don't notice any of it and just go along with it, or we'll lose him.'

I've started to wonder, Francine: what would Tim say if I were to kill you, and if I then told him I'd done it? Instead of writing letters in which I speculate about who else might do it and when, I could do it myself. In an ideal world, I'd do it purely to experience the feeling, then undo it immediately afterwards. I'm not sure I want you gone, from a personal point of view. Having you here like this protects Tim, and he's all I care about. But, as

Sophie Hannah

contradictory as it might sound, that doesn't mean I wouldn't enjoy putting an end to your life.

Would I ever have the courage, Francine? Would I be brave enough to make your last memory of all?

19

Sunday 13 March 2011

'I'm going to show you the first photograph,' says DC Simon Waterhouse. 'I want you to tell me if you've seen this man before.'

I'm in a police station. There are police everywhere. He can't hurt me here.

'It's only a picture,' Charlie Zailer says quietly next to me. 'You're totally safe in this room. And you don't have to look till you're ready. Simon won't turn it over until you say the word.'

I nod. Nothing happens. Is he waiting, literally, for a word rather than a gesture?

Should I tell him to go ahead? I don't want to try and identify the man who attacked me anywhere near as much as I want not to have to see his face again, but DC Waterhouse set out the order of events when he came in and took over: first the photographs, then some questions, then he'll take me to see Tim.

I would rather drive to HMP Combingham myself, or have Charlie drive me. If she and I were alone, I might be able to persuade her to tell me what's changed. She left the room to take a call, and when she came back she looked rattled and had DC Waterhouse with her. Now she's moved round to my side of the table. Either she can't stand to be near him or she thinks I need protecting from him. She has seemed nervous since he joined us, and it's making me want to get away from her, from both of them. I thought I'd feel safe in the same room we were in yesterday, but everything's wrong today: the hard table and chairs are where the armchairs should be, the blind's not down, the grilles of the ventilation units are visible through the window; I can see their multiple slat-mouths, hear them breathing at me.

I'm struggling to get my own breathing under control, and my body temperature. My feet are painfully cold, as if I've been planted in ice.

What if I'm like this in front of Tim? I can't be. Somehow, I must leave this room with more strength than I brought in here.

'Gaby?' says Charlie. 'You okay?'

'Show me the photograph.'

Waterhouse turns it over and places it on the table in front of me. It's all there: the same short hair, small square forehead, thin lips; the same brown skin tags on the neck. I couldn't think of the name for them on Friday, but that's what they're called.

I lunge for the picture and rip it in half, and again. I carry on tearing until I can't any more because the pieces are too small. 'Sorry,' I say, not meaning it.

'Have you seen him before?' Charlie asks. Clearly a non-verbal answer won't do.

'On Friday, outside my house.'

'He was the man who warned you to keep away from Lauren? Are you sure?'

'Yes.'

Charlie sweeps the fragments of the photograph across the table, away from me. I'd like to be able to set fire to the disconnected parts of his face. Together, they still add up to him. Burning would sort that out.

'Gaby? Is there anything you'd like to ask us?'

'Is Lauren all right? Where is she? Tell me you haven't left her at the Dower House.' *Why am I the only person who cares about her safety?*

'Why are you so worried about Lauren?' Waterhouse's question is a mirror image of my unspoken one.

'Because she's married to Jason, who's a killer, and who sends his heavies round to people's houses to . . .' My throat closes, choking off the end of my sentence.

'To what? What did he do to you, the man in the picture? He

did more than warn you, didn't he? Or else why did you tear up his photo?'

I could say that I object to being given orders by strangers, which is true. Or I could say nothing.

'You haven't asked us anything about him,' says Waterhouse. 'Is that because you already know who he is? Gaby?'

'How could I know?'

'Don't you want to know his name? Most people would be curious.'

'Would they? I'm sure Jason Cookson's got lots of thuggy friends, any of whom'd be willing to intimidate a woman on his behalf. I don't care what Thug X's name is – he could just as easily have been Thug Y or Thug Z.'

'Do you care about us finding and punishing X, Y or Z for what he did to you? You don't seem to.'

'It's not illegal to warn someone to stay away from someone else, is it? No, I don't care about you punishing him.' *Whatever you did wouldn't be enough. I'd rather not have to know his name.*

'Please, Gaby, can you seriously consider telling us what really happened on Friday?' says Charlie. 'It would help us so much, and it might help Tim. If you'd rather speak to me in private, DC Waterhouse can leave us alone for a bit.'

Is this how the police make people talk when they don't want to: by misrepresenting them until they feel they have no choice but to protest and set the record straight? 'The reason I'm holding back has nothing to do with embarrassment or an inability to say the word "vagina" in front of a man. I told you: I wasn't sexually assaulted.'

'Then why not tell us exactly what happened?' Charlie asks.

'How do I know you won't tell Tim? He can't find out.'

'Why is that so important?'

'I'm worried he'll see me as damaged goods if he finds out that Jason's thug friend violated my honour – that's what I'd say if I were a simpering cliché, right?'

'And if you were you?' Charlie asks.

No idea, sorry. I haven't been me for a long time. In order to be me, I need Tim. Which makes me a different kind of cliché.

Waterhouse is trying to cut the plastic surface of the table with his thumbnail; he has absented himself without leaving the room. Was it my reference to the female anatomy that sent him into automatic shut-down mode, or doesn't he know how to handle women who behave like men? I've met that before: I meet it nearly every time I leave the house. Until Friday, I met it when I returned to the house as well, but not any more, not since I left Sean.

Never again in my own home.

It would be dishonest not to acknowledge the downside: that I no longer have a home.

'I don't want Tim to feel guilty, and I know he would,' I tell Charlie, who is a better interviewer than Waterhouse even when he isn't ignoring me. He makes me feel as if everything I say is the wrong answer; Charlie does the opposite. 'What happened to me wasn't Tim's fault any more than it was mine. It was Jason's fault and the man who . . . did what he did to me, but Tim wouldn't see it that way. He'd trace it back to himself and feel responsible: if he hadn't confessed to Francine's murder, Lauren wouldn't have turned up in Dusseldorf and said what she said to me. I wouldn't have gone to the Dower House on Friday and met Jason, who wouldn't have decided he needed to keep me quiet by whatever means necessary.'

'What means?' Waterhouse asks.

'Give me a cast-iron guarantee that whatever I tell you will go no further than this room.'

'You care more about Tim's feelings than you do about your own,' says Charlie. It doesn't sound like a question. 'So do Kerry and Dan Jose.'

'You won't understand, not knowing Tim, but however much he matters to us, it'll never be enough to compensate for how little he matters to himself. We're his ego: me, Kerry and Dan.'

And I wish I didn't have to be. I wish he were stronger. I wish I could say for certain that he'd drop everything for me as I have for him.

I crush the thought in my mind, tell myself I'm being unreasonable. I can't expect everyone to be as bold and reckless as me.

'You need to tell us what happened to you on Friday.' Waterhouse's deep voice has the force of an unexpected blow. 'This is about a whole lot more than Tim Breary, his ego and his dead wife, as of last night.'

'What? What do you mean?'

His flat stare contains no willingness to compromise: if I want to be told, I first have to tell.

I direct my answer to Charlie. 'Jason's emissary put a plastic bag over my head and taped it round my neck. I thought I was going to suffocate, but then he tore a hole in the plastic near my mouth so that I could breathe. He'd taped my wrists together behind my back. I don't know when he did that. I think I must have blacked out from the shock. I know he put his arm round my neck and squeezed. That was his first move when he came up behind me: crushing my windpipe.'

'I should have insisted on taking you to the hospital,' says Charlie.

'Would have been a waste of time. Physically I'm fine.'

'Carry on,' Waterhouse says. It feels like an intrusion, though the three of us are supposedly taking part in the same conversation.

'When you're ready, Gaby.' Charlie gives him a look that makes me wonder if she's tired of being his antidote.

Like me and Tim? No. I push the thought away.

'There's no rush.'

'Thanks, but I'd rather get it over with.' Why do people always want you to linger over the bad stuff? *Take your time recounting the details of the worst experience of your life at a rate of one word per day, make the story last for three years instead of an hour. No thanks.* 'He said he'd come to teach me a lesson. I asked what it was, but he wouldn't tell me straight away – that would have been too quick and easy. I had to suffer first, so that the lesson would make an impression on me. He undid my belt and my trousers, pulled them down to my knees, pulled my underwear down. At that point I thought he was going to rape me and kill me, but he didn't. Instead he asked me all kinds of sick questions: what was the worst thing he could do to me? What's the most frightened I've ever been? Was I more frightened or more humiliated by what he was doing to me? That sort of thing.'

'Twisted fuck,' Charlie mutters.

Did Lauren hear my answers? I can't go anywhere near the possibility in my mind: the idea that there was an audience. I block it out.

'His plan was to scare me, then spare me,' I say. 'Fill my mind with the worst that could happen, then release me, give me a chance to be good and follow his orders: to stay away from Lauren, say nothing to anyone about what he'd done to me. Or else next time would be worse. He didn't say that, but it was clear what he meant.' *And here I am telling the police.* My vision rocks; I have to close my eyes. Am I trying to prove to myself that I'm not scared of next time? It won't work. I'm petrified; every cell in my body knows it.

'What happened then, after he warned you?' Charlie asks.

'Once he was satisfied I'd learned the lesson he wanted me to learn, he cut my wrists free and walked away.'

'I'm so sorry, Gaby.'

'Thanks.' Is that the appropriate response? I've always hated the linguistic fusing of apology and sympathy. There's something messy about it. I'd have preferred her to say, 'That's the most horrendous thing I've ever heard.' Except it isn't; she'll have heard far worse stories than mine, the sort that generate shocking headlines: 'Raped and Abandoned to Die', 'Raped, Tortured and Left to Starve'. Who'd bother to read 'Not Raped and Not Even Injured'?

'I'm going to show you another picture,' says Waterhouse. Six seconds later, he reaches into his folder. I wait for his hand to reappear but it doesn't, not straight away. 'Are you ready?' he asks.

I wish he'd just show me instead of trailing it. If I need to be warned, that must mean there's something to dread.

He holds up the photograph in front of me. 'That's Jason Cookson,' I say, as repelled as I was on Friday by the coiffed-pubes beard and the kink in the shoulder-length hair. Maybe it's not from being worn in a ponytail; maybe that's just how it grows.

'For clarity, can you tell us if and when you've met this man before?' Waterhouse says.

'I told Charlie yesterday. I met Jason on Friday at the Dower House. The gates opened as I arrived, and he drove out.'

'Did he identify himself to you as Jason Cookson?'

'No. He didn't need to. I knew it was him.'

'How?'

'The tattoo on his arm: "Iron Man". Lauren told me in Germany that Jason had done the Iron Man Challenge. Three times,' I add unnecessarily.

'Aside from the tattoo, did you have any other reason for believing the man in the car was Jason Cookson?' Waterhouse asks.

'Yes. The way he talked about Lauren and warned me off going anywhere near her. It was . . . proprietorial, protective. Why? What does it matter how I knew?'

'You didn't know. You can't know something that isn't true.'

He looks at Charlie. I can't make sense of his words, but I can read his eyes, and hers: they're having a silent argument about which of them should tell me. Tell me what?

'The man in this picture isn't Jason Cookson,' Waterhouse says eventually. 'He's Wayne Cuffley, Lauren Cookson's father.'

The room tips. I close my eyes until the feeling passes, until I'm ready to put things back in the right order. Could I have been wrong? I can't think. I need to be scientific about it: measure my certainty before I speak. First I need to track it down.

'But . . . he's too young. He's about forty, isn't he?' I know this proves nothing. I hear Lauren's voice in my head: *In twenty years' time, I'll be forty-three. No forty-three-year-olds have great-grandkids.*

Some forty-year-olds have twenty-three-year-old daughters, though.

'Wayne Cuffley is forty-two,' Waterhouse says. 'He's only six months older than Jason Cookson.'

'Yesterday you said Jason might as well have had "Thug" tattooed on his forehead to add to his collection,' says Charlie. 'It didn't sink in until this morning. I realised you must have meant his collection of tattoos, and I knew he didn't have any. There are no tattoos anywhere on Jason's body.'

How can she know? Has she seen every part of his body? The idea makes me want to throw up.

All I have to work with is a strong desire to tell her she must be mistaken, her and Waterhouse. I want the man I met at the gates of the Dower House to have been Jason because I hate being wrong. It's not enough. I can think of no reason why Lauren's dad shouldn't have completed the Iron Man Challenge at least once. And I know he's a fan of tattoos; Lauren had 'FATHER' tattooed on her arm at his request – her spare arm, the one that hadn't already been appropriated by Jason's name. I wonder if Wayne Cuffley has a 'DAUGHTER' tattoo that I didn't spot on Friday. Jason didn't reciprocate; maybe Wayne didn't either. Do all the men in Lauren's life treat her as their own personal graffiti wall?

'All right,' I say eventually. 'I drew a stupid conclusion.'

'The other picture, the first one . . .' Charlie leaves the sentence hanging.

'I tore up the other picture. It doesn't exist any more. Thug X. I don't want to know. I don't want to hear it.'

'The man in the photograph you tore up was Jason Cookson,' says Waterhouse.

'I knew you'd say that. I knew it.'

'I'm saying it because it's true.'

It should make no difference. I walked in here knowing Jason Cookson was responsible for what happened to me; why do I feel as if he's used Waterhouse as a conduit to attack me all over again, as if evil has crept one step closer?

'Gaby, there's something I need to tell you that might come as a shock,' says Charlie.

Can you be shocked when you're already in shock? In an ideal world, the second shock would cancel out the first. Jason Cookson would cancel out Wayne Cuffley; neither of them would exist.

'Gaby?'

'What?'

'Jason Cookson's dead. His death wasn't natural or accidental.'

Good. Good to both statements.

'Gaby? Did you hear what I said? Jason's been killed.'

'I heard,' I tell her. 'I'm glad.'

20

13/3/2011

'Jason Cookson and Francine Breary.' Proust stood in front of the whiteboard where their enlarged photographs were displayed. 'What do they have in common? Come on. No answer too obvious.'

'Both murdered,' said Sellers.

'Except that one, detective. Try harder.'

Sam had nothing to offer, obvious or otherwise. The two glasses of wine he'd poured down his throat when he got home last night had taken the edge off the image of Jason Cookson's dead body in his memory, but he was paying for it this morning. I must be getting old, he thought. Since when were two glasses of wine enough to give him a fuzzy head the next day?

'Two people you wouldn't want to be in a relationship with,' Gibbs said. 'Both abusive to their partners in different ways.'

'Evidence?' said Proust.

'Kerry Jose's description of Tim and Francine Breary's marriage, and a catalogue of horrors from Cookson's ex-girlfriend.'

'Hearsay,' said Proust. 'Still, I don't think we doubt any of it, do we? So, now that we're all but certain it was Cookson who terrorised Gaby Struthers, it'll be interesting to hear what she has to say about what happened on Friday, assuming Waterhouse and Sergeant Zailer manage to get anything out of her. If she won't talk, it's probably because she's too embarrassed to go into the kind of detail we've had this morning from Cookson's ex Becky Grafham: forced to stand naked on a chair in the middle of the room with a noose round her neck attached to a light fitting, stripped and penetrated with a tube of lipstick for going out with too much make-up on. Et cetera. Put that together with what Kerry Jose told Sergeant Zailer about the suffering inflicted on Tim Breary by Francine, and we might conclude . . . what? Oh, come on, it's not hard! Is the world any worse off without these two in it?' Proust hit the whiteboard with the back of his hand.

'So we're on the killer's side?' Gibbs asked.

'We're on the law's side. That said, we're probably not looking for the usual self-seeking pond scum, but for an altruist with a strong sense of justice. Anyone fitting that description spring to mind?'

'Lauren Cookson,' said Gibbs.

Sellers chuckled.

'I'm being serious. When Gaby Struthers came in on Friday, I suggested to her that Lauren might have killed Francine Breary. Gaby said no, Lauren would think it was unfair to murder someone.'

'She might have made an exception for Jason, assuming he subjected her to the same kind of torture he put Becky Grafham through,' Sellers pointed out.

'She's got an alibi,' said Sam. 'Jason was killed between midnight and 4 a.m. on Friday night, provisionally. Lauren was—'

'It's not possible to kill someone provisionally, Sergeant.'

'The timing's provisional, I meant. The post-mortem will confirm it.'

'And when it does, Lauren Cookson's alibi will still be worthless and an insult to every serving police officer and every victim of violent crime in the Culver Valley, because the same liars providing that alibi, Dan and Kerry Jose, also said that Jason Cookson was at home on Friday from 4.30 p.m. onwards. Perhaps he was, but if so, he was also being murdered during that period, which no one mentioned. I'd call that a significant omission – wouldn't you, Sergeant?'

'Yes, sir. I tried to ring the Joses and Lauren first thing this morning. I drove round there too. No one's answering any phones or doors.'

'Good,' said Proust.

'Good?'

'What's the point in talking to them?' the Snowman barked. 'What's the point in listening to them? They do nothing but lie. Let's discount everything they've told us and use our brains instead. Lauren Cookson *doesn't* have an alibi for Jason's murder – not one that's worth anything.'

Sam nodded, embarrassed. He wouldn't have needed to be reminded of this if he hadn't been hungover.

'The Dower House Disobligers didn't report Jason Cookson missing on Friday night,' said Proust. 'This tells us what?'

'They knew why he wasn't at home,' said Gibbs. 'They knew he was busy being killed somewhere else, and they knew who was killing him. It could have been one of them, or someone known to them: Gaby Struthers, maybe. Either way, they knew.'

'Wouldn't it have made sense for them to report him missing, in that case?' Proust asked. 'That's what they'd have done if they were innocent and had no idea where Cookson was.'

'It's possible they needed time to cover their tracks,' said Sam. 'They wouldn't want anyone looking for Jason while they did that, so they pretended he wasn't missing. Though obviously that contradicts what happened next.'

'So, what, they changed their minds?' Proust frowned. 'Decided to roll Cookson's body across our car park in the direction of your feet instead?'

'The decision to dump the body at the nick could have been a deviation from the original plan,' said Gibbs.

'It was certainly a deviation from Cookson's plan to help his friend renovate a house on Saturday,' Proust said. For a few seconds, the hint of a smile hovered around his lips. 'All right, let's search everywhere Cookson's likely to have been killed: break into the Dower House if you have to. Sean Hamer's home, Gaby Struthers' hotel room . . .'

'Gaby's work?' Sellers suggested. 'Lauren's parents' places?'

'All of the above,' said Proust. 'And . . .' He stopped and leaned to his right, looking past Sam. 'PC Meakin, that door ought to be closed. Since it isn't, I suggest you put yourself on the other side of where it would be if it were. And assume the bearing of a man who's happy to be ignored until the end of a case briefing, keeping in mind that no one cares if you're happy or not.'

'Sir, there's a man downstairs asking about Francine Breary's murder. I thought I should nip up and tell you. He wants to talk to a detective.'

Proust inhaled ominously: the breathing equivalent of pulling back the bow in anticipation of firing the arrow. 'There are four men *up*stairs asking about Francine Breary's murder, Meakin. You've just interrupted them.'

'He also wants to confess to a murder, sir. Nothing to do with Francine Breary, he says.'

'I see. One of those. He wants to stand in reception and say, "murder" as often as he can?'

'He could be a crank, sir, but he reckons he killed someone on Friday night – a man called Jason Cookson.'

'What?'

Meakin took a step back as Sam, Sellers and Proust all moved towards him at the same time.

21

Sunday 13 March 2011

Jason Cookson, dead. Lauren's husband. The man who attacked me.

'Right,' I say for the sake of saying something. The sound of my voice is proof that I'm not alone; if I were, I wouldn't bother to speak. I can't let Charlie and Waterhouse see how much trouble I'm having processing each new piece of information. It's lucky mind-reading is impossible; mine at the moment would be illegible. They'd probably have me sectioned.

I wish Wayne Cuffley were dead too, though he probably had nothing to do with what happened to me on Friday. His warning was the same as Jason's: stay away from Lauren. That's enough to make me wish him dead. He might not have done what Jason did to me, but I'm sure he would have approved.

'Who did it?' I ask.

'You mean who killed Jason?'

For about five seconds, I wonder if I might have murdered him, then filed the memory in an inaccessible part of my brain to avoid giving myself away.

I wish I hadn't ripped up the photograph. An urge grips me: to look at his face and savour the knowledge that it's rotting in a morgue somewhere. Nearby, probably; it would make sense for the morgue to be near the police station.

I would like to see Jason in the cold lifeless flesh, stripped naked on a tray in a long, silver drawer. Is there a tactful way of asking?

'Jason was killed between midnight and 4 a.m. on Friday night, early hours of Saturday morning,' Waterhouse says. 'Exactly when we can't account for your whereabouts. I'd like to know where you were. I think Sergeant Zailer's already spoken to you about legal representation . . .'

'I don't want a lawyer. I wish I had murdered Jason Cookson, but I didn't. If I were a plagiarist like Tim, I might try and take the credit.'

'Gaby, we don't for one second think you killed Jason,' says Charlie. 'I know you didn't.'

'No, you don't. You'll only know for sure if I tell you where I spent Friday night.'

'Go ahead,' says Waterhouse. 'The sooner you do, the sooner I stop asking myself if you pretended not to be able to identify a man you had good reason to want dead.'

'Between midnight and 4 a.m.? I was in the Proscenium Library's car park on Teago Street.'

'In your car?' Charlie asks.

'Most of the time, yeah. I arrived at about eleven and stayed till seven fifteen the next morning.'

'Teago Street?' Waterhouse frowns. 'I've been to the Proscenium – it's on The Mallows.'

'The entrance to the car park's on Teago Street, behind the library,' I tell him. 'It's a private car park with a big gate and a keypad. Only staff and members know the code. It's generally pretty empty after six when the library closes, and always totally empty after eleven, eleven fifteen. Any members who've parked there to go out for dinner or to the cinema or theatre are gone by then. Talk to the librarian, May Geraghty. Ask her for Friday night's CCTV footage from the car park – she'll be in ecstasies. She's prouder of her top-notch security system than any normal person who isn't obsessed with rare books could possibly imagine.'

'CCTV?' Waterhouse passes another silent message to Charlie with his eyes.

'There were two break-ins last year,' I tell him. 'All the members clubbed together to pay for the cameras – a fiver in most cases. People whose lives revolve around antiquarian books aren't generally very well off. I put in more than half of the money. It felt worthwhile at the time, to protect the Proscenium's collection, and it feels even more worthwhile now.' Without my contribution, the cameras wouldn't have been affordable; I wouldn't be able to prove I didn't kill Jason Cookson.

'So if I watch this footage, will I see you?' Waterhouse asks. 'Or just your car?'

'You'll see the car drive in and stay there all night. That'll be exciting viewing for you. Once or twice you'll see me get out of the car, stand next to it crying, then get back in. You'll be in the middle of your seat. As in: not at all on the edge of your seat,' I say in response to Waterhouse's puzzled frown. 'That's what Tim used to say about boring films: "I was in the middle of my seat throughout."'

'Why did you get out of the car once or twice?' Charlie asks.

'To prove to myself that I wasn't trapped in a small metal box. It was more than twice. Three or four times, maybe. Mostly, I felt safest in the car with the doors locked, but then I'd start to panic about not being able to breathe, running out of oxygen. What if I couldn't open the door and get out if I needed to? What if the locks had jammed? I had to get out into the open air when I started thinking like that.'

'But then you'd get back in and lock the doors again, knowing the effect it would have on you. Inviting the panic to recur.' Waterhouse sounds unimpressed.

Is he serious? 'I was inconsistent, yes. Well spotted. Sorry, are most victims of terrifying attacks more focused than I am? Do they dust themselves off and immediately set about pursuing a coherent goal?'

'No,' he says. 'Though you're not what I'd call typical.'

'Really? I suspect I'd have to visit another solar system to find anything you'd call typical.' I turn my chair so that I'm facing Charlie. 'I couldn't stand next to the car all night. It was freezing. I couldn't . . . I felt as if the cold would kill me if I stayed out in it, and I didn't know where he was – Jason. He could have crept up on me again. I was in an empty car park in a silent part of town, no one around. I know it sounds stupid.'

'It doesn't at all,' Charlie says.

'He attacked me outside my house when I thought I was totally safe. There was no warning, I didn't hear him coming. What was to stop him doing it again?' I laugh, surprising myself as much as Waterhouse and Charlie. 'If I asked myself that question now, I'd have an answer, wouldn't I? Violent death. The best possible answer to the Jason Cookson question.' I like the sound of my voice saying those words: as if I coolly planned his extermination. 'How was he killed?' *Did he suffer enough?*

'Can you fill in a gap for me?' says Waterhouse. 'You were attacked behind your house early evening, but you didn't arrive at the Teago Street car park till eleven. Where were you in between?'

'Driving. I drove to Combingham airport and back, twice.' More atypical behaviour; I wonder if Waterhouse will be able to cope. 'I didn't want to risk going to the Proscenium car park too early in case anyone else was there and saw me.'

'Why Combingham airport?'

'No reason in particular. I drive there all the time. I couldn't think of anywhere else.'

'Why not park up somewhere? On a side street, in a lay-by?'

'Someone who knew me could have seen my car. People walk down streets, don't they? *He* could have walked past, or anybody. If someone had knocked on the window, I'd have had to talk to them.'

'Why the Proscenium car park as a destination for the night?' Waterhouse asks. 'Why not a hotel, or a friend's house?'

'You're not listening to me. I didn't want to have to deal with anyone. I knew no one would drive into the car park at that time of night, and you can't walk in when the gate's shut – it's physically impossible.'

'It's okay, Gaby. We do understand.'

'You might. He doesn't.'

'I don't,' Waterhouse backs me up. 'Two minutes of talking to a receptionist in a light, warm hotel lobby and you could have locked yourself in a comfortable room for the night. Instead, you chose a cold deserted car park.'

'Yes. You're right. That's what I chose – not being *typical*.' I spit the word at him. 'So what? You'll soon be watching a black and white silent CCTV movie starring me not killing Jason Cookson, all night long. You wanted proof, and I've given it to you.'

'And now I want something else,' says Waterhouse quietly. 'I want to be confident that you had nothing to do with Jason's murder. Not killing him and not being involved are two different things.'

I laugh. 'You think I whipped out my BlackBerry and quickly arranged to have him killed? My assassin of choice happened to have a free slot at short notice?'

'You're not short of money for a nice hotel,' Waterhouse tells me. 'You've got parents or siblings you could go to, presumably. Colleagues, friends at the Dower House – Kerry and Dan Jose. I'm wondering why you made a point of spending an uncomfortable night under the square eye of a state-of-the-art security camera when you had so many other options.'

'She didn't want to see anyone, Simon,' Charlie says impatiently.

'There's something she's not telling us.' Waterhouse keeps his eyes on me.

'You think I went to the Proscenium car park knowing I'd be filmed, to give myself an alibi?' I ask him.

'Did you?'

'No!'

'I don't believe you.'

Why isn't Waterhouse a photograph I can tear up? Why does he have to be real?

'I assume you still want to go and see Tim today?' he says.

'Simon, for God's sake,' Charlie murmurs.

Be gentle with the almost-rape victim, that's what she means; don't threaten the human wreckage – it might release harmful toxins.

If she's trying to make him feel guilty, it's not working.

I don't require special treatment, and I want them both to know it. 'If you really want to know, I'll tell you, but don't blame me when you wish you hadn't asked. During the attack, I was sick all over myself. I also lost bowel control. When it was over, once I was sure he'd gone, my first thought was "How do I clean myself up?" The most basic thing, but I couldn't think of a way. If I hadn't just walked out on Sean—' I break off. 'No. Even if I hadn't, I wouldn't have gone back into the house in that state. Sean's never made me feel better about anything. The more difficult the situation, the worse he makes me feel.'

'I wish you'd come straight here,' says Charlie.

I ignore her. It's an unreasonable wish that doesn't take any of mine into account. She probably only said it to sound sympathetic and because she knows Waterhouse won't try; I've struck him dumb again. 'I had clean clothes with me in the bag I'd packed before I left, but I was filthy. I needed to wash, but I couldn't think of anywhere to go where I wouldn't have to come into close contact with anyone. If I couldn't wash, then I didn't want to be seen, obviously. The Proscenium car park was the best idea I had – the only idea. I thought about the camera, how much it would reveal, if anyone watched the footage. Not that I thought they would in a million years.'

'Simon? I think you should tell Gaby that you believe her now.'

'She hasn't finished yet,' he says stonily. 'You interrupted her.'

'There's not much else to say.' Hasn't he heard enough? What if he's still not convinced? I've told him everything now; there's nothing more I can do.

Yes, there is.

One small but crucial detail will prove I'm telling the truth. 'I turned the car round before getting out of it the first time,' I say. 'Watch the CCTV footage. You'll see that I came in, parked, then about an hour later I did a three-point turn and reversed back in again, into the same parking space, but with the car facing in the opposite direction. I did it so that the car would be a barrier between me and the camera, when I got out on the driver's side. I didn't want to be filmed in that state, even if no one was ever going to see it.' *Pitiful, isn't it?* 'Why else would I have done that? Can you think of a single other reason?'

'No. Where did you go when you left the car park at seven fifteen on Saturday morning?'

No. He definitely said it; I didn't imagine it. Does that mean he believes me?

'I went home. My former home,' I correct myself. 'Sean goes to the gym every Saturday: sets off seven fifteen, gets there seven thirty, stays till nine thirty. I let myself in, washed, bagged up my dirty clothes. Then I had to drive somewhere to dispose of them, and . . .'

'What?' Waterhouse pounces on my hesitation.

'I'd been sitting on a pile of old cardboard all night, from the boot of the car. I needed to get rid of that too.'

'Thank you for being so honest with us, Gaby,' says Charlie. 'I'm going to give you the phone number of someone I think you should get in touch with. A counsellor.'

'Really?' I feign excitement. 'Why didn't you say so before? That'll solve everything.'

'You've been through the worst kind of hell. You should speak to someone who can help you deal with it.'

Waterhouse pulls an envelope out of his file. My envelope, with Lauren's name on it. He puts it down on the table between us. 'We haven't given this to Lauren Cookson.'

'So I see.'

'I've read it, though. I'd like you to give it to her in person if you can.'

'Did Lauren kill Jason?' *Did she kill him because of what she saw him do to me?* Would I rather she hadn't seen, if that meant Jason would still be alive?

'We don't know. Lauren does – that's the problem. She knows everything I want to know and everything you want to know: who killed Jason, who killed Francine Breary, why Tim Breary doesn't belong in prison, why he's ended up there and seems to want to stay.' Waterhouse sighs. For a few seconds, he sounds and looks human. 'If we give her your letter, we run the risk of her associating you with us. If she does that, she'll tell you no more and no less than she's telling us.'

'Lies, fuck all, and more lies,' Charlie chips in.

'If she thinks you're nothing to do with us, if you can convince her that you'll keep her secrets . . .'

'It won't work,' I say. 'Lauren's stupid but she's not that stupid. She knows I'd do or say anything to get Tim out of prison.'

'Wrong,' says Waterhouse. 'She knows you'd do anything *for* Tim, and she knows he wants to stay where he is. You could try to persuade her that if that's what he wants, then you want it too. Then she might feel safe telling you the truth.'

Tears prick my eyes. 'How do you know that's what he wants?' I ask. 'How could anyone want to take the blame for a murder they didn't commit? I don't care what Tim wants! If he wants to be in prison when he's done nothing wrong then he's *insane*!'

I don't want to love a man who's that crazy. I want to invent a better version, one that doesn't do any of the infuriating, baffling things the real Tim does.

He lied to me when he said that I'd invented him. He was banking on appealing to my vanity, and it worked. The truth is that I failed to invent the Tim I wanted – the ideal Tim – though I tried for years.

Can't stop trying now. Gaby Struthers didn't get where she is today by giving up.

'I can persuade Tim to tell you the truth,' I say. 'I know I can.' *Take me to see him.*

'Going back to Lauren,' says Waterhouse. 'I've read the notes DC Gibbs made after speaking to you on Friday. You told him something Lauren said to you, her outburst at Dusseldorf airport.

Sophie Hannah

I'm going to read it back to you. Tell me if it's correct, as you remember it. "Little Miss Stuck-Up Bitch, you are! So much better than me. Course you are! I bet you'd never let an innocent man go to jail for murder."'

'Word perfect,' I confirm.

'You assumed – like I did at first, and like Gibbs did – that Lauren was criticising herself for being unethical: she was letting a man be framed for a crime he didn't commit, and she felt guilty about it. You took her outburst as a flare-up of guilt that she couldn't keep down.'

'Not quite,' I say. 'There was some guilt, definitely, but it slipped out by accident. Her intention was to accuse me of ivory-tower cluelessness.'

'Explain,' Waterhouse orders. *Half man, half Dalek.*

'She was implying that I couldn't possibly understand how hard things are for her. I might think she's unethical for letting Tim go to prison, I might think I'd never do something so immoral, but I've got a nerve congratulating myself on my superiority when I don't know what she's up against. A case of "Don't throw stones until you've lived in my glass house."'

'Interesting,' says Charlie.

'Here's another interpretation,' says Waterhouse. '"You think you're better than me, but that's crap. You'd assume it was always wrong to let an innocent man go to jail for murder, whereas I understand that it's right for Tim to do this. You never would because you're too conventional, too black and white. Not ethically sophisticated or nuanced."'

I laugh. 'Ethically nuanced? You've met Lauren Cookson, right?'

'She used the word "let". "Let an innocent man go to jail for murder." True, she could have meant stand by and allow it to happen. Or she could have meant grant his wish.'

'That would explain a lot,' Charlie says. From her face, it's clear she hasn't heard this theory of Waterhouse's before. More worryingly, it's equally clear that she's happy to buy into it on the basis of no proof whatsoever. 'Kerry and Dan Jose, Tim's best

342

friends – they're also granting his wish by letting him stay in prison. Their lies are keeping him there; their lies and his.'

'How can it be good for Tim to go to prison for his wife's murder when he didn't do it?' Waterhouse asks me. 'Why's that what he wants? Any reason you can think of, Gaby, however unlikely it seems, I want to hear it.'

I nod, numb inside, trying to ignore the voice in my head that's telling me things I don't want to hear.

He wants to be in prison because he needs a way of avoiding you, now that Francine's dead.

No. Can't be. I know Tim loves me. I know it.

Really? Is that why his principles and his fear of Francine meant more to him than you did? Is that why he told you to get out of his life, and hasn't been in touch since?

Waterhouse reaches into his file again and pulls out a crumpled sheet of A4 paper. He unfolds it and hands it to me.

'Tim asked me to give you this,' he says. 'It's a poem.'

I take the page from his hand. Mine is shaking.

'He told me to tell you it was from The Carrier. Do you know what that means?'

You bastard, Tim.

I can't concentrate on the poem at first. Tim's writing is all I see; its only significance is that it's his. He held the pen, touched the paper, folded it . . .

'Yesterday you told Charlie that Tim's not The Carrier, and that Kerry Jose is. What did you mean?'

Waterhouse can wait until I've finished reading. I start to cry halfway through. I read the sonnet again and again.

'Gaby?' Charlie says gently.

I shake my head.

'Does Kerry know that she's The Carrier?'

'Oh, yes. She knows.'

'Carrier of what?' asks Waterhouse. 'A disease? A burden of some kind?'

I wipe my eyes. 'Neither. I don't want to talk about it. It's personal.'

'Who and what is The Carrier?' Waterhouse asks again, as if he hasn't just heard me say I'm not going to tell him. 'Do you know why Tim wanted you to have this poem? What it means?'

Falling in love's a paradox like this. / Either it happens like a thunderbolt, / So when it makes our lives make sense, it lies . . .

'That's easy,' I say.

'What does it mean?'

Or we had long been hoping for the kiss / That changed us, and, aware how it would jolt / Our beings, we could suffer no surprise.

'I can't speak for the poet, but I can tell you what Tim means by it.'

Ridiculous and immature though it is, I have a sudden urge to run to the Proscenium and search every volume until I find the perfect poem to send back to him. Stupid; I'm about to see him in person. Anything I want to say to him I can say directly and not in rhyming quatrains.

And he won't hear it as clearly.

'It means that he doesn't trust love,' I tell Waterhouse.

22

13/3/2011

Sam took a deep breath before going back into the interview room. Wayne Cuffley had brought a cloud of bad smell in with him, and it wouldn't leave until he did: a combination of strong aftershave, stale smoke and clothes that hadn't dried soon enough after being washed. 'Your brief's on her way,' Sam said. 'Her name's Rhian Broadribb. If you want, we can wait till she arrives before continuing with the interview.'

'What's the point?' said Cuffley. 'I've got nothing to hide.'

Sam sat down so that he was facing Cuffley across the large table. The nick's audio-visual equipment grew ever more sophisticated, and each interview room had a different set-up. This one could only be operated with a remote control. Sam picked it up and pressed the button that meant, though unhelpfully didn't say, record. 'DS Sam Kombothekra interviewing Wayne Cuffley on Sunday 13 March 2011. Interview resumed at 2.15 p.m. Mr Cuffley, you've confessed to the murder of your son-in-law Jason Cookson. Is that right?'

'Yes.'

'I'd like you to repeat what you told me before we took a break.'

'Why? To check I don't slip up and say something different?'

'It's standard. You might have inadvertently left out an important detail.'

No reaction from Cuffley apart from a visible tensing of the arm muscles. His 'Iron Man' tattoo shifted, stretched. Never had body art been more guilty of false advertising, Sam thought. Cuffley was no hulking superhero. His head was too small for his short, wiry body, and his rats'-tails hair made it look even smaller.

'I killed Jason, I wrapped his body in bubble-wrap, I put it on the back seat of my car and I brought it here, to the police station. My wife Lisa drove the car. I sat in the back seat with the body. I pushed it out of the car in the car park, then we drove away, back home.'

He'd left out a detail he'd included first time round.

'Had you done anything to your car before setting off?' Sam asked.

'You know what I did to the car. I told you: I took off the number plates.'

'Why did you do that, Mr Cuffley?'

'Didn't want the car traced back to me. I wasn't planning to give myself up at that point.'

'So what changed your mind?' This was new territory.

'Lauren. She was panicking. She had no idea where Jason was, and she's not good with stress. She was going out of her mind, not knowing what had happened to him. Best she knows as soon as possible, I thought.' Cuffley exhaled slowly. 'Look, I didn't want to give myself up, but . . . Lauren's my daughter and I love her. She deserves to know the truth about what happened and why. If I didn't owe that to my daughter, you'd never have known it was me. You'd never have found that cunt's body, for a start.'

Sam had come across this phenomenon many times before: killers facing long sentences, keen to let you know how easily they could have got away with it.

'Lisa supported my decision. She said, "What's the point of doing what you did if Lauren's still living in fear of him walking back in at any moment?"'

'That explains why you gave us Cookson's body,' said Sam. 'It doesn't explain why you're confessing.'

Cuffley folded his arms. He looked as if he was trying to stare Sam down. As if he couldn't believe Sam had had the nerve to make such a trivial point. Or perhaps Cuffley's objection was that he didn't know how to respond to it.

'I couldn't have Lauren thinking someone else might have done it, could I?' he said, just as Sam was about to give up hope of getting an answer. 'If she knows it's me, she knows I'm not going to come after her. I did it for her, to protect her – she'll understand that. If she thinks it might be one of Jason's crew, some vendetta, she's going to worry about them targeting her next, isn't she?'

Crew? Did handymen-cum-gardeners have crews?

'They often target the wives, even when they're nothing to do with anything,' Cuffley said.

'Was Lauren scared of Jason?' Sam asked.

'Me and Lisa thought so. She always denied it. Look, can you let me tell her he's dead?'

That he's dead and that you killed him? Talk about two for the price of one.

'I'm afraid that won't be possible, Mr Cuffley. I'm sorry. I need you to tell me what happened between you and Jason Cookson on Friday night.'

'What do you want to know?'

'Where and how did you kill him?'

'In the house.'

'Your house?'

'Yeah. Stabbed the cunt through the heart.' Cuffley smiled as if at a fond memory.

'Where did this happen?'

'I told you: at home.'

'Which room?' Sam asked.

'Lauren's old bedroom.'

'When?'

'Friday night. Bit after midnight.'

'I need the full story, Mr Cuffley. What happened?'

'Me and Lisa were watching telly, about to go to bed. Suddenly there's all kinds of loud banging on the window. Jason. We knew it was, soon as we heard the noise. No one else we know'd turn up at that time.'

'What time was it?' Sam asked.

'I don't know – eleven thirty? He'd come from the pub, pissed up, shouting all kinds of shit about Lauren.'

'What did he say?'

'It was disrespectful to my daughter. I'm not repeating it.' Cuffley sneered. 'What are you going to do, send me to prison? I'm going there anyway.'

'All right, so . . . Jason was shouting unpleasant things about Lauren. Had anything like that happened before?'

'Once or twice,' said Cuffley. 'When he was drunk, which didn't happen very often. This time he was so drunk, his guard was down. He said too much. I'd always thought he probably did worse than get pissed now and then and come round asking me if Lauren was shagging someone else. Which she wasn't, and she never would have, either. She's no slag, my Lauren. She's loyal as anything.'

Sam waited, sensing Cuffley hadn't finished.

'I asked her all the time: is he treating you nice? She always said he was, said he just needed to get it into his head that she wasn't interested in anyone else. He was the jealous type, you could say. Lisa used to worry about it – so did I – but Lauren'd say, "Please, Dad, just leave it." So what could I do?'

Kill him? Had Cuffley forgotten the solution he'd eventually arrived at?

'You say Jason said too much on Friday night. What did he say that was too much?'

'He was mouthing off about what he'd done to Lauren – in the fucking street! Any of our neighbours could have heard. Some probably did. And you can ask me as many times as you like, I'm not telling you what he did to her. Bang me up for a hundred years – I don't give a fuck. My daughter's been through enough. I'm not having her shown up any more.' Cuffley clenched both fists. 'I went to open the door, drag him inside before he made any more of a show of us all. By the time I got there he was on the floor. He'd passed out. I dragged him inside. Lisa said to take him up to Lauren's old room. Best ring Lauren, she said. No way, I told her.'

'Because?'

'I didn't want Lauren coming round to fetch him home. I wanted to fucking kill the twat. And I did,' Cuffley reminded Sam, scratching his Iron Man tattoo. 'I went to the kitchen, got hold of the biggest knife I could find, went back upstairs and stuck it in him – all the way in. Lisa wasn't involved. I didn't tell her what I was planning. She'd have stopped me. You know what women are like.'

Not so much women as people who disapprove of murder, thought Sam. He stood up, walked over to the window. There were metal bars across it, top to bottom. He was tired of spending so much time in this room and others like it. Whatever his next job was, its windows needed to offer a view that was uninterrupted by grey stripes. 'Where did the bubble-wrap come from?' he asked.

'You what?'

'That you wrapped Jason's body in.'

'Oh, right. I bought a roll from Brodigan's yesterday. Look.' Cuffley reached into the pocket of his jeans and pulled out a small white piece of paper. He handed it to Sam.

A receipt.

Sam managed not to thank him. 'When forensics search your house, what evidence will they find that Jason was killed where you say he was?'

Cuffley was unfazed by the question. 'We got rid of the bedding, but the mattress is still there. Lisa won't come back till it's gone. She's taken the kids and gone to her mum's. Put it this way, no one'll be looking at that mattress and imagining someone cut themselves shaving.'

'You and Lisa have children?'

'Two. They're not mine.'

'Were they in the house when you killed Jason?'

'They were asleep,' said Cuffley defensively. 'They saw nothing. I wouldn't have let them see anything. Lisa got them up, dressed and out first thing Saturday morning.'

Oh, well, that's all right, then. Here's your Stepdad of the Year award back. Sorry I doubted you.

'How did Lisa react when you told her what you'd done?' Sam asked.

Cuffley shrugged. 'She'd rather it hadn't happened in her house, but she won't miss Jason. We both had a feeling he wasn't treating Lauren right. We're solid, me and Lise. She drove me here, when I needed to . . . you know, with the body, and she's said she'll stand by me whatever happens. She knows I did what I did for Lauren.'

Something was bothering Sam. It took him a few seconds to pin down what it was. 'How long was it between you killing Jason and telling Lisa what you'd done?' he asked.

'I don't know,' said Cuffley. 'Not long. Few minutes.'

'Why didn't you also tell Lauren?'

'She wasn't there.'

'You could have phoned her. Or gone round to see her – it's not far, is it, from your house to the Dower House?'

Cuffley shrugged.

'You asked me before if I'd let you tell Lauren, and I said no,' Sam reminded him. 'You could have told her yourself, any time between when you killed Jason and when you turned yourself in. Why didn't you?'

'I don't know. I just didn't. I've got a few questions for you.' Cuffley jabbed his finger at Sam. 'Did Tim Breary kill his wife or not? Lauren won't tell me what's going on, but I know something's not right. Did Jason kill her?'

This Sam had not been expecting. He opened his mouth, but Wayne Cuffley was on a roll. 'Why did Lauren end up in Germany and then miss her flight back, so that I had to pay for another one? And who's Gaby Struthers?'

'Tim Breary's been charged with Francine's murder,' Sam said neutrally. 'Do you have any reason to think he might be innocent?'

'No, but I know Lauren's not been right since Francine died. She won't tell me what it's all about. Clams up whenever I ask.'

And when I do. 'Why did you ask who Gaby Struthers is?' said Sam. 'You've met her. You knew who she was before she introduced herself.'

'I know fuck all about her apart from she met Lauren at an airport and hassled her, wouldn't leave her alone. And she's posh and up herself – that's what Lauren said when she rang from Germany in a right state: Gaby Struthers, a snooty bitch. Lauren's shit-scared of her, but she won't tell me why. She said she'd come looking for her at the Dower House, and she did. That's got to be something to do with Francine Breary.'

'I can't discuss the case with you,' Sam told him. Cuffley's questions had put a new one in his mind. 'Why were you at the Dower House on Friday, when you met Gaby? You must have known Lauren wasn't back yet if you'd booked her flight home.'

Cuffley closed his eyes, shook his head. 'I was fucking stupid. Lauren was in such a state about this Gaby Struthers, I couldn't get any sense out of her. I thought Jason might know who she was, and what Lauren was doing in Germany. Course, Lauren hadn't said anything about anything to him, so I fucked up there. I should have realised she was ringing me because she couldn't ring him, because he didn't know.'

'He was angry?' Sam asked.

'He didn't want to lose his cool in front of me, but I could see what was going on underneath,' said Cuffley. 'He could barely keep it together. Guy was a psycho – same since he was eight years old.'

'Eight?' said Sam, surprised.

'We were at primary school together. And secondary.'

'What did he say when you told him about Gaby Struthers?'

'I never did,' said Cuffley. 'I only got as far as asking why Lauren was in Germany. Jason stared at me like he didn't have a clue what I meant. Then he walked off, saying he was going to ring her. I shouted after him did he want me to pick her up from the airport. He said no, he'd do it. The way he said it, it didn't sound right. I nearly went to the airport but . . .' Cuffley stopped. Shrugged. 'It's not like he was going to start smacking her about in the Arrivals Hall, is it? What good would I do by going there? I couldn't stop him taking her home.' He smiled suddenly, as if he and Sam were on the same side. 'I've stopped him now, though.'

'Where were you on Wednesday 16 February?' Sam asked him.

'That when Francine died? I was working. Lauren was lucky: I'd have been working on Friday if I hadn't taken the week off to redecorate the front room. I wouldn't have been able to sort out her flight for her.'

'What's your job?'

'Delivery driver. For Portabas.'

'Which is . . . ?'

'Courier company.'

'I'm going to need to contact them,' said Sam.

'You think I killed Francine? Why would I ask what was going on if I knew *I'd* killed her?'

Sam's questions were different: why would Cuffley have wanted to murder Francine? What motive could he possibly have had? 'You said something interesting to Gaby Struthers at the Dower House on Friday. You said, "Never bullshit a bullshitter". What did you mean by that?'

Cuffley ignored the question and asked one of his own instead: 'Is there a chance Jason could have done it?'

'Killed Francine Breary?' said Sam. 'Why do you ask?'

'If he did it, I want it made public.' Cuffley lifted his head, looked past Sam as if imagining a bigger audience. 'I want the world to know I did us all a favour,' he said.

23

Sunday 13 March 2011

Tim. Tim Breary, standing in front of me.

He doesn't seem big enough, somehow. No, that's wrong. Not what I mean.

His face . . . Is it a face that can explain everything I feel? I used to be sure it was, but after all this time . . .

This isn't an emotional response I'm having, it's an assault: so many sensations screaming in the air that don't feel like mine. I don't recognise their harshness, can't get a firm hold on any one of them. All I can do is stand here as they whirl around me in a thick storm, cutting me off from my surroundings. I'm closer to Tim and further away from myself than I've been for a long time.

'I can't believe you're here,' he says.

I listen for clues in the silence that follows his words. *Who were you then, Tim? Who are you now?*

'Gaby?'

I open my bag, pull out the Valentine's card with the e. e. cummings poem in it.

i carry your heart with me, i carry it in my heart . . .

'Who was The Carrier?' I ask Tim.

Counting the seconds before he answers: *one, two, three, four, five, six, seven* . . .

'Me.'

'No. You didn't send me this card. Kerry did.'

'Me,' he says again. 'I'm The Carrier, Gaby. I wished I'd sent it. As soon as I knew about it, I wished I'd thought of it. Kerry sent it on my behalf, but I'm The Carrier. You must see that. I *do* carry your heart, Gaby. I always have.'

'It was stupid of me to believe it could have been you,' I say. 'I suppose we believe what we want to believe, right?'

'Please sit down.' Tim edges towards the door, as if to block it. He thinks I might walk out.

There are chairs: comfortable ones. What is this room? It's not how I imagined a prison would be.

I sit. 'I didn't work it out until I went to the Dower House and found the e. e. cummings book in your room. I'd read the poem hundreds of times in the card, but it was different when I saw it printed in a book. I thought about all the other poems I'd read in books, all the ones you'd shown me, and I realised the card couldn't have come from you. There's no way you'd have chosen that poem.'

'"And it's you are whatever a moon has always meant / and whatever a sun will always sing is you,"' Tim quotes. '"And this is the wonder that's keeping the stars apart / i carry your heart (i carry it in my heart)".'

He sits down opposite me. He could have come closer. Could be touching me now. There's a free chair next to me.

Simon Waterhouse is outside. Our invisible chaperone. Francine always used to play that role.

This is too strange.

I don't want poetry quoted at me. I want Tim's arms around me. I want to claw at his face in fury. Jason Cookson wouldn't have come after me if Lauren hadn't followed me to Germany. That happened because of Tim: the worst thing that's ever happened to me.

I'm not going to say any of that. I'm going to talk about a poem instead.

'It's nonsense,' I say. 'Moons don't mean anything. Suns don't sing, the stars aren't kept apart by wonder. The poem you asked Simon Waterhouse to give me – that's much more your style: literal. If a poet has something important to say, he says it as simply as he can. Remember?'

Tim nods.

I open the card. My turn to quote. '"To Gaby, I love you. Happy Valentine's Day, with love from The Carrier." Those words were written by Kerry. Not you.'

She knew I'd think you'd sent the card. She knew I'd respond in kind and declare my love. She wasn't trying to help you say what you were too timid to say – she was trying to force a crisis that would break us up. And she succeeded: if there had been no card from The Carrier, I wouldn't have rushed to your office and told you I loved you too. You wouldn't have confided in me about your dream, I wouldn't have gone to Switzerland looking for clues . . . You wouldn't have panicked and told me to get away from you and stay out of your life.

'I should have told you the truth,' Tim says. 'I know that, I just . . . what could I say? I'd have sounded pathetic: "Actually, it's from one of my friends, but coincidentally, that *is* how I feel about you."'

'Did you know Kerry had done it?'

'Dan told me as soon as it was too late to undo. Kerry was too embarrassed to tell me herself. I don't know why she expected me to be angry. I was grateful for her impatience. She knew how I felt about you. Better than I did.'

He believes she did it with the best possible motive. Of course.

'Turns out my literal style isn't suited to realistic human emotions.' Tim smiles sadly. 'Turns out moons do mean something. Suns do sing.'

Feelings. More feelings. I've got too many of my own to deal with without adding Tim's to the mix. What I'm short of is facts.

'So,' I say. 'Who else's handiwork have you taken credit for, more recently? Whose burden of guilt has The Carrier been carrying?'

'I killed Francine, Gaby.'

'Lauren doesn't think so. Neither does Simon Waterhouse. Neither do I.'

'Lauren?' Tim looks at me as if I've said something blasphemous. 'You trust her more than you trust me?'

I don't want to have to answer that question. Love and trust aren't the same thing.

'Tell me, then: why did you do it?'

Uncertainty flickers in his eyes. Then he forces it aside. 'I told the police I didn't have a reason, but that wasn't true.'

'Nothing you're saying is true, Tim. I know you didn't kill Francine.' I open my bag, take out a piece of paper. 'My poem for you,' I say, handing it to him.

'"Lied to like a judge I stepped down,"' he reads aloud. '"My court cleared to the shrieks of the set free. / I know the truth, I know its level sound. / It didn't speak, or didn't speak to me." Glyn Maxwell, "The Sentence".' He smiles. 'Good choice.'

If I smile back at him, will that change the course of the conversation? Of the rest of our lives? Will he relax, see who I really am and tell me the truth, or take it as a sign that I'm willing to live with the lie and pretend it isn't one? *Two roads diverged in a yellow wood . . .*

Who, really, are you, Gaby Struthers? Are you someone who can promise you'll still love him once you know what he's hiding from you, whatever it turns out to be?

Who, really, is Tim Breary? Do you know? What if it's an unattainable fantasy you're in love with and not the flesh-and-blood man in front of you.

'Gaby, you have to believe me.' He leans forward. 'I killed Francine. I picked up a pillow, pressed it down over her face and smothered her. I had a motive – one I didn't tell the police because it won't help me get out of here any quicker. I'm willing to be punished, but that doesn't mean I need to add years to my sentence by admitting why. There's nothing admirable about my reasons for doing what I did, and they're no one's business but mine. And yours. I killed Francine because I've wanted to for a long time. Ever since I told you I never wanted to see you again.'

I can hear how much he wants what he's saying to be true. I still don't believe him.

'I can't explain why I waited years, or why I chose that particular day. Maybe I got tired of not listening to my instincts, not doing what I wanted to do. There was no particular catalyst.' He sounds as if he's reading from a script.

'You don't have to lie to me,' I say. I hate it when people with choices imagine they don't have a choice.

And when people who could leave their wives, or be unfaithful to them if they really wanted to, pretend that they can't?

'Gaby, listen.' Tim sits down beside me, takes my hand. My body buzzes as if in response to an electric current. I want him to kiss me.

I don't mind what the truth is. If he killed Francine, I will still love him. If he didn't kill her but did something worse that he's trying to hide, I'll still love him. Same difference.

'It wasn't only the dream,' he says, his breathing fast and ragged around the words. 'That day at the Proscenium, the last time we saw each other . . . you were so excited about working out what it meant. I didn't want to know. Living with my suspicions and a recurring nightmare was bad enough. I thought knowing for sure would be worse.'

'It won't be. You can still know for sure.'

He carries on as if I haven't spoken. 'Next thing I know you're telling me you've been to Switzerland, to Leukerbad . . .'

'I shouldn't have done that, not without telling you,' I say.

'I'm glad you did. Now. Then, I couldn't get past the dread – of finding out what the dream meant, partly, but it was more than that. You'd gone all the way to Switzerland for *me*. That was how much you loved me, how important I was to you, and there I was: trapped in a miserable marriage that, yes, I'm well aware any other man would have walked out of without a backward glance, but I knew I never could. I never would have, Gaby.'

But you did. Am I missing something?

'You knew I loved you long before I told you about going to Switzerland.'

'I thought I did,' Tim says. 'When I heard you'd gone all the way to Leukerbad for my sake, it . . . I don't know, it kind of brought it home to me. How strongly you must have felt about me.'

'You keep saying "all the way". All the way to Leukerbad, all the way to Switzerland, as if it's New Zealand or something. I'd go to Leukerbad for a lunch or a spa treatment if there were good ones to be had. And if your dream had been set in New Zealand, I'd have gone there. Flying's nothing to me. I do it five times a week.'

Tim sighs. I wish I could tell myself that I don't mean to give him a hard time, and believe myself. Part of me wants to make him suffer, pay him back for all the pain he's caused me.

'Is there anyone apart from me whose recurring dream you'd fly even to London Heathrow to investigate?' he asks. 'Or take a break in your busy schedule to think about for five minutes?'

'No.'

He looks relieved. We understand each other again.

'Gaby, what we had . . . it was the best part of my life without a doubt, but it wasn't real. It was the perfect fantasy. That day, when you told me about going to Switzerland, I thought, no, I don't want this, it's too much. I don't want to know if Francine tried to kill me. Or the guilt of knowing you love me more than you should. I'd let things go too far, and there was no future in it. For both of our sakes, I had to get you away from me and make you stay away.'

'Don't pretend anything you did was for my sake, Tim,' I say carefully. *Stop*, a voice in my head commands. If I don't stop, the bitterness will pour out of me like lava from a volcano. It could destroy everything.

Tim rubs his forehead with his thumb and forefinger. 'You're right. Want to know what I really thought?'

Yes. Also, if you really murdered your wife.

'For years the dream had been bothering me and I'd done nothing about it. Taken no steps to find out what it meant, just hoped it'd go away. Even though I knew it never would. It still hasn't. And you, a few days after hearing the story, you hop on a plane to Switzerland, and you come back saying you've found the answer! It scared me, Gaby. I thought, if she can do that, she can make me leave Francine, and eventually she will.'

'Only if you'd wanted to,' I say, hurt by what I think he's accusing me of.

'I did want to, more than I've ever wanted anything,' Tim says. 'The temptation was getting too dangerous. You think I didn't know what a coward I was? I knew, Gaby. I knew that if I didn't force you away from me, you'd grow to hate me like I hated myself. Why wouldn't I leave a woman I didn't love? We didn't have any children together. What made me think I had to stay? Only the dream? Did I think Francine would hunt me down and kill me, do the job properly second time round?'

I wish I could answer that question.

And the rest.

'You might not want to hear this, but if I'd known how I'd feel as soon as I'd told you we were finished, I think I'd have been able to do it. Leave her. I did, very soon afterwards, when I realised that aching to kill her wasn't a feeling that was going to go away.' Tim looks at me to check I'm taking in what he's saying. 'I was never happy with her, but after I lost you . . .'

'You didn't lose me. You threw me away.'

Tim tries again. 'After that day when we . . . said goodbye, my feelings towards Francine changed. Instantly. It was as if someone had flipped a switch inside me. I couldn't have imagined what a strong urge to kill someone felt like until I experienced it myself. All my energy was going into making sure it didn't happen. I couldn't eat, couldn't sleep, couldn't work. Have you ever wanted to kill someone? No, not wanted to – *known* you're going to? That it's just a matter of when, because, ultimately, you can't stop yourself and actually it's the only thing you want or care about?'

The only person I want to kill is already dead: Jason Cookson.

'I left Francine to save her life,' Tim says.

'Why didn't you tell me? If you weren't with Francine, you could have been with me. Why didn't you make contact?' If I were playing fair, I would warn him that I won't find his answer acceptable, whatever it might be.

He tries to smile, but it doesn't take. 'You'd have told me to fuck right off, wouldn't you?'

I force myself to wait a few seconds before speaking.

'How can you think that? You don't think it – it's an excuse.'

'Yes, you would, Gaby. Your pride wouldn't have allowed you to do anything else. I knew you were way out of my league: Gaby Struthers the genius, the brilliant success story. Whereas I was a nondescript accountant who was one day going to kill his wife.'

'You couldn't be nondescript if you tried,' I tell him, knowing it will make no difference to how he feels about himself.

'I never wanted to be a murderer,' he says quietly. 'I moved halfway across the country to try and make sure I didn't become one. Tried to kill myself instead of Francine, but that didn't work. I chickened out and rang Kerry and Dan, soon as I'd done it. I didn't want to die, Gaby – only because of you. I'd given up on us ever being together, but I knew I couldn't leave a world that had you in it.'

Yet you did nothing. You let me think you and Francine were still together, all those years.

'Why did you go back when Francine had the stroke?' I ask.

'I wanted to be closer to you. If she was bedridden, an invalid . . .'

'What? What, Tim?'

He sighs. 'If I no longer had to be scared of her, then I no longer had to be scared of you – the danger that I'd leave her for you. What could she do, lying in a bed, unable to move or speak?'

'But you didn't make contact. You were back in the Culver Valley, Francine had no power over you any more . . . why didn't you get in touch?'

'I didn't think you'd want to know me, after the way I'd treated you. To be honest, I was happy just knowing you were nearby.'

'I might have been happier too, knowing you'd moved back,' I say angrily. 'You didn't give me the chance, though, did you?'

'I'm sorry, Gaby. I hoped I might . . . I don't know, bump into you in the street one day. I know how pathetic it sounds, believe me. Look on the bright side: when I killed Francine, I was reborn as a man of action, albeit a cold-blooded murderer.'

Not funny.

'You didn't come back to the Culver Valley for me,' I say. 'You could have felt the way you felt about me from anywhere. Francine was the irresistible pull, wasn't she? New, damaged Francine. How desperate were you to see it first-hand?'

'Honestly?' Tim's voice cracks on the word. As if too much truth could break him. 'Pretty desperate. Not for the reason you think. It wasn't about gloating or revenge, not at first. I wanted to see if I was still scared of her. God.' He closes his eyes. 'You have no idea how much I needed the answer to that question. It was like a scientific experiment. I was told before I saw her that her mind was still functioning. Her personality too, presumably. But she couldn't speak at all, could hardly move. So how could she have the power Francine used to have over me?' He shrugs. 'It could have gone either way.'

'What do you mean?'

'I might have been as cowed by her as I'd always been. She was still her, still there, alive. Or . . .' Tim takes a deep breath. 'I might have looked at her lying there and thought, "Fuck you. You have no hold over me now."'

'And? Which did it turn out to be?'

'Neither.' Tim smiles. 'Life's never as simple as you hope it'll be. I knew straight away that I wouldn't be able to answer my question unless I spent more time with her. As much time as I could. I needed to get used to the new Francine if I wanted to shake off the old feelings. I suspected that if I did, if I really immersed myself, the time would come when I wouldn't fear her at all. When I'd be able to say, "You know what, Francine? I'm in love with a woman called Gaby Struthers. You probably don't remember the name – I mentioned her a couple of times, years ago. She used to be a client. Anyway, I want to ask her to marry me, so . . . any ideas about how we sort out a divorce? Obviously you're laid up, so I'll take care of all the admin."' Tim covers his face with his hands and rubs. Trying to rub himself out. 'Sorry,' he says through his fingers.

'Did you still want to kill her?'

He stares at me, unblinking. 'You missed the point,' he says eventually. 'I'm asking you to marry me.'

And if I say yes straight away, I'll lose what little bargaining power I have.

'I love you, Gaby. My wife is dead. Thanks to me. I'm going to be spending the next five to ten years in prison, at a minimum. If that doesn't kill your love for me, then, please, marry me.'

My heart pole-vaults in my chest. I repeat my question. 'Did you still want to kill Francine, when you saw her after she'd had the stroke?'

'I did kill her,' Tim says. 'That's all you need to know.'

'I operate on a want-to-know basis.'

He sighs. 'Yes, I still wanted to kill her. It wasn't the same, though. I also wanted to know whether I was right to want to kill her. Whether the "her" I'd be killing was the same woman I'd been unhappily married to. The more time that passed with her in that state, I just . . . I found it harder to be certain I'd be killing the Francine I wanted to kill. I don't expect it to make sense to you.'

'It makes perfect sense,' I tell him. 'So, what, you watched her for signs? Clues? What could she have done to prove she was the same old Francine? Or to prove she wasn't?'

Tim's staring at the floor. He doesn't like where I'm heading: too close to the truth.

'That's why you didn't kill her,' I say. 'She could have been changed by what she'd been through, or not. You had no way of knowing. All you could do was sit by her bedside and . . . what? Watch for the sign that you knew would never come? Try to interpret the look in her eyes, gauge the emotional atmosphere around her? Meanwhile, the Francine who'd made you suffer was receding further and further into distant memory, where no one could touch her. Getting away with it. I'd have hated her more at that point, I think. Though, like you, I wouldn't have been able to murder the body, not without knowing if the woman I hated was still in it.'

'Please stop,' Tim whispers.

I stand up, pull my hand away from his.

'Do you think I'm perfect, Tim? I'm not. Whatever it is that you're so scared to tell me, whatever you're trying to atone for and think is *worse* than killing Francine, maybe I've done something as bad.'

'I doubt it.'

'And if I had? Would you stop loving me?'

'I'd love you whatever you did.'

I hold up my hands. Why can't he see it? I can't bring myself to tell him what he should know by heart.

'Do you know why I left you alone for so long?' I say. 'It had nothing to do with you telling me it was over. I'd have put up a fight, but . . . I felt unworthy. Of you. All the time we were together, or whatever you want to call it, you never took anything from me.'

'What do you mean?' Tim asks.

'You never asked for anything. It was as if you existed solely for my benefit. You didn't drain me in the way Sean did: expecting things, requiring me to behave in a certain way, making me feel as if I was a resource, put on earth for his convenience – a malfunctioning resource that stopped doing its job properly years ago. You were the opposite: you helped me with my business, you talked to me about poetry. Every single effect you had on my life was a good one, without exception.'

'How does that make you unworthy?' Tim asks.

'My feelings for you were too strong. They felt . . . unnatural. I thought, maybe I'm a selfish bitch who can only love someone who gives constantly and asks for nothing in return.'

Tim's shaking his head. 'I don't know how you can think that. I might have asked for nothing, but nothing wasn't what I got. The opposite.'

'Sean had money,' I say quickly, wanting to get the confession out there before I can change my mind. 'Inherited money, like Dan's. Not as much. Fifty grand. He didn't want to invest any of it. I didn't ask him, obviously . . .'

'Why's it obvious?' Tim sits forward in his chair. 'He was your partner, and it was a brilliant investment opportunity. Put those two things together—'

'The company was nothing to do with Sean. If he'd wanted any part of it, he'd have offered. He knew I was looking for investors.' Why does this still hurt, when I don't love Sean and haven't for a long time? 'I could see his point of view. What I assumed was his point of view, I mean. I never asked him, we never talked about it. He had fifty grand and that was it, the extent of his savings. If my company had nose-dived . . .'

'I knew it wouldn't,' says Tim. 'Sean would have known too, if he'd taken an interest.'

'If he'd thought I could turn his money into ten times as much, he'd have invested,' I say. 'When he didn't offer, I knew he had no faith in me. I let it kill our relationship, and I never said a word, never gave him a chance to explain.' It's a relief to be telling someone. 'Doesn't that make me the lowest of the low? And if you add in the fact that I fell in love with you as well, round about the same time you were hatching brilliant plans to bring in the millions for me . . . And Dan and Kerry, whose money made Sean's seem like small change, were suddenly my second and third favourite people in the world, after you. I liked them so much more because of something that had nothing to do with them, because they'd demonstrated so clearly that they were the opposite of Sean: willing to back me when he wasn't, even though they hardly knew me.'

Tim smiles. 'Are you saying you fell in love with me because I was a talented fundraiser?'

I want to keep that smile forever. I fell in love with him, among other reasons, because he has always known how to make me laugh. 'I don't think I did, but how do I know? It's a bit of a coincidence, isn't it? Sean doesn't offer me so much as a tenner and I fall out of love with him; you solve all my problems and I fall for you head over heels.'

'This one's easily sorted out,' Tim says. 'Do you still love me? I haven't been an accountant for years. I've lost all my contacts. You're unlikely to get any more money out of me.'

'Yes,' I say.

'Then you must want me for me.'

'I want you out of prison,' I tell him. 'I don't care what you've done, Tim. I care that you don't trust me enough to tell me.'

He looks up at me. 'Other people are involved, Gaby. It's not only me.'

'Aren't I one of those other people? The one you want to marry?'

'Yes, of course. I just meant—'

'Then tell me the truth,' I talk over his doubts. 'And don't propose to me again until you have.'

24

14/3/2011

Don't take one. Don't.

Sam stared at the neatly stacked leaflets in the display rack while he waited for the librarian to return. Leaflet, rather, since the rack was stuffed with multiple copies of only one: stiff and expensive-looking, glossy white with black print and a black and white photograph on the front. 'Join the Proscenium Library today', it urged. Sam thought about taking a break between leaving the police and finding a new job. A year spent whiling away the weekdays, doing nothing but reading – it was an appealing prospect, but he doubted Kate would share his enthusiasm.

Sam hadn't read poetry since school. It wasn't the book collection that attracted him so much as the beauty and coolness of the building. The Proscenium was like a church that belonged to the religion of literature. A church with a top-notch restaurant. And totally silent. How was that possible, when Rawndesley city centre was outside? Sam wondered how Gaby Struthers and Tim Breary had managed to start a relationship in a place where raising your voice above half a decibel was forbidden. Did whispering make it more romantic? Did people join the Proscenium in order to hide from the world? Block out reality?

Sam pushed these thoughts from his mind as he saw the librarian approaching. May Geraghty was a tall, thin woman of around sixty with straight, heavy-fringed grey hair. She was mouthing words as she crossed the room, but Sam couldn't make them out. She must have known he wouldn't be able to. Sam recognised the type: awkward, easily flustered, incapable of walking towards somebody face to face without starting a conversation in transit. Feeling her unease, Sam crossed the room to meet her halfway.

'This is a little awkward,' she whispered. The very word that had been in Sam's mind. 'The sonnet you're looking for is by a poet called Lachlan Mackinnon. It's in his 2003 collection *The Jupiter Collisions*.'

Sam wondered if she was having him on. Or if it was some kind of strange test. 'Yes, I know,' he said. Lowering his voice further in response to May Geraghty's pained expression, he whispered, 'You told me that already.' *I thought you were going to find the book*. He'd been impressed when she'd taken one look at his photocopied sheet of paper and immediately recognised the poem.

'Yes.' May nodded, as if the decision to give him the same information twice had been a deliberate and sensible one. 'The thing is, I'm afraid I can't bring the book to you at the moment.' She nodded again. A fan of repetition, evidently.

'Right,' said Sam. 'That's okay.' It was the longest of long shots, in any case. 'Perhaps I could—'

'I can't bring it out to the desk, because it's rather popular today. Our newest proprietor is sitting in the drawing room reading it. If only all our books were as much in demand!' she whispered emphatically.

Newest member. Sam felt a prickle along the back of his neck.

'However,' May Geraghty beamed at him, 'I've just spoken to the gentleman, and he's assured me that he'd be delighted if you'd join him briefly. He'll be more than happy to let you have a quick look. Shall I show you through? And while you're talking to him, I'll get you the film from the CCTV for Friday night.'

'Yes, please,' said Sam.

He followed May Geraghty across the room and along a roped-off corridor, trying not to think about the man he would find at the end of it.

Only one person it can be . . .

Behind the mustard-coloured rope on one side there was a large antique wooden writing desk. Newspapers and magazines covered its surface, laid out in four neat columns, collapsed-domino style. As he and May Geraghty moved further away from the Proscenium's restaurant, the foody smell gave way to the more library-appropriate odours of chalk, dust, old paper. It was a pleasant combination, Sam thought. Comforting.

'Sergeant Kombothekra.' Dan Jose appeared in the doorway ahead. There was a book in his hand. 'I'm not sure if this can accurately be called a coincidence, but it feels like one.'

'Sssh!' May Geraghty hissed, startling the elderly man and woman who were sitting at a table by one of the drawing room's large sash windows.

In a corner to the left of the unlit fire, a red and grey canvas rucksack that Sam had seen at the Dower House leaned against a high-backed green leather armchair – one of a cluster of three arranged around a small circular occasional table.

'Have a seat,' Dan said. 'I can order us some coffee if you'd like? Or tea?'

'No, thanks,' said Sam, who had never understood why he often refused drinks he would have liked to accept. He noticed a trainer protruding from the rucksack, a lace spilling over the side. 'I walked here,' Dan said, looking down at the polished brown leather shoes he was wearing. 'Took me exactly an hour and a half. Another good reason for becoming a member. Or a "proprietor", as May prefers to call us. Good for the body, good for the mind.'

'Is that why you joined?' Sam asked.

'No. Not really. Pretty obvious why I joined, isn't it?'

'Because Tim's a member?'

'Well, not so much that he's a member as . . .' Dan looked down at his lap. 'I don't know. I know how much this place means to him. For as long as he can't make use of it . . . And, if it's all right . . . ?'

'What?' Sam asked.

'I didn't tell Kerry I was coming here. I wasn't planning to tell her I'd joined. Not that it's a secret or anything. I'd just rather she didn't know.'

Sam wondered about Dan Jose's definition of the word 'secret'. It was obviously different from his own.

'She'd disapprove?' Sam asked.

'No. She'd say it was the best idea, and wonder why she hadn't had it herself.' Dan chewed the inside of his lip. 'She'd want us to come here together. Which wouldn't be so bad. It wouldn't be bad at all.' He sounded as if he was trying to convince himself.

'But?' Sam said.

'I don't know. I wasn't planning to join. Like you, I came in to ask about this.' Dan held up the poetry book. 'Spur of the moment, I thought, why not? When Tim's back at home, we can come here together, for lunch.'

'Without Kerry?'

'No, all of us. Of course.'

'But until then, you'd rather come here alone?' Sam persisted.

'I needed some space,' Dan's voice dropped from quiet to barely audible. His face coloured. Did he imagine that the elderly couple by the window were listening avidly? They were doing a convincing impression of two people who had no interest in other human beings, least of all one another.

'I suppose I was trying to test out what it might feel like to be Tim,' Dan said. 'To sit here reading. Thinking the kind of crazy thoughts only Tim would think. Wondering if any of them make sense, when you really examine them.'

Sam wanted to know more, but his instincts told him he'd do better if he changed the subject. 'Can I see the book?' he asked.

Dan handed it to him. 'It's the last poem you're after. "Sonnet", it's called.'

'How do you know what I'm looking for?'

'How do I know Tim gave you a copy of that poem and asked you to pass it on to Gaby Struthers?' Dan answered with a question.

'That too,' Sam said. He flicked through *The Jupiter Collisions*. The sonnet was where Dan had said it would be: at the end. There was no message for Gaby Struthers tucked between the pages, though of course Dan would have got to it first and might have removed it.

Highly unlikely. Sam had always thought so. And having the idea in front of Simon, as Charlie had suggested, had achieved nothing as far as Sam could tell. Simon had grunted non-committally and walked away.

'I know because I let Tim down,' Dan said. 'That's why he had to ask you to give Gaby the poem – because I hadn't done it. He asked me the first time I visited him in prison. He'd written the poem out by hand. For Gaby. I promised I'd give it to her, but when I told Kerry about it she said no, I mustn't, it would be the worst thing I could possibly do.'

'Why?'

Dan sighed. 'It's complicated. The last time Tim sort of sent Gaby a love poem, everything spiralled out of control. Tim ended up trying to take his own life. I think Kerry didn't want to risk that happening again. I'm sure she was right, even if I couldn't follow the logic myself.'

Sam couldn't either. 'So you came here . . . what, to see if you could find the poem?'

Dan nodded. 'I thought there was a reasonable chance, since I knew the poet's name.'

'I didn't,' Sam told him. 'Luckily, the librarian seems to have committed to memory every poem that's ever been written.'

'I thought I might copy it out, since there's no photocopier here,' Dan said. 'Make sure Gaby gets it this time. Or at least try to work out my own opinion, instead of obeying Tim or obeying Kerry. Use my judgement for once.'

'Only about the poem?' Sam asked.

The answering silence lasted nearly ten seconds. Then Dan said, 'No. About everything.'

Sam waited. The words he heard next sent a jolt of adrenaline straight to his heart.

'We've been lying to you. All of us.' Dan flinched as if at bad news. 'I'm not telling you anything you don't know, am I?'

'No.' *Not yet.*

'We all knew what Jason had done to Gaby on Friday night. Sick bastard. We always wondered about him and Lauren, what went on between them, but . . . Look, you have to believe that Kerry and I would never have given Jason an alibi if we'd thought there was even a fractional chance he'd get away with hurting Gaby. Since he was dead—'

'How did you know that?' Sam interrupted.

'We knew.' The shut-down expression on Dan's face told Sam not to push it. 'I don't want to lie to you any more. That means I'm not going to be able to answer every question you ask me.'

Then you're still lying. How's it any different?

'Who killed Francine?' Sam asked, struggling to contain his disappointment.

Silence.

'Was it Tim?'

'I didn't witness Francine's murder,' Dan said, after giving it some thought. 'So all I know is what I've been told. One of the things I've been told is that we all have to lie, and keep lying. I've been told that by more than one person. At first I thought it must be true. Now I'm not so sure. I doubt very much that Gaby Struthers would agree, and she's certainly the cleverest of everyone involved, if we're talking intellect. Or is that too elitist a way to look at it?'

Sam's phone had started to vibrate. He pulled it out of his pocket and glanced at the screen. *Sellers.* 'Dan, I'm grateful for any honesty I can get, but if the only truth you're willing to tell me is that you've been lying, that doesn't really help me. Excuse me, I have to take this call.' Sam hurried out into the corridor with the mustard-coloured rope, wondering how long it would take Dan Jose to progress beyond the stage of suspecting that Gaby Struthers would want the truth told to the crucial next stage (without which all the others were sodding pointless, frankly) of actually telling it.

'Sorry,' Sam said to Sellers, instead of 'Hello'.

'I forgive you, Sarge. You still at the library?'

'I am. I can't really talk.'

May Geraghty had appeared at the far end of the corridor and was peering at Sam disapprovingly. *Oh, get a life, you old bat*, he thought, knowing that if he said it out loud he'd be plagued by remorse for months.

'You can listen, though, right?' said Sellers.

'Go on.'

'I've been to Wayne Cuffley's work. They can account for his whereabouts for the whole of 16 February, so he's ruled out for Francine Breary. I thought it wouldn't do any harm to check on his wife's alibi too, since she helped him dump Jason Cookson's body.'

Good thinking. Never hurts to be thorough. Sam would have said so if he hadn't been subject to May Geraghty's Trappist restrictions.

'Lisa Cuffley's a nail technician, works at a place called Intuitions in Combingham. It's a right dive. I've just been there.'

And?

'Lisa was at work on 16 February too – all day. Sarge, I don't know what made me think of it, but I asked about Friday and Saturday nights just gone, not really expecting anything, and guess what? On Saturday night, Lisa Cuffley had a private booking she'd taken via the salon – a hen party in Spilling, all the girls wanting their nails done and a lesson on how to do it themselves. Obviously she could have been mistaken, but Lisa's boss reckons Lisa was at this party on Saturday from nine till after midnight.'

And therefore not available to give Jason Cookson's dead body a lift to the police station.

'Did you talk to Lisa about it?' Sam asked Sellers. 'Was she there?'

'Not yet. Yeah, she's there now, but I wanted to tell you first, see what you thought.'

'Get back onto Wayne Cuffley's work, ask them about Friday and Saturday nights too,' Sam told him. He turned his back on

May Geraghty's glare of profound and enduring disappointment, pleased to be able to demonstrate that he could withstand a stranger's disapproval in a public setting for up to ten seconds.

'Cookson's blood's all over Cuffley's house and car,' said Sellers.

'So he was probably killed in one, and transported to the nick in the other, but let's not take anything on trust,' Sam said. *Ever again*, he added silently. 'If Cuffley's lying about Lisa being with him when he dropped the body, what's to say that anything he's told us has been the truth?'

25

Monday 14 March 2011

Knocking. Loud. Tim would never knock like this. Which means this can't be him, so I might as well stay where I am: lying on the bed in my hotel room with the curtains shut and the TV screen flickering mutely from its wood veneer cabinet. At least I can't hear the drivel I'm watching.

If I loved Tim less, I'd be working now. Doing something important. I can't imagine ever again being able to concentrate on anything apart from him. It scares me.

More knocking.

I haul myself off the bed, gearing up to yell at another member of hotel staff. Most of them seem to think my 'Do Not Disturb' request applies only for a limited period; that it's impossible for anyone to want to be left alone for as long as that sign's been hanging from my door. I haven't moved from the bed for nearly eight hours.

The maid would only be disappointed if I let her in. There would be nothing for her to do. I haven't had a bath or a shower, no room service, no cups of tea or coffee. I've barely disturbed the bedclothes; the outer cover is still in place, uncreased. I've hardly slept, apart from when I've lost consciousness, fully dressed, for the odd half hour here and there. Each time, I've woken with my heart pounding and Jason Cookson's sickening voice in my head.

Tim's fault.

No. That's not fair. I mustn't let myself think that.

The knocking has developed a threatening tone. Best Western housekeeping wouldn't be so confrontational. I open the door half an inch and see a thin tear-streaked face.

Lauren.

Fear surges up inside me, all the way to my throat.

He can't be with her. He's dead.

She starts in on me from the corridor. 'What the fuck are you playing at? Is this some kind of joke? You tell me to come here and then you won't let me in?'

'I'll let you in.' *Just not yet. I'm not ready.* I stand in front of the door so that she'd have to knock me over to force it open any further. I'm heavier than she is, even after three days of near-starvation. She'd never manage it.

I'm having difficulty believing she's here. I did as Simon Waterhouse asked and delivered my letter to her first thing this morning, but I never thought she'd respond. I added my new contact details thinking I was safe: hotel name, address, room number.

She ran away from me. And now she's back.

Ready or not, I need to talk to her. I have to let her in.

I open the door fully and stand to one side. 'Come in. Sorry. It's . . . I didn't think it'd be you.'

'Well, it is.' The door swings closed behind her, taking with it the light from the corridor. 'Fuckin' hell, Gaby, are you going to open the curtains or what? I can't see a fucking thing.'

Should I give her a hug? The idea embarrasses me. She'd probably punch me in the face.

'I'll open them,' I say. It's true: I would, if I could move. I'm trying to understand why having Lauren here is making me feel so churned up. Nearly as bad as when I first saw Tim in prison. It doesn't make sense: she's nothing to me. She should mean nothing.

I watch as she walks over to the window and yanks open the curtains as if she's trying to rip them off the rail. 'Jason's dead,' she says matter-of-factly.

'I know.'

She picks up the remote control from the bed, turns off the TV. 'Who told you? The police? They tell you who did it?'

Do they know? Obviously they do.

'My dad's turned himself in.'

I look at her 'FATHER' tattoo, then quickly look away. I want to ask all kinds of questions. Should probably wait. Express sympathy first. 'Lauren, I . . . I don't know what to say. That's terrible. Are you . . .' No. Of course she isn't okay.

'I'm fine.' She wipes her eyes.

'I'm not close to my family, and I'm not married, but if my father killed my husband . . .' Once upon a time, I would have been confident that that sort of thing would happen in someone like Lauren's world, but never in mine.

'I begged him not to do it.'

'You were there?' Jesus Christ, did FATHER kill Jason in front of his own daughter?

'Course I was there. I begged him to stay out of it – Lisa did too. He ignored us both. Said he was doing it for me, but I didn't want him to. No one cares what I want – ever. No one listens!'

I stand and watch helplessly as she works herself up into a state.

'I don't want my dad going to prison, Gaby! Another innocent man in prison – I don't want that!'

'What do you mean "another innocent man"? If he killed Jason—'

'Killed Jason?' Lauren laughs bitterly through her tears. 'He didn't. He's *saying* he did, the fucking . . . stupid lying bastard! Haven't you been listening?'

I freeze, my breath suspended in my chest, Lauren's words going round in my mind. Yes, I've been listening. But not under-standing. Not until now.

Course I was there. I begged him to stay out of it.

'You begged your dad not to take the blame,' I say.

Lauren nods frantically. 'At first he was on about burying the body – that was okay, I was all right with that. But then he started saying I'd worry myself sick if Jason stayed missing for long, wondering if he was dead, and some shit about turning himself

in so's the police don't suspect me. Don't ask me what the fuck
he was on about!'

'Did he mean that was what he could tell the police?' I ask.
That's the only way it makes sense.

And it can only mean one thing.

'It's fucking daft if you ask me,' Lauren says. 'I wasn't worried,
was I? I knew Jason was dead.'

She doesn't get it. No surprise there.

'And you knew who killed him,' I say. 'Who killed Jason,
Lauren?'

'Me! I killed him!' Her voice rocks as if someone's shaking her
body.

'Did you . . .' My throat closes on my words, choking them
off. 'Did you do it because of what he did to me?'

'No. Not everything's about you, you know. I did it for Francine,
and Kerry – and for me, mainly, because I was fucking sick of
the bastard, all his shit I'd put up with for years. Maybe a bit
for you,' she adds grudgingly. 'You were the lucky one last Friday
– I got the worst of it in the car, once he'd finished with you.'

'What do you mean you killed him for Francine? She was dead
long before last Friday night.'

'Nothing,' Lauren mutters.

'Revenge?' It's a guess, nothing more.

For Francine, and Kerry.

'Did Jason attack Kerry?' I ask.

Lauren stares at me as if I'm deranged.

'You said you killed him for Kerry.'

She looks as if she's considering denying it.

'Please tell me, Lauren.'

She sits down on the bed. Her legs, in black jeans, look like
two thin pipes. I'm surprised she managed to stand on them for
so long. I'm amazed I'm still standing on mine.

I have an idea. More of a superstition, really. Not based on
anything solid. *If I sit down next to her on the bed, she'll start
to talk.*

Worth a try.

She looks at me oddly. Shuffles to one side, putting more distance between us. 'When we got home on Friday, after . . . When we got back, Jason went upstairs, locked himself in the bathroom,' she says. 'Walked straight past Dan and Kerry, really ignorant, like they weren't there. I knew he wasn't going to be out for at least half an hour. Kerry asked me if I was all right. I must have looked a bit off. You know when someone asks if you're all right and it's just the worst fucking thing they can ask?'

Yes. Know it well.

'I couldn't hold it in, Gaby. I went to pieces, told Kerry everything: what Jason had done to you, forcing me to watch. Look, I thought you were a snobby cow in Germany, I won't pretend I didn't, but you didn't deserve *that*. Ah, you should have seen Kerry, Gaby. She was in pieces, hearing that had happened to you, but what could she do?'

I flinch. She could have contacted the police. She didn't. Because Jason Cookson knew the truth about who killed Francine, and keeping that truth hidden was more important to her.

So that Tim would stay in prison. So that he and I couldn't be together, now that Francine was dead and he should have been free.

'Seeing Kerry like that, I couldn't stand it,' Lauren sobs. 'She's always been good to me, and there she was: a wreck because of Jason, *my* husband. I had to do something, didn't I, to put things right? It was my fault, everything. What he did to you was my fault.'

'No, it wasn't, Lauren. How? You couldn't have stopped him.'

'You'll hate me if I tell you.'

'You tweeted for help.' Later I will thank her. I can't bring myself to do it now.

'You'll think I'm an evil bitch and you won't forgive me,' she insists.

'Forgive you for what, Lauren? Yes, I will. Course I will.'

She covers her face with her hands. 'I said the only thing I could think of, to make him angry with someone else, not me. He found out I'd gone away without telling him. I did that whole lying thing like you said, about being sick at my mum's, and then my dickhead dad went and ruined it all, mouthing off to Jason about me being stuck in Germany, so of course he phones me! I was at the airport, waiting to board the flight Dad had booked me on. "I know where you are," he says. Fuck, I nearly had a heart attack and dropped dead on the spot, I swear. I'd never lied to him before – I wouldn't dare. And then he's like, "What the fuck, she's gone to fucking Germany and told me she's at her mum's?" I don't even know what I said to him, I was that panicking. I started on about wanting to see you because of all this shit with Tim, not that I was ever going to do anything or tell you anything, I just—' She breaks off, shakes her head.

There are so many questions I want to ask, but I'm afraid to interrupt her.

'Jason starts yelling his head off: how fucking mental am I, and what do I think I'm playing at, why can't I keep my nose out? How can he ever trust me again? He wanted to know what I'd told you. I was in bits. I had to tell him I'd not said a word about Tim or Francine. When Jason's in that mood, you tell him what he wants to hear, whatever, doesn't matter. Being honest, I didn't give a shit about Tim *or* you, or even Francine, soon as I heard his voice. I knew he was going to go off on one 'cause I'd lied – worse than anything I'd had from him before. For Jason, thinking I'd ever hide anything from him or sneak around behind his back, that'd be his worst nightmare. I had to think of something.'

I still can't see where she's going with this. What will I never forgive her for? 'So you told him . . . what?'

She swears under her breath, almost reverently. The way some people pray. 'What you said about how you were going to become a lesbian in the middle of the night. If we shared a bed.'

'What?' My voice rings in my ears. Shock comes out as a hollow laugh. A lesbian? This is the very last thing I expected her to say. Then I remember. 'Lauren, I didn't say I was going to become a lesbian. You thought I was coming on to you? I was making a joke.'

Her features have set in a stubborn expression. 'You said you might turn into a lesbian,' she insists. 'Why would you say that if you didn't mean it?'

'Jesus, Lauren, fucking . . .' I can't believe this. I cannot believe it.

'I'm not into anything like that.'

'Neither am I! I was *joking*. You were worried about us sharing a bed. I said, "Don't worry, even if lesbianism overpowers me in my sleep, my good taste will protect us both." Or words to that effect.'

'Yeah, and now you've just said it again! You've admitted it.' *Oh, God.*

I take a deep breath. 'Lauren. What I meant was, even if I suddenly became a lesbian – which never happens to any sleeping heterosexual woman, by the way . . . That was the bedrock of my joke, that absurd hypothetical premise.' Seeing her puzzled frown, I say, 'Oh, forget it! Look, my point was: even in the unlikely event of it happening to me, I wouldn't try my luck with you because I would be a lesbian with good taste. I wouldn't fancy you.'

'Oh. Right.' Hurt flickers across her face. Now she understands.

'Lauren, I'm sorry. I was in a foul mood and I shouldn't have taken it out on you. Tell me what you told Jason. Word for word.'

'I've told you!'

'You told him I threatened to . . . what, molest you? Have my wicked way with you?'

'Yeah! That's what I heard,' she says tearfully. 'How was I supposed to know you were just being a bitch as usual, saying you wouldn't shag me even if you were . . . like that? I told him I'd been straight up about that not being my cup of tea and you said you were going to . . . whatever it was that you said. Overpower me in the night.'

'No. Just . . . *no*.' I'm shaking. Trying to understand why this makes it so much worse. The needlessness of it. The stupidity.

'I'm so sorry, Gaby.'

'And that's why Jason did what he did to me? Because he thought I was some kind of sexual predator, pursuing his wife?'

'I only told him because he's obsessed with it anyway: lesbians. He's always asking me about my mates, even about Kerry – if any of them's ever suggested anything like that with me. Looking for someone else to take his anger out on, to put in his sick pervy fantasies. I didn't realise how far he'd take it, Gaby, I swear. I thought you'd be okay. You're strong – not like me. And I'd never *seen* it before, what he did. It's different when it's you. You don't see it, do you? Not like watching, like when it's someone else.'

I stand up, walk over the window. I want to open it, but there's no way of doing that. Unopenable windows; every claustrophobically crap hotel has them. Four floors down, an endless spool of cars loops round the roundabout. 'Jason didn't attack me because I was asking questions about Francine's death,' I say, hoping that by speaking the truth aloud I'll be able to come to terms with it, make it part of a reality I can live with. 'He didn't do it because he killed her and didn't want me to find out.'

It's your fault, what he did to you. You made a cruel joke at Lauren's expense. What goes around . . .

'He did it because he's a fucking pervert,' Lauren says fiercely. 'Always has been. Always been jealous as fuck, too. I used to like it, first few months. I thought, "All this fuss over me", until he turned nasty with it. He didn't give a fuck if Francine lived or died, didn't care who got sent down for her murder as long as *his* life carried on like normal. He liked having the power over us all: "I keep the secret, you'll do whatever I say."'

'Jason's dead. You don't have to keep any secrets any more.'

Lauren sniffs. 'Are you going to tell the police I killed him?'

'No.'

'Why not? I want them to know. He deserved what he got.'

Sophie Hannah

I can't argue with that. 'Do Dan and Kerry know you killed him?'

'Yeah. They won't say anything. Never do, do they? Stupid bastards. Like me – we're all fucking stupid!' Lauren shudders and pushes her fingers into the corners of her eyes. Tears spill over her hands, down her arms.

'Who killed Francine, Lauren? It wasn't Tim, was it?'

'No,' she says scornfully. 'I told you that the first time I met you. It wasn't him, but he told the police it was, and he wouldn't let any of us say different. He begged me. Kerry did too. Gaby, he got down on his knees, grabbed me round the waist. He was in bits. I couldn't say no, not after what he'd done for me.'

So Simon Waterhouse was right. 'Tim wants to be in prison,' I say, praying I've misunderstood. 'He wants to be convicted of Francine's murder.' *Not to protect someone else. He's pretending he killed her for no one's sake but his own. Taking advantage of someone else's crime, turning it to his own advantage.*

Tim the opportunist. Yes, I can see that.

But why? For God's sake, Tim, or even just for mine – why?

I wonder how Francine's killer feels about it. Does he resent Tim taking credit for his handiwork? Or is he – or she – relieved? Not many murderers are so lucky.

'He's doing it for *you*!' Lauren blurts out. 'All this is because of you, and you haven't got a clue what's going on? That's mad, that is.'

'What do you mean?' How can it have anything to do with me?

'Why don't you ask Kerry? She knows. No one's told me fuck all – they all think I'm stupid, like you do. You lot are all so clever-clever, aren't you?' This is the voice she used with Bodo Neudorf at Dusseldorf airport, the tone that made me dislike her instantly. 'So clever, you think it's okay for an innocent man to get banged up and a killer to walk around free! That's not clever, that's all wrong, that is. I might not be clever enough to book my own flights to Germany, I might have had

382

to get Kerry to do it for me, but I was the one who knew you were going there! If Kerry's so much cleverer than me, how come she believed me when I said I wanted to visit a mate? What mates have I got in Germany? No one! I wouldn't want any German mates, either.'

I want to shake her. 'Who's walking around free, Lauren? Who killed Francine?'

'Don't ask me! I promised Tim I'd never say anything, *never*. I promised Kerry.'

'Lauren, you don't need to be scared of me.'

'I'm not scared,' she fires back, insulted, wrapping her arms around herself for protection.

'I am,' I tell her. 'More than I've ever been. But you don't need to be, not of me. I just want to understand. You read my letter. You know how I feel about Tim.'

'Yeah.' She sneers. 'That's how I felt about Jason when I met him. Thought the sun shone out of his arse. Can't think about that now, or it'll do my head in.'

'What did Tim do for you?' I ask her. 'You said, "After what he'd done for me".'

'He knew about Jason. What he used to do to me. He . . . saw something. It was after we'd been talking one time, me and Tim. Arguing. About Francine. We were losing it with each other, just the two of us in a room together, trying to keep our voices down so Kerry wouldn't come nosing in. Jason got the wrong idea.' Lauren's eyes widen. 'It *was* the wrong idea, Gaby, I swear – there's never been anything like that between me and Tim. Between me and anyone! As if I'd risk it, married to Jason. Kerry and Dan thought Tim ignored me because he was too much of a snob to bother with me, but it wasn't that – he knew Jason'd take it out on me if he paid me any attention. Maybe on him too. That scared the shit out of him. That's why he ignored me, to keep us both safe.'

She's looking through me, as if I'm not here. I'm afraid to move in case I interrupt her train of thought.

'I begged him not to tell Kerry and Dan, and he didn't. They'd not have wanted Jason in the house if they'd known, and if he'd lost his job, he'd have been ten times worse. Most of the time I could keep him under control, no problem. I thought Tim'd be shocked but he understood. Said you never know what goes on in marriages and it's no one else's business.'

Did you say that, Tim? How very fucking convenient. How respectful of Lauren's privacy, to leave her in the clutches of a monster.

'What did you and Tim argue about – the row Jason overheard?'

'Tim heard me talking to Francine. I used to . . . you know, tell her stuff. About Jason, mostly. I couldn't tell anyone else, not without getting a load of hassle: why don't I leave him, why don't I go to the police, find myself someone better? Even you said it to me and I'd told you nothing!'

Because you're so obviously the sort of woman who'd waste her love on a man who doesn't deserve it.

Takes one to know one.

'I didn't blame you for saying it. It's what anyone would have said, except Francine: leave him, he's not worth it. Francine never said anything. She couldn't.'

'You confided in her.'

'Didn't matter what I said to her. She never said anything back.' Lauren smiles. Her words are ambiguous but her expression makes it clear: Francine's unresponsiveness was a point in her favour. The main attraction, even.

I remember thinking something similar on the coach to Cologne: that Lauren was so thick, it didn't matter what I said to her.

'I just needed someone to know, Gaby. Not do anything about it, just *know*. All the worst things that have happened to me in my life – no one knows about them! It was like, I'd look at my mum and dad and Lisa and my mates and think, "Why am I bothering talking to you when you haven't got a clue?"'

'I've felt exactly the same,' I tell her. 'Not being able to tell Sean or any of our friends about Tim.'

'Yeah, you get it,' Lauren says approvingly. 'So did Francine. I could feel it. She didn't judge me like anyone else would have. I could say stuff to her, I could say anything, things I'd never dare say to anyone else. She's the only one who knows . . . knew . . . the whole story about me and Jason. The things he used to do.' Lauren wipes her eyes. 'I don't see why Tim couldn't just leave me alone. He had to stick his fucking nose in.'

'What did he do?' I ask.

'He's like you, Tim.' Lauren frowns. 'I never understand half of what he says, all that saying bits of poems, like talking in riddles. I knew what he was trying to do, though: turn me against her.'

'Against Francine?'

'He didn't like us being close. Said I wouldn't have wanted to tell her anything if I'd known her before. She wasn't kind or understanding, she wouldn't have been my friend. Horrible things I didn't want to hear. Francine *was* my friend, my best friend.' Lauren scratches at her tears with her fingernails, as if they're insects on her face. 'So what if she couldn't talk? If you spend that much time with someone, you *know* them. You know what's in their heart. You pick it up. They don't need to say anything. There was a bond between Francine and me. She knew how hard it was for me, like I knew it was hard for her. But I . . . for a long time, I thought . . . I mean, like, the worst had already happened to her, you know? I never thought that one day she might not be there and I'd be back to having no one. Never prepared myself for it. Stupid, isn't it: thinking nothing shit can happen to someone if something really shit already has?'

'It's natural,' I say automatically. I'm not sure if I understand or mean any of the things I'm saying any more. Part of me has shut down.

'I couldn't stop them, Gaby. There was nothing I could do. I'm just a care assistant, and those three . . . no one would have believed me! No one cared about Francine but me!'

'Stop what? Lauren, calm down. Tell me. I'm on your side.'

She shakes her head violently. 'I wish I could tell her about Jason,' she says.

About killing Jason: that's what she means.

'Tell me,' I say. 'I won't say anything. I'll just listen.'

'You?' She laughs. 'That's a joke. Only person you want to listen to's yourself.'

'No. I want to listen to you.'

'What do you want to know?' she asks sullenly. 'I took him down the pub, got him pissed up, took him round my dad's. He passed out. I sat with Dad and Lisa, watched telly for a bit. I didn't tell them what I was going to do. They had no idea. I told them I was off to make a brew, got a knife out of the kitchen drawer, went upstairs and just . . .' She holds her hands together above her head and mimes stabbing. 'Like that. I didn't feel anything when I did it, just, "How the fuck am I going to tell Dad and Lisa what I've done?" In their house. I couldn't have done it at home, though.' She lets out a high-pitched squeal of a laugh. 'Can you imagine it? Kerry and Dan aren't the kind of people who'd want someone stabbed to death in their posh house, are they?'

'Francine was murdered in their house,' I remind her. *Who? Who did it, Lauren?*

'There was no blood, though,' she says, as if I've completely missed the point.

This is really happening. I'm debating messy and tidy murders and the kinds of houses they belong in. With Lauren Cookson.

'Do you think I'm evil for killing him?' she asks me.

'I think you should get a medal,' I say honestly.

'Really?' The hope in her eyes is painful to see.

'Why do you care what I think? I'm just a snooty cow you hardly know.'

'That's true.' Lauren smiles through her tears. 'I don't know. Everyone else seems to think the sun shines out of your arse and you'll have all the answers. I wanted to see if they were right. You asked me why I followed you to Germany, in your letter. That's why.'

I'm at a loss. Did I miss the part where she explained? 'What do you mean?'

'Whenever I heard Kerry and Dan at each other's throats after Francine died, it was always about you. Never in front of Tim, but whenever he wasn't earwigging, they started up. Kerry kept saying what about talking to you, that you'd know what to do. Dan said no, Tim'd never forgive them. Sometimes it was the other way round – they swapped sides. Went round and round in circles. And you should have heard Tim, the way he used to go on about you. I was sick of the lot of them. I thought, right, let's find this Gaby Struthers. Everyone keeps saying how great she is and how she'll know what to do, so let's see if she does. Maybe I'll tell her, I thought. It wasn't right, what was happening – whatever Tim wanted, however good he was at making it *sound* okay. I was in a right state. You saw me. I was losing it, doing my head in with it. I wanted to see you, see what all the fuss was about. Soon as I did, I thought, "No way can I talk to that fucking snooty bitch." Sorry, but you know what I mean.'

'You heard Tim talking about me to Dan and Kerry?' I say.

'No.' Lauren looks confused. 'Why?'

'You said you'd heard him talk about me.'

'Not to Kerry and Dan. Only to Francine.'

'Francine?'

Lauren nods. 'I wasn't the only one who used to talk to her. Tim did too. Didn't like sharing her with me, either. He wanted her all to himself.'

No. He hated her. He left her. He went back, yes, but not because he wanted her.

'Who killed Francine, Lauren? Please.'

She looks at the door. 'If I tell you who, you'll want to know why.'

'Yes. I will.'

'I should have showed you the letters in Germany.' She starts crying again. 'If I wasn't such a fucking chicken-shit bastard, I'd have showed you then, told you everything.'

'What letters?'

'They were under Francine's mattress. Then when she died and they chucked out her bed, Dan moved them. Hid them in Tim's room, under his mattress instead. No one knew I knew where they'd got to, but I did. They all thought I wouldn't notice what was going on right under my nose. Kerry knew I knew and she knew I didn't like it, but she didn't think I'd do anything. Stupid twats! I bet they all think those letters are still there. I thought, one day one of them's going to decide they want burning and then I'll never be able to explain why Francine died. I haven't got the gift of the gab like Kerry or Tim. Or you. That's why I took them: they explain it better than I could.'

'So you took the letters with you to Germany? So that Kerry and Dan couldn't destroy them?'

Lauren nods. 'I was going to give them to you. But then I just . . . couldn't.'

'Where are they? Show me them, Lauren. Please.'

'I can't. I haven't got them any more.'

No. Don't let her say what I think she's about to say.

'Where are they?'

'In that bathroom, in that crappy hotel. I took my bag in with me. They were in there. I put them in the toilet whatsit, that bit on top. I thought, they won't get wet – I had them in a plastic thing. I wish I hadn't left them now. I panicked when you started going on about Tim, trying to get the story out of me.'

I pull my BlackBerry out of my pocket, key in the number Simon Waterhouse gave me: his mobile phone.

'Do you think they'll still be there?' Lauren asks. 'I should have given them to you. I knew I should.'

'Hello? Gaby?' Simon Waterhouse sounds startled, as if I've woken him from a nightmare.

How will he feel when I tell him there are letters he needs to read in a toilet cistern on the top floor of a shabby hotel by the side of a dual carriageway in Germany?

POLICE EXHIBIT 1437B/SK – TRANSCRIPT OF HANDWRITTEN
LETTER FROM DANIEL JOSE TO FRANCINE BREARY DATED 13
FEBRUARY 2011

Francine, there's something Kerry and I haven't been doing enough
of in our letters, and that's telling you things you don't already
know. We seem to be mainly giving you our perspective on past
events. Maybe that's okay, I don't know. But the point of our doing
this letter thing is to support Tim. There's supposed to be only one
difference between what he's doing and what we're doing: he's
saying it out loud, sitting by your bedside day after day, and we're
writing it down so that Lauren can't overhear anything.

I've eavesdropped on Tim's one-sided conversations with you. He
doesn't tell you anything you already know – he's careful about
that. I could be wrong, but I think he plans what he's going to say
to you in advance, before going into your room. There's a neatness
to his monologues. Each one contains a revelation of some kind,
even if it's only that he and Gaby first kissed in the porch of the
Proscenium Library on this or that date. No big deal to anyone
apart from Tim, Gaby and you: the long-suffering betrayed wife.

At least you're not bored, I suppose. Tim wants you on the edge of
your seat (sorry – you know what I mean), scared of what you're
going to hear next. It's all what a stand-up comedian might call
new material, though there's nothing funny about it. Gaby's his
only subject matter, and he's incapable of anything but total
seriousness when it comes to her. He never runs out of new things
to tell you: how she built up her company, endless technical detail

about her creation, Taction, that no one but an expert or someone in love with an expert could hope to understand, her amazing website, witty remarks she made four years ago about trivial things. Tim must have a photographic memory. Or nothing else in his life that matters to him.

Having said that, I've never heard him come out and tell you he loves Gaby, not in so many words. Still, you'd have to be pretty dense not to have worked it out, Francine. No man wants to talk endlessly about a woman unless he's got it pretty bad. Kerry and I didn't quite realise the level of Tim's obsession with Gaby until we heard him talk to you about her.

Since I can't be bothered doing any more work today, I'm going to follow Tim's example and tell you two things you don't already know. And like him, I've planned both in advance. One is something no one knows: I'm starting to think I've been wasting my time for the past God knows how many years. I want to give up on my PhD, with immediate effect, and never see the damn thing again. Kerry doesn't know. She's against giving up on anything and would try to talk me out of it. And probably succeed. The truth is, I'm not sure I can be bothered thinking or writing any more about how the kinds of archetypes and stories we're attracted to affects our attitudes to financial risk. It's too interdisciplinary-messy and, at the same time, just too sodding obvious: person number 1's worst fear is that he'll end up having to tell a story about himself in which he was too timid to grab an amazing chance, and, as a result, missed out on the rewards enjoyed by those braver than him. Person number 2's least favourite hypothetical life narrative is the one in which he stakes all his hard-earned savings on a long shot and is left regretting his recklessness in abject poverty. Person number 1 is obviously more likely to invest £100,000 in a high-risk illiquid start-up than person number 2.

There: I've said it in roughly a hundred words. Even you'd understand, Francine, though I'm sure you'd find a way to condemn persons 1 and 2 equally. But you'd grasp the basic concept. Any fool would. So why am I devoting years to writing a PhD on it, months drafting questionnaires and gathering data to prove what I already know? What's the point? Even if I finish and publish it, all that'll happen is a load of economic theory windbags'll queue up to shout me down in journals no one reads. They're already gearing up, apoplectic with rage because I've brought a wishy-washy imposter like narrative archetype into their precious economics.

You must be wondering why I'm telling you something that's nothing to do with you, Francine. If I give up on my PhD or if I don't, what do you care? Tim wouldn't waste time telling you a random piece of news, would he? At the risk of sounding big-headed, I think there's something he's forgotten to take into account: how affronted you always were when someone else took centre stage, even for five minutes. You were incapable of sitting and listening to another person's news without starting to seethe and act up because you'd lost the spotlight. Kerry and I noticed it the first time Tim brought you round to ours for dinner, the first time we ever met you. We were mystified and couldn't for the life of us work out what had happened to him. Suddenly, his long, entertaining rants that had always been the best part of the evenings we spent together were no more. Every question we asked him, he answered as succinctly and humourlessly as possible before turning the focus back to you. 'Fine, thanks, not much happening at the moment.' The 'fine, thanks' was weird enough in itself. Even weirder was 'Francine's having an exciting time at work, though, aren't you, darling?'

An exciting time at work. Never mind the fact that you were a pensions lawyer, Francine – it was such an un-Tim thing to say. Kerry and I couldn't work out what the hell had happened to him at first. Then we realised. Actually, it was a bit of a horror film moment: the way the trusting heroine feels when she stumbles across a cobwebby black and white photograph album and finds a picture of her husband lying in a coffin with the undertaker's sutures all over his body, and realises he's been dead for years and that's why he's got that strange stitched Y-shape on his torso that he's always claimed was a tennis injury. (Please pardon facetiousness and intrusion of random narrative archetype. As I said, I've been working on the PhD all morning.)

I think it would wound you, Francine, to have to listen to me chunter on about my career anxieties. It would cause your ego pain to be forced into a minor role – mute listener – especially knowing you won't get your turn when I'm through.

Moving on to my second planned agenda item, the one that directly relates to you: remember when you and Tim got me *Imperium* by Robert Harris for my birthday? It's funny, I've read Kerry's latest letter to you and she didn't even mention the Robert Harris aspect of the evening. Making Memories Night, to give it its official title. You told me as I was opening my present from you and Tim that I probably already had it, but that Tim had insisted I didn't. You said it as if Tim, being Tim, was bound to be wrong. In fact, he'd been spotlessly correct until earlier that same day when not one but two people had presented me with copies: my boss and my secretary. Kerry laughed when I told her. 'You'll have to start putting the word about that you've gone off Robert Harris, otherwise you're going to be getting twenty copies of his latest book for birthdays and Christmases for the rest of your life.' (Incidentally, I'm sure a quick statistical analysis would reveal that your biggest flare-ups were on other people's special occasions, Francine.)

I ripped off the paper in one corner, saw the '*Imp*' of the title at the same time Kerry did. She was sitting next to me on the sofa. We both knew what had to happen. Impossible as it would have been to explain to anyone who wasn't part of our crazy foursome set-up, we knew it was inconceivable that we'd laugh and say, 'Actually, this is the third copy to arrive so far.' Tim had assured you I didn't have it. If he turned out to have been mistaken, you'd have made him suffer. Thanks to him, you'd have been someone who'd messed up the buying of a present, which, in your eyes, would have made you look bad in public.

I launched into a pretence of never having seen *Imperium* before and, for added security, not even knowing Robert Harris had a new thriller out. Kerry stood up and said she was just nipping to the loo. I knew it was an excuse. She wasn't willing to risk you going upstairs for some reason and seeing the two *Imperium*s in our bedroom. (Imperia?) Do you know what she did, Francine? She got the other two copies of the book, wrapped them in a shirt and stuffed them under the mattress of our bed. I'd have done the same if I hadn't needed to stay put and make an elaborate show of loving your present more than I loved life itself, to make sure you felt properly appreciated.

Tim was trying to look relaxed, but I knew he knew too. He'd guessed from my face, and Kerry's, though he probably thought it was only one other copy of *Imperium* we were afraid of you finding and not two. Imagine that, Francine: that level of panic, over something so ridiculously trivial. That's what you did to the people around you. That's why I don't worry, like Kerry does, that Lauren knows what's going on. She thinks Lauren might have seen her shove a letter under your mattress. 'And that matters why?' I asked. 'What can Lauren do that can harm us?' It's not about harm for Kerry, though. It's about guilt. She couldn't bear for Lauren (or anyone, actually) to think she was doing anything wrong. She's also scared Lauren might confront Tim and make him feel guilty. I can understand that. In Kerry's mind, Tim feeling bad equals Tim probably ending up dead.

Hence she's always encouraged his long 'chats' with you, Francine. She talks about it as if it's a kind of therapy for him. And hence this: our one-sided correspondence with you, and with the proviso that all our letters must be written in your room, sitting by your bed. This is how Kerry decided she and I would support Tim.

The drawback of these letters, from my point of view, is precisely what Kerry thinks is their best feature: you can't read them, and we can't read them aloud to you – Kerry's rules. So you don't know what's in them. It's the only way of being fair to everyone, in the opinion of my wise wife.

Who I think and have always thought, Francine, is in love with your unwise husband. It's lucky she's not his type physically or I might have lost her years ago.

I don't especially want to be fair to you. When were you ever fair to Tim? Or any of us? I think I'm going to read you this letter. Kerry's out. She won't know. I'll feel guilty about keeping it from her, but that's not enough to stop me.

Here goes.

26

16/3/2011

Sam took the last of the letters from Simon. They were sitting on the floor of a chairless attic room in the Haffner Hotel in Germany, the room Gaby Struthers and Lauren Cookson would have shared when their plane was delayed, if Lauren hadn't fled. Who wouldn't run, Sam thought, from a room like this? It was a space no one would choose to enter, let alone spend time in, unless what they had in mind was a death pact or the filming of a movie in which everybody was supposed to be depressed all the time. The curtains were mottled with filth, the carpet was a collage of shiny bald patches. A previous resident of the room had discarded a shrivelled pink Elastoplast in a corner that the cleaners, assuming any ever came up here, had failed to spot and remove. There was nothing on the walls apart from jagged lightning-flashes of plaster where the paper had peeled off. Actually, the walls reminded Sam of Simon and Charlie's living room, but he'd kept that thought to himself.

A stale smell hung in the air: old alcohol and sweat. It made Sam wish he'd never left the civilised Proscenium Library.

He passed the letter back to Simon once he'd read it. 'More of the same.'

'I'm sorry.'

'No, it's not your fault. You were right: a plastic wallet full of hidden letters in a hotel toilet cistern in Germany, brought all the way from Lower Heckencott in the Culver Valley – it *sounds* as if it's going to be useful. Sounds as if it could hardly fail to be significant. Yeah, we could have sent uniforms to pick it up, but—'

'Not what I meant,' Simon cut him off. 'I'm sorry about . . . you know. How I've been. You were unlucky, that's all.' He dropped the pile of letters on the floor as if they were nothing but an irritation, and drew his knees up to his chin. He looked like someone waiting for a giant to reach down and whack him over the head.

Sam waited.

'I'm low-level angry most of the time, never really know why,' Simon told him. 'You got the brunt of it. This time.'

Sam wanted to meet him halfway, but was afraid that if he said, 'Well, to be fair, I should probably have told you sooner,' things might take a turn for the less cordial; Simon might retract his apology. 'Let's put it behind us,' he said instead, pleased to be forgiven whether he'd done anything wrong or not.

'It was useful,' said Simon.

'For you, maybe.' Sam smiled to take the sting out of his words. 'You thrive on conflict and drama.' *You thrive on not thriving. Turn your own negative energy and everyone else's into . . .* Sam didn't know what.

'No, I meant the wallet. The letters. Read them again.'

Sam picked up the one nearest to him. 'What, you think they tell us something?'

'I think they've told me something they've not told you. They might if you ask nicely.'

'Not who killed Francine?' Sam wouldn't have missed that.

'Something more important than who. They tell us why.'

'I can't see it. I see hearts and grudges and insecurities and regrets poured out on paper, that's all.' Sam fanned out the pages on the floor in front of him. Odd words jumped out: 'memories', 'hammer', 'twist'. He knew looking like this wasn't going to help, but he was too impatient to read the whole lot again. Was Simon going to make him?

Any chance of cutting me a bit of slack, as I'm resigning soon? In a few weeks it won't be my job to work things out any more. Sam had been trying to think of a way to broach the subject all day; the last thing he wanted was for Simon to take his decision personally, and he couldn't think how to phrase it to ensure that didn't happen.

'I can't see any motive here.' He gestured at the letters. 'Can't see a why.'

Simon nodded. 'You won't do. Because you don't know who.'

'But we agreed these letters don't tell us who.' *Which means* . . . 'You know who killed Francine?'

'You would too if you weren't thinking of killing her in the wrong way.'

It took Sam a few seconds to disentangle the grammar: 'thinking in the wrong way about killing her'. That had to be what Simon meant.

'Who? Dan Jose?'

'Dan?' Simon grinned at the idea. 'The man who took a brave moral stand against the deception that's landed his best friend in prison by admitting he's been lying about everything and then still refusing to tell you the truth? He'd never kill anyone – he'd never do anything. Kerry Jose?' Simon anticipated Sam's next question. 'No. You read Dan's assessment of her: wants to be fair to everyone. Needs to be seen to be good. She admits in one of the letters that she'd quite like to kill Francine, but it's a fantasy – she knows she never will. Lauren: the only one in the Dower House who actually liked Francine. If you can like a slab of meat lying prone in a bed,' Simon added as an afterthought. 'Lauren never knew the bitch who made everyone's lives a misery. She missed out on her family Christmas to be with Francine, lobbied to have her included in the Dower House celebrations. And tended to her needs, day after day – paid extremely well for it, too, with the perk of five-star accommodation and a job for her husband thrown in. Why would Lauren want to murder Francine? She wouldn't. There's no way.'

'Then . . . Jason?' Sam asked, knowing that it was the wrong answer and that was why Simon was steering him towards it. He was ruthless when he had something to show off about. Sam had come to the conclusion that he enjoyed making other people feel stupid; he was an intellectual sadist. This knowledge did nothing to diminish Sam's affection for him. 'Do you also know who killed Jason?'

'That was Lauren,' said Simon, as if it was obvious and hardly mattered. 'Wayne Cuffley might have been trying to protect her, but he gave the game away with his inconsistencies, asking you if he could be the one to tell her Jason was dead. As you pointed out, he could have done it already before turning himself in. According to him, he's first taken the plates off his car and delivered us the body so that Lauren doesn't have to worry if Jason's dead or alive, then he's come and handed himself in so that she doesn't have to live with the uncertainty of not knowing who knifed her husband. If he's that bothered about Lauren being kept up to speed, there's no way he wouldn't have told her what he'd done while he was still free and in control. His story doesn't add up. Only purpose of telling it was to drum it into our heads: Lauren doesn't know what's happened to Jason – one, she doesn't know he's dead; two, she doesn't know who killed him. All bullshit.'

Lauren cared about Francine. Lauren killed Jason. Put the two together . . .

'Jason didn't kill Francine,' said Simon, apparently reading Sam's mind. 'He saw who did, though. Through a window.'

Awe wasn't an emotion Sam felt often, but he felt it now. 'How do you know?'

Simon frowned, running through his theory one last time before presenting it, to check the logic was sound. 'Obvious. The lie about where Jason was when Lauren found the body and screamed, the one parroted by everyone at the Dower House. Since Jason didn't kill Francine, why not tell the truth about where he was and what he was doing when she died?'

'But . . . how do you know he didn't kill her?' Sam asked again. If he'd already been given the answer, he'd missed it.

'Because I know who did,' Simon said. All so simple, if your name was Waterhouse. 'So did Jason. He knew before everyone else, apart from Francine herself and the person who smothered her with a pillow. He was outside, cleaning the windows like everyone said in the *second* version of the story. Except it wasn't the lounge windows at the front of the house, it was Francine's bedroom windows. Also ground floor, but at the back. When Charlie started grilling Kerry about what exactly Jason had been doing in the lounge – had he been repairing something, and if so, what? – Kerry panicked, and reached for what she hoped would be a more plausible lie: Jason had been cleaning windows. True. Any good liar knows to pack as much truth as possible into a lie. Kerry changed one detail: lounge, she said, instead of bedroom. It was crucial that no one found out Jason was an eyewitness. He'd have been asked to describe what he saw. We'd have grilled him too hard, expected too much detail. His version would have been checked against Tim Breary's confession – it was too risky, when what he'd have been describing would have been a lie. He could easily have slipped up over any number of tiny points. Simpler to have him not witness anything and just recite Tim's version of what happened, like everyone else at the Dower House.'

Tim Breary. In all the speculation, Sam had almost forgotten him.

'So if it wasn't Kerry, Dan, Lauren or Jason, then . . .'

'Tim must have murdered Francine?' Simon completed Sam's question for him. 'No. He mustn't and he didn't. Tim wanted Francine alive, not dead. After what she'd put him through, he couldn't get enough of the new balance of power between them. Of not being scared of her, of making her suffer for a change. Words can be weapons just as much as a knife or a gun is, and Francine couldn't fight back. Tim was addicted to tormenting her: telling her stories about Gaby Struthers, the woman he really loved. Reading her poems about decaying forty-year-old bodies. Knowing that, however much Francine hated hearing it all, she couldn't get away. He wouldn't have put an end to that, I don't think – ever. Why do you think he didn't make a beeline for Gaby Struthers, soon as he moved back to the Culver Valley after Francine's stroke?'

Did Sam need to bother shaking his head in bafflement, or would Simon take it as read?

'He still wasn't free, that's why. Still wasn't available. He craved Francine in a way he never had before she was laid low, got a power kick out of punishing her. The urge to carry on was so overwhelming, even the thought of Gaby nearby wasn't enough incentive to give up. Breary was addicted. Didn't want to face up to it, though, so he told himself he was conducting an inquiry: was Francine the same Francine he'd known, or not? How to arrive at an accurate ethical evaluation of her? Some inquiry, that never gathers any data,' Simon said dismissively.

Sam was only half listening. He was trying to think. Gaby Struthers had an alibi; she couldn't have done it. *Who, then?* 'I'm out of ideas,' he admitted. 'Even desperate ones. If you want me to know who murdered Francine, you're going to have to tell me.' *Sorry to be a disappointment. Again.*

'No one murdered Francine,' said Simon.

'*No one?* But . . .'

'You've seen her dead body?' That infuriating half-smile again.

'Yes!' *More than once.* What the hell was he implying? It had to be a joke.

'She's dead, for sure,' Simon said. 'Legally, it might or might not be murder. Depends on the judge, I suppose. Or a jury. I wouldn't call it murder, though, personally. I'd call it the opposite.'

'Who killed her?' Sam asked. Simon couldn't quibble about the word 'killed', surely.

'The person who'd have wanted to murder her least of all. Her only ally at the Dower House.'

'You mean . . . Lauren?'

Simon nodded.

But a minute ago, he'd said . . . No, Sam realised. Simon had said only that Lauren hadn't murdered Francine. Not that she hadn't killed her.

'What I'm wondering is, did Kerry and Dan Jose share the addiction? Did they get the same sadistic kick out of writing these letters that Tim Breary did from his little bedside chats, or were they doing it just to give Tim moral support, like Dan Jose says in the last letter?'

Sam was at a loss. He decided to sit it out, be a good listener, since he couldn't contribute. *Like Francine Breary.*

'Moral support,' Simon repeated with contempt. 'Letters that very thoughtfully and analytically rip Francine's character to pieces – taunt her and condemn her in any and every way they possibly can. Talk about kicking a person when they're down. Meanwhile, Breary's doing the verbal equivalent – torturing his wife, basically. What else can you call it? There she is, trapped in a bed, can't move or speak, and he's telling her all the things he knows are going to make her wish she was dead if she doesn't already. It's psychological torture. And Kerry Jose, who knows all about it – she thinks it's good therapy for Tim! Tim's processing his fear, she thinks – getting it out of his system, making progress. How sick is that? Kerry decides it's okay to let him punish and emotionally torture an invalid who can't fight back, and Dan goes along with it.'

Simon swore under his breath, looked up at the ceiling. 'Day after day, a punishment that never ends. Francine gets it rammed down her throat over and over again that her life was never what she thought it was, her husband never loved her like he said he did. She's become nothing more than a receptacle for his bitterness. And Kerry's, and Dan's. The letters, which are Kerry's idea of *fair*, let's not forget! That's balanced, in their crazy heads. The well-adjusted moderate response: writing long vicious denunciations that are oh-so-polite and articulate and sensitively worded, so it's almost impossible to spot what's really going on.'

He was right. Right that it was hard to spot, too. Kerry's and

Dan's accounts painted Tim as the chief victim, with the two of them coming a close joint second. The first time he'd read the letters, even knowing Francine had been murdered, Sam had had little sympathy for her; such was the skill of Kerry and Dan Jose's narrative.

'Kerry and Dan want it both ways,' Simon went on angrily. 'They want to show solidarity with Tim, but they don't want to harm Francine, or so they imagine. So they never read her their letters. But they write them – sit there for hours by her bed, writing them, stirring in all their resentment. Does it occur to them that Francine might wonder what the fuck they're doing, sitting there writing shit she never gets to see? And then stuffing them under her mattress! So she knows she's lying on it, whatever it is.'

'If Francine was as much of a control freak as the letters suggest, she'd have hated that,' Sam said, pleased to be able to contribute something at last. 'Maybe they knew that not knowing what they were writing would torment her. That could have been part of the buzz.'

'For Kerry, yeah,' Simon agreed. 'Could well have been. If you think you're too good and fair to ever hurt anyone deliberately, you've got to find a way of doing it that you can hide – even from yourself. Especially from yourself. I think that's what the letters were, for Kerry. Dan . . . I don't know. Best-case scenario, he was trying to support his friend and his wife, and Francine was a means to that end. If he didn't want to make her suffer, then he treated her like an object. Like a . . . muse for bile and hate. It might not be the same straightforward emotional torture Tim Breary was serving up, but it's still pretty depraved.'

'So Lauren knew what they were all doing?' Sam asked. 'She must have done.'

'Must have,' Simon echoed. 'Course, part of the motivation behind Kerry's rule about her and Dan never reading their letters aloud was that: she couldn't risk Lauren hearing. She must have known Lauren had overheard Tim a fair bit – in Francine's room, persecuting her with his stories about Gaby. Kerry didn't want Lauren to realise Francine was being assaulted from all sides – not by one person but by three. Three clever, articulate attackers who saw nothing wrong with making a woman who couldn't move or speak lie there day after day, soaking up all their venom.'

'Do you think that's what Kerry meant when she wrote that someone would kill Francine soon, but she didn't know who?' Sam asked. 'Was she thinking of Lauren?'

'Lauren or Tim,' Simon answered without hesitation. 'Kerry was terrified one of them'd do it, but she didn't know which. Lauren, to get Francine the fuck out of that house where she was being abused and mistreated, or Tim because once he wasn't scared of Francine any more and he'd said everything he wanted to say to her, once she served no function for him—'

'But – sorry, I'm interrupting – in one of the letters Kerry begs Francine to stop breathing.'

'Yeah, but not because she wants her dead and gone.' Simon shuddered. 'That's Kerry being fair again: "Spare yourself the ordeal of getting murdered, Francine – and don't forget to be grateful to me for the tip-off." And don't forget . . .' – Simon jabbed his finger in the air to make it clear that he meant Sam this time – '. . . all these letters are performance pieces. Everyone's editing themselves, thinking the others are going to be reading the results at some point. They all know where the letters are hidden – why wouldn't they read each others'? Dan's hoping Kerry'll be pulled up short by what he wrote about her being in love with Tim Breary. If she brings it up and tells him there's not a single grain of truth in his suspicion, he'll feel better. If she doesn't mention it, he'll feel worse.'

'So . . .' Sam struggled to keep up. 'Kerry *didn't* want Francine to die?'

'Did she fuck! Oh, she probably kidded herself sometimes that it was what she wanted, and maybe part of her did. Or wanted Tim to think she did, when he read her letters to Francine. Mainly, though, she didn't want there to be nothing stopping Tim and

Gaby Struthers shacking up together. She wanted Tim living with her and Dan, at the Dower House. His addiction to the wife he hated and tormented suited her down to the ground – she still got to be the good woman in his life, the one he relied on. Once he was blissfully happy with Gaby, she'd have been relegated to second place. She'd have hated it.'

'Why kill Francine?' Sam asked. 'If Lauren cared about her and wanted to protect her from . . .' He stopped, reluctant to use the word 'attack'. Though Simon was right: there was no word that better described what Francine Breary had been subjected to. A sustained attack, albeit written and verbal rather than physical. 'Why didn't Lauren . . . I don't know, report Tim's mistreatment of Francine to Social Services?'

'What could she have said? It's just talking, isn't it? Not even shouting, not aggressive. Calm, quiet. She's overheard a man chatting to his invalid wife, that's all. And she's read some letters that people have tried to hide, and, yes, she knows they're bad news. Very bad.' Simon hauled himself to his feet and started to walk round the room. He was limping; pins and needles.

'Instinctively, she knows exactly what the letters mean,' he said. 'They mean deliberate cruelty, but someone like Lauren, not the brightest in the world, how's she going to put that into words and make sure she's believed over the likes of Tim Breary with his collection of poetry books and exclusive library membership, and Dan Jose with his economic theory research and his old-fart tweedy suits? Educated millionaires who write touchy-feely letters full of anecdotes and insights and therapeutic airing of everything that's been bothering them that they've never had the guts to express until now. Poor fucking them! Who do you think Social Services are going to prioritise in that situation? The husband and best friends, or the chippy hired help? Lady-of-the-Manor Kerry, with her original art on the walls of her listed building, or tattooed, anorexic Lauren who can't open her mouth without a stream of foul language spilling out?'

'When you put it like that . . .' Sam muttered.

'Lauren can *feel* exactly what's wrong, but she can't think it through,' said Simon. 'And she's married to Jason, which is confusing for her. *That's* what abuse is, she probably thinks. Psychological torture's what Jason does, so how can this be the same and as bad when it's so different? She can't answer her own questions, she's getting more and more desperate. Then, I'm guessing, one day she overhears Dan Jose read a letter aloud to Francine for the first time. The cruelty's escalating, she thinks – though not in those precise words. How bad could it get? Answer: very. She has to get Francine out of the Dower House. So she does it the only way she knows how – she takes a pillow and puts an end to an unremittingly miserable life.'

'A mercy killing,' Sam said quietly.

'In the truest sense, yes.'

'What about Tim Breary's confession?'

'I can't say for sure, but I think there's a good chance Francine's death broke the spell,' Simon said. 'The addiction, whatever you want to call it. Think about it: Lauren tells Tim what she's done and she tells him why. She's distraught. He sees his behaviour through her eyes. Feels guilty, maybe. Hard to see how he could feel good about turning a basically decent young woman into a killer. Hopefully it brought him to his senses.'

'He confessed to protect Lauren,' said Sam. 'Or Jason strong-armed him: "You caused all this trouble for my wife and therefore me; you're taking the blame."'

'Partly, maybe,' said Simon, staring out of the window. 'Could have been a bit of both, but neither was the main force driving him.'

'Gaby,' said Sam, not knowing quite what he meant.

'Gaby,' Simon repeated expressionlessly. 'Breary still wanted her, and with Francine dead, there was nothing to stop him, except his conviction that he didn't deserve her.'

'Even more so now, presumably,' Sam said.

'Right. Soon as Gaby found out the truth about how he, Kerry and Dan had been treating Francine, she'd want nothing to do with him – that's what he thought.'

'So he pretended he'd killed Francine,' said Sam. Finally, he felt as if he was getting somewhere. 'It's still bad – it's murder, it's worse – but in a different way. In a way that seems less grim and repellent, somehow. More . . . honest.'

'More male,' said Simon. 'Less humiliating. Straightforward evil of the masculine variety: brutal, yes, but over quickly – not endlessly sick and spiteful, not pathetic. You murder the person you hate. It's a show of force. There's something effeminate about subtly torturing your helpless wife with carefully chosen words. If Lauren had admitted to killing Francine, the truth would have come out – Breary would have been certain that'd scupper his chance with Gaby. At the same time, he didn't want Gaby to be under any illusions about his moral character – he wouldn't have seen that as being fair to her.'

'So he tells Lauren he'll take the blame,' Sam took over the story. 'In doing so, he protects her, which, given the circumstances, feels like the right thing to do, and he can finally be honest with Gaby, he thinks, even though he's being anything but. Still, he feels as if his . . . badness is out in the open. So many of Kerry and Dan's letters mention his lack of self-esteem.'

'Exactly,' said Simon. 'He's going to be labelled a murderer and punished, and it'll wipe his slate clean. He can say to Gaby, "Look, this is how bad I am. I've done the worst thing a person can do. Can you forgive me?" Whereas he wouldn't have dared ask her the same question in relation to what he'd *really* done.'

'Yes. That makes sense, doesn't it?' Sam asked. He still wasn't sure.

'Perfect sense,' he heard a woman's voice say. He turned.

Gaby Struthers stood in the doorway. 'Correct in every detail,' she told Simon.

'How do you know?' Sam asked her.

'How do you think?'

'Tim told you?'

Gaby nodded. 'And Lauren. She so desperately wanted to tell the truth and be told she'd done nothing wrong. Tim deprived her of that chance by insisting on protecting her. He begged her to let him take the blame. Jason backed him up. So did Kerry and Dan, once they saw how desperate he was to bury the truth. He convinced them that the only thing he had to live for now was me, that I'd want nothing to do with him if I found out he'd mistreated his bedridden wife until her care assistant had been driven to kill her out of pity.'

'But he thought you'd forgive him for killing her,' said Simon.

'You don't need me to explain the difference,' Gaby told him. 'You've said it all already: a sudden murderous impulse on the one hand, and on the other, constant passive-aggressive victimisation over a period of years, slow and insidious.' She looked very serious suddenly. 'You were right when you called it an addiction. Tim didn't plan to torture anyone. He just got caught up in something stronger than he was. I'm not justifying what he did – it was wrong, but—'

'There's no "but",' Simon said.

'If you were Tim, if you'd had his exact life experiences and been through exactly the same formative psychological process that he went through, can you honestly say you'd have behaved differently?'

Did that question make sense? Sam wondered. If Simon were Tim Breary, would he have behaved as Tim Breary behaved? Yes. Obviously.

'What about Lauren?' Gaby asked. 'Is there a "but" for her? She also killed Jason.'

'We know,' Simon said.

'He attacked her on Friday, after he attacked me. She decided enough was enough. Another life she felt she had no choice but to take.'

'I'm sympathetic, but I'm not sure the law will be,' said Simon. Sam had been thinking the same thing, but hadn't wanted to say it.

'I'm sure it wouldn't be,' said Gaby. 'Still. The law will have to find her first.' A smile played around the corners of her mouth.

'I don't know, obviously – I'm just guessing – but I'd imagine that Lauren might be out of reach by now. It could be that when you go to the Dower House to look for her, you'll find it empty.'

'If you know where she is, you'd better tell us,' said Simon. It could have been intended as a threat, but Sam heard only weariness.

'I don't know anything,' Gaby replied smoothly 'I'm speculating.'

'Are Kerry and Dan with her?' Sam asked.

'I don't know where any of them are, but I doubt Lauren would be capable of getting far without support. Or of staying hidden indefinitely. Don't you agree? You've met her.'

'We'll find her,' Simon told Sam: a show of bravado, for Gaby's benefit.

'I'm sure you will, if you look long and hard enough,' she said. 'Or you could not look quite so hard, and catch bad guys instead. Isn't that what you're supposed to be for?'

Before Simon or Sam could answer, she'd gone.

27

Tuesday 5 April 2011

'Marjolaine,' Tim says, staring at the door at the far end of the corridor. He's stopped several feet away from it, white-faced. I know how hard it's going to be for him to come any closer. I'm not going to try and persuade him. It has to be up to him. I tried to solve the mystery of his nightmare years ago, when he wasn't ready, and I drove him away.

'I'd forgotten that the rooms had names and that ours was called Marjolaine,' he says, almost whispering. 'They're all named after flowers, or herbs. I remember Francine saying.'

'You don't have to come with me, but I'm going to go inside,' I tell him. 'Okay?' I booked the room for one night in order to have the access I need this afternoon, even though Tim and I aren't staying. We're here for the day only. Tim would never have agreed to stay at Les Sources des Alpes in any case, even if I'd suggested it. If he's wondering why I booked us outbound and inbound flights on the same day instead of suggesting we stay overnight at a different hotel, he hasn't mentioned it.

Another thing he hasn't mentioned since getting out of prison: that I've spent every night at the Combingham Best Western and he's spent every night at the Dower House, both of us alone. I know and understand his reasons. He doesn't want to rush me.

Damn his reasons to hell. They make no difference.

Be fair, Gaby. He's the one who suggested this, coming here. That's huge, for him.

Huge for Tim isn't good enough for me any more. I need him to do things that are huge by my standards. Nothing less will do.

The key is gold, heavy, shaped like a bell. I unlock the door and walk in. To anyone but Tim, this would look like an ordinary hotel room. He calls my name from the corridor, anxious because he can't see me.

I can't stand this. What if I wait for him to decide to come in and he never does? 'The walls aren't even plain white,' I shout back. They're wallpapered: a pattern of pastel coloured squares against a cream background. 'Tim, I promise you, you won't be scared of this room the second you set foot inside it. It's not the room from your nightmare. It's enormous, for one thing.'

He's moving. I feel the vibration in the floor. When he comes in, I expect him to stop in the doorway but he strides over so that he's standing right next to me, our arms touching. He looks around. I listen to his jagged breathing.

'Are you . . . ?' He stops to clear his throat. 'You're sure this is where me and Francine stayed? The right room?'

'You told me your room was called Marjolaine. This is Marjolaine.' In case he needs any more grounding, I say, 'You recognised it just now when you saw the name on the door.'

'Yes. Sorry.' He wipes his forehead with the back of his hand. 'You're right. It's not . . . This isn't the room in my dream.'

'No. It's not. Nor is any other room.'

'What?'

'The room in your dream isn't a room, Tim.'

'What do you mean?'

'Follow me.' I pick up the key and move to leave.

He pulls me back. 'Wait.'

'No. I've waited. I'm sick of waiting.'

His eyes fill with tears. 'Gaby, I understand that, but I need to stay here for a few seconds. Not much longer than that, not even five minutes, just . . . I need to stand here and know that it's not this room I'm scared of. It never was.'

'Right. It never was.'

'But . . . now you want to take me somewhere else,' Tim says, his voice full of shadows: the shadow of a handbag against a white wall. Except it wasn't a wall. 'You want to take me to the place I should have been scared of all this time, the place I thought was this room. I don't know if I can do it, Gaby.'

'What place, Tim? Where is it? *What* is it?' No point asking; I can see from his face that he has no idea.

'It's here, in Leukerbad. It must be if you're about to show it to me, but . . .' He shakes his head. 'There isn't anywhere else. We didn't go anywhere else that wasn't a public place. She wouldn't have tried to kill me in a public place.'

'She didn't try to kill you,' I tell him. 'That never happened.'

'Then why do I dream that she did?'

I take a deep breath. I don't know if it's going to be worse or better for him when he has the answer. 'You're taking the dream too literally,' I say. 'Come. Let me prove it to you.'

This time he doesn't protest.

We walk along the corridor in silence. Into the lift, down to the ground floor, outside and down the red-carpeted stairs. We turn left, Tim following me as if he doesn't know where I'm going. Can he really not know? Where else might I be going?

I wish the walk were shorter. I could end this now and just tell him, but I want to give him every chance to get there on his own. As we walk up the hill, past shops, restaurants and wooden chalets, I say, 'In the dream, does the size of the handbag's shadow change? Does it get bigger or smaller?' The weather's bright and sunny where we are, but there's snow on the mountains above us. I take care not to look at them.

Tim stops for a second beside a fountain that's spilling warm water. Leukerbad is famous for its hot springs and likes to show them off, I discovered last time I came here.

I carry on walking.

'No. The handbag stays the same size,' Tim says, picking up his pace to catch me up.

'You said Francine's walking towards you in the dream, diagonally across the room, getting closer and closer.'

'Right.' The wounded expression on his face as I force him to think about his nightmare is too much; I can't look at him.

'So the handbag's shadow ought to grow or shrink, depending on the source of light,' I say. 'It ought to get smaller, or bigger and more blurred as she gets nearer.' I find this immovable law of nature comforting. I doubt Tim does. 'If she's walking diagonally across the room towards you, the bag's either going to be getting further from the wall or closer to it.'

'It's a dream, Gaby,' Tim says. 'Not a scientific trial.'

He's almost right: there's nothing scientific about a symbolic representation of danger in a dream, which is why I'm determined to cling to the one scientific detail: the shadow of an object travelling across a white surface will only stay the same size if the distance between it and the surface doesn't change as it moves.

We turn another corner and I freeze. Here we are, sooner than I expected. I throw out an arm to stop Tim going any further. 'What?' he says. 'What, Gaby?'

'Look. Have you been here before? Did you come here with Francine?' The answer has to be yes. Ahead of us are tall snow-covered mountains. A cable runs from the peak of one of them down to a small wooden building at the bottom of another. There's a square car sliding down the wire, a slow diagonal through the air.

Tim's breathing as if it hurts him.

'There's your small room,' I say.

'The cable car. But . . . I don't understand. Yes, Francine and I went up in it, but we weren't alone. There were other people there, a family of four, a Russian family. She wouldn't have . . .' His words run out. He's staring. Trying to piece it together.

'Wouldn't have tried to kill you in front of them? No, she wouldn't. I told you: she didn't try to kill you at all, in front of anyone or no one. Not in the way you mean. What happened in that cable car, Tim? Did you and Francine talk? Did anything important happen?'

'She proposed to me. I told you.' He's distracted. Can't keep his eyes still.

'You told me she proposed, but not where.'

'She asked me at the top, when the car set off. She said . . .' He shakes his head.

'What? What, Tim?'

'I didn't answer straight away.'

'What did you want to say?'

'I didn't want her to have asked.' I force myself not to turn away from the pain in his eyes. 'She said I had until we got to the bottom to give her an answer.'

A proposal immediately followed by an ultimatum. Nice.

'I said yes.'

'When? On the way down?'

'When we got to the bottom. I'd run out of time. She was my girlfriend, Gaby. What was I doing with her if she wasn't the right person? I didn't know there *was* a right person.'

'All the way down the mountain in the cable car, you were getting closer – not to a handbag containing something that was going to kill you, but to the moment when you handed over the rest of your life to a woman you knew would crush all the joy and hope out of it. That's what was going to kill you.'

'She made herself more miserable than anyone else, always,' Tim murmurs. He's angry with me.

'Francine's crooked arm in the dream – that's the cable,' I tell him, needing to have it out in the open. 'Crooked because the car's hanging from it and making a dent in its straight line, dragging it down as it moves along. The white wall isn't a wall, it's the mountain, covered in snow. The car was at the same distance from the mountain all the way down, and you were watching its shadow moving along the white mountain – that's why the shadow of what you thought was a handbag stayed the same size. But it wasn't a handbag, it was a cable car, the one you and Francine were in, Tim.'

'I can't stay here.' Tim starts to march back in the direction of the hotel. I run after him, into the oncoming wind. It stings my face. 'All this time, thinking she tried to kill me,' he says. 'I really believed it.'

'I know.'

'It was so vivid.'

I grab his arm, pull him round to face me. 'It wasn't too late,' I say. 'You could have left her. You *did* leave her, but you didn't come and find me. You never came looking for me!'

'You had Sean.'

'Yes, I did, didn't I? How did you feel about that?'

Tim stops walking. 'I thought he was wrong for you. Part of me was glad you had someone, even so. I'd have felt guiltier about not being able to leave Francine if you were completely on your own—'

'Stop!' I can't stand to listen.

'What do you want me to say, Gaby? That I was jealous of Sean because he had you and I didn't? Of course I was.'

'But you didn't say that, Tim. You said something different. Shall I tell you how I felt about Francine? I *hated* her. Not for being a bitch and putting you through hell every day. For being your wife. She could have been the kindest, loveliest woman on the face of the earth and I'd have loathed her every bit as much. I used to wish she'd drop dead. I Googled her five times a day, looked at the photo of her on her firm's website, stared into her stony eyes. I'd imagine you in bed with her, watching TV with her, clearing away the supper things together, and I'd wish her dead. Next to you, Francine's the person who's inspired my most passionate feelings. There – how do you feel about me now?'

How would you feel if I told you I love Lauren for killing her, and always will, however wrong it is?

'Wow,' Tim says.

'You didn't feel that way about Sean, did you?'

'No, I didn't. But that doesn't mean what you've decided it means.'

'You can live without me, Tim.' *I can't forgive that.* 'All those years of no contact—'

'Gaby, you lived without me perfectly well!'

'It's not the same. I thought I had no choice. You'd made it clear you didn't want me anywhere near you.'

'You could have thought, "Fuck that", and hunted me down,' Tim says. 'You could have turned up on the doorstep and told Francine the truth, provoked a crisis. Can't you see how unreasonable you're being? I could live without you, yes, but I don't want to. I choose not to – ever. What about you? You can live without me, and you're about to prove it. You're leaving me, aren't you?'

I say nothing.

Tim grabs my hands. It hurts. 'Tell me what I can do to change your mind,' he says. 'I'll do anything.'

'No. You tell *me* what you can do. Or, better than that, don't tell me – just do it. Change my mind.'

'I will.'

'Goodbye, Tim.'

I walk away, down the hill without looking back. I don't have to hurry; he won't follow me. Though I can't see him, I know he's still where I left him, deciding we're doomed, that it's too late – there is nothing he could possibly do that would be big enough. *Run after me, refuse to let me go. Turn back the clock, do everything differently.*

There's a taxi rank outside a pizzeria at the bottom of the hill path. I get into the first cab in the line, tell the driver to take me to Geneva airport. 'Which airline are you flying with, miss?' he asks me in English.

Good question. I think back to Dusseldorf airport, Sean asking me, 'Who's the carrier?'

I don't know who I'm flying with. I'm booked onto the same return flight as Tim, but that's impossible now. 'I don't know,' I say. 'Take me to any departure gate.'

'You are going to book a flight when you arrive?' The driver's not giving up easily. 'There are different gates for different destinations. What is your destination?'

'I don't know. Sorry. I'll decide when I get there.'

If I get there. Maybe Tim will stop me; maybe we'll decide to stay in Switzerland for the rest of our lives. A new start. Not three hundred and sixty-five minus ninety midnights, but as many as we've got left. If I'm lucky – and I have been in my life so far, mostly – I'll never have to make the decision of where to fly to, never have to face the realisation that there's nowhere I want to go without Tim.

That's what I'm going to keep thinking all the way to Geneva airport. I've got about two hours, a bit longer if I'm lucky. Two hours is a long time.

28

6/4/2011

'Stop where you are! Permission to approach denied.'

'I'm . . . here, sir.' Sam was standing directly in front of Proust's desk. Any closer and he'd have been touching it. He stared at the inspector's upside-down signature on the bottom of a form. The ink was still wet. Shiny.

'I meant metaphorically stop where you are. I don't want it.'

How could he know? There was no way. 'I think we're at cross purposes,' Sam said, trying to work out what Proust thought he was about to give him.

'You mean you're making me cross on purpose?' the Snowman snapped, removing the signed form from the top of the pile in front of him and signing the one beneath it without looking at it. 'I don't want your letter of resignation, Sergeant.'

'My—'

'The one you were about to produce from your jacket's inside pocket and put on my desk.'

Give it to him. You don't need permission. It's not up to him.

With an unsteady hand, Sam extracted the letter from his jacket and held it out for Proust to take.

'Put it through the shredder,' the Snowman barked. 'I'm not interested.'

'You want me to stay?' Sam asked.

Proust smiled in the way that an adult might smile at a child's sweet but naïve suggestion. 'Neither of us *wants* you to stay – not you and not me – but we'll both have to put up with you being here. I'm not one for lavish compliments, Sergeant, but you're the only member of my team who's halfway normal. Reliably unremarkable.'

'Sir, I—'

'If you leave, I won't be able to avoid having Sergeant Zailer working for me again. Waterhouse would hate it, but he'd have to pretend it was what he wanted. His marriage would hate it even more, and would hasten to its inevitable doom. You don't want that on your conscience, do you?'

'You want me to stay,' said Sam. This time he wasn't asking.

Proust looked up at him. Sighed. 'Would you like me to send a bunch of flowers to your dressing room? Yes, Sergeant, I want you to stay. You're the only person I work with that I never have to think about. And I do mean *never*. I'm not thinking about you now, for example. I'm thinking about more important things.'

Sam prayed the Snowman couldn't read his mind. What did it say about him that he felt flattered when he ought to feel insulted? He would tell Kate later and pretend to share her outrage, while secretly believing Proust wanted to make him feel valued in the only way he knew how.

'I'm going to have to think about it, sir.'

Proust chuckled. 'Think all you like. I won't be thinking about you thinking. I won't be thinking about you at all, Sergeant, and I'll be enjoying it very much.'

'Sir, if you want me to stay . . .'

'In the immediate short term, I'd rather you left. My office, I mean. Off you go, and take your pointless letter with you.' Proust waved elaborately, as if for a press photograph, without looking up from his paperwork.

Sam went.

He took his pointless letter with him.

Acknowledgements

As always, an enormous thank you to my ace publishers Hodder & Stoughton, especially my fantastic editor Carolyn Mays who expertly saves every book from much-less-good-ness. Also to Francesca Best, Katy Rouse, Karen Geary, Lucy Zilberkweit, Lucy Hale, Jason Bartholomew, Alice Howe, Naomi Berwin, Al Oliver – the whole team. Nobody does it, or could do it, better than Hodder. Julia Benson deserves a special mention, for supplying me with certain football-related facts. Thank you, also, to my wonderful international publishers who do such a great job of translating and publishing my books abroad.

Thanks to Dan, Phoebe and Guy for really believing every book is worthwhile and important, and for putting up with the increasingly dishevelled madwoman in the attic for another year.

Thanks to Luke Hares, who provided not only scientific expertise but also an alibi for my heroine, and who allowed me to be part of a very exciting gang. May the force feedback be with you (even if I don't have a clue what that means).

Thanks as always to my two research stalwarts: Guy Martland, who told me what I needed to know about strokes, and Mark and Cal Pannone, who provided police procedural and curry.

Thank you to Jonathan Walker-Kane – I think this book would have ended up being a different and worse book if it weren't for you.

Thanks to BW and DR for the original inspiration for PUE.

Thanks to Chris Gribble for The Slack Captain – the perfect name.

Thank you to all my jolly Twitter followers who have answered many a useful question, especially the one about football team support! And thank you to my readers – everything I do, I do it for you (as Bryan Adams once said. Though not about psychological thriller writing).

Reading group questions for *The Carrier*

1) Which of the characters in the book is most responsible for the death of Francine Breary? Do you think the person who physically killed her is the person most guilty of murder?

2) Do you agree with Kerry Jose that 'a tyrant is someone whose death would liberate somebody, even if it's only one person'? Does it make sense to talk of tyrants in the domestic sphere, or is 'tyrant' a label that sounds more political? Is there a different between a bully and a tyrant? Is Francine a psychological tyrant, and if so, how does her particular kind of tyranny work? What hold does she have over the other characters in the novel?

3) Gaby and Sean's relationship is a not a happy one. How has it ended up in such a bad state? Do you think either Gaby or Sean is more to blame for this, or were they simply incompatible from the start?

4) Who matters more to Tim Breary, Francine or Gaby?

5) Is there any sense in which Francine's murder could be seen as a mercy killing, or does/should that concept only apply to cases of terminal illness and/or extreme physical pain?

6) When Gaby and Lauren first meet at the airport, it's fair to say that they don't get on very well. How does their relationship change over the course of the book?

7) Charlie and Simon become entangled in the problems of the Proust family in this book, which leads Charlie to worry if her relationship with Simon might be as dysfunctional as Proust and his wife Lizzie's marriage. Is there any truth in this? How does one measure whether a relationship is healthy or unhealthy?

8) At the end of the novel, were you surprised by Gaby's decision with regard to Tim? What do you think will happen between Gaby and Tim following the end of the book? What do you think should happen? Did you find this aspect too unresolved or ambiguous? Would you have liked a more definite resolution?

9) How did you feel about the role played by poetry in the book?

10) Olivia, Charlie's sister, has a strange philosophy with regard to romantic infidelity. She believes that lying in order to keep everyone happy for as long as possible, so that you can sustain your double life and maximise the personal fulfilment of everyone involved, is the best way forward – better than either ending one's affair or leaving one's spouse for one's lover. Do you agree with her? Why, or why not?

11) *Murder on the Orient Express* by Agatha Christie is referred to several times in the book. Why do you think this is (apart from the fact that the author is an Agatha Christie fan)? Is there any link or thematic connection between the solution to this murder mystery and the solution in *Murder on the Orient Express*?

12) Money is a character, a theme and a motive in *The Carrier*, though in a very unconventional way. Discuss.

13) 'This is a novel about what happens when human beings unreasonably impose upon one another, both in major and minor ways.' Do you agree? Is it inevitable that people will impose on those close to them in ways that will sometimes be unpleasant, or is it simply that the characters in this particular book don't know how to behave properly?

14) For how long is it reasonable to hold a person responsible for past bad behaviour? Is it fair to think of Francine, after her stroke, as the same woman she was before? Should Tim, Kerry and Dan have forgiven Francine as soon as she became the helpless victim of her own ill health?

15) When Simon expresses his shock and disgust at the end of the novel about what was done to Francine Breary, did you, as a reader, experience any kind of 'parallax view' feeling? Did you suddenly feel differently about Francine or the other characters, or see anything differently from how you'd seen it up to that point?

Look out for Sophie Hannah's next unnerving
psychological thriller

THE TELLING ERROR

Stuck in a traffic jam on her way to deliver her son's forgotten
sports kit to school, Nicki Clements sees a face she hoped never to
see again. It's definitely him, the same police officer; he's stopping
all the cars on Elmhirst Road one by one, talking to every driver.
Keen to avoid him, Nicki does a U-turn and takes a long and
inconvenient detour, praying he won't notice her panicky escape.

He doesn't, but a CCTV camera does, as Nicki finds out when
detectives pull her in for questioning the next day in connection
with the murder of Damon Blundy, a controversial newspaper
columnist and resident of Elmhirst Road.

Nicki can't answer any of the baffling questions detectives fire at
her. She has no idea why a killer might sharpen nine knives at the
murder scene, then use two blunt ones to kill, in a way that involves
no stabbing or spilling of blood. She doesn't know what
'HE IS NO LESS DEAD' means, or why the murderer painted it on
the wall of Blundy's study. And she can't explain her desire to avoid
Elmhirst Road on the day in question without revealing the secret
that could ruin her life. Because, although Nicki is not guilty of
murder, she is far from innocent . . .

Coming out in hardback and ebook in 2014

HODDER &
STOUGHTON

If you enjoyed the compelling psychological suspense of *The Carrier*, we think you'll enjoy *The Burning Air* by Erin Kelly. Here, Sophie Hannah recommends the novel.

If you're looking for a great psychological thriller to read, I would thoroughly recommend *The Burning Air* by Erin Kelly. It's the story of a family get-together from which a baby is stolen – apparently by Kerry, the new girlfriend of the youngest MacBride sibling. Kerry is a completely unknown quantity whom none of Felix's relatives has ever met before. Sophie wasn't convinced about whether she ought to leave her new baby with the enigmatic and uncommunicative Kerry, but, persuaded by her husband and sister that everything would be all right, she finally agrees – only to regret it when she and other family members return from their night out to discover that the baby and the mysterious babysitter have disappeared.

The novel begins with an intriguing confession from Lydia MacBride, the elderly matriarch of the clan, as follows:

Of course it was my love for my children, love for my son, that caused me to act as I did. It was a lapse of judgment. If I could have foreseen the rippling aftershocks that followed I would have acted differently, but by the time I realised the extent of the consequences, it was too late . . .

Motherhood was my only excuse. I was trying to do right by my son and it made me momentarily blind to the interior laws I have always tried to live by. We all want the best for our children, but I crossed the line between protection and offense.

As the novel progresses, we discover more about the past history of the MacBride families and about the person or people who might wish to destroy them. The quality of the writing is what sets *The Burning Air* apart from most psychological thrillers. The texture, atmosphere and psychological sophistication are truly impressive and ensure that readers will be glued to the page. There is an amazing twist that strikes not at the end of the novel but halfway through, which is a risky manoeuvre, but thankfully it works beautifully because there is an equally gasp-inducing revelation saved for the end of the book.

A novel about the damage jealousy and deceit can do to good people, *The Burning Air* will have you on the edge of your seat.

S O P H I E
H A N N A H

kind of cruel

Amber Hewerdine knows more than she is telling.

She knows that she hasn't slept since the arson attack which killed her best friend.

She knows that it is not normal for four members of your family to disappear one Christmas morning, and then reappear the next day, refusing to explain or ever speak of it again.

And she knows that somewhere, buried deep in her subconscious, is the key to what happened all those years ago at Little Orchard.

Kind, cruel, kind of cruel.

These are the words she keeps coming back to.

But what do they mean?

And why is she arrested within hours of first saying them, for the murder of a woman she has never met?

Available in paperback

HODDER

SOPHIE HANNAH

lasting damage

It's 1.15 a.m. Connie Bowskill should be asleep. Instead, she's logging on to a property website in search of a particular house: 11 Bentley Grove, Cambridge. She knows it's for sale – there's an estate agent's board in the front garden.

Soon Connie is clicking on the 'Virtual Tour' button, keen to see the inside of the house and put her mind at rest once and for all. She finds herself looking at a scene from a nightmare: in the living room, in the middle of the carpet, lies a woman face down in a pool of blood. In shock, Connie wakes her husband Kit. But when Kit sits down at the computer, he sees no dead body, only a pristine beige carpet in a perfectly ordinary room . . .

Available in paperback

HODDER

SOPHIE HANNAH

a room swept white

TV producer Fliss Benson receives an anonymous card at work: sixteen numbers arranged in four rows of four – numbers that mean nothing to her.

On the same day, Fliss finds out she's going to be working on a documentary about miscarriages of justice involving cot death mothers wrongly accused of murder. The documentary will focus on three women: Helen Yardley, Sarah Jaggard and Rachel Hines. All three are now free, and the child protection zealot who did her best to send them to prison for life, Dr Judith Duffy, is under investigation for misconduct.

For reasons she has shared with nobody, this is the last project Fliss wants to be working on. And then Helen Yardley is found dead at her home, and in her pocket is a card with sixteen numbers on it, arranged in four rows of four . . .

Available in paperback

H
HODDER

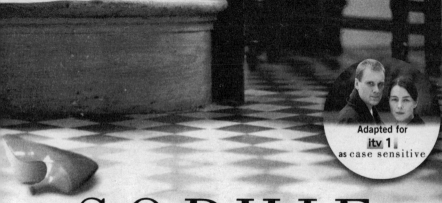

SOPHIE HANNAH

the other half lives

Why would anyone confess to the murder of someone who isn't dead?

Ruth Bussey knows what it means to be in the wrong and to be wronged. She once did something she regrets, and her punishment nearly destroyed her. Now Ruth is rebuilding her life, and has found a love she doesn't believe she deserves: Aidan Seed. Aidan is also troubled by a past he hates to talk about, until one day he decides he must confide in Ruth. He tells her that years ago he killed someone: a woman called Mary Trelease.

Ruth is confused. She's certain she's heard the name before, and when she realises why it sounds familiar, her fear and confusion deepen – because the Mary Trelease that Ruth knows is very much alive . . .

Available in paperback

HODDER

SOPHIE HANNAH

the point of rescue

Sally is watching the news with her husband when she hears a name she ought not to recognise: Mark Bretherick.

Last year, a work trip Sally had planned was cancelled at the last minute. Desperate for a break from her busy life juggling her career and a young family, Sally didn't tell her husband that the trip had fallen through. Instead, she booked a week off and treated herself to a secret holiday. All she wanted was a bit of peace – some time to herself – but it didn't work out that way. Because Sally met a man – Mark Bretherick.

All the details are the same: where he lives, his job, his wife Geraldine and daughter Lucy. Except that the man on the news is someone Sally has never seen before. And Geraldine and Lucy Bretherick are both dead . . .

Available in paperback

HODDER

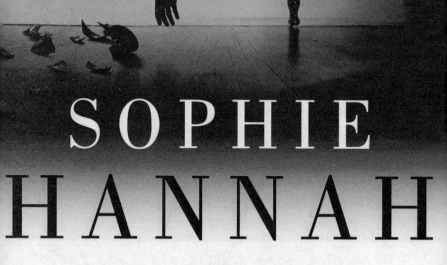

SOPHIE
HANNAH

hurting distance

Three years ago, something terrible happened to Naomi Jenkins —
so terrible she never told anyone.

Now Naomi has another secret — her lover, unhappily married Robert Haworth. When
Robert vanishes, Naomi knows he must have come to harm. But the police are less
convinced, particularly when Robert's wife insists he is not missing.

Naomi is desperate. If she can't persuade the police that Robert is
in danger, she'll convince them that he is a danger to others.
Then they'll have to look for him — urgently.

Naomi knows how to describe in detail the actions of a psychopath.
All she needs to do is dig up her own traumatic past . . .

Available in paperback

HODDER

SOPHIE
HANNAH

little face

She's only been gone two hours.

Her husband David was supposed to be looking after their two-week-old daughter.
But when Alice Fancourt walks into the nursery, her terrifying ordeal begins, for
Alice insists the baby in the cot is a stranger she's never seen before.

With an increasingly hostile and menacing David swearing she must either be mad
or lying, how can Alice make the police believe her before it's too late?

Available in paperback

HODDER

In the best books, the ending often comes as a shock.
Not just because of that one last twist in the tale,
but because you have been so absorbed in their world,
that coming back to the harsh light of reality is a jolt.

If that describes you now, then perhaps you should track down
some new leads, and find new suspense in other worlds.

Join us at www.hodder.co.uk, or follow us on
Twitter @hodderbooks, and you can tap in to a
community of fellow thrill-seekers.

Whether you want to find out more about this book,
or a particular author, watch trailers and interviews, have
the chance to win early limited editions, or simply browse
our expert readers' selection of the very best books,
we think you'll find what you're looking for.

And if you don't, that's the place to tell us what's missing.

We love what we do, and we'd love you to be part of it.

www.hodder.co.uk